MINE ALL MINE

by

Christy St. Romain Marchand

Copyright © 2020 by Christy St. Romain Marchand

ISBN Number 978-0-578-66272-5

Library of Congress Control Number 2020905356

Printed in the United States of America

For Man, Adam and Amanda

and for Eloise and Jeanie,
my real life inspirations for Rosie

MINE ALL MINE

Prologue

The dark blue sedan slowly pulled down the driveway and came to a stop. Tyler glanced at his grandmother at the wheel, then over the seat where his brothers and sisters sat quietly in a neat row.

"Well, here we are," Grandma Rosie announced gently. "Why don't we go inside and have something to eat?"

Four doors opened simultaneously. Tyler climbed out and stepped around the open back door to unfasten Hope, his baby sister, from her booster seat. The toddler wrapped chubby arms around Tyler's neck and clung. "Ty, want mommy," she pleaded, her childish voice cutting through the thick silence. Tyler met Leanne's anguished eyes over the toddler's head and felt his own chin quiver. Leanne blinked and spun on her heel, running for the door into their grandmother's house. The screen door banged like a gunshot in her wake. Ten year old Joel kicked at the gravel in the driveway and muttered something unintelligible before setting off at a brisk pace down the driveway. Helplessly Tyler watched him go.

"Where's Joel going?" His grandmother closed her car door and took Allison and Robb by the hands. Ally's face was pale, and there were tear stains tracking down Robb's cheeks.

"He's just going for a walk," Tyler replied, reaching down to squeeze Robb's shoulder. "He'll be back."

Grandma Rosie nodded. "Well, come on, let's go in and change out of these clothes and have something to eat." Propping Hope on his hip, Tyler nodded and followed her indoors. Ally and Robb trudged toward the back of the house to the bedrooms where their overnight bags had been deposited, where Leanne had disappeared. While Grandma Rosie put her purse away and began taking covered dishes from the refrigerator, Tyler set Hope into her high chair and poured some dry cereal into a bowl for her. Wiping his hands on his dark pants, he slipped outside and walked to the end of the driveway to look for Joel. There was no sign of him in either direction.

Tyler dragged his feet back to the house and sat down heavily on the wide steps of the front porch. Was it just seven days ago when their world had been turned upside down? He shook his head slowly in bemusement. One minute everything was normal, and then a knock on the door, and poof, nothing would ever be fine or normal again.

He recalled how excited his parents were about the long weekend trip they had planned for their anniversary. They were going to go back to the same place they had honeymooned and it was the first trip they had ever planned just for themselves. His mom had been looking forward to it for weeks. She even bought some new clothes. Tyler recalled how she swept into the kitchen while his dad finished up the dishes, modeling a pretty blue dress that reached the floor, and his dad's whistle of appreciation. Tyler squinted in concentration. Had he told his mom how pretty she looked? His eyes stung. Probably not.

And his father had taken enough time off from work so that when they got back, he, Tyler, Joel and Robb could go on a camping trip. In fact, the tent and all their equipment were piled neatly in the garage just waiting to be tossed into the back of his dad's truck upon their return Sunday night.

But they didn't return. About the time he began to wonder where they were, Mr. Hanley from next door came over along with their minister and a policeman.

Tyler swallowed. As long as he lived he'd never forget the way the men filed into the living room and sat in a row on the sofa, their faces grim, waiting until Grandma Rosie, who was staying over, could round up them all up. Then their minister told them all, haltingly, how there was an accident on the highway and five people, including their parents, were killed. Tyler remembered listening carefully to the words, and how he still couldn't exactly put them together right away. He remembered thinking how glad he was it happened at the end of their trip, not the beginning. Then he realized his parents were never coming home.

Tyler heard a soft noise behind him and turned to look. His grandmother slipped through the front door onto the porch. He tried to give her a smile but it probably didn't look like one. His face felt stiff and unnatural.

"Any sign of Joel?" She sat down carefully on the top step beside him.

"No, ma'am," he replied quietly.

She sighed. They sat together silently for a few minutes, then Tyler swallowed past the lump in his throat and voiced his unspeakable fear. "I heard Aunt Patricia talking about taking the twins," he blurted. "She said she couldn't take us all but she wouldn't mind taking the twins. And then Aunt Jessie said she wants Hope." He broke off and stared at his hands. Aunt Patricia lived in Alabama and Aunt Jessie lived all the way across the country in New Mexico. The idea that they would be split up and shipped off was making him sick to his stomach, but it could happen. Things like that didn't just happen to other people, he knew that now. And these days nobody wanted six kids, especially somebody else's six kids. That was the impression he clearly received from his mother's older sisters.

"Well, they can just go jump in a lake, both of them," his grandmother replied swiftly.

Tyler looked at her in complete surprise. Grandma Rosie had a tone to her voice he'd never heard before, and he'd sure never heard her say somebody could go jump in a lake.

"The very idea!" She took his big hands in her small, creased ones and met his gaze squarely. "You're not going to be separated and you're not going to go anywhere. We're staying together. The seven of us."

Tyler stared at her incredulously, his heart skipping a beat. "Can we do that?"

She squeezed his hands. "You bet we can. Who's going to tell us we can't?"

He shook his head fiercely. "Nobody." For the first time since he'd overheard his aunts, the tightness in his chest eased a fraction, and he felt like he could breathe halfway normally again.

"We'll manage just fine," she added, as though she were trying to convince herself as well. "I'll have to rely on you a good bit, Tyler, to help me out. You know, get organized about things, getting all of you to the places you're supposed to go. That reminds me, we'll have to see about getting your permit pretty soon."

He nodded. A week ago he'd turned fifteen, and his dad was going to take him to get his learner's permit after the camping trip. He'd been so excited about getting his stupid permit. That was all he had to worry about then. It felt like a million years ago. The lump rose in his throat again.

"We'll try to keep things as much the same as we can," Grandma Rosie added. They exchanged sad glances because, of course, things could never be the same. She patted him on the knee and changed the subject. "Did I tell you that your coach spoke with me?"

"I won't play ball anymore," Tyler offered quickly. "It takes too much time and you're going to need a lot of help."

She squeezed his hands again. "Of course you're going to play, Ty. He said you've got amazing potential. We're going to manage just fine, wait and see."

Tyler looked at his grandmother, really looked at her, for the first time. It hadn't been all that long since Grandpa died, and he recalled his parents talking about how worried they were about Grandma Rosie, how hard she was taking it. He now realized, guiltily, he hadn't understood or even thought much about how sad she must really be. And his dad was her only child. He wasn't the only one hurting so bad. Maybe his grandmother needed a friend, one who understood and cared, as badly as he did. Clumsily he draped his arm around her shoulders and squeezed gently. "Sure we will, Rosie. We'll be fine." He wondered if she'd mind him calling her just Rosie. It seemed right, all of a sudden.

She slipped her arm around his waist and leaned against him. "I think you're right. I think between you and me, Ty, we'll be just fine."

Chapter One

The fifth floor employees of Conrad, Berkley and Burns didn't know whether to gawk in amazement or run for cover when the door to Eleanor Haley's office burst open so vigorously that the heavy wood banged against the paneled wall.

"Gracie, are you positive he said 'lead counsel'?" Eleanor was only dimly aware of the glances lifted over low divider walls as she shot down the corridor at a white hot clip. "Absolutely positive? No mistake?"

Shaking her head anxiously, Gracie Whittington hurried to keep up. "No mistake, Eleanor."

"It's unthinkable." Eleanor continued on her path toward the elevators. The senior partner's offices were on the top floor and she would get her answers there. Jabbing the elevator button, she spun to face her worried assistant. "Tell me again."

"Wayne Patterson said he was replacing you as lead and told me to give him the files. I told him I took my orders from you and you haven't said a word about giving him anything. I grabbed them up and he got all red in the face and said to tell you to be in his office in an hour."

Eleanor narrowed her green eyes at the elevator control panel. "We'll just see about that." The doors finally slid open and she strode inside. "We'll just see about that right now."

Impatiently she watched the floor numbers change on the panel above the doors, her mind racing. She was the lead on the Wilford case. It was hers, damn it. And now that her case strategy was laid out as neatly as surgical tools on a tray, they were taking it away from her? Never mind she knew the case inside out and backwards, that she was capable of so much more than digging for details, that she had graduated at the top of her class, editor of Law Review. The bottom line at CBB was she was female.

Her common sense kicked in and Eleanor snorted. Wayne, lead counsel? It was ridiculous. His lack of ability was legendary. Unfortunately he was the nephew of the firm's most senior of senior partners, Philip Conrad, so it didn't take a rocket scientist to figure out whose idea it was to swap her for Wayne.

The elevator chimed to announce its arrival on the tenth floor. Eleanor squeezed through the doors and marched down the hallway. She had to believe Philip would listen to reason. Wayne might be his nephew, but Philip had standards and he liked to win. She would simply explain why he couldn't afford to replace her. How she knew each tiny detail and every possible loophole. When it came down to the bottom line, surely Philip would put the firm first. She drew to a stop at the mahogany desk outside his office.

"Morning, Eleanor." Amelia Landry looked up from her paperwork. "How are you today?"

She didn't have time for pleasantries. She wasn't all that good at them, anyway. "Amelia, I have to see Philip."

"I'm afraid that's impossible," Amelia replied smoothly, rising and rounding the front of the desk to stand purposefully between Eleanor and the closed door to Philip's office. "He's with a client."

Eleanor spied a familiar umbrella in the copper stand beside Amelia's desk and felt a curling trickle of apprehension. "Looks like Mr. Wilford's umbrella, Amelia. My client."

Amelia stood her ground. "The firm's client."

Eleanor eyed the closed door. This was her break-out case, the one that would force the partners to take her seriously.

The telephone on Amelia's desk began to ring. Amelia glanced at it, and back at Eleanor. Eleanor felt a ripple of impending triumph. She stood still and waited.

Mistaking Eleanor's hesitation for compliance, Amelia made an error in judgment and stepped out of the path to the door.

Eleanor bolted for the door. Amelia gave a gasp and lunged for her, but Eleanor had just enough time to toss a hasty, half victorious, half apologetic glance over her shoulder before slipping inside the heavy paneled door.

"Eleanor!" Eleanor heard Amelia's cry of dismay as she shut the door behind her.

"Eleanor." Philip Conrad, whom Eleanor had once heard accurately, if not unkindly, described as a walking cadaver, gave her a terse nod from his position behind his wide expanse of desk. "Now's not a good time."

Mr. Wilford, ordinarily jovial, looked distinctly ill at ease, his gaze carefully aimed out the window.

Ignoring Philip's directive, Eleanor strode into the room and perched on the arm of the nearest wingback. She shot what she hoped was a confident smile at Mr. Wilford, who gave her an uneasy nod in return. "There seems to be some confusion, Philip.

Perhaps you can clear it up." Philip raised an eyebrow. "Wayne Patterson just told my assistant that he's replacing me as your lead attorney." Eleanor tried to gauge Mr. Wilford's response and felt a wave of fresh alarm when he glanced away again.

Philip gazed at Eleanor imperturbably. "He is replacing you, Eleanor."

She felt as though she had taken a heavy blow straight to her stomach.

Mr. Wilford heaved himself out of the matching armchair. "Think I'll be going now."

Eleanor watched as her client rushed for the door. When the door closed in his wake, she turned her head slowly back to Philip.

Philip glared at her coldly. "Eleanor, your behavior is disgraceful."

Eleanor's temper began to bubble. "I'll tell you what's disgraceful, Philip. Finding out through the grapevine that I've been taken off my own case."

"Mr. Wilford feels more comfortable with a man leading his defense."

"And who decided Wayne would be that man?"

Philip's expression turned stony.

"You did, didn't you? Be real! You know as well as I do that Wayne can't argue his way out of a paper bag!"

"That's quite enough, Eleanor. It's certainly not your place to---"

Gathering steam, Eleanor cut him off. "Not my place, Phillip? Where exactly is my place? Out of sight, gathering dust? Giving Mr. Wilford's suit to Wayne is a joke!" A wave of pure fury swept over her. "Do you know how long I've worked here, Philip?" She didn't allow him time to respond. "Eight long years. I've worked ninety hours a week, including every weekend and almost every holiday. I did the grunt work, I took the dog cases, I built my reputation, and I've generated a lot of billable hours for this firm."

Philip began to interrupt but she continued heedlessly. "Nobody wanted the Wilford case, Philip. It was nothing, which is why you agreed to give it to me, but now it's something, and damn it, it's mine." Eleanor slapped her hands down on the edge of Philip's desk and leaned over the polished surface. "There's a word for this, Philip. Discrimination."

Philip's brows met dangerously and he deliberately pushed his chair back. Rising, he circled the desk and rounded the corner, glaring down at her silently. Eleanor recognized the intimidation ploy; it was used on her all the time because of her tiny stature and she was sick and tired of it. She flung her hands on her hips and glowered up at him in reckless return. "That's right, discrimination."

Philip abruptly changed tactics. "Now, Eleanor, don't overreact. We still want you to be involved. You can assist Wayne every step of the way."

It occurred to Eleanor that she had nobody to blame but herself. She'd been passive since the day she crossed the threshold and now she was being mistaken for a doormat. No more. She'd swing naked from the flagpole of the federal courthouse before she'd take a back seat to Wayne Patterson.

Apparently Philip thought she was calming because he relaxed and leaned against the edge of his desk. "Frankly, I'm the first to admit Wayne doesn't have your thorough knowledge of the case but the firm expects you to be a team player. We expect your understanding and cooperation. The trial will demand a strong personality. You know as well as I do that your strength lies in research and preparation, not at the forefront of a courtroom battlefield. But, I agree, you deserve to sit at that table and be part of it. In fact, I think the two of you will make a great team. Perhaps off the job as well as on. He admires you very much, you know."

Eleanor stared up at him, speechless for a moment. Was Philip actually trying to manipulate her by waving Wayne under her nose like some kind of prized male specimen? Did he think she was stupid *and* desperate?

"You know," Philip added confidingly, "Your father and I both think you'd make a good match."

Her father. Eleanor blinked. Her father was a master of manipulation but there were some things even the Honorable Julius W. Haley, III, would never accomplish. "Are you insane?"

"Excuse me?"

She was marching right into career suicide but the unfairness of the situation was more than she could stand. "You want to give Wayne the case, then give it to him, but don't delude yourself into believing that I would, for one minute, hold his hand and waltz him through every motion and objection and sidebar conference. And, for God's sake, don't delude yourself into thinking I'd ever hold your nephew's hand for any other reason, either!"

Philip folded his arms across his chest, his expression apoplectic. "Eleanor, I don't believe you have a choice where the Wilford case is concerned."

For once in her life, Eleanor deliberately refused to think about the consequences of her actions and she felt a strange, giddy excitement. "Oh, I believe I do, Philip." She gave him a decisive nod before spinning on her heel. "I'll be out of my office by close of business today."

Had she really said that out loud? Judging by the flush of purple in Philips face, she sure had.

"You're making a mistake, Eleanor," he bit off. "At the very least you owe this firm some notice!"

Insufferable chauvinist. "Notice this, Philip. Notice me walking out the door." Eleanor yanked the door open and slipped through, resisting the temptation to let it slam behind her.

Her heart was threatening to pound right out of her chest. Biting back an inappropriate and slightly alarming giggle, she closed the door and leaned against it for a moment. The giggle erupted.

Amelia, sitting stiffly at her desk, turned a chilly, curious eye in her direction.

Eleanor wondered if she was about to be hysterical. She'd never been hysterical before so she didn't know how it felt but she imagined it was something like this: slightly light-headed and a touch feverish, on the edge of either bursting into heaving sobs or maniacal laughter. She clasped the sides of her face for a moment and drew in a deep, shaky breath. And if she was, would it be hysteria from horror or exuberance? At this moment it was hard to tell. Adrenalin still pumping through her veins, she caught Amelia's stare and gave her a trembling smile. "I just quit," she announced in a whisper.

Vexation forgotten, Amelia's eyes opened wide and she rolled her chair around in Eleanor's direction. "Quit?" She gaped at Eleanor as though she had just announced she was joining the Marines.

Eleanor nodded. "Just like that." She snapped her fingers weakly in illustration. "Bye, Amelia."

* * *

Man, it was good to be home in Baton Rouge, even if just for one night. Tyler Hurst slung his suit bag over his shoulder and punched the security code into the panel beside his back door before jamming the key into the lock. Hopping around the country took its toll. Hotel beds that were too hard or too soft, food that was too rich, meetings and flights that were too long, with no time in between for any significant exercise. That had to be the worst of it. His body, abused for fourteen tough years on the Denver Renegade's defensive line, had a tendency to complain when he quit moving. Like his old Mustang, he couldn't sit in the garage for too long or the motor had a hard time cranking.

He barely turned the key in the lock before the door wrenched open from the inside.

"Ty!"

Tyler lifted his head and caught the young woman hurtling herself through the doorway. His youngest sister, staying at his place for a couple of days, hugged him tightly. "I thought you told me you weren't coming home until Wednesday or Thursday."

"Change of plans," Tyler replied easily, dropping his bag on the floor. "Anyway, if I didn't get home till Wednesday or Thursday, I'd completely miss seeing you, wouldn't I? I'll fly to Denver tomorrow." He squeezed her waist, then held her away and gave her a considering, thorough inspection. "I can feel your ribs. You're too skinny. Gain some weight." Hiding a grin, he headed through the cavernous great room toward his office.

On his heels, Hope laughed at him. "Quit bossing me. I have to fit in my wedding dress, you know."

Tyler flicked the overhead light switch and circled the partner's desk to pick up his stacked mail. When Hope dropped onto the sofa and patted the tan leather beside her, he shook his head and began flipping through the envelopes. "I've been sitting too long as it is. What's this about a wedding dress?" he asked, quirking an eyebrow innocently. "Somebody getting married?"

She leaned forward, blue eyes shining. "Oh, quit teasing, Ty. It's only six weeks away. That reminds me, you still have to be fitted for your tux."

"But I already have a tux," he protested, enjoying the exchange. "Why would I want to rent another one? And who says I agreed to wear one, anyway?"

"You're impossible," she retorted cheerfully. "Do it today."

He folded his arms across his chest and narrowed his eyes. "Bossy wench."

"Big bully." She stuck her tongue out at him.

Tyler grinned in spite of himself. His menacing game face had absolutely no effect on his baby sister.

Hope changed the subject. "Are you going to go over to Rosie's this afternoon?

"Yep. Have you seen her yet?"

She made a face at him that plainly inferred he was silly for asking. "Of course. We went straight there when we got in on Saturday to take her out to dinner. We wanted to take her someplace special but she had her own ideas."

Tyler raised his eyebrows curiously. Rosie always had her own ideas. Usually harmless, often amusing, occasionally horrifying. "Not Mongolian barbecue again?" Just the idea made him shudder. Everyone got violently sick after that auspicious outing; everyone, that is, but Rosie.

"Heavens, no. She wanted to go to Hooters." Hope delivered her deadpan announcement and sat back to enjoy his reaction.

"Hooters!" Tyler grinned broadly. "Why on earth did she want to go to Hooters?

"The billboard along the interstate made her curious."

Tyler shook his head in amusement. "Well, what did she think?"

Hope giggled. "She said she'd never seen so many healthy girls in one place in her life. Adam suggested they might not all be, well, 'natural,' and Rosie was absolutely horrified. She started pointing out different waitresses and asking us if their chests were real, as if we'd know, and then she began asking the waitresses."

Tyler laughed out loud. "I'm sorry I missed it." It sounded like a classic Rosie outing. "Where's your bridegroom, anyway?" He picked up an envelope and ripped it open.

"He's helping his dad with something. Ty, put that down and come sit for a minute. I want to talk with you." She patted the sofa again, her tone suddenly serious.

Tyler picked up on the change instantly. He raised his eyes from the correspondence and searched her face, but she gave away nothing.

She patted the sofa again. "Come sit down."

He frowned, disliking the idea he had to sit down for whatever Hope wanted to tell him. Dropping the mail, he obediently crossed the room to join her on the sofa. His body protested at being bent into a sitting position again. "Is something wrong, honey?"

"No, nothing's wrong, Ty, it's just that I want to tell you about some changes to our plans." Hope twisted the sparkling engagement ring on her left ring finger.

"Changes to the wedding plans?"

"No, changes about where we're going to live and what we're going to do."

He relaxed. "You've decided to let me help you buy Letty's house." That was good news. When his grandmother's friend and long-time next door neighbor passed away and left her house to Rosie, he and everyone else in the family wholeheartedly supported her plan to sell the house to Hope and Adam for a fraction of its value. Tyler further enticed them with the offer of a wedding gift in the form of a healthy down-payment, but his efforts had so far proved futile.

Convinced he could persuade them to accept the offer, Tyler had charged full steam ahead and sank a hefty chunk of change into updating and remodeling the house. Hope had always admired Letty's home with its gingerbread trim and wide, curved porch, and Tyler felt confident that when she saw it in its restored glory, she'd convince her fiancée to accept the offer.

"No, that's not it," Hope replied, twisting her ring again. "We still feel the same way about that, and I made Rosie promise to put it up for sale right away and tuck the money into her rainy day fund. Now, listen, I want you to be open-minded about what I'm going to tell you."

She was starting to make him nervous. Tyler folded his arms across his chest and eyed her carefully. "Just spit it out, Hope."

She drew in a deep breath. "Okay. We're not moving back to Baton Rouge. We're staying in Chapel Hill and Adam is going back to school in the fall." Dismayed, Tyler opened his mouth to interrupt but she continued hurriedly. "I know, I know, everybody expected us to move back but we think this is best. So this is the plan. I'll work while he goes to school, then when he graduates, he'll get a job and I'll go back."

Tyler glared at Hope. "No, you won't."

"Yes, I will," she replied calmly, unperturbed by his scowl. "We're staying in North Carolina and we're taking turns going back to school."

"You're not going to take turns," Tyler retorted. "If he goes to school, you go to school. I can't make you come home, Hope, but I can damn well afford to pay for graduate school."

"Nope. One of us has to make money to live on."

"I'll give you money to live on."

"Listen to me, big brother. You've already put me and everybody else through school, and while I adore you for wanting to do more, you have to remember I'm all grown up now. In just six short weeks I'm going to be Mrs. Adam Whittington, and finally out of your hair."

Tyler screwed his face in distaste. "I don't recall complaining about having you in my hair." He liked Adam well enough but he still rebelled at the idea of walking Hope down the aisle and handing her well-being over to a twenty-two-year-old kid. To him she would always be his baby sister, impossibly sweet and innocent. The oldest and youngest of a flock of six, they shared a special bond, and it added extreme insult to injury to accept the fact that Adam was soon going to have a voice in what Tyler could or couldn't do for her.

"Adam has every bit as much pride as you have, Ty. It's important to us that we do it on our own. And you know darn well you'd hate it even more if I was marrying somebody you could bulldoze."

"Yeah, yeah, but I don't like it."

"Well, hold on, because you haven't heard the worst of it yet." Hope straightened her shoulders slightly.

There was more? Tilting his head against the wall behind the sofa, Tyler slowly rubbed his forehead. He felt the unmistakable twinges of a headache coming on. "I'm listening."

"Adam has been accepted into law school."

Tyler tensed. He turned his head and viewed his sister through narrowed eyes. "Law school?" He breathed the words in a low, careful monotone.

Hope nodded. "He wants to study law." She watched him closely, gauging his reaction. "Actually, he always has."

"Call off the wedding," he said bluntly. Lawyers were bottom feeders of the worst sort and he wasn't going to allow one in his family. It was bad enough Adam had balked about Letty's house. It was worse he wasn't bringing Hope back to Baton Rouge. But this was too much. It went way over the top of too much. In fact, it simply wasn't going to happen.

Hope laughed, and then faltered when Tyler fixed her with an unblinking glare. "You're kidding, aren't you?"

Tyler eyed his little sister, her expression anxious. Hell, no, he wasn't kidding but he could see he had to handle this carefully.

"Because I know how you feel about lawyers and I know you've got good reason, but this is Adam we're talking about. You know Adam. He's like you, Tyler. Honest to a fault. He wants to specialize in environmental law."

Tyler leaned back and rubbed his throbbing brow fiercely. An honest lawyer. Now there was an oxymoron. A sideways glance at his sister made him grit his teeth and swallow. She looked like she was about to burst into tears.

"Yeah, I'm kidding." Like hell he was kidding. There were other ways to handle this situation. There were thousands of careers in the world and he was personally going to help Adam pick out another one. "But I don't like it," he couldn't resist adding.

Hope hugged him, relief washing over her face, then jumped up from the sofa and headed for the doorway. "Well, I can't make you like it, Ty, but it really means a lot to me that you'll still give us your blessing." She caught his narrowed glare and sighed. "Give me your blessing, Tyler."

"You have it," he said, rising and picking up his mail again. More than anything he wanted this miserable conversation to be over with. He had to plan his strategy for dealing with Adam. He tore another envelope open and asked casually, "Where'd you say Adam was? Is he coming back by here this afternoon?"

Hope gave him a stern look. "There'll be no pulling Adam off to the side, do you hear me?"

He gave her a wounded look but she didn't buy it.

"I mean it, Ty. No evil looks, no guilt trips, and especially no lectures. Promise me."

"You're asking a lot." She had no idea how much.

"I love you a lot, o' great intimidator of bridegrooms." With a wave she disappeared through the door.

Tyler leaned forward, dropping his head into his hands. What a homecoming.

Chapter Two

Tyler turned onto Magnolia Drive and grinned when he saw Mrs. Tuminello whipping around her front yard on her oversized riding mower. She still drove that thing like she was competing in the Indy 500, he noted, the same tattered straw hat with plastic flowers dangling from the brim pulled down low on her gray head like a race helmet.

Continuing on, he spied Rosie, standing on the brick walkway to her front porch, speculatively eyeing the beds of petunias lining the sides. As always his heart warmed at the sight of his diminutive grandmother. She stood five feet nothing, was all heart and humor, and was the best friend he'd ever had. There was nothing he wouldn't do for Rosie.

In a way he and his grandmother had grown up together, and in a hurry, because Rosie had been lovingly sheltered by both husband and son until his parents died. The realities of dealing with skimpy finances, insurance battles and legal problems, not to mention his five brothers and sisters, had created a bond between the unlikely pair that had enabled them to survive it all.

There was absolutely nothing he wouldn't do for Rosie.

He tapped the horn lightly as he approached. Her softly lined face lit up, and she hurried to meet him as he came to a stop at the end of the driveway. He unfolded himself from the seat of his old Mustang and met her halfway.

"Tyler! You're home early!" She reached up and put her soft hands around his face, pulling him down for a kiss.

Tyler hugged her gently in return. "Well, yes and no. I'm leaving again tomorrow night for Denver but I ought to be back by Sunday or Monday."

His grandmother gave him a concerned look. "I thought you were going to be able to sit still for a while once you came back home, but I declare, I don't think I see any more of you now than I did before." Stretching, she straightened his collar and brushed an invisible piece of lint from his shoulder. "When are you going to stop all this running around?"

"Soon, Rosie. That's what all the traveling's about, remember? Tying up loose ends."

She reached up to pat his jaw. "I hope so, honey. Well, tell me, how were Hank and Warren and their families? Did you boys like the property in Phoenix? Did Hope remind you about your tuxedo fitting? Are you hungry? Come inside and I'll fix you something to eat." She turned toward the side porch, confident he was following.

His grin widened at the predictable barrage of conversation. "Let's see, that would be 'fine, yes, yes, and no, I already ate.' Hold on, Rosie. I want to talk with you about Hope and Adam."

She shot a careful glance over her shoulder but didn't slow down. "Well, you may not be hungry, but I baked a chocolate cake and it's been calling my name all morning. At least sit down and keep me company."

Giving up, he followed along, crossing the wide expanse of deck and ducking through the doorway into the screened side porch that led to the kitchen. "Did Hope tell you she and Adam are planning to stay in North Carolina? That Adam wants to go to law school?" He was counting on Rosie being as horrified as he was. After all, his first and possibly worst experience with an unscrupulous lawyer had deeply affected Rosie, too.

Rosie pushed him toward a chair at the kitchen table and lifted an aluminum dome to show him a homemade chocolate cake with thick fudge icing. He lifted his eyebrows in appreciation. "Maybe a little slice," he said.

Giving him a "told you so" look, she deftly hacked off an enormous slab and plopped it onto a plate. The term "little slice" meant nothing to her, Tyler thought with amusement. Never had, never would.

"About Hope---," he began.

"It's what Adam's always wanted to do, Tyler," Rosie interrupted. "He wants to specialize in environmental law." She handed him the plate, then turned to pour milk into a tumbler. Slowing slightly on her return trip to the table to seize a napkin, she pulled out a chair beside Tyler and sat down, pushing the tumbler and napkin in his direction. "That's a good field, don't you think?"

He ignored her hopeful question. "If it's what he always wanted to do, how come it's the first I've ever heard of it? What were they doing, keeping it a secret from everybody or just me?" He was beginning to suspect he was the last to know, and secrets really ticked him off.

Rosie confirmed his suspicion. "Because Adam knows how you feel about attorneys in general. We all do. Who can blame him for not announcing it? In fact, I told them they ought to wait until after the wedding to tell you."

Tyler choked on his first bite of cake, and stared at his grandmother, eyes watering. Rosie whacked him on the back energetically. Just like he thought, dead last to know. "I feel the way I feel for good reason, Rosie."

"I know, I know. Don't get all bent out of shape, hon. The important thing to remember is Adam is a nice boy. He's going to make a fine husband and a fine attorney." She caught his skeptical glance and folded her arms across her slight bosom. "Oh, don't give me that look, Tyler. There are such things as good attorneys. What about the ones who work for you now? You like them, don't you? You need to remember that one bad apple doesn't spoil the whole barrel."

"No, but three bad apples might make you wonder exactly what they teach nice boys in law school," Tyler retorted, working steadily on the chunk of cake. "And, no, I don't like my attorneys. They're a necessary evil and they know I don't like them and that I don't trust them any farther than I can toss them. That's exactly how I want it, too. That way they don't get any ideas. Do you want to see Adam turn into a Rodney Stineman or a Louis Terrell? How about a Thomas Mattingly?" Just the names made him grit his teeth. He drained the tumbler of milk and set it back down on the table with more force than necessary. He looked down at his plate which was startlingly bare, and back at Rosie. "And how come I'm the only one eating around here? What about cake calling your name?"

Rosie winked and patted him on his broad shoulder. "He's not going to turn into anything. You need to put all that behind you, Tyler. Get over it."

Get over it? If he lived to be a hundred he'd never get over his loathing for lawyers but there was no point debating the issue with Rosie. "What about their plan to stay in North Carolina?"

Rosie sighed. "Well, I see the sense of it since Adam's been accepted into law school there, but of course I'm disappointed. You've got Letty's house fixed up so beautifully and it seemed to be the perfect plan." She picked up his plate and empty tumbler and carried them to the sink. "I called a real estate agent friend of Leanne's and told her to put it on the market. No point in hanging onto it now that Hope and Adam have made other plans." She ran water over the dishes and placed them in the dishwasher. "Her name is Amanda Howard. She and Leanne were in the same class in high school. Do you remember her?"

He shook his head warily; pretty sure he knew where the conversation was headed.

Rosie sat back down. "Well, she remembers you. Apparently she's a big fan because she went on and on about watching you play on television. She said to tell you hello and she hopes to see you sometime." She looked at him expectantly.

Tyler folded his arms across his chest and leaned back in his chair, the front legs lifting from the floor. "Quit it, Rosie," he said, eyes narrowed.

"Quit what?"

"Quit matchmaking."

She didn't bother to deny it. "Leanne was sure you'd remember Amanda because she's tall and blonde and pretty. I think she was a cheerleader. I have her telephone number. You could call her and invite her out to dinner."

Tyler drew in a deep, long-suffering breath and put the chair back down on all four legs with a thump. "Rosie, you're really going to have to give me a break here. I know you probably find this hard to believe but, honest to God, I don't have any trouble meeting women on my own." No way was he about to go into any details with his grandmother about just how easy it was. Some things were better left unsaid.

"Nice women?" She pinned him with hopeful blue eyes.

"Yes, of course, nice women. Now, listen, about Letty's house---"

"Then why don't I ever get to meet any of them?"

There was no dodging the bullet so he changed tactics. "Well, let's see, now, Rosie," he drawled playfully. "Do you think maybe the twelve hundred or so miles between Baton Rouge and Denver might've had a little bit to do with it?"

He could tell by the way she drew up her shoulders and sat up straight in her chair that she didn't appreciate his attempt to deflect her favorite topic with humor. "All I know is that neither one of us is getting any younger and if you've got any notion at all about getting married again someday, I sure wish you'd put it on the front burner so I can meet your wife before I pass to the great beyond."

The great beyond. Tyler sighed.

Satisfied she'd made her point, Rosie promptly returned to the topic of Letty's house. "Anyway, Amanda has already got a sign in the yard."

Tyler was more than glad to change the subject. "Sounds good. It should sell quickly."

"Maybe a young family will buy it," Rosie remarked hopefully, covering the cake. "It's nice when young families move into the neighborhood. It keeps us old fogies on our toes." She wiped the already clean counter with a dishcloth.

CHRISTY ST. ROMAIN MARCHAND

Tyler smiled at the idea of Rosie requiring any boosting to stay on her toes. She ran circles around them all, zipping from one end of town to the other for more clubs and classes than he could keep up with. Almost every evening some part of the family was at her house because she constantly cooked enormous quantities of food and then called around, nonchalantly mentioning favorites they couldn't possibly resist. Her story was she couldn't learn how to cook for just one and they would just have to get on over to eat. They always got on over and ate. Now that he was home he found he was as susceptible to her wiles as the rest of his family. A fearless traveler to boot, she had thought nothing of jumping onto planes at the spur of the moment, alone or with other family members in tow, to watch him play in Denver and around the country. His teammates had been completely enamored with her. He smiled again at the memory. No, Rosie was not your standard little old white haired lady.

Still, a young family with small children next door would be ideal. Tyler rubbed his jaw thoughtfully. Not only would his nieces and nephews have some other kids to play with but, more importantly, the adults could keep an eye on Rosie when he and his brothers and sisters weren't around.

Leaning, Rosie wiped the crumbs he'd managed to disperse on the tabletop, and then surveyed his crisp slacks and button-down shirt with a critical eye. He glanced down and brushed at his chest. "What's the matter? More crumbs?"

"I was just wondering how you were going to help me dig up my poor, tired pansies wearing those nice clothes." She patted the top of his head affectionately. "How can I put you to work when you come over dressed like a model from GQ?"

26

Tyler leaned back in his chair and grinned at her. "I'm sure you can find something else I can wear."

"I've got an extra apron," she teased. "Would you prefer floral or polka dots?"

"No aprons. Can't you scare up some manly stuff?" He flexed his arms comically.

She nodded. "Robb rushed by day before yesterday, running late as usual, to change on his way to meet Nancy at Austin's program and I washed his work clothes. I'll get you outfitted for digging, wait and see." She headed into the living room. "I'm thinking about putting in more petunias. Or maybe yellow lantana. It blooms all summer and shows up so nicely from the street." Her voice trailed off as she disappeared into the back of the house.

He rose and stretched, pleasantly stuffed with cake and milk, and surveyed Rosie's kitchen. His new house beside the golf course was nice enough but he didn't really feel at home yet. He still expected to see the mountains through the windows, not a swimming pool and golf course. Anyway, this small house was his real home. He'd convinced Rosie to let him handle the upkeep, and had bossed her into some much needed renovations, but the bones were familiar and unchanging. The scent of lemon furniture polish, the floral china, the vast collection of childish paintings and misshapen crafts projects proudly displayed on every surface and wall, and most importantly, Rosie. Wherever Rosie was, was simply and irrevocably home.

* * *

Eleanor heaved a box containing her most personal belongings into the passenger seat of her car and closed the door. Gracie, dear, loyal Gracie, was going to bring the rest of her stuff over later in the evening. Word of her resignation had spread like wildfire, and the effort required to maintain her composure, console Gracie, pack her things and answer the barrage of questions posed by curious colleagues all at the same time had proved to be too much. Yes, it was true, Philip gave Wayne her case. Yes, she really did quit on the spot. No, she didn't have a clue about her future. The last admission to Gracie made her stomach twist and, in the end, she grabbed her one packed box and fled.

She knew one thing about her future, though. The days when Eleanor Haley stood back instead of standing up were over.

Circling to the driver side, she opened the door and slid inside. For the last time she eased out of her parking space, casting a scowl at Wayne Patterson's ostentatious Jaguar.

The bright sunlight at the upper end of the basement garage ramp stung her eyes and she reached for her purse, only to remember she'd lost her sunglasses some time back and never bothered to replace them. Hadn't needed to. A girl who never saw the light of day didn't need sunglasses.

Eleanor pulled out to the edge of the street and stopped at the stop sign, suddenly anxious again. Now what? She drew in a deep breath. Perhaps she should look at this as just some temporary time off, like a vacation. She hadn't had a vacation since---Eleanor frowned, thinking back. Certainly not since she began working at CBB. And before that, during law school, she hadn't had a minute to call her own. Maybe back when she was earning her bachelor's degree. Her face wrinkled in concentration. Nope, not then, either. She'd been living at home, under her father's eagle eye, always cognizant of the fact she was expected to maintain a minimum 4.0 grade point average. No, there had been no vacations that she could recall.

She glanced at her wristwatch. Two-thirty in the afternoon. What exactly did people do at two-thirty in the afternoon if they weren't at work? What did it say about her, that she didn't have a clue? Eleanor frowned, her hands gripping the steering wheel. She had no hobbies, no real friends beyond Gracie, and certainly no love life. There simply hadn't been time for anything but work as she dedicated herself to her education and then to her career as she worked toward becoming the firm's first female senior partner. A vital step toward making her father proud.

Her father. She winced. She'd be surprised if he didn't already know about her fall from grace, thanks to his longtime friendship with Philip, and she imagined he would have a few choice things to say when he called. And she knew he would call. Not ready for that, she put her phone on silent and dropped it back into her bag.

A horn sounded behind her and she jumped. "All right, already," she muttered, turning onto the boulevard.

She'd like to think her father would applaud her refusal to sacrifice her role in the biggest case of her career. Stand behind her and offer sympathy and support in the face of Philip's blatant chauvinism. Closing her eyes briefly, she knew she was being unrealistic. The truth was he would be livid at her display of temper and recklessness.

Eleanor sighed. She would disappoint him again.

She drove towards home, taking the longer route she had discovered accidentally a year or so earlier; one that wound through a lovely established neighborhood in an older part of the city. The very first time she drove down the main oak-lined avenue, she fell under the charm of the storybook like homes. The railed porches, swings, and lush flowerbeds conveyed time and tradition and lots of love, and were infinitely more appealing than the haughty estate that had been her childhood home. In the past year or so she had come to know the individual houses in the old neighborhood as well as she knew the rooms in her apartment. After a day spent focusing on facts and strategies and the seamier side of humanity, it was strangely therapeutic to ease up and down the broad streets and make little discoveries, like just last week when she saw that the family who lived in the house on the corner of Foxglove and Camellia was building an elaborate tree house, and that bright striped awnings had been installed on the house at the end of Wisteria.

The streets were all named for flowers, lovely old-fashioned southern flowers, and while she knew less than nothing about flowers, southern, northern or otherwise, it was cheerfully clear that the homeowners there were experts. Summer had exploded with a colorful vengeance, the evidence spilling from window boxes and hanging baskets and oversized pots, and curving around houses in sweeping flowerbeds.

This was the first time she'd driven through the neighborhood during the middle of the day and the sidewalks ribboning through the shady yards were busy with activity. A bright flock of gangly little girls bobbled their way down the sidewalk of Violet Street in skates and a boisterous game of softball was in full swing in one of the larger front yards on Viburnum. Eleanor slowed as she passed. There seemed to be some disagreement about whether the runner on third, a boy with shocking red hair, was safe. Maybe they needed a mediator. She smiled at the thought. Had she ever been that lively? Of course not. From the time she was old enough to understand, it had been drummed into her to sit still, hold her tongue, act like a lady and mind her manners.

Of all the homes in the neighborhood, there were two in particular to which she was most drawn. At the end of Magnolia Drive, they sat side by side, farther from the street than the rest of their neighbors. The first house exuded an air of welcome and whimsy that was hard to resist, from the pink flamingo mailbox to the electric blue chairs clustered beneath the biggest oak tree Eleanor had ever seen. The flower beds there were without equal, even in the competitive flower laden neighborhood.

The second was something of a mystery. The front yard, rimmed by a lacy, old-fashioned wire fence, was lined with ancient, overgrown shrubs that almost shrouded the little house. Last winter when some of the shrubs lost their foliage, she had been able to see a bit more, and what she saw was intriguing. A glimpse of a curved porch, a flash of twinkling windows. The other houses were of a gregarious nature with open lawns and open windows, while 421 Magnolia struck Eleanor as almost shy, definitely endearing.

But something was afoot at 421 Magnolia. Last week she discovered the fence was gone and herculean efforts were underway to tame the overgrown yard. A massive pile of debris and trash waited street side for the next garbage day, but most telling were the service trucks lining the driveway. Eleanor thought it likely the old house had new owners, energetic people who wanted to give the old home the love and attention it deserved. She hoped so. Maybe today she would find out.

Turning down Magnolia, she barely spared a glance for her other favorite in her eagerness to check out the progress at the mystery house. How much would be visible today? Would it live up to her expectations? She hoped, inexplicably, the house wouldn't disappoint her. A boost would be nice today, even a vicarious boost.

She spotted something staked beside the mailbox. A garage sale sign, perhaps? Leaning forward, Eleanor squinted to make out the lettering and then exhaled with a breathless whoosh. No, it was a "for sale" sign. The mystery house was for sale.

"Oh, my," she whispered, goose bumps prickling her arms. She eased down the driveway at a snail's pace and came to a complete stop before lifting her eyes to the house that was finally exposed to view.

Eleanor's breath caught in her throat, then escaped in a long, heartfelt gasp. She felt a funny, almost familiar thrill of recognition, and the goose bumps returned in renewed force. It was a storybook house straight out of the simple books she read as a child, before textbooks took the place of the romantic tales that always had a happy ending. Unconsciously Eleanor turned off the key in the ignition and leaned forward. Every wretched remembrance of her miserable morning was completely swept away as she drank in the details of the house.

It sat back from the street in the shade of an enormous old moss laden oak tree, and wore its lush green lawn like an apron. Painted a sunny yellow, the house boasted wide bricked steps leading to an intricately railed porch that stretched across the front and curved gracefully around the left corner. Comfortable old rocking chairs flanked a wide bay window that dominated the right side of the house. A cheerful little window with diamond panes blinked out of the pitched eave and a stocky little cupola sat on top like a pert hat. The wide front door boasted a stained glass panel of a creamy magnolia bloom, there was a small storybook window next to the door, and the whole house dripped in gingerbread trim.

Almost mesmerized, Eleanor swung open her door and climbed out of the car to get a closer look. She walked up the brick walkway and broad brick steps, feeling an unfamiliar anxiousness, and drew to an abrupt halt a foot away from the door. The stained glass window in the front door was a work of art. Eleanor reached a tentative hand to touch the creamy opaque magnolias against a glossy green background. Smiling gently, she pulled her hand back and wrapped her arms around her waist, drinking in the charm of the wide door with its lovely window. Then she reached out and tested the ornate brass knob. Locked, of course. She laughed self-consciously. What did she expect? That it would be open, just for her, like in Goldilocks and the Three Bears? Her imagination was truly getting the best of her.

Eleanor slowly retraced her steps down the walk and driveway back to her car. She slid inside, propped her arms on the steering wheel, and eyed the house speculatively. There was just something about it. Something familiar, something enticing. She wanted to see inside. In fact, she simply had to see inside. Inexplicably determined, she climbed out again, and then faltered. What on earth was the matter with her? She was getting carried away. It wasn't as if she could buy it. The house was adorable, certainly, but she already had a perfectly acceptable apartment. She was settled and comfortable there. True, it seemed a little austere compared to this frilly Victorian candy box, but it suited her just fine. It fit the needs of her lifestyle.

Of course, her lifestyle had just taken a drastic turn in an unknown direction.

Well, she was just curious, that was all. There was nothing wrong with curiosity. And since old houses almost always looked better on the outside than they did on the inside, she might as well just go ahead and peek inside a window or two, satisfy herself that it was more trouble than it was worth, and go home. Nodding to herself, Eleanor shut the car door. That's what she would do. Just peek inside and get it out of her system.

After clumsily circling the house in her heels, she discovered with dismay the only opening not obstructed with shades or shutters was a pair of arched windows high on the left side of the house. She gazed up at them thoughtfully and then glanced around for something to stand on.

* * *

The pansies were history, and the soil in the wide flowerbed was primed for the next planting. Tyler wiped his forehead with his arm, leaned on his shovel, and watched a little gray hybrid ease past Rosie's house and turn into Letty's driveway. The single occupant sat in the car for a long moment before stepping out and heading toward the front porch at a healthy clip. His curiosity piqued, Tyler stabbed the shovel into the loosened earth and walked toward the dividing hedge of azaleas for a better look. He watched a lone woman tentatively make her way onto the porch and draw to an abrupt halt at the front door. He watched her examine the stained glass insert. It really was a nice window, he thought with satisfaction. One of his favorites.

"What are you looking at, honey?" Wiping her hands on her cheerful smock, Rosie spoke to him through the screen door. "Somebody over at Letty's?" She pushed through the door with a rounded shoulder and trod carefully down the wide planked steps, a tall glass of iced lemonade in each hand.

Nodding, Tyler wiped his hands on his borrowed, uncomfortably tight jeans and stepped over to take one of the glasses from her. "There's a woman taking a look around on the porch."

Rosie peered in the same direction. "I can't see her."

Tyler grinned down at her. "'Course you can't, short stuff. What does your real estate agent look like?"

Rosie swatted his sleeve for his impertinence. "I already told you. She's tall and blonde."

The woman on the porch was small and dark haired. "Then that's not her." Placing a gentle hand at his grandmother's elbow, he tried to steer her toward the circle of enamel lawn chairs sitting in the shade of the old oak tree that shaded her house as well as Letty's. The enamel chairs were ancient and had sat in the same spot under the tree for as long as Tyler could remember. Every year or so he coaxed Rosie into letting him give them a fresh coat of paint, any color she wanted, and the last time around she picked turquoise blue. A slightly startling shade, he thought, but he'd have painted them with polka dots if that was what she wanted.

"Maybe the ad was in the paper this morning," Rosie suggested. "Amanda was very enthusiastic." She swatted again at his hand at her elbow and continued toward the hedge

Tyler eyed his grandmother carefully. It was hot outside and she looked a little too flushed for his comfort. He knew she liked to keep busy but she tended to forget she was pushing eighty-seven.

"My goodness," he heard her say.

"What is it?"

Rosie stepped nearer the shrubs and pushed back a branch with her free hand. "I do believe she's trying to climb up to Letty's kitchen windows."

Blinking, Tyler jumped up. "The hell you say." Hastily he placed his glass on the wrought iron table and spun in the direction of Letty's house.

"Tyler! Language!"

"Sorry," he replied automatically, pushing his way through the narrow path between the azaleas. He cleared the shrubbery, and then halted, standing silently on the edge of Letty's green lawn.

His grandmother was right. The woman was indeed trying to climb into the window but there wasn't a snowball's chance in hell she was going to succeed. Tyler bit back a smile and ducked back into the cover of the shrubbery. This could be interesting. For one thing, she was about a foot and a half too short and, for another, her clothes were all wrong. From the tips of her Barbie doll high heels, to the stiff collar of her expensive suit, she was way overdressed for breaking and entering. He slid behind the tree to avoid her notice. She sure was little. Bordering on scrawny, in fact.

The woman stared up at the window for a long moment, hands on her hips, and then glanced around speculatively. Tyler glanced around, too, wondering what she had in mind. Surely she didn't think she could scale the wall without a ladder? The woman caught sight of the garage at the end of the driveway and headed toward it purposefully. Don't go in there, he warned her mentally, it hasn't been cleaned out yet. She pushed the door open carefully.

Hesitating only a brief moment after pushing the creaky door open, the woman tiptoed inside.

All right, hard-head, he thought wryly. Wait till a rat runs across your little tiny shoe.

She emerged moments later with an armload of grimy plastic crates. She dropped them near the window and then returned to the shed for another load. Tyler watched as she struggled, in her severe suit, to toss the crates over the top of the overgrown azaleas lining the side of the house.

He had to give her credit; she was a tenacious little thing. The branches of the old azaleas were thick and gnarled and provided a formidable barrier between the open lawn and the house. She managed to toss the crates over the top and then took on the battle of pushing her way through the wall of shrubbery. Once successful, the only proof for a moment that there was someone behind the azaleas was a rustling of branches and an occasional, indecipherable mutter. Suddenly her head reappeared, then her shoulders, and finally she was visible to the hem of her slim skirt. Giving her points for stacking and scaling the crates, Tyler noted without surprise she still lacked the height required to see inside the window. Her nose was barely at a level with the ledge.

Tyler felt a pang of conscience. He could save the woman a lot of sweat and bother, and quite possibly injury, by simply interrupting and offering to fetch the key that Rosie held to Letty's house, but he hesitated to speak. Not just because he might startle her and cause her to tumble off her crate tower, but also because anybody crazy enough to fight their way through sixty year old shrubbery to see inside a house deserved the chance to try. He admired determination. Tyler continued to watch and wait, leaning against the trunk of the old oak that shaded both yards, his arms folded across his chest, fingers tucked beneath his armpits.

She strained to peer inside the window, face upturned and hands gripping the ledge.

"Rats."

He grinned at her mild curse. Apparently she had figured out it wasn't going to work. Curling the fingers of one hand on the edge of the window ledge and flattening the other against the exterior siding, she began the awkward backwards descent down her makeshift scaffolding. Her narrow skirt hampered her flexibility and she struggled. Headed for trouble, no doubt about it. One foot stretched downwards, feeling in vain for the ground and safety, but the gnarled azalea limbs thwarted her movement.

"Stupid, stupid, stupid." Again he heard her mutter, more vigorously and with a decided self-derisive tone as she strained to touch the ground. One particularly aggressive limb caught itself on the hem of her skirt, hitching it upwards as she tried to scoot downwards. He heard her curse, colorfully this time, when she realized she was snagged. Keeping her grip on the ledge, she swatted carefully at the limb with her free hand.

She was in big, big trouble, Tyler grinned, noting the brief view of slim legs the errant branch afforded him. He started forward unconsciously. Her chances of reaching the ground unscathed were slimmer than a snake's shadow. He would have to help. She swatted again at the limb and it broke away from her skirt, snapping against her leg noisily.

Ouch, he thought, wincing. Bet that stung. She yelped and her balance shifted suddenly, causing her tower of crates to shift as well. Shrieking in earnest, she grabbed the window ledge with both hands just as the crates toppled over sideways. The knot of dark hair at the nape of her neck slipped and unrolled slightly as she hung from the ledge like limp laundry for a brief moment and though Tyler leapt in her direction with the agility he'd honed through the years, he couldn't cross the few yards separating them before she gracelessly tumbled into Letty's aged azaleas.

Chapter Three

Eleanor landed among the scattered crates in the cool margin of space between the shrubs and the house with a painful, teeth-jarring thud. Carefully motionless for a moment, she drew in a deep breath and took stock of her situation.

She had banged her elbows, jabbed her ribs, and lost a shoe and several hairpins. Apparently she'd lost her mind, too, for even trying such a stunt. A normal person would call the real estate agent and make an appointment to see the house. A normal person wouldn't rummage around in a creepy old shed and then try to climb a stack of flimsy crates just to peek inside a house they had no intention of buying. Honestly, she didn't know what had gotten into her.

Small mercy it was an azalea she fell into and not something with stickers, Eleanor thought disjointedly as she struggled to push the crates out of the way and twist into a sitting position on the cool ground. She carefully dusted the dirt from her hands and smoothed back the hair that had begun to come loose from her chignon. Bigger mercy she hadn't broken a bone or given herself a concussion. God knows how long she'd have lain there, comatose or worse.

She shuddered. What a day. It was definitely time to go home and pull the covers over her head. Maybe she'd wake up and find that the whole morning was nothing but a terrible nightmare. That she still had a job, both her shoes, and her dignity.

She scrambled to her knees and began to feel beneath the low growing limbs for her lost shoe. She peered into the dense foliage. No shoe. It was probably lost forever inside the hungry, man-eating azalea. Suddenly she didn't even care; the shrub could keep the shoe. She just wanted to stumble back to her car and drive away as quickly as possible.

She debated whether to rise and fight her way out on foot, or crawl out beneath the lower branches. Since she was already on her hands and knees, she decided to opt for the latter.

"You okay in there?" A deep voice, humor undisguised, rumbled way above the screen of foliage.

Eleanor's hand went to her throat. Two enormous work boots, mud clumped around the soles, appeared on the other side of the shrub. .

"Yes, I'm fine," she replied. "I'll be right out," she added, and then resisted the immediate temptation to thump herself on the side of the head. What an asinine thing to say.

"Take your time." Amusement seemed to ooze from the voice.

"If you don't mind, I'd just as soon climb out without an audience." Eleanor hated the note of desperation she heard in her voice.

"Too late. I saw the whole thing and must admit, I'm very impressed. I'm no expert, mind you, but I doubt many women can climb a stack of crates in high heels. Where'd you learn to do that?" The man spoke with a warm, lazy drawl.

Eleanor cringed with embarrassment and wondered what he saw when the limb snagged her skirt. "Listen, if you're a gentleman, you'll go away right now. I'm really fine. I don't need any help."

He laughed, a wonderful rumbly sound, and Eleanor's skin tingled in spite of herself. "Aw, come on out. Don't you want your shoe?"

So that's where it was. How had it managed to clear the azalea? "Just leave it on the ground," she replied.

The boots moved closer and the branches above her head began to rustle. "Don't be shy, now," he wheedled. "Stand up and let me help you get out."

"I can get out by myself. Really. Go away."

Paying no attention whatsoever, he simply laughed again. "Come on, honey, rise and shine."

Honey? Eleanor frowned, her brow wrinkling.

"Hellooo?" The shrubs rustled insistently.

She sighed. Okay, let's get this over with. Climb out, get your shoe from Mr. Helpful and get the heck away. Reversing her direction, she scooted backwards and clambered awkwardly to a standing position against the side of the house. Strangely hesitant to put a face to the voice, Eleanor smoothed her jacket sleeves and tugged at her skirt before raising her eyes to her insistent rescuer.

She looked where she expected to see his face, and saw his chest. A broad chest. She tilted her head, lifting her hand to shade her eyes against the glare of sunlight at his back.

He was big. No, not simply big. Huge. She was resigned to feeling small beside average people and tiny compared to tall people, but this man, even across the width of the azaleas, made her

CHRISTY ST. ROMAIN MARCHAND

feel downright miniature. Eleanor pulled herself up as tall as she could on one shoe and stiffened her shoulders in unconscious reaction as her gaze traveled over the extraordinary length of his body. Her heart thumped slowly, painfully.

He was nothing like any man she'd ever seen before.

Tight faded jeans were molded to long, long legs, and the fabric of his navy blue pullover stretched tightly over bulging biceps and shoulders that looked about three feet wide. His hair, closely cropped in an almost military style was too light to be considered brown but wasn't quite blonde either, and dipped on his wide forehead in a well-defined widow's peak. Reflective sunglasses accentuated his sculpted cheekbones and hid his eyes but she had the uneasy feeling they were twinkling to coordinate with the amused tilt of his lips. Completely dumbstruck, Eleanor stood and stared up at him, then realized her mouth was hanging open. She snapped it closed.

"Hi." He pulled off his sunglasses and hooked them into the collar of his shirt. "You okay? Still in one piece?"

His eye color, like his hair, defied common description. Not exactly blue or green, they were a striking blend of both with shots of hazy gold, and they were definitely twinkling. She continued to gape at him across the top of the azalea bush, and then realized he'd asked a question.

"Yes, of course I'm okay." It took some effort but she managed to respond in a cool, slightly impatient tone.

Raising an eyebrow in skeptical amusement, he held up her shoe. It looked tiny in his big hand. "Yours, I believe."

"Mine," she agreed. He reached across the shrub to hand it to her. Planting her free hand against the house for balance, she jammed it onto her sandy foot. "Thank you."

He took a step between two of the overgrown shrubs. "My pleasure. Come on, Supergirl, let's leap over tall shrubbery." Taking a second step, he planted himself firmly in the middle of the foliage and reached for her.

Eleanor edged away hastily, bumping into the unyielding wall. "I can get out by myself," she protested. "Really. If you'll just move---"

He took a third step that carried him into the tiny aisle of space against the house. Breaking out into a sweat, Eleanor flattened herself against the wall and cursed the impulsiveness that had placed her squarely into this sorry situation. The man could be a mass murderer for all she knew. She was cornered against a wall with a potential mass murderer who was bigger than Paul Bunyan. Bigger even than the blue ox. She craned to monitor his expression. "I can get out the same way I---"

"I know," he interrupted her placidly. "But it's so much easier my way." Effortlessly he scooped her up, lifting her high against his chest as he backed out of the shrubbery. "Besides, haven't you've had enough excitement for today?"

Excitement? He gave a whole new meaning to the word. Eleanor felt as though electricity was flashing through every nerve in her body, as though her own body was foreign and the only thing that still belonged to her was her ridiculously muddled mind. She clutched awkwardly at the fabric of his shirt with clumsy fingers, her breath caught in her throat. Never had she been handled so casually yet personally. The trip back out of the azaleas took only seconds but she was so acutely aware of the man and his muscled arms that it seemed to take much, much longer.

"There you go." He straightened one arm and leaned again, allowing her legs to slide toward the ground. For a millisecond

Eleanor was pressed against him, chest to chest, her legs dangling, and she thought she could actually feel his heart beat through the damp fabric of his shirt. She felt a profound rush of relief when her feet touched the ground and her legs held her up. Her skirt had ridden up on her trip down to earth and she tugged at it jerkily. The tiny bit of common sense she was able to corral screamed at her to turn her back on the man and run like the wind for her car, but the charges of electricity still zipping through her body forced her to lift wide eyes up to him instead.

He wasn't looking at her. He was looking down at her legs, his mouth quirking in suppressed amusement. She glanced down, too, and her humiliation belly flopped to new depths when she discovered the matching ragged holes in the knees of her sheer black hosiery. The heat running rampant in her body zoomed north to scorch her face. "Well, thanks," she managed, refusing to meet his eyes as she began to edge toward the driveway and the safety of her car.

The man ambled along beside her. "Did you want to see the house? Because if you do---"

"No." Eleanor interrupted him quickly. "I don't want to see it. I don't have time. I have to go."

He lifted an eyebrow dubiously. "If you don't want to see the house, why were you trying to climb up to the window?"

Because she was a total idiot, but surely he'd figured that out all on his own. Eleanor decided to try another tack. Reaching her car, she stopped and peered at the script lettering stitched onto his pocket. White monogramming against navy blue fabric announced his association with Southern Heritage Nursery and Landscape.

A yard boy. She felt a rush of self-confidence. She was running away from a yard boy. Well, maybe the term "boy" wasn't exactly accurate but the fact was he really had no more right to be there than she did. No right at all to question her motives. Eleanor raised her chin and used her haughtiest tone. "Actually, you know, I don't see how it's any of your business. Don't you have work to do?"

Instead of looking suitably chastised, the man broke into a wide, breathtaking grin. Eleanor felt her knees wobble slightly. "Oh, I always have work to do, but I have this policy about rescuing damsels in distress." Reaching down, he opened the car door for her and then stepped aside. "Crashing into azaleas seemed to qualify, but maybe for you it's an everyday thing."

Eleanor stared at him blankly. He was supposed to apologize, not tease. "I see," she finally, inanely, replied. Oh, what a witty comeback, she castigated herself. Be careful you don't overwhelm him with your razor sharp wit. Flushing, she slid into her seat.

Muscles bulged without any effort on his part when he rested his folded arms on the top of her car door. "Hey, if you change your mind, the lady next door has a key. I think you'll find it's a lot easier going through the door." He gave her a decidedly playful wink before slipping his sunglasses on.

Eleanor gave him what she hoped was a nonchalant nod and tugged at her door. "I'll remember that," she replied.

After giving the top of her door a neat rap, he closed it and stepped back.

Eleanor turned the key in the ignition with a trembling hand and managed to back out of the driveway without banging into the mailbox. She couldn't seem to help sending a little tiny glance in his direction as she rolled forward. He was still firmly planted on the lawn beside the driveway, shaking his head slightly at her undignified departure.

Once out of his sight, Eleanor pressed her hand against her chest. Her heart was pounding ferociously; in fact, it hadn't slowed since she first looked up and saw him, haloed by blinding sunlight. It was easy enough to explain. He had given her quite a start when he appeared out of nowhere, a voice without a body.

That's not it, an impudent voice in her head piped. It was natural feminine reaction to six and a half feet of a live super hero wearing tight jeans and a toothpaste commercial grin.

Well, at least she hadn't been working so hard she didn't recognize an exceptional male specimen when it picked her up and put her down, she retorted mentally. Maybe there was hope for her, yet.

* * *

"Answer the door, Hazel!" A frenzied flapping accompanied the shrieking voice.

Fuzzily, Eleanor lifted her head and swatted at a piece of paper stuck to her damp cheek. Straightening into an upright position in her desk chair, she rubbed her aching neck and wondered for the briefest of moments why she was at home instead of at the office. She picked up the piece of paper and squinted at the scribbles. Information to include on her résumé. The memory of her miserable morning returned and she dropped her head down again with a thud.

She heard banging on her front door and a familiar voice.

"Eleanor, I'm starting to get worried. Open the door!"

"Answer the door, Hazel!"

Gracie. Eleanor rose, rubbing her stiff neck, and hurried downstairs. "Quiet, Walter." The white cockatoo clung to the side of its cage and looked the other way.

She unlocked the door. The look of relief on her friend's face was marked. "Geez, Eleanor, I'm blue in the face from yelling." Gracie edged inside carefully, holding one box in her arms and nudging another through the door with her tennis shoe clad foot. "There's more in the car."

Eleanor took the box from Gracie's arms and placed it on the sofa. "I really appreciate your bringing my stuff over, Gracie."

"Let's watch the Wheel!" Walter paced back and forth on his perch, his beady eyes fixed on the television in the corner. "Let's watch the Wheel!"

Gracie shoved the box along the floor until it bumped against the wall, then turned toward Walter's cage. "Hiya Walter, how's it going?"

Eleanor sighed. "He's not doing very well. Look at all the feathers." She gestured at the bottom of the cage that consumed a fair portion of her living room. "The vet says he's stressed. He misses Mrs. Dunlap."

"I still can't believe you're keeping the cranky old thing."

Eleanor shrugged. "What else could I do? Mrs. Dunlap couldn't bring him to the retirement home, and her daughter is allergic."

Gracie grinned. "I think Mrs. Dunlap's daughter is allergic to his bad temper and loud mouth."

Now that Eleanor had come to know Walter, she suspected the same thing. "I hope you didn't have too much trouble, packing and getting over here."

"Not a bit. It was a good thing you left when you did, though, because you just escaped Wayne Patterson by sheer minutes. He got wind of your resignation and came running downstairs in a panic." She gave Eleanor a cheeky grin. "It was a wonderful sight to see." Dusting her hands on her hips, Gracie opened the front door again. "I brought a pizza. We can carry the rest in after we eat. I bet you haven't eaten all day, have you?" Without waiting for a reply, Gracie turned back toward her SUV.

Resisting the urge to smile, Eleanor shook her head. She couldn't remember how many times she would have worked through the day without lunch if it hadn't been for Gracie; nagging and reminding, and usually simply taking matters into her own hands by appearing with food Eleanor never remembered requesting but always obediently ate. She held the door open and watched Gracie hoist the pizza box and a grocery bag out of her vehicle, then took the bag and led the way toward the kitchen table. "What are Ben and Lexie doing tonight?"

Gracie slid the pizza box onto the table. "Stuart's helping his dad with some do-it-yourself project and his mom wanted to take Lexie to see the new Disney film, so I'm footloose and fancy free." She lifted the pizza box and inhaled happily. "Life is good."

Eleanor wished she had a fraction of Gracie's wealth of perpetual cheerfulness. She peered into the bag and discovered two cartons of peach ale. "What's this? Are we having a party?"

Gracie laughed. "I know you don't drink, Eleanor, but I thought, what the heck. It's not every day Philip Conrad gets what he deserves. We have to celebrate properly."

Eleanor pulled one of the bottles from the carton and considered it. She had never enjoyed alcohol but this looked intriguing. "What the heck," she murmured. Twisting the cap off, she sipped tentatively. It was delicious. "Mmm!" She wiped her hand across her mouth. "This is wonderful." She took another swallow, much longer than the first, her eyes closed. "Tastes just like peaches."

Gracie's mouth dropped open. "Eleanor! It's got alcohol in it, you know." Grabbing the pizza box, she pulled a piece out and held it toward Eleanor. "Here. Eat."

Eleanor accepted the pizza and pulled out a chair. "Here. Sit." She stepped into the kitchen and returned with paper plates and napkins in one hand, her slice of pizza in the other. Pulling out a chair for herself, she sat and examined the slice of pizza. "This looks good." She drank another swallow of the ale, enjoying Gracie's slight consternation. "Well, you brought it for me to drink, didn't you? Aren't you going to have one?"

"Yes," Gracie replied, helping herself to a bottle. "I want to make a toast." She untwisted the top and held the bottle up. "Here's to the first day of the rest of your life."

"Hear, hear." Eleanor clinked her bottle with Gracie's.

"Have you talked to your father yet?" Gracie posed the question nonchalantly.

Eleanor nodded, her smooth brow furrowing. "Briefly."

Gracie leaned forward. "Did he give you a hard time?"

Eleanor shrugged. "Well, he's not happy with me."

Actually, she was guilty of first degree understatement. It had been even worse than she had anticipated. Her father had gone on and on about his disappointment in her rash behavior, and how Philip had every right to be furious with her. Then he went on to say that he had convinced Philip to take her back. Years of obedience had threatened to choke her, but Eleanor somehow found her tongue and startled both her father and herself when she told him wild horses couldn't drag her back to Conrad, Berkley and Burns. Her dramatic statement was met with a long, barren silence on the other end of the line, and Eleanor could just picture her father's face. Red. Apoplectic.

"What did he say?"

Eleanor imitated his clipped, cold tone. "I will not support you in your decision to throw away the fruits of your eight years with Conrad, Berkley and Burns, Eleanor. You would be well advised to give this matter your most careful consideration before you make a very rash mistake, one that will affect both your livelihood and your reputation."

Gracie made a face. "Eeew. He gave it to you with both barrels, huh?"

Eleanor nodded. "He told me to apologize and ask for my job back."

"You're not going to, are you?" Gracie's look of horror was almost comical.

Eleanor shook her head emphatically. "CBB has seen the last of me." She gave Gracie an apologetic shrug. "I really hate leaving you there, you know. They're probably going to assign you to Wayne."

"I hope so," Gracie said firmly. "I really hope so."

Eleanor blinked in surprise. "You do?"

"Yes." Gracie gave Eleanor a bright grin. "He'll think he's died and gone to secretarial hell." She fidgeted with her earring. "Maybe when you get settled someplace else, you can call me to come work for you again."

"You'd leave CBB?"

"In a heartbeat," Gracie replied crisply. "Just let me have a little fun with Wayne first, okay? He'll be crying over his doughnuts and coffee before I'm done with him." She bit off a big piece of pizza.

Eleanor smiled at the mental picture Gracie created. "I'd love to see that," she admitted. "But wait, you haven't heard everything yet. Philip started talking about how much Wayne admires me and how we'd make a nice couple."

Gracie, her mouth full, made a rude noise.

Eleanor had to laugh. "Really," she insisted. "I think I was supposed to be honored."

Slapping her pizza on her plate, Gracie swallowed and found her voice. "You and Wayne? That's awful. That's disgusting. Wayne's such a, such a, such a---" She shrugged helplessly

"Doofus?"

"Doofus doesn't begin to adequately describe Wayne," Gracie replied, blue eyes wide with humor. "So, what are you going to do about getting another job?"

Eleanor took a sip and realized her bottle was empty. She looked at it in dismay and tugged the carton closer to withdraw a second bottle. "You know, I was thinking that maybe I'll take some time off before I start job-hunting."

Gracie scooted forward in her chair, her eyes brightening. "And do what? Travel? Oh, I know! You could take a cruise."

"By myself? I don't think so."

"Well, what do you want to do, then?"

"I want to buy a house." The unexpected announcement popped out, startling Eleanor as well as Gracie. It was true, though, she realized. She wanted that little house more than she could ever remember wanting anything.

Gracie's mouth dropped open. "Did you say 'buy a house'?"

Eleanor leaned forward, suddenly eager to tell her all about it. "Yes. There's a house on Magnolia Drive that just went up for sale."

Forgetting both the pizza dangling from her hand or the fact Eleanor was guzzling ale like a parched sailor, Gracie eyed her in amazement. "You've never said anything about wanting a house before."

"That's because I never did before. This one's special." And she could buy it, too, Eleanor realized with increasing enthusiasm. There was no reason why not. She sat up abruptly, her mind racing. There was nothing tying her to this apartment. Nothing tying her to anything. The time it would take to move wasn't an issue now that she was unemployed, and neither was money, thanks to her habit of socking away a big chunk of her salary every month and a little trust fund her maternal grandparents had set up years ago. Maybe it wasn't so little anymore.

Gracie looked dubious. "Owning a house is a lot different from renting an apartment, Eleanor. There's no manager to call when something breaks, and then there's stuff like yard work."

"I can hire people to take care of the yard." Suddenly the gorgeous lawn man came to mind. Eleanor felt a warm flush and blamed it on the drink.

Gracie, always quick to come on board, sat upright, too. "Well, let's go see it!"

Eleanor blinked. "Right now?"

"Why not?"

Why not? Eleanor giggled, and then clapped a hand over her own mouth in surprise.

* * *

Tyler carefully lowered himself into the hammock hanging between two old pines in the farthest corner of Rosie's back yard. It dipped perilously from his weight and he put a hand to the ground to stop the swaying. Through the spiky branches the early evening sky was clear, pinpoints of stars beginning to pierce the darkness. The neighborhood was quiet, with only crickets and the occasional hoarse bullfrog speaking out in the stillness.

Though he had planned to take Hope and Adam out for a nice dinner, he was relieved when Hope apologetically explained she and Adam had made plans to see some of their old friends. She invited Tyler to join them, but he wasn't about to suffer through an evening of holding his tongue with Adam. The best way, in fact, maybe the only way, to keep his promise to Hope was to avoid Adam right up until the minute he had to walk Hope down the aisle.

He and Hope spent a nice hour or so catching up, but when she glanced at the clock and mentioned Adam was due to arrive shortly, he took his cue and promptly departed. The relief on her face might have been comical under other circumstances.

Rosie wasn't at all surprised when he showed back up at her house. She immediately began bustling around in the kitchen while he filled her in on the plans he, Hank and Warren were making for their next sporting goods store. After supper they played Spite and Malice, and she beat him soundly and triumphantly, three games in a row. By that time it was late, and he felt lazy, so he decided to spend the night in his old double bed. It was smaller than he remembered, though, and after tossing and turning for a while, he decided to sneak out and head for the hammock.

Shifting carefully, he propped his head on his arm and gazed at the back of Letty's house. With any luck, it would sell quickly to a nice, settled young family. Mr. Lemoine across the street wasn't any prize as neighbors went, and the Tuminello's and Melancon's were getting up in age just like Rosie. As often as he and the others dropped by, he still worried she might need help, and neither he nor his brothers or sisters would be able to respond quickly enough.

Tyler smiled slightly, thinking of his brothers and sisters and their numerous offspring. He was glad to be back in the middle of the rowdy bunch again. After fourteen years in Denver, overseeing their well-being from that frustrating distance, it was past time to come home. He wouldn't admit it to his ex-teammates for anything, but it was something of a relief to put the mental and physical stress of professional ball behind him. To most of them, retirement was the equivalent of the death penalty, and he had subscribed to that same sentiment until last season, when a change of coaching staff, combined with a string of injuries, changed his point of view. Like it or not, he was thirty-five years old, and the players in the pit kept getting younger and bigger and faster. His body had been trying to get the message across to him for quite a while that enough was enough, and his last trip to the hospital, when he separated his shoulder again, had finally convinced him the time was right. Tyler shifted in the hammock, rolling his shoulder carefully.

His brothers and sisters were all educated and settled and happy, his investments were solid, and his business ventures were paying off, and his grandmother, if she weren't so damned stubborn, could live the life of embarrassing extravagance she deserved. His life as a Denver Renegade had made it all possible, just the way he planned, but now that part of his life was over, and it was time to think about a new direction for himself. He thought about Hank and Warren, his longtime friends and business partners. Like him, they'd played the game as long as they could, but unlike many others, they'd done so with an eye to the future. Hank, a rangy wide receiver, came to Denver out of Oklahoma the same year Tyler was drafted from LSU, while Warren, the meanest tackle he'd ever had the pleasure to line up with, came from Penn State. While their rowdier teammates partied, the unlikely threesome made plans designed to carry them into the great unknown that was life after football. Seeing them this past week with their affectionate wives and rambunctious children made Tyler feel a little lonely, a little adrift. He'd like to have a wife and kids of his own to spoil. He knew just the kind of woman he wanted, too. He wouldn't make the same mistake he'd made the first time.

Tyler sighed, unwilling to dwell on his debacle of a marriage. He had to remind himself he had been just a kid. It wasn't something he was proud of, but nobody could say he hadn't learned from his mistake. In fact, he'd been burned so badly he'd avoided serious relationships like the plague ever since. Trust was a real problem with him. He was up front about it, though. A good time, sure. Long term commitment, no. There had been a few women along the way who had begun to believe they could change his mind, but they had been quickly replaced by others without such aspirations.

But now he was home and things were different here. He'd find a nice southern girl, pretty and sincere and honest, who liked the idea of a big family as much as he did. He'd like to have a wife and children of his own to spoil. What Hank and Warren had looked really good.

* * *

"Oh, that's it! Turn here!" Eleanor pointed out of the window. She felt wonderful; light-hearted and practically breathless with eagerness. She downed the last swallow of her fourth ale as Gracie veered into the driveway with a screech.

The headlights of the van illuminated the house. Gracie leaned forward. "Oh, Eleanor, it's so pretty."

Eleanor nodded vigorously and struggled to unbuckle her seat belt. This was the most fun she'd had in years. "Leave your lights on, Gracie. Let's go look at it. I want to show you the front door. You have to see the front door." With a little difficulty she managed to extricate herself from the passenger seat and stumble out of the SUV. "Come on." She hurried up the pathway to the front porch. "Come see the front door. It's got a stained glass window. It's a magnolia design. Get it? A magnolia and this is Magnolia Drive. Get it?"

Gracie rounded the front of the van, giggling. "Shh, Eleanor. I get it, really, I do."

Eleanor waved her arms impatiently. "Come on, come on." She skipped up the walkway and did a pirouette on the top step. "Just look at this porch. At all that curly wood. Doesn't it look just like Cinderella's cottage?"

Gracie nodded admiringly from the walkway. "Don't you mean Snow White?"

Eleanor laughed boisterously. "One of those!"

"Shh!" Gracie giggled again. "You'll wake the neighbors."

* * *

Tyler was jarred from his thoughts by a pair of slamming doors and voices wafting around the front of Letty's house. Two voices, both feminine, he concluded as he sat up carefully.

One voice was far more audible than the other; in fact, it was downright raucous. Perplexed, Tyler swung out of the hammock and made his way, barefoot, toward the corner of the house. Magnolia Drive was ordinarily the quietest street in the entire neighborhood.

Headlights shone from a SUV he didn't recognize, parked halfway down and halfway off the driveway, front wheels on the lawn and angled toward the porch of the house. The driver door was ajar, and he could hear the persistent buzzing of the door alarm.

"Oh, Gracie, isn't it beautiful? I'm just dying to see inside."

Tyler listened carefully. The pair was on the front porch and one voice sounded vaguely familiar.

"I tried to see in a window today, but, well, you wouldn't believe what happened." The voice broke off, giggling. "I fell into the bushes and met a Viking."

"Into the bushes? A Viking?"

"Yes, really!"

Both females went off into wheezing gales of laughter.

A Viking? Was she talking about him? Immediately the image of the tiny brunette popped into Tyler's mind, but the voice was so much more animated than he remembered that he had trouble believing his ears. It had to be her. He hadn't fished anybody else out of the bushes lately. He slipped around the azaleas to carefully peek around the corner.

Yes, indeed, little Miss Breaking and Entering was perched on the front porch railing in what looked like her same plain suit, arms twined around one of the carved posts, head thrown back in paroxysms of laughter. Her cohort sat on the bottom step, hugging her sides in mirth.

"Actually, you know, he was even bigger than a Viking. He was a Viking god!"

There they went again, into hiccupping gales. Tyler edged a little closer, taking care to stay in the shadows. It was hard to fathom that this chortling pixie was the same tongue-tied woman who ran off in a panic earlier in the day. He moved in enough to hear the second woman implore the first to give up the entire story.

"Well," the brunette began, her voice clear in the still night air. "I still don't know what happened. It was a very good plan. I piled some boxes against the house under these windows, but they were kind of high up and then the branches started attacking me---"

"Who's there? Who's making all that racket?" The light on the porch across the street blazed on. Tyler watched from the shadows as Mr. Lemoine, perennially cantankerous, stomped out onto his porch across the street and called crossly into the darkness. "Keep it quiet or I'll call the police!" He went back inside with a slam of the door.

The woman on the step drew in her breath and scrambled up. "Ooh, I was afraid we were going to wake somebody up. Come on, Eleanor, let me take you home. It's time to call it a night. You've had a big day, you know."

Eleanor? Tyler had to grin. That was the perfect name for such a plain little woman. He backed away, sorry he wasn't going to hear the rest of her story.

Eleanor waved away her friend's suggestion and tilted on the railing unsteadily. "I'm going to buy this house, you know." She hugged the post tightly and gave it a loud, smacking kiss. "It's going to be mine. All mine."

Tyler raised his eyebrows in surprise. He hoped she wasn't serious. She wasn't what he had in mind for a neighbor for Rosie at all. She was completely unsuitable.

The friend tugged on her sleeve. "I know, I know. I also know you're going to have a whopper of a headache tomorrow and it's all my fault. Come on, let's go."

Tyler watched Eleanor obediently slide off the railing. She began to follow her friend, and then hesitated. Tyler craned to see what she was doing and watched in bemusement as she turned and hurried back up the steps to give the stained glass window a gentle stroke. "It's true," she said softly. "I'm buying you. See if I don't."

Patting the window once more, she turned and hurried across the lawn to catch up with her friend. Tyler watched her climb clumsily back into the SUV and close her door. The vehicle backed up, disappeared down the street, and Mr. Lemoine turned off his porch light. Peace was restored.

Jamming his hands into his jeans pockets, Tyler walked to the front porch and sat down on the top step to think about the woman's second wacky visit. Stopping in broad daylight to take a look was one thing; this late night sojourn was something else. It smacked of strong intentions and made him very uneasy. He'd have to talk with Rosie first thing in the morning. She needed to call Leanne's friend to explain the kind of neighbor she wanted. Impulsive little brunettes need not apply.

Chapter Four

The next morning, Eleanor pulled her car back into the driveway at 421 Magnolia Drive as though she had done it a million times and smiled over her steering wheel at the house she already thought of as her own.

When Gracie dropped her off last night, she'd dashed straight inside to call the real estate agent. This morning, as she nursed her aching head, she wondered whether her babbling message had made any sense at all because everything after her fourth peach ale was just the tiniest bit fuzzy. Who knew the innocent-tasting drinks carried such a punch? Gracie could've warned her.

To be fair, Gracie *had* warned her. At any rate, she must have made some sense, because the agent returned her call and they fixed a time to meet at the house. Eleanor glanced at her wristwatch. The time was now.

Climbing out of her car, she set off toward the front porch. She had a few aches and bruises from yesterday's humiliating tumble into the shrubbery to complement her ale headache, but her enthusiasm for the house hadn't faded a whit. Today she was going inside, and she was going through the front door like a normal person. Already she was off to a better start, and it was impossible to feel anything but optimistic. She glanced at her wristwatch again. Where was that agent?

As if in answer to her query, a glossy Mercedes turned into the driveway and came to a smooth stop behind Eleanor's Prius. Eleanor watched the driver, a tall, expensively groomed blonde, emerge. The real estate agent was just the kind of polished southern belle who invariably made Eleanor feel like a troll.

"Miss Haley?" The blonde, as graceful as Eleanor suspected, smiled in greeting as she made her way up the walk. "Good morning. I'm Amanda Howard."

"Good morning," Eleanor replied, pasting a smile on her own face. Come on, move it, sister, she thought, resisting the urge to tap her foot restlessly. Let me in.

"It's so nice to meet you." Ms. Howard held out an impeccably manicured hand. "I hope I haven't kept you waiting. It's a lovely morning, isn't it?"

Yes, yes, yes. Save the charm and unlock the door. "Nice to meet you, too," she managed, shaking Amanda's hand.

The agent tapped a code into the lock box on the door before giving Eleanor an apologetic look. "I hope you don't mind if I don't go through the house with you. This appointment was rather last-minute and I have a meeting in half an hour."

Eleanor suddenly felt a great fondness for her because now she could poke around to her heart's content. "I quite understand," she replied. "I appreciate your taking the time to accommodate me. Shall I just lock it when I leave?"

The blonde smiled in relief. "No, that's not necessary. Mrs. Hurst, who lives next door, will come by later to lock up." She pushed the door open slightly, and then dug in her smart little purse. "Here's my card. I'm sure you'll be delighted when you look around because the seller has spared no expense in remodeling and updating the interior to make it every bit as charming as the exterior."

"What's the asking price?"

Ms. Howard quoted the amount. Eleanor nodded but gasped inwardly. It was more than she had expected. Clearly homes in the old neighborhood, however small, were choice real estate.

"Why don't we talk later, after you've seen the interior and thought about it?" Miss Howard was oblivious to Eleanor's internal turmoil.

"That's fine". When the agent reached her car, Eleanor gave her a little wave before turning to the unlocked front door.

At last. Goose bumps prickled her arms. She ignored the whisper of common sense that suggested she leave without going inside and forget all about it.

Not a chance. Eleanor pushed the door open and stepped over the threshold.

She was inside a gracious, airy living room, and the dining room, which boasted the wide front window, was on her left. The staircase hugged the dividing wall and overlooked the living room from a narrow landing. I'll be up in a minute, Eleanor thought fancifully, hugging her waist. She paused to admire the marble trimmed fireplace and recessed, arched bookcases on her way into a sunny breakfast area and kitchen. The kitchen was a tiny jewel of a room. Amanda Howard hadn't exaggerated a bit about the extensive remodeling. Eleanor could certainly see why the house was listed at such a high price. She crossed to gaze through the pair of arched windows over the ceramic sink. The infamous windows, she realized wryly, that had caused her predicament the day before. A door from the kitchen led in one direction to a small covered porch, with steps down to the back yard, and the other to a little hallway that led to two bright bedrooms and a shared bath.

Circling back, Eleanor felt an odd sense of peace stealing over her as she slowly climbed the stairs to the second floor. Even vacant, this house felt like a home. Upstairs was a small landing and a door to the master bedroom. It was large, with windows that overlooked the shady side and back yard, polished hardwood floors and ornate trim. Eleanor peeked into the bathroom and stared in wonder at the marvelously old-fashioned footed bathtub. The thing was as big as a boat. What would it be like to own that tub, to fill it with bubbles and go for a swim? Surrendering to temptation, Eleanor gleefully kicked off her shoes and climbed in. She rested her arms along the high curved sides, stretched out her legs, and giggled.

"Hello? Amanda?"

Eleanor started in surprise at the voice wafting from the first floor and scrambled out of the tub. Snatching up her shoes, she jammed them on and started out of the bedroom. "No, Miss Howard had to leave," she called, rounding the bedroom door to the landing.

* * *

Rosie Hurst stood at the bottom of the staircase, waiting eagerly for the girl to appear. She knew perfectly well Amanda wasn't there because she was the one who arranged for the agent to make her excuses and leave. When she phoned earlier to tell Rosie she'd already received a call on the house, Rosie just knew it was going to be that girl again, the one who made such a mixed impression on Ty. Yesterday afternoon he'd gone into detail, with great amusement, about the young woman's fall into the azaleas, and that was the end of it until this morning when he'd started expounding about the kind of neighbor she needed. Rosie was accustomed to his inflexible black and white opinions on everything under the sun, and his indefatigable need to try to bring everyone in line with his own thinking, but by the time he made his third or fourth pass on the subject, she'd finally fixed him with an exasperated eye and demanded to know what in the world had put him so squarely on top of his soapbox. He was reluctant to explain, possibly because he was afraid that the girl's intoxicated late night visit would do more damage to his cause than good. Someone who fell headlong into azaleas and was affectionate with porch columns sounded absolutely fascinating to Rosie. Her interest was piqued and Tyler, unhappily, knew it.

He'd lectured her a while longer about not taking any action on the house until his return, and Rosie did what she always did with her eldest grandson; she made agreeable noises without actually agreeing. Life with Tyler was much simpler that way. She could tell he was feeling a little nervous about the fact she had power of attorney and could make decisions about the house in his absence. Many months back she had concurred with his proposal that they transfer ownership of the house to his investment company, and to allow him to oversee the expense of the renovations, because it made good sense. Tyler's business decisions always made good sense; it was his personal decisions that often kept her awake at night. Not because they were impulsive or irrational; oh, no, just the opposite. Everything he did was based on logic and reason, and once he had decided on a course, there seemed to be no force on earth that could stop him. But just once, how she'd love to see him throw his stockpile of reservations to the wind and do something impetuous.

She'd been watching avidly through a gap in the azaleas for Amanda to arrive and leave again, sure that the girl who so effectively alarmed Tyler was the same girl who was upstairs right now. Rosie smiled, reflecting again on Tyler's behavior. He had been quite adamant. Not for the first time, she wondered how she was going to manage with him living in Baton Rouge again. Not that she wasn't thrilled to have him home but he did have a problem with being, well, bossy.

When the girl appeared at the top of the stairway, Rosie knew her instincts had served her well. She was tiny, almost fragile looking, with dark hair sternly pulled back behind her head just as Tyler had described. He had neglected, however, to mention the wide green eyes that seemed to take up most of the girl's heart-shaped face, or the fact that her thick hair was boisterously trying to escape the confines of the severe twist.

"Oh, I'm sorry," Rosie lied cheerfully. "I thought Miss Howard was here and thought I'd say hello. You're looking at the house, then."

"Yes," the girl replied. She stepped gracefully down the stairway, her hand on the carved rail. "Miss Howard let me in. She said the neighbor would lock up."

"I'm the neighbor." Rosie held out her hand. "Rosalie Hurst, but my friends call me Rosie."

"I'm Eleanor Haley." Reaching the bottom step, Eleanor took Rosie's hand and then took the last step down to the hardwood floor.

My, my. Rosie had almost forgotten how nice it was to look eye to eye with another adult. It certainly made a nice change from looking up all the time. "Do you like the house?" She glanced nonchalantly at the girl's left hand. A wedding ring would be a huge disappointment.

"Oh, yes," Eleanor replied, gazing around the living room. "It's amazing."

Rosie nodded, pleased with her sincere response and even more delighted with her ringless hand. "Did you see the master bath? The tub?" She liked the bit of mischief she saw in Eleanor's quick smile.

"I couldn't help climbing in," Eleanor admitted as she crossed to the fireplace and turned to view the room. "Every detail is perfect." She ran a hand along the mantle. "I thought, from the condition of the yard these past months that the house would be falling to pieces."

Rosie decided against explaining that her General Patton of a grandson had spared no expense in renovating it from top to bottom. "So you've been down this street before?"

"I drive through this neighborhood all the time on my way home from work. I always wondered about this house." She crouched and examined the ornate brass fireplace fender. "It seemed shy, maybe even lonely. Different from the others." Giving Rosie a quick look, as though she were embarrassed by her fancifulness, Eleanor rose abruptly. "Do you live in the house with the pink flamingo mailbox?"

Rosie smiled. She did love that silly mailbox. "Yes, that's me." The mailbox had been one of countless no-occasion gifts, mailed overnight-delivery from Denver. Over the years Tyler had spent far too much money on similar, outrageous gifts, all the while paying no attention to her protests. Perhaps because she could never hide how much she enjoyed receiving them.

Eleanor looked at Rosie with renewed interest. "It's my other favorite. Anyway, I just happened to drive by yesterday and see the 'for sale' sign. Somebody put an awful lot of time and trouble into fixing it up, didn't they?" She examined the carved columns of the fireplace. "I was almost hoping it would be a mess on the inside," she confessed. "Seeing how beautiful everything is makes it harder."

"Makes what harder?"

"Finding out the price," Eleanor smiled ruefully. She looked up to wistfully survey the chandelier. "It's a bit steeper than I expected and I'm temporarily unemployed."

"Oh?" Rosie took advantage of Eleanor's interest in the chandelier to study her clothing. Excellent quality, but, well, unimaginative. Her navy blue linen slacks and matching blazer were a bit baggy; her blouse, stark white and buttoned to the chin, didn't do a thing for her pale, almost translucent skin. She wasn't unattractive, not at all, but she did need a little guidance, some good advice, about color and style. Rosie felt supremely qualified for the challenge. She hadn't beautifully outfitted three granddaughters on a shoestring for nothing.

Eleanor nodded. "I quit yesterday. I can still hardly believe it myself. I just up and quit."

"Really?" Rosie was fascinated. Her intuitive feeling about Eleanor was growing stronger by the minute. Tyler, so predictable and responsible, would be horrified by someone who quit their job on a whim. She resisted the temptation to rub her hands together with anticipation.

Despite Tyler's assurances that a slower pace was what he craved, and her profound relief that he wasn't going to be injuring himself on the football field anymore, Rosie didn't think a relaxed lifestyle was going to satisfy her over-achieving grandson for long. She had tried to convince him to give retirement in Baton Rouge a trial run before selling his mountaintop home, but he had made up his mind, and that was that. In typical Tyler fashion, when his fourteenth and final season ended, he'd focused on the task of neatly severing all ties to Denver so he could move home and be completely available to his family.

And therein lay the problem. Rosie sighed. Tyler believed his brothers and sisters still required some measure of oversight, and she didn't like to think about his reaction when he realized they were happily self-sufficient. Always a man with purpose, he was going to be restless and bored. The very thought filled her with dread. When Tyler was bored, he drove them all crazy.

But here, standing inches away was just the little live grenade she could throw at him. "So you had a big day yesterday." Rosie debated mentally whether she should confess any knowledge of Eleanor's fall and rescue.

Eleanor laughed ruefully. "I'll say. Quit my job, found this house, and---" She broke off, her face coloring, and crossed the room to touch one of the lacy balusters, as if to put some distance between herself and her recollections.

"And what?" Rosie prompted, following her. Perhaps she wouldn't say anything just yet about her connection to Tyler. Perhaps she'd learn more of what she wanted to know that way.

Eleanor turned to Rosie, the corners of her mouth lifting impishly. "I made a remarkable fool of myself with the most gorgeous man I've ever seen in my entire life."

That definitely fit under the category of 'promising reactions.' Rosie tilted her head questioningly. "Surely not?"

Eleanor nodded, green eyes sparkling. "Yes, I did. It was awful. I tried to climb on top of some crates to look into the window and, the next thing I knew, I was flat on the ground. He saw the whole thing." She covered her face with her hands. "I was never so embarrassed in my life. Not only was I a complete klutz, but I couldn't even string three words together." She stared off across the room for a long moment before blinking and returning her flustered gaze to Rosie. "I can't believe how I'm rattling on and on. You must think I'm crazy." She gripped her purse with both hands. "I'm beginning to think I'm crazy, myself. I think it's this house. It seems to affect me. I ought to leave." She headed toward the front door.

"Wait," Rosie said hurriedly. Eleanor couldn't run away yet. Things were just beginning to get interesting. "Maybe the house is trying to tell you something."

Eleanor turned her head and gave Rosie a puzzled look. "Excuse me?"

Rosie nodded emphatically. "Maybe it's not just a coincidence that you quit your job and found this house in the same day. Maybe it's fate. Maybe this is supposed to be your house."

Eleanor's laugh didn't quite correspond with the wistful look in her eyes. "I'm not sure I should want a house that makes me behave like an imbecile."

Rosie reached to take her hand. Eleanor looked down in surprise but didn't pull away. "Eleanor, this house deserves someone who truly appreciates it. I think you're that someone and I think you should make an offer." She gave Eleanor's hand a gentle squeeze before letting go.

"Do you really think so?" Eleanor felt a rush of hopefulness.

"I do," Rosie said encouragingly. "I happen to know the house is owned by a corporation." Nothing untruthful about that, she consoled herself cheerfully. No reason to mention the company belonged to her grandson. "They might need to sell quickly. You never know." Rosie squashed the mental picture that kept rising in her mind of Tyler clutching his head in dismay.

"That's true," Eleanor agreed slowly. "I guess it's worth a try."

Wonderful! "It's definitely worth a try. When things are meant to be, they have a way of working out. Why don't you come over to my house for a cup of coffee and you can give Miss Howard a call?"

"Right now?"

"No time like the present," Rosie replied briskly, her mind racing. She mentally counted the days before Tyler's return on Sunday. Only five. Heavens, she had a lot of work to do between now and then, and so did Eleanor, though she didn't know it yet. Rosie opened the front door and tugged gently on Eleanor's arm.

* * *

"Here are the last of your boxes, Miss Haley. Where do you want them?"

Eleanor blew a delinquent strand of hair out of her eyes and watched the moving foreman carefully roll a dolly loaded with more unlabeled boxes up the ramp and over the front porch steps. There hadn't been time, in the whirlwind of the past few days, to worry about little details like labels. "Just stack them up here in the living room, Mr. Moses."

He nodded obligingly. It occurred to Eleanor she needed to pay him, but the location of her purse was anybody's guess. Maybe Gracie, battling sticky shelf paper in the kitchen, would know. "Gracie, have you seen my purse?"

"Upstairs in your bedroom," Gracie called back. "I'll go get it." She appeared around the corner, arms laden with shelf paper, scissors jammed in her pocket. "I'm done in the kitchen and I think there's enough paper left for your bathrooms." Lopsided ponytail bouncing, she ran up the stairs.

"That'll do it, Miss Haley." The foreman reached into his back pocket and carefully unfolded an invoice before handing it to her.

"Time for Jeopardy!" Walter watched her with a beady black eye from his cage by the front window. She hoped he'd be happier here than in her apartment. She also hoped he'd be a little less vocal.

"Time for Jeopardy! Time for Jeopardy! Time for Jeopardy!"

"Okay, Walter, settle down," Eleanor murmured, casting an apologetic glance at Mr. Moses. She glanced at the figure on the invoice, then back at Mr. Moses. "I don't think this is the right amount. It should be more. Somebody's made a mistake."

"Here it is, Eleanor. Catch." Gracie dropped the bag over the railing. Eleanor caught it and sat on a box to dig out her checkbook.

"No mistake, Miss Haley." He grinned cheerfully. "You don't know me but I know you. You helped my sister a while back."

Eleanor looked at him questioningly.

"Antonia Moses," he clarified. "Her boyfriend was giving her trouble and you got a restraining order and helped her find a place to live. She still talks about how nice you were. I was working in Atlanta then, didn't know anything about any of it or I'd have been more help."

Eleanor nodded in remembrance. Antonia was a soft spoken girl, visibly uneasy in the plush offices of CBB. Eleanor had been happy to try to help. She hadn't been able to fit in many pro bono cases at CBB. There, everything boiled down how much income and positive image you were generating for the firm, and clients like Antonia Moses generally didn't have a lot of capital to throw around. "How's she doing?"

"Real good. Went back to school and is going to graduate next year." He beamed with brotherly pride. "She'll be teaching elementary school."

"I'm so pleased," Eleanor replied sincerely. It was nice to hear about a happy ending. "Please give her my regards." She scribbled out the check and handed it to him.

"I sure will." He glanced around the bright living room. "I'm glad I could help you get moved into your new place. You need something, anything at all, you call me." He pointed a finger at the business card attached to the invoice. "Gerald Moses, at that number. Anything at all."

"I'll be sure to do that," Eleanor replied. She walked him to the front door, propped open to admit both movers and the gentle breeze. His crew waited by the big moving van. She gave them a wave, shook his hand, and watched as they piled into the cab and drove away. Turning, she admired her stained glass door for a moment, gently tracing the lead curving around one of the magnolia petals. It was nothing short of a miracle, but the house was hers and she was in. Well, almost hers. She was actually leasing until the closing but that was good enough for her. Rosie said possession was nine-tenths of the law, and Eleanor was happy to subscribe to that slightly inaccurate but cheerful sentiment.

Thinking of her new neighbor always made Eleanor smile. She was convinced that getting Rosie for a next door neighbor was the best part about her new house. When she had discovered the older woman at the bottom of the stairs, she'd felt a funny zing of recognition, as though Rosie was an old friend she hadn't seen in a long, long time. That same afternoon---was it just four days ago?--- at Rosie's urging, Eleanor had followed her through a gap in the row of azaleas between the two homes, through a screened porch and into a comfortable kitchen, to call the real estate agent. That kitchen was a wonder, an amazing contradiction of sleek equipment and homey clutter. After placing her call, Rosie hadn't turned her loose right away. No, indeed. Instead, Eleanor found herself seated at a big round kitchen table, armed with a fork, facing down the most intimidating chunk of chocolate cake she'd ever seen in her life. And while she worked on the cake, Rosie, in turn, worked on her. Gently, but oh, so expertly, she set out on a fact-finding mission that would have made any investigative attorney proud. Eleanor didn't mind, not a bit.

Between bites, she told Rosie all about Philip Conrad and Wayne Patterson, the circumstances that led to quitting her job, and how she thought she might like to take some time off to enjoy her new home before returning to work. Rosie had been affronted, amused and encouraging, in all the right places. Looking back, Eleanor wondered if there hadn't been an unusual lull in their comfortable conversation when Eleanor mentioned she was an attorney; but the conversation picked up speed again before she could give it much thought.

And in return, Eleanor learned about the six grandchildren Rosie had raised, and their combined flock of five, almost six great-grandchildren, all of whom Rosie clearly adored. She seemed to take for granted that Eleanor would meet them all, and right away. The thought was as tempting as it was intimidating.

Then, when Miss Howard phoned Tuesday night with the remarkable news that her offer had been accepted, albeit with some curious stipulations, Eleanor had automatically called Rosie to share the exciting news. Rosie hadn't seen anything all that bizarre about the condition that Eleanor had to be moved in by Sunday, and she even helped her set the many wheels in motion that enabled her to meet that odd requirement. Lease papers were signed, calls made, and Gracie even took a day off to help her hurtle her belongings into boxes.

The only low point had been her father's reaction. She'd phoned, cautiously, to tell him she was moving---after all, she couldn't just move and not give him her new address---and he had treated her to another lecture. He couldn't understand, not even a little bit, her desire to buy a home of her own. He didn't want to hear what it looked like, where it was located, or what was so special about it. All he wanted to hear were assurances that she would think long and hard about returning to CBB. Consequently, they reached an uncomfortable impasse, and she was down in the dumps by the time the conversation, such as it was, ended.

But never mind that now. She was in. Only happy thoughts allowed today.

"Knock, knock." Ben, Gracie's amiable young husband, announced his arrival at the open front door.

"Answer the door, Hazel!" Walter edged to the end of his perch to crane his neck toward the front door. "Answer the door, Hazel!

Ben and Lexie, their two year old daughter, laughed out loud.

"Down, daddy. Want to see the bird," commanded Lexie.

Her father obediently put her down. "Hi, Eleanor. You and Gracie ready for a lunch break?"

Eleanor trailed the child to the bird cage to make sure Walter didn't decide he had a taste for little fingers. "Absolutely," she replied. "I'm starved." And she really was, she realized with surprise. Apparently, chaos and upheaval did wonders for the appetite.

Ben nodded cheerfully. "Where's that wife of mine? I know

she's hungry. She's always hungry." He joined them beside Walter's cage. "This is some noisy bird, Eleanor."

"That's Walter Cronkite," she replied with a grin, dusting her hands on her hips, eyeing the cockatoo. "He's quite the talker. I never know what he's going to say." She leaned toward the cage. "Hi, Eleanor. Say hi, Eleanor."

Walter, pacing back and forth, ignored her.

Eleanor sighed. "He doesn't like me." It was embarrassing to be disliked so heartily by a bird.

Ben grinned. "Where'd you get him, anyway?"

Eleanor perched on the arm of her sofa and studied Walter. "He belongs to a sweet old client of mine, Hazel Dunlap, who just recently moved to a retirement home. They say she can't keep him, and her daughter is allergic."

Ben burst out laughing. "Yeah, right. Like I'm allergic to shopping."

Eleanor smiled. "I'm trying to convince the director to make an exception for Walter but until then, he's stuck with me." She waved him toward the stairs. "Gracie's upstairs battling shelf paper."

"My money's on Gracie," he grinned, scooping Lexie into his arms and starting up the stairs. "This is a great house, Eleanor." Lexie gave her a coquettish smile over her father's shoulder. Eleanor waggled fingers at her in return.

Another head, this one silvery-white, peeked through the open front door. "Eleanor?"

Eleanor turned toward the doorway again. "Hi, Rosie!" She waved over the disarray. "Come on in."

"It looks like you're making a lot of progress," Rosie said, making her way through the maze of furniture and boxes. She came to a stop beside Eleanor and surveyed the room.

"To me it looks like a big mess," Eleanor smiled, looking around. She sighed again at the jarring effect of her modern gray leather sectional sofa in the old-fashioned room. No matter which way she turned it, it looked ungainly. "I hardly know where to begin."

Ben and Gracie appeared at the top of the landing. "I'm hungry," Gracie announced. "Let's go get something to eat. Oh, hello," she added, spying Rosie.

Eleanor introduced her friends to one another, inwardly marveling that she had a houseful of visitors.

"I've heard lots of nice things about you," Gracie said to Rosie.

"Likewise," Rosie smiled. "Can I convince you all to join us for lunch? Nothing fancy, just barbecue. Robb and Joel should have the pit fired up by now, and everyone's looking forward to meeting you, Eleanor." She bent to address Lexie. "Would you like to play on my swing set?" Lexie nodded vigorously.

Meet Rosie's family right now? Eleanor didn't feel prepared at all. She was dusty and wrinkled and---suddenly very nervous.

Rosie sensed her anxiety. "It'll be fine." She put a hand beneath Eleanor's elbow and began steering her toward the front door.

As they crossed the lawn, Gracie skipped a step or two to catch up with Eleanor, and gave her arm an encouraging squeeze. "Nice lady," she mouthed. Eleanor nodded. It was comforting to have Gracie and Ben along for support, but they were just accidental side servings to the main course. She was the one Rosie's family wanted to inspect.

Rosie slowed to walk alongside Eleanor. "You look worried,

and you needn't be," she said kindly, in a low voice only Eleanor could hear. "They're going to like you as soon as they meet you, just like I did."

Eleanor summoned a smile. This was so important. Rosie's family wasn't meeting the poised creature Eleanor had invented at CBB, they were meeting the fledgling real-person Eleanor, and it was anybody's guess how the new version would go over. Be interesting, she commanded herself. Do not sit in a chair like a lump. Remember to smile. She lifted a nervous hand and patted the knot at the nape of her neck as they cleared the shrubbery. A group of three women and three men, relaxing on the deck winding around the side and back of Rosie's house, turned with curiosity as they approached.

"Leanne, Joel, Robb, bring your better halves to meet Eleanor," Rosie called. "But for heaven's sake, don't call the children just yet." She winked at Eleanor. "The six of you are quite enough for the first go-round." She introduced Leanne, the second oldest, and her husband Elliot; Joel and his wife Sonya, who was very pregnant; and Robb and his wife Nancy. The eldest, Tyler, and Joel's twin, Allison, and her husband Dave, and the youngest, Hope, were the only members of the family absent.

A few smiles and handshakes later, Eleanor and Gracie were herded to the cluster of enamel chairs beneath the massive oak tree. It was easy to tell who were Rosie's grandchildren and who were the spouses, Eleanor mused on the short trek, because the handsome siblings shared a distinct family resemblance. There was something about that alikeness, something disturbing, that Eleanor couldn't quite put her finger on, but she didn't dwell on it because, once seated, it was much more interesting to listen to the energetic stream of conversation flowing around her. She felt like she had been injected directly into an impossibly colorful commercial, or maybe into the Land of the Giants, she thought with a twinge of amusement, looking over at Joel and Robb who were conversing with their brother-in-law, Elliott, and Ben, at the barbecue grill. Well over six feet, both of them, and easy nines on the feminine-appeal Richter scale. And Leanne was very tall for a woman, probably close to six feet herself. What on earth had Rosie fed her grandchildren?

And in the middle was Rosie, in constant motion. After nudging Eleanor along with the others to the sitting area, she flitted indoors, shooing away offers of help, delivered a bowl of chips to the men, gently corrected one grandchild, scooped another up for a hug, and finally returned to the ring of chairs. She took the seat on Eleanor's left and leaned forward. "Do you like my family so far?" she asked in a whisper.

Eleanor smiled. "I do, very much," she whispered back.

Rosie patted Eleanor on her arm, and then turned to Leanne. "Did I tell you that I talked Tyler into participating in the bachelor's auction?"

Leanne brightened. "That's great news, Rosie. I knew if anyone could talk him into it, it would be you. The planning committee is going to be thrilled. They want to make him the grand finale."

"Tyler is the oldest of your family." Eleanor felt brave enough to pipe in, and glanced around for confirmation.

"That's right," Leanne smiled. "He's thirty-five. You haven't met him yet?"

"No," Eleanor replied, trying to recall what Rosie had told her about Tyler but drawing a complete blank. She turned to Rosie, embarrassed. "I've forgotten what you told me about Tyler, Rosie. What does he do?"

She was startled by the surprised expressions that swung in her direction. Robb, en route from the deck, came to an exaggerated stop. "You've never heard of him?" he asked.

Tyler Hurst, Tyler Hurst, Tyler Hurst. Eleanor racked her brains furiously. Nope, the name didn't mean a thing to her. She shook her head, painfully aware she was now the object of everyone's startled attention. "I'm afraid not. Should I have?"

"I don't know who he is, either," Gracie said, too quickly. Bless Gracie's heart, Eleanor thought, glancing over at her friend's earnest face. She's the worst liar on the face of the earth, and everyone knows it but her.

Joel, Elliott, and Ben ambled over to join the group. "Eleanor doesn't know who Tyler is," Robb told them. He propped a hip on Nancy's chair and grinned.

"No way!" Ben's amazement was comical. "Man, he's only the best sacker in the league!"

Well, that was absolutely no help. Eleanor tried not to glare at Gracie's husband. The only thing 'sacker' brought to mind were the grocery store clerks who bagged her groceries.

"He played football," Joel said helpfully, head cocked as he gauged her response. Everyone looked at her intently. "Defensive end, for the Renegades."

What she knew about football could fit inside a thimble.

"Not everybody lives and breathes football," Rosie said matter-of-factly.

"That's true," Nancy added quickly. "I knew zip before I met you, Robb. Football games were just social events."

Eleanor bit her lip. Rosie hadn't told her very much about Tyler, she realized, just that he had recently moved back from---"Denver," she said, seizing the one bit of information she could recall. "He just moved back from Denver."

Robb nodded encouragingly, but unfortunately, no brilliant

flash of knowledge followed. Eleanor shrugged apologetically. "To be honest, I don't really follow sports," she admitted. Like they hadn't figured that out for themselves.

Robb dropped into the chair beside her. "Tyler has played for the Denver Renegades for the past fourteen years. He's played in the Pro Bowl eleven times, was the Renegade's all-time sack leader, and led his division in sacks for five years."

What in blue blazes was a sack? Clearly something impressive. Eleanor tried to summon an appropriate expression of awe.

Joel sat down in another chair. Steepling his fingers together, he continued the mantra. They've been NFC champs three times in the past eight years, and won the Super Bowl year before last. . ."

"You don't say," she murmured. She had heard of the Super Bowl, of course, but beyond that, Robb may as well have been speaking in a foreign language.

The men stared at her as though she had just landed in a space pod on the back lawn. Clearly she wasn't impressed enough to suit them. "That's really wonderful," she added weakly. It was obvious they were very proud of their big brother but suddenly she felt very annoyed with Tyler Hurst. Until his name came up, she was blending in nicely, just as she'd hoped. But not anymore. Oh, no. Her unfamiliarity with the ridiculous testosterone-generated, society-sanctioned excuse for violence made her stick out like a big fat sore thumb

"I need some help with the actual plan for Tyler's auction date," Leanne said quickly. "He told me to think up something simple." Eleanor recognized a diversionary tactic when she heard it and was very grateful.

Nancy took the hint. "If we left it up to Tyler, he'd probably drag the poor woman who wins him to Baxter's."

"Do you honestly think his date would complain?" Sonya

asked with a rueful laugh.

"You'll have to come with us," Leanne told Eleanor. "It'll be a fun night."

"Fun for everyone but Tyler," Joel said with a grin.

A bachelor's auction. It was safe to say that Eleanor wouldn't be participating at a bachelor's auction. "Do you think you'll raise a lot of money?"

The women laughed. "Oh, yes. I think, with Tyler, we'll break our record," Leanne replied. "In fact, I'd bet on it."

"Well, I'm looking forward to meeting him," Eleanor said lamely.

"He'll be here in a little while," Robb announced casually, winding his way back through the chairs toward the deck.

"What?" Rosie sat up abruptly. "No, Robb, he's not due back until tomorrow. That's what he told me. I'm sure of it."

Robb shrugged carelessly. "Apparently his plans changed. I forgot to tell you he phoned when y'all were at Letty's---" He smiled at Eleanor. "I mean, Eleanor's." He cocked his head attentively. "In fact, I think I hear him coming now."

Rosie spun on her chair and, clasping her hands together, fixed a worried gaze on Eleanor. "There's something I need to tell you, Eleanor."

Alarmed by Rosie's anxious tone, Eleanor sat up straight. "Yes?"

"You bought the house from me."

Eleanor blinked, trying to assimilate Rosie's rushed announcement. The house was Rosie's? She was confused. The lease papers indicated a corporation owned the house. There had been no mention of Rosalie Hurst. Why wouldn't Rosie have told her? "I don't understand."

"What, she didn't know that?" asked Robb. He turned to

Eleanor. "You didn't know that?"

"Never mind," Rosie told him. "No time to explain now."

"I don't understand," Eleanor repeated, rising in confusion. "Rosie, why didn't you tell me the house belonged---"

"There he is now," Robb interrupted, pointing his basting brush toward the driveway.

The rumble grew louder until an enormous motorcycle, all wheels and chrome and deafening noise, turned into the driveway and thundered to a stop a few feet away from the cluster of chairs. The rider, a big man clad in well-worn jeans, black tee shirt, scuffed boots and a shiny black helmet, silenced the machine and lifted the helmet from his head. Dropping it gently on the ground, he raked a hand through his short hair and grinned at the group.

Eleanor gaped. It was the big, handsome lawn man. The lawn man was Tyler. Tyler was Rosie's grandson.

Chapter Five

Breathe, Eleanor told herself. She felt winded, as though she had just run up the stairs at the courthouse. Breathe or faint, it's your choice.

So that's why Leanne, Joel and Robb seemed so familiar. Tyler was the common denominator. In one way or another, they all resembled their eldest brother. Surely Rosie had surmised from her description that the man who plucked her from the azaleas was her own grandson. It wasn't as if there were men like him roaming loose all over the place. Why hadn't Rosie said so? Why was it a secret? Another secret, like the house really belong to Rosie, and not some corporation---what was the name? T-something-H Investments. A light bulb blazed on in her head. Tyler-something-Hurst Investments? She sent a bewildered glance in her new neighbor's direction and found Rosie watching her, her expression both concerned and apologetic.

"Uncle Ty! Uncle Ty!" Eleanor's gaze was pulled back toward Tyler, and the excited children who were falling over themselves in an effort to reach him first. He swung one long leg over the seat of the gleaming motorcycle, and pretended to collapse under their noisy attack. It was, apparently, routine behavior because the adults didn't bat an eye.

"Gee, I wish he'd sell that thing." Sonya shook her head and sighed. "Every time he dusts it off, Thomas and Shawn fight all afternoon about whose turn it is to ride around the block with him, and then for days they play motorcycle races on their bikes and I go through a box of Band-Aids doctoring boo-boos."

Joel chuckled and patted his wife on the shoulder. "He'll never sell it, hon. Just keep buying Band-Aids."

"Damn right he'll never sell it." Robb shook his head in mock dismay. "You women, you just don't get it. That's no ordinary motorcycle; it's one of a kind. A classic." The conversation hummed around Eleanor but her attention was riveted on the scene playing out yards away.

"Aw, come on, you monsters, no fair!" Tyler protested in the deep, drawling voice she realized she would recognize anywhere, as he lay on his back on the grass and allowed the children to trample him. They shrieked with laughter as he caught first one, then another, and tossed them high into the air. "Who wants to go for a ride?" His question was received with increased pandemonium. Rising like Gulliver in the land of Lilliputians, he swiped grass out of his short hair and set one of the smallest children atop his shoulders. The child clutched his uncle's ears and Tyler let out a playful bellow. He hoisted two more into his arms, and the remaining child stood on his foot and wrapped chubby arms around his legs. Covered with giggling children, he stomped with exaggerated movements toward the adults. Eleanor thought she'd never seen a more appealing sight. The first time she'd seen him, he'd struck her dumb with his chiseled face and rugged masculinity. Today, his antics with the troop of adoring preschoolers put every one of her hibernating female hormones into screaming red alert. Breathe, she reminded herself. Breathe.

"I see Robb's at the pit," he called as he approached. "What's for lunch? Burnt burgers or charred chicken?" He grinned unrepentantly and used one of the children as a human shield when Robb flicked a potato chip in his direction. "What's everybody doing here on Saturday, anyway? Special occasion?"

Leanne and the others began to offer simultaneous explanations but it was Robb's voice that rose above the rest. "It's a welcome-to-the-neighborhood party for Rosie's new next-door neighbor."

Tyler, grin vanishing, stopped in his tracks. "What?"

He scanned the group and spied Gracie, sitting between Nancy and Sonya. Gracie gave him a bright, unaffected smile. Tyler nodded back, and when he saw Ben, standing with Robb and Joel, with Lexie hoisted on his hip, his wary expression relaxed visibly. "That was quick," he said. "You had me scared for a minute, thinking maybe that little lunatic came back."

The sudden, uncomfortable silence sent a funny signal to Eleanor. Little lunatic? Was he referring to her? Surely not. Glancing toward Rosie, Eleanor watched her exchange a grimace with Leanne before schooling her face and aiming a bright smile somewhere over Eleanor's shoulder.

Then again, maybe he was. Eleanor suddenly felt rubbery.

Tyler was the only one who didn't notice the lull in conversation or the worried glances. He strode toward the grill with his human cargo and, depositing a nephew on the ground, extended his hand to Ben. "Tyler Hurst," he said by way of introduction. "Nice to meet you. When are you moving in?"

Ben shook his head. "Ben Whittington," he replied, clearly awed. "It's really nice to meet you; too, Mr. Hurst, but we're not the new neighbors. Eleanor is." Happily unaware of any consequences to his announcement, he nodded toward Eleanor.

She swallowed.

Swinging back toward the seated group, Tyler raked the group with his eyes again. This time he saw her, and his grin froze, and then vanished. "The hell you say!"

There was no mistaking the horror in his tone. Eleanor felt her blood run cold. She straightened her back and gripped the armrests of her chair.

He carefully shed himself of all five children and, frowning, advanced.

Eleanor felt like a mouse caught in a trap. This was bad. This was very, very bad.

"And we're all just delighted," Rosie added, an encouraging tone to her voice as though she were prompting him to remember his manners.

Oh, no, we're not, Eleanor thought. Rosie's eldest grandson was not delighted at all, and he didn't give two hoots for manners. There was a lot she didn't understand; why Rosie kept her in the dark about owning the house, and why she hadn't clued Eleanor on to the fact that the man she mistook for a yard boy was, in fact, her grandson, but one thing was crystal clear; Tyler was definitely not part of the Hurst family welcome wagon.

He glared at her for a long moment, and then turned his gaze toward his grandmother. "Rosie, can I talk to you inside for a minute." It wasn't a request; it was a steel-coated command. Without waiting for a response, he began striding toward the house. Sighing, Rosie gave Eleanor a reassuring smile before rising and following him. Silently, Eleanor and the others watched them disappear into the side porch, the screen door squeaking and clattering behind them.

There was an uncomfortable pause. Eleanor, finally able to breathe normally again, decided to take the bull by the horns. "Well, that was interesting," she began, pasting a nonchalant smile on her face. "Was it my imagination or did your brother just look at me like I have the sign of the devil tattooed on my forehead?" She gave herself points for sounding unperturbed, even slightly amused. Inside she still quaked from Tyler's reaction.

Leanne sighed and leaned to give Eleanor a pat on the shoulder. "Don't worry," she began, "He was just a little surprised, I think. He's protective of Rosie---well, actually, of all of us, and it tends to make him a little---" She broke off awkwardly.

Eleanor leaned forward anxiously. A little what? Tell me why your brother looked at me like I'm glowing with radioactive cooties.

"Apparently, Tyler had some ideas about the kind of neighbor he felt was best for Rosie. You all know how he is." Hearty nods all around. They were amused nods, Eleanor noted, but also long-suffering. Leanne patted Eleanor again. "He wanted Rosie to wait until he got home before making any decisions about the house. But Rosie wanted Eleanor in the house, and, well, you know Rosie."

Her reply seemed to satisfy everyone but Eleanor. Still baffled, she stared at Leanne. "So you feel he objects to me because I'm---what?" She jerked her head toward Gracie. "Not married with children?"

"And maybe a lunatic," Robb grinned.

The women glared at him.

Leanne nodded. "In a nutshell. Not," she said quickly, "that we agree or that it even makes any sense."

The anger Eleanor felt trickling down her spine was a definite improvement over her previous paralysis. "But he doesn't even know me."

"Don't worry about it," Joel said soothingly. "He'll come around. He's just got this need to be in charge." The others nodded in agreement. "He likes to tell us what to do. Not that we ever pay any attention," he clarified, grinning. "In fact, we were talking just the other day about how it's going to be interesting now that he's back home again."

"He might just be too close for comfort," Leanne said, making a face. "Hopefully he'll find a lot to keep him busy."

"He's always been this way," Robb added. "It's a big-brother control kind of thing."

A control thing. Eleanor took a moment to consider Robb's remark, tapping the armrests of the metal chair with her fingertips. She was certainly familiar with controlling men. In fact, hadn't she just decided that her life had been overrun with them for far too long? "He's inside talking to Rosie about me."

Nobody disputed her remark.

Suddenly determined to include herself into the conversation inside the kitchen, Eleanor jumped out of her chair and hurried toward the house. A chorus of voices called after her to wait, to let Rosie handle him, but she continued on heedlessly. She'd been left out of too many conversations lately. Anything Tyler Hurst had to say, he could say in front of her. She eased through the screened porch door carefully. The door between the porch and the kitchen was ajar. Tyler stood just a foot or so beyond the threshold, his back to her, hands propped on his lean hips. "You've got to be kidding, Rosie," he said in his Southern Comfort drawl. "I've only been gone four days!"

"A lot can happen in four days," Eleanor heard Rosie reply smoothly. Detecting a hint of smugness in Rosie's tone, Eleanor relaxed fractionally. She tiptoed across the enclosed porch so she could hear more easily.

Tyler was too focused on his grandmother to notice Eleanor behind him. "I distinctly remember having a conversation about the kind of neighbor you need, about how inappropriate this---," he hesitated, apparently at a loss for words. "This Eleanor creature is."

Eleanor frowned. This Eleanor creature?

"As I recall, Tyler, you did all the talking. I never actually agreed with you." Tyler's hands fell from his hips at his grandmother's casual insurrection. Rosie continued mildly. "There's no point in raising a ruckus. What's done is done, and I, personally, am delighted with my new neighbor."

Tyler shook his head. "She's all wrong, Rosie. She's not normal.".

Eleanor shifted indignantly from foot to foot.

Rosie's tone sharpened. "That's not a nice thing to say."

"It's nothing against her, Rosie," he backpedaled swiftly.

Oh, sure, nothing against me, Eleanor thought wrathfully. I'm just abnormal.

"I'm sure she's a very nice person---"

Rosie interrupted him. "But?"

He sighed and shifted his posture. Leaning a little, Eleanor could just see Rosie. She was glaring up at her grandson.

"But you need stable neighbors. People you can count on, who you can call at a moment's notice if you need something."

"It sounds like you think I need a babysitter." Rosie pursed her lips. "Really, Tyler. And what on earth makes you think that Eleanor's not stable?"

"Okay, maybe that's too harsh. How about scatter-brained?"

Scatter-brained? Eleanor curled her hands into fists.

"Eleanor's a simply lovely girl, Tyler. You'll see when you get to know her better." Rosie's tone was smooth and encouraging.

"I don't want to get to know her better," he shot back. "I don't want anything to do with her."

His open disdain stabbed the tiny piece of Eleanor's heart that had secretly daydreamed about their first meeting. In her daydream, she was witty and alluring, not tangled and torn, while he was captivated, not amused. Eleanor pressed her cold hands against her suddenly hot cheeks. She didn't want to hear anymore. He was going to hear from her now.

Her jaw so tight it ached, she stepped forward and rapped him on his broad back as if she were knocking on a door. "Let's see if I caught everything," she chimed, anticipating his start of surprise as he swung around. Glaring up at him, Eleanor felt a tinge of satisfaction at his surprised expression. "I'm a lunatic, all wrong, unstable, and scatter-brained. Is that everything?"

His chagrin was fleeting. Pinning his narrowed eyes on her, like a lion zeroing in on its prey, he was quick to strike back. "Well, now, let's see," he drawled, "you're pretty clumsy, and you don't have any qualms about eavesdropping on private conversations, so I guess that means your ethics are questionable, too."

Clumsy! Questionable ethics! Eleanor struggled to think of a biting response but her tongue and brain seemed to be at direct odds with one another. It had been much easier to think straight when facing his back.

Rosie was dismayed by the battle breaking out in her kitchen doorway. "Now, Tyler, Eleanor, let's just calm down. Tyler, apologize right this minute."

"Yes ma'am." One eyebrow arched in a decidedly derisive manner, Tyler leaned against the wall and surveyed Eleanor. "I'm sure sorry it hurts your feelings to hear the truth when you're eavesdropping, Eleanor."

"Tyler!" Rosie wasn't pleased with his apology.

Eleanor gaped at him. The big lout. She didn't care anymore that he was Rosie's grandson. He wasn't going to call her names to her face and get away with it. She snapped her mouth closed, slapped her hands on her hips, and took a step closer. "Not half as sorry as I am that Rosie has a control freak Neanderthal for a grandson, Bubba."

Tyler stiffened, and folding his arms across his chest, advanced a step.

"You don't know anything about me," she added, craning her head to maintain eye contact.

He took one more step and glowered down at her. "I know you're impulsive and reckless, and you don't think before you act. And I know you have a tendency to show up in the middle of the night, drunk as a skunk, waking up the neighbors." He imparted his last shot triumphantly.

Eleanor stared up at him. His hazel eyes, dark and smoky, bored right back into her. How could he know that? "What were you doing, spying on us?" she spluttered indignantly. The peach ale might have sanded the edges off her inhibitions a little but she hadn't been intoxicated. Just cheerful. There was no law against being cheerful.

"Who had to spy?" he asked. "You were making enough noise to raise the dead. Mr. Lemoine was going to call the police. You would have been arrested for disturbing the peace if your friend hadn't dragged you off. And what about that big kiss you laid on the porch column? How normal was that?"

Eleanor vaguely remembered hugging the porch column, but had she kissed it? She couldn't recall. Well, so what if she had? "It was simply a gesture," she replied haughtily, trying not to be distracted by his arching eyebrow. "Not that I expect you to understand."

"A damned odd gesture, if you ask me," he retorted. "Some might say unstable."

"I didn't ask you!"

He squinted at her as if he was trying to decide how to deal with her. "Be that as it may, Rosie needs someone who's home during the day, to keep an eye on her." Grimacing, as though he regretted his words immediately, he shot a cautious, sideways glance at Rosie. Then he frowned at Eleanor as though it was her fault he was putting his foot in his mouth.

Snorting, Rosie began to interrupt, but Eleanor was gathering steam, and gave her no opening. "Who says I won't be around?"

Rosie gave Eleanor an approving nod, which Tyler noted with exasperation. "What, you don't have to work for a living?"

"Of course, but I'm taking the summer off." He didn't have to know she was currently unemployed.

"She quit her job," Rosie volunteered. "Just this week."

Eleanor glanced at Rosie in dismay. If she didn't know better, she'd think Rosie was starting to enjoy this awful exchange.

Tyler looked triumphant. "Quit your job? So no income? Then how do you think you're going to be able to buy the house?"

"I gave her a good deal," Rosie offered mildly.

"You did what?" Tyler gaped at his grandmother. "What kind of a good deal? How much of a good deal?"

Suddenly Eleanor understood why Rosie had kept her identity as the owner secret from her. If Eleanor had known Rosie owned the house, she would never have made such a low offer. The house was worth every cent of the original asking price, and Eleanor knew Tyler wasn't going to like it one bit that Rosie was selling it for less. Heaven help them both if he found out she was only leasing it until closing. She was sure he could put a stop to the purchase if he wanted to. Maybe he wouldn't find out. The adrenalin pumping through her body flagged and she felt a little weak.

"She's leasing it until closing next month."

Oh, no. Eleanor grabbed a chair and sank into it.

Instead of exploding, Tyler closed his eyes and pinched the bridge of his nose with his thumb and index finger. "Leasing it, you say," he repeated carefully.

"That's right," Rosie said cheerfully. "It's all signed, sealed and notarized, and I couldn't be happier."

He stared at her dumbly for a minute, the pulse at his temple jerking, before closing his eyes again.

He had a lot of self-control, she gave him that. Eleanor glanced at Rosie. Completely unruffled by Tyler's reaction, Rosie opened the refrigerator and removed a covered bowl. "Potato salad," she announced blithely. "Can't have barbecued chicken without potato salad."

"That's ridiculous," he finally said, lifting his head and glaring first at Rosie, then at Eleanor. "You gave it away."

"It's mine to give away," Rosie replied easily, and Eleanor watched Tyler's jaw tighten. "Letty left it to me and I'm selling it to

Eleanor. And you may as well know that, after the closing, I plan to reimburse you for all the money you spent renovating it." She peered up at him and patted his cheek fondly. "Are you getting a headache, hon? Want some aspirin?" Without waiting for his response, Rosie crossed the kitchen and swept a bottle of pain reliever from the kitchen window sill. She sat it on the table and turned to Eleanor. "Tyler took charge of all the renovations." She patted Tyler on his broad shoulder. "He did a beautiful job, didn't he? She loves the bathroom, Ty."

"Great," he said sarcastically. "That makes me so happy."

Rosie chose to pretend he was being sincere, and beamed at him. "Now, I want the two of you to put this bad start behind you. Make up and be friends."

Eleanor wrinkled her nose. Sure, right after she phoned Philip Conrad and asked for her job back. Judging by the disgusted expression on his face, Tyler didn't think much of Rosie's suggestion, either.

Sighing loudly, Rosie tugged Eleanor from her chair and, catching Tyler by the hand, pulled them toward one another. Eleanor hung back, but Rosie pressed their hands together anyway. Ignoring the tingle that zapped her down to her toes, Eleanor gave Rosie a weak smile and tried not to notice how her hand was swallowed inside Tyler's big, warm hand. It was much wiser to view their clasp as the requisite handshake before a prizefighter's boxing match.

Rosie gave their joined hands a squeeze. "There, isn't that better? Come on, now. Let's go outside and have lunch."

The instant Rosie lifted her hand, Eleanor snatched hers away from Tyler's unenthusiastic grip. Satisfied, Rosie crossed the kitchen to retrieve the bowl of potato salad.

"This isn't the end of it," Tyler said in a low voice meant only for Eleanor's ears. "You're not moved in yet."

Rosie stepped around them on her way back outdoors, unaware of Tyler's inflammatory remark. "Looks like we're almost ready to eat. Bring the bread when you come, Ty." The door closed behind her.

So he thought he could prevent her from buying the house. Well, he thought wrong. Eleanor reached for the bottle of pain reliever on the tabletop with one hand and caught his hand again with the other. "Brace yourself for more bad news," she murmured, pressing the bottle into his palm and curling his fingers around it. "As a matter of fact, I am." Startling herself with her audacity, she reached up to pat his lean cheek. "All moved in, that is." As gestures went, she thought, even as her legs wobbled, it was beautifully insolent. "Now be a good boy for your grandmother and bring the bread."

He was standing still as a rock, but her flippant command sparked a flash of something---outrage? bloodlust? ---in his eyes that sent a healthy charge of foreboding down Eleanor's spine. Pulling her hand back before he bit it off, she veered hastily toward the doorway in Rosie's wake.

* * *

Clenching the plastic bottle inside an iron grip, Tyler watched Eleanor swagger out the door, across the porch and deck, and down the steps before drawing in the breath he'd been holding since she reached up and touched his cheek. She was one twisted bit of work, that was for sure. Frowning fiercely, he rubbed his cheek. Plain as a dust mop and about as shapely, but for a scary moment there, when she lifted her hand to his face, he felt glued to the floor, oblivious to the bottle she had slapped into his palm, oblivious to anything but the dare in her tilted green eyes. He had been very tempted to respond to that dare. He had been very tempted to--

Shuddering, he popped the cap on the bottle, and swallowed four tablets without benefit of water. He needed help if he was remotely tempted, even for a split second, by the likes of Eleanor Haley. She was the most unattractive little mouse of a woman he'd ever seen, and talk about your Jekyll and Hyde personality! Apparently she had two modes; mute or smart-mouth. So far there was no sign of any normal in-between.

Crossing the kitchen, Tyler returned the bottle to its place on the window sill and stared at it. He seemed to be popping pills like clockwork since he'd moved back home. Somehow that didn't seem to be a good sign. He leaned over the sink and surveyed his family through the window. Correction; his family and Eleanor Haley and her entourage. She sat on the glider right beside Rosie, their heads bent together in deep conversation. Tyler frowned. He guessed his ears ought to be burning. There wasn't any doubt they were congratulating one another on their successful double-team effort. Tyler noticed for the first time how like they were in size. In temperament, too, apparently. Neither one was the least bit repentant; not Rosie, for happily and blatantly disregarding his advice, and not Eleanor Haley, either, for stealing the house for a fraction of its value.

Turning away from the window, he crossed the kitchen and sat in the nearest chair, the one Eleanor sank into when Rosie dropped the bomb about leasing her the house in advance of the closing. She'd looked as though she was going to faint when that particular cat got out of the bag.

A fraction of the house's value. All that work, ostensibly for Hope, not a sneaking little stranger. Tyler inhaled deeply. Don't think about it right now, he cautioned himself. He'd rather think about how depressing his trip to Denver had been than to dwell on Rosie's questionable coup.

And flying back for the closing on his home in Denver had definitely been depressing. He'd stayed with his friend, Garrett Long, the Renegade's golden quarterback who, unlike Tyler, still had a lot of good years left in him. Staying with him had been a personal test of sorts and Tyler was pretty sure he'd failed it. It wasn't supposed to bother him to hear Garrett talk about the upcoming season, but it did, a lot more than he expected, because while it was just another off-season for Garrett, for Tyler, it was off-season from here on out. He had felt disconnected and a little bummed. Truthfully, completely bummed.

And then there was the closing. Tyler rose and opened the refrigerator to search for an IPA. Rosie usually tucked one or two someplace safe for him, and he smiled when he found one hidden in the vegetable drawer. Returning to his seat, he propped his feet up on another of the kitchen chairs and twisted off the cap. The long cold swallow felt good going down and made the recollection of the closing less grim.

The buyers, an impossibly perky young couple in trendy designer sportswear, had annoyed the hell out of him by gushing endlessly about their excitement over the transaction. They told him how impressed their friends were that they were buying his house, which made Tyler wonder what kind of friends they had. He had played football, for God's sake, not discovered a cure for cancer. The guy, some kind of specialized dentist, tried to talk football while they signed papers. Tyler snorted in remembrance.

He wanted to talk football with him about as much as he wanted to hear the wife talk about her plans to put a gas insert inside his beloved stone fireplace. Then the wife asked him for his address so she could send him an invitation to some housewarming thing they were planning once they moved in. While he was thinking how intolerable it would be to go to their party with their friends in his home, she'd put her hand on his thigh beneath the table, another kind of invitation altogether. He couldn't wait to get away from them both.

He had some time to kill before catching his plane, so he got the bright idea to take one last look from the deck of the house that didn't belong to him anymore. It seemed like an okay idea at the time, but the closer he got to the turnoff, the more hesitant he became. He felt uneasy as he drove up the winding driveway, and downright depressed when the house came into view. The yuppy couple looked at it and saw property value and lavish parties and their own self-importance. When he saw it, he remembered tinkering with the plans for months to make sure every detail was perfect, he remembered the satisfaction and pride he'd felt after the last nail was driven, and he remembered the beauty of every morning of every season.

He had walked around the empty house, climbed the steps to the deck, and braced his hands on the rail like he had done a million times before. With nothing but mountains and trees and sky for company, he'd second-guessed his decision to retire and return home, and, like now, wondered what the hell he was going to do with himself back home in slow-moving, sultry Baton Rouge. For all his talk about enjoying retirement, he was pretty sure he was going to hate it.

Chapter Six

The trip back across the lawn seemed endless. Eleanor could feel Tyler's eyes boring holes into her back while his family waited for her return with blatant curiosity. As she approached, she offered a weak smile.

"Is everything all right, Eleanor?" Leanne rose, her brow furrowed in concern. "You look a little pale."

Robb caught her gently by the arm as she edged through a gap in the cluster of chairs. "Well, we see you're still in one piece," he teased, moving behind her to lift her arm and rotate it gently. "Nothing's chewed off that I can see."

Eleanor flexed it a time or two. "Still working," she agreed, and then rubbed her neck. "It's the head I'm worried about. Any bite marks?" Her shaky attempt at humor had the effect she wanted; Robb and the others laughed and resumed their casual conversations. Eleanor sat beside Rosie on the glider. "You never told me the house belonged to you, Rosie," she whispered. "Why not?"

Pushing the glider into motion, Rosie patted her on the arm. "I decided right away I wanted you to have the house, Eleanor, and I was afraid you'd decide against making an offer if you knew."

Eleanor shook her head in dismay. "You shouldn't have accepted my offer. It was way too low."

"Money was never the issue, honey. I want you for a neighbor. Please don't let Tyler make you feel awkward. I was going to make my grand confession this evening, really, I was."

"TDH Investments belongs to Tyler, doesn't it?"

Rosie nodded. "We transferred the house to the company long ago, for business reasons, but it was still mine to sell. Don't waste a minute worrying about it. It's yours now in every way that counts, and I'm as pleased as punch."

"Tyler's not." It shouldn't matter, Eleanor thought grimly, but it does.

"Tyler will come around, you'll see." Rosie nudged Nancy's foot, and tilted her head toward Eleanor. Nancy was quick to take the cue. "Rosie tells us you're not working this summer," she said, conversationally. "Are you a teacher?"

Eleanor shook her head. "No, up until last week I worked for Conrad, Berkley and Burns. It's a law firm downtown." She caught what seemed to be looks of dismay flashing between the others.

"A secretary?" Sonya asked hopefully.

"Nope, associate," Eleanor replied.

Joel leaned forward. "You're an attorney?"

Eleanor nodded. "An unemployed one right now, though."

Nancy stared at her, open-mouthed. Joel let out a long whistle and Robb leaned back in his chair, grinning.

"Oh, boy," Sonya said, rubbing her round stomach absently. "Things are about to get even more interesting around here."

Puzzled, Eleanor glanced around. With the exception of Rosie, and Robb, who looked tickled pink, the others reacted as if she'd just admitted she was the head of an underground militia.

"Lord have mercy," Leanne breathed. "Tyler cannot know. We all have to agree, Tyler cannot know."

Eleanor didn't like the sound of that, not one bit. "Why not?"

"Well, it's like this. Tyler's sort of, um, preinclined to be suspicious of---" Nancy began carefully and trailed off. She looked toward Sonya for help.

"He's got a pretty strong bias against---" Sonya struggled with her words as well.

"He hates lawyers." Robb made his startling announcement easily. "Hates 'em with a black passion. No ifs, ands or buts about it."

Blinking, Eleanor absorbed his matter-of-fact announcement. "Tyler hates lawyers? All lawyers?" How ridiculous. He couldn't just hate a whole group of people like that. Nobody was that narrow-minded.

"Hey, Eleanor, have you heard the one about 'what's black and brown and looks good on an attorney?'"

"Robb!" Rosie, Nancy and Sonya gave him collective scalding glares.

"A Doberman pinscher!" He grinned at Eleanor unrepentantly. "Here's another one. Two lawyers are walking down the street and one of them---"

Nancy jabbed him in the side. "That's enough, Robb! You're not being any help at all."

"You have to understand about Tyler," Sonya began, clearly uncomfortable. "He's got good reason for feeling the way he does. Tell her, Rosie."

"Please do." Eleanor scooted forward to the edge of her chair.

"Let's don't go into all of that right now," Rosie said earnestly. "We can explain why later. He'll be coming back outside any minute. Let's agree it's best if he doesn't find out just yet."

Eleanor frowned. "You mean, purposely keep it from him?"

The women nodded emphatically, even Gracie, Eleanor noticed wryly. Joel shrugged skeptically while Robb continued to grin, thoroughly entertained by the dilemma.

"I don't know," she said reluctantly. "He's bound to find out. Wouldn't it be better to tell him now and let him deal with it?"

"No!"

The united chorus startled her.

"Eleanor's right, you know. Better to get it out and in the open and over with," Joel calmly advised. "Think about his reaction later when he finds out we all knew, and kept it from him. He hates secrets."

"I agree with Rosie; let's cross that bridge later," Nancy said. "First, let him get over---" She broke off and clamped her mouth closed.

"Let him get over today's shock." Eleanor summed up Nancy's unspoken sentiment.

Nancy grimaced and patted Eleanor's hand.

The porch door opened and banged closed. Eleanor turned her head and saw Tyler, expression still grim, heading their way.

"We're all in agreement, then," Rosie hissed through her bright smile. "Not a word. Not a single word."

* * *

Eleanor had no inkling a house could be so quiet and so loud all at the same time. Noises in her old apartment were familiar and easy to dismiss. The creaks and squeaks in this old house, on the other hand, were going to take some serious getting-used-to. Not to mention the sounds outside, she thought with a shudder. Her first trip down the dark driveway, loaded with empty boxes, quickly became her last when something rustled inside the nearby shrubbery. Stricken with foolish terror, she had flung the boxes in the air and dashed back inside.

A glance at her phone told her it was very nearly midnight. Too bad, she told herself ruthlessly, dragging another box across the floor and hoisting it to the top of her bed. About a dozen boxes to go, and then, and only then, would she call it a night. She pried the box open and lifted an eyebrow in relief. Towels, finally. She cast a longing look toward the old-fashioned bathtub. A bottle of bubble bath and her favorite pajamas were waiting, and now she finally had the towels. Soon, she promised herself. The first soak in that amazing old tub was the carrot she'd been dangling before herself all evening.

Not that she couldn't stop now, if she really wanted to, she reminded herself, carrying a stack of towels to the built-in cherry dresser in the bathroom. She glanced at her reflection in the mirror, and leaned forward. What little make-up she wore had worn off hours and hours ago, there were shadows beneath her eyes, and her hair---big surprise here--- had fallen down again. Wearily she pulled the remaining hairpins out. There, she snorted in self-disparagement, that truly completed the picture of style and beauty. She was too old to have such a tangle of hair, as her father routinely pointed out. It was more trouble than it was worth but, as always, she balked at the notion of cutting it. Sometimes she felt like the wild curls were all that kept her from becoming invisible.

She turned back to her room and considered calling it quits. There wasn't really any reason for working like a madwoman. She had all the time in the world. The reasonable thing to do would be to get some rest and start again in the morning. But the truth was, she didn't feel reasonable. Not at all. Eleanor vigorously stuffed the towels inside the cabinet, and then crossed the room for another armload. Ever since she'd come home from Rosie's that afternoon, she'd been going ninety to nothing, fueled to the top of her tank with pure, unleaded spite. If she had to stay up all night long, every single box was going to be unpacked, and there was going to be a mountain of cardboard boxes stacked beside the street by noon on Sunday. She wanted them to be the very first thing Tyler Hurst saw the next time he turned onto Magnolia Drive.

Eleanor ripped open another box and frowned at the jumble of plain pumps inside. Today she'd noticed Leanne and Nancy, and even pregnant Sonya, all wore pretty, strappy sandals that showed off tanned legs and painted toenails. That's what she wanted, some sandals, and some nail polish. And bright socks and quirky athletic shoes like Rosie wore. And shorts, and tee shirts, and, while she was at it, some bright red lipstick.

She pushed the box across the room and upended the contents onto the closet floor. There, she thought crankily, another box unpacked. Grabbing the two empty containers, she stepped through the bedroom doorway and tossed them down the stairs to join the rest that were waiting for morning for a trip to the curb.

Oh, how she wished she could see the look on Tyler Hurst's face when he saw all her empty boxes, thumbing their noses at him. They would be proof of just how settled she was, of how little his opinions and objections affected her. She was going to be so damned entrenched a hurricane couldn't uproot her. And then she was going to prove to him what an excellent neighbor she was going to be for Rosie. That's what she was going to do.

Trudging back to her room, she gave in to temptation and flopped on top of her bed to rest for just a minute. In her mind, she still saw Tyler glaring at her, his eyes steely and cold. She draped an arm across her eyes to block out the vision, but it didn't work. She hadn't been able to block him out at Rosie's, either. After he came back outside, she'd done her best to ignore him, but every single time she'd glanced up, she'd found him studying her like she was some kind of mad science experiment gone awry. His hard-boiled scrutiny made her go hot, then cold, and an awful time or two she had completely lost her train of thought and actually stuttered. Eleanor groaned in remembrance. She'd been fitting in so well until he showed up and ruined everything.

The odd thing was, nobody else seemed to notice the way he gazed at her, censure written all over his face, underscored by his posture. That was another thing. Couldn't the man stand up straight? All he did was lean, with his big, brawny arms folded across his big, brawny chest, one long leg crooked behind the other. He leaned and he stared, his expression inscrutable, until she was reduced to stuttering. Grabbing a pillow, Eleanor punched it a time or two and clasped it around her head.

That wasn't the worst of it, though. The worst occurred when she took her plate to the oversized picnic table where she slid in beside Gracie. Purposely choosing the near side of the table so she wouldn't have to see Tyler, she took her first bite of the mouth-watering barbecued chicken and then looked up to find him settling in directly across from her. He lifted a mocking eyebrow and she responded, probably just the way he planned, by choking on the chicken and promptly knocking over her glass of sweet tea.

While Gracie pounded her on the back and Nancy mopped up the table, he leaned back, shook his head slowly, and mouthed something. It took Eleanor a moment to realize what it was.

'Clumsy.'

Eyes still watering, Eleanor had gaped at him in speechless outrage.

Clearly satisfied, he then picked up his plate and stepped easily back over the bench. "Too much commotion over here," he announced cheerfully, and ambled off again.

The big beast.

* * *

Despite the impromptu get-together the previous day, Sunday afternoon barbecues were a Hurst family tradition, something to look forward to when he was in town, but today Tyler found himself dreading the gathering. He was still bent out of shape about Rosie's sneaky sale of the house but knew he was alone in his disapproval. His siblings had fawned over Eleanor the day before and he was grumpily aware that there was a good chance she'd be on hand again today. Don't think about her, he told himself, taking a deep breath.

Normally the first to arrive, today he was the last, and even the onslaught of his nieces and nephews racing to greet him did little to improve his mood. He made his way toward the deck where Ally, her husband, David, Leanne, Joel and Sonya stood talking. There was no sign of Eleanor, he noticed right away, but that didn't mean she wasn't inside. He hoped she was next door, where she belonged. Not that she belonged there, either, he quickly corrected himself.

Tyler stopped in front of Sonya and hunkered down on his heels. "Hello in there," he said to her stomach. "How's the world treating you?"

Sonya grinned down at him. "I think she's got some complaints because she's been kicking the devil out of me all morning."

Rising, Tyler lifted an interested eyebrow. "Do we know for sure she's a 'she'?"

Sonya grimaced. "She better be, or else you'll have a nephew named Stephanie."

Tyler laughed. "You hear that?" he asked her stomach. "I think she means it." He looked up. "Is she kicking right now?"

"Oh, yes." Sonya took his hand and pressed it against the side of her firm abdomen. "Feel that?"

Tyler concentrated, and felt a tiny ripple beneath his hand. Smiling, he shook his head in wonder. "Yeah, I do feel it. What is it?"

"Maybe a knee, maybe an elbow," Joel replied, grinning. "Some pointy little part." He pulled Sonya close and began massaging her shoulders. She leaned back against him and they shared a private smile.

Tyler felt an unexpected jolt of envy. Joel, five years younger, was about to be a dad for the third time, while he, the eldest, wasn't even out of the starting blocks. He needed to quit wasting time and start looking for wife and mother material. Like Rosie was fond of pointing out, he wasn't getting any younger.

Pushing the disturbing thoughts aside, he leaned down again. "Just remember, little lady," he said to Sonya's stomach, "if your brothers ever give you any trouble, you just call your Uncle Tyler and I'll straighten them out for you. That's a promise." He rose and looked toward the house. "Where's Rosie?"

"Inside with Robb and Nancy," Allie replied, heading toward the door. Tyler held it open for her and followed her into the kitchen. Robb, sitting at the table with papers spread before him, looked up. "Hey," Tyler said. "Where's Rosie?"

"In the back, helping Nancy try on her bridesmaid dress," Robb replied, leaning back in his chair.

"Oh, I want to see it," Ally said.

Robb laid his pencil down. "Isn't it exactly like yours?"

Ally grinned. "What's your point?" She disappeared through the doorway.

Perplexed, Tyler sat down at the table. "And why does Nancy need help?"

Robb shrugged. "Beats the hell out of me. They've all gone into overdrive on this wedding, in case you haven't noticed. I'll sure be glad when it's over." He gave Tyler a considering glance. "You're the only one left, you know."

"Left for what?"

"To get married."

Tyler lifted an eyebrow. "I hear it enough from Rosie, Robb."

Robb grinned. "She's determined to see you married, Ty, you know that."

Unfortunately, Tyler did know that. "Well," he said, "You can be sure if and when I do decide to get married, I'm not going to put everybody through another one of these ordeals. This kind of commotion is for the birds."

"What commotion?" Rosie entered the kitchen with Ally and Nancy on her heels. "What are you two talking about?"

"Nothing important," Tyler said, rising to receive his usual hug. Rosie gave him a brief, un-Rosie-like pat and then pushed him away. "What's wrong?" he asked

Rosie faced Allison. "Tell Ty what you just told me."

"That I'm looking forward to meeting Eleanor," Ally said, opening the refrigerator and helping herself to a soda.

Uh, oh, not safe in here, Tyler thought abruptly.

"When's she coming over?" Ally popped the tab and drank a swallow, her blue eyes innocent over the top of the can.

"She's isn't," Rosie replied, withdrawing a serving spoon from a kitchen drawer and closing it with a bang. Tyler flinched. "She doesn't feel welcome here."

Allison lowered the can and gaped at Rosie. "Why not?"

Tyler began to ease back toward the door.

Rosie put her hands on her hips and glared at him. "Tell Ally why not."

He shrugged innocently. "How would I know?"

Rosie's gaze narrowed.

"You do have an awfully guilty look on your face, Ty," Ally said, the corners of her mouth tilting.

"Gee, thanks, Al," he said, reproachfully. A guy could always count on his sisters to dig him a deeper hole.

"As well he should," Rosie said. "He outdid himself yesterday."

He hadn't done anything wrong, Tyler thought indignantly. In fact, if anybody ought to be feeling guilty, it was Eleanor Haley, for sneaking up behind him. A guy was entitled to be a little bent out of shape when he just found out his grandmother had given away a small fortune. He should be allowed to rant and rave a little without worrying that some beady-eyed little mouse was standing in his shadow.

Leanne and Sonya banged through the screen door. "Rosie, Joel wants to know if you're ready for him to light the grill," Leanne said. She glanced around the room. "What's going on?"

"I'm trying to find out why the new neighbor isn't coming over this afternoon," Ally explained. "Rosie says Ty knows, but he won't say."

Sonya pulled out a chair and sank into it, frowning. "Eleanor's not coming?"

"She's home," Leanne said, glancing out of the window by the table. "I see her car. She's not sick, is she, Rosie?"

"Maybe she's still got a lot of unpacking to do," Nancy suggested. "We ought to go insist that she come over and eat, though. I mean, we have all this food," she nodded toward the counter top, covered with dishes, "and she's awfully thin."

"Is she expecting company of her own? Family maybe?"

"Her friend, Gracie, told us she hasn't really got any family to speak of," Sonya confided.

Her announcement was met with a chorus of feminine sighs and clucks. Dismayed, Tyler glanced around at the women in his family. Too warm-hearted and maternal for their own good, all of them.

"You know, someone should go and insist she join us," Robb piped in. "It's just too pretty outside to be cooped up inside."

Tyler shot a seething look at his brother. "You're inside," he bit off.

Grinning, Robb rose and opened the back door. "Not anymore."

Tyler, trapped behind the lines, listened and fumed as more clucking and debate about Eleanor followed. It was turning into a damned federal case. What a shame; poor Eleanor home alone. Such a pretty afternoon; wasted on unpacking. Oh, I was so hoping to meet her. Tyler made a face, and then looked away hastily when he realized Rosie was studying him. Cut and run, he thought, quickly. "Maybe she wants to be home," he suggested mildly. "Maybe she wants to enjoy her new house. That's why she bought it, isn't it? To live there? She lives there," he said, gesturing with exaggeration out the window. "Not here." He waved his arm to take in the kitchen.

The women of his family, women he spoiled at every opportunity, all stopped and stared at him.

"What?" he demanded. He hadn't said anything ugly; just stated facts.

"Who is this man?" Ally asked Leanne.

"You got me," Leanne shrugged, studying Tyler thoughtfully.

"Everybody out," said Rosie, galvanized back into action. "Everybody but you, Ty. Go on, out, right now."

He glanced around, dismayed, but nobody spoke up in his defense.

"One too many head-butts without a helmet, maybe," Sonya said, heaving herself out of the chair.

"I heard that," he called. The others laughed and disappeared through the door.

Rosie pulled out a chair. "Sit down, Tyler."

He sat.

She sat beside him, a troubled expression on her soft face. "Your brothers and sisters are willing to---no, eager to welcome Eleanor. Why aren't you?"

"She took advantage of you," he shot back. "Probably gave you some sad story and cranked up your sympathy. He didn't reiterate all his personal objections to Eleanor; that she was erratic and klutzy and irritating. Nobody else seemed to get that about her. "And I hate surprises," he added stonily.

Rosie nodded sympathetically. "I know you do, hon, but you have to get over it. And if you're upset with anyone, be upset with me. She didn't know it belonged to me. As a matter of fact, I purposely kept her from finding out. I planned to explain it to her last night but then you showed up before I had a chance. Poor thing, she was as shocked as you."

Tyler frowned. ""You went to a hell of a lot of trouble, didn't you?"

She tried not to look pleased with herself but he could tell she was smirking beneath the surface. "Amanda Howard was Eleanor's only contact and all the papers were in your company's name. The only reason she's moved in already is because I made it a condition of the agreement. It was really quite difficult for her, but I wanted her in the house before you got home. You would have done everything in your power to throw a wrench in the works."

No doubt about that. No doubt at all about that. Tyler could barely fathom his grandmother's plotting.

"Does knowing that I was the instigator change your perspective at all, Tyler? Because I'm already fond of Eleanor," she said, patting his arm, "and I don't want to have to worry every time you two bump into one another."

Tyler sighed and rubbed his jaw forcefully. "We probably won't bump into one another often, Rosie."

She lifted an eyebrow. "Tyler. She lives next door and you come over all the time."

Well, she'd just have to learn to stay out of his way.

"I want you to be nice," Rosie said. "You can do that for me, can't you?"

"Yeah, sure," he said resignedly. "I'll be nice. Just as nice as she is to me," he clarified.

Rosie was satisfied. "Then everything will be just fine. Now I want you to go next door and invite her to come over."

Not going to happen. "Send Leanne or Nancy."

Rosie shook her head emphatically. "No. You have to do it, because you're the reason she won't come."

"Did she come right out and say that?"

"Of course not. She said she didn't sleep well her first night in the house and wouldn't be good company but I know better." She touched his arm. "Please, Tyler."

Somehow he didn't think the amount of rest Eleanor Haley got was going to affect her social skills. "And this is something you really want me to do," he said, rising reluctantly.

"Yes. It's important to me that you make amends."

It was inherently unfair. All he was guilty of was looking out for his family but Rosie didn't see it that way and no amount of reasoning was going to convince her. Eleanor Haley had weaseled her way into Rosie's affections already and he was the odd man out in his own family. He recalled Eleanor's horror when he sat down across the table yesterday, and the whole funny string of events that followed. Downright panicky, she choked and promptly sent the table into an uproar by sending her drink flying, and then, as plates were lifted and puddles were sopped, she received a well-intentioned but overly energetic beating from her friend. Quite a show. And, well, maybe he should be a little ashamed of himself, even if he was stating the obvious when he mouthed the word 'clumsy' but who knew she could read lips? Her eyes had flashed pure green venom, and he had felt considerably cheered.

Rosie looked at him solemnly, for a long moment. "You know, Tyler, I miss Letty."

His thoughts interrupted, Tyler drew up short. "I know you do, Rosie." His grandmother and Letty had been closer than sisters. He'd flown home right after a Monday night football game, exhausted and limping, to make Letty's funeral, but Rosie had looked ten times worse than he did.

"I think Eleanor might fill some of the void that Letty left."

His sly little grandmother was bringing out the big guns now. "Do you, now?" He thought about kidding Rosie that there couldn't be much void, not with all her hobbies and classes and friends and family, but abruptly changed his mind. Rosie and Letty had lived next door to one another for over fifty years, after all. Fifty years of canning vegetables, planting flowers, sharing pots of coffee, laughing and crying. No, he wouldn't make light of that. She had lost many friends during the last few years, but none who were such an integral part of her life as Letty.

"I really do. She has a lot to learn and I have a lot to share."

Tyler eyed his beloved grandmother with resigned affection. "Is she going to become one of your pet projects?"

His grandmother smiled back. "Maybe."

He gave a great sigh. If tucking one dowdy little bird under her wing was what Rosie really wanted to do, he supposed he could live with it; annoying squawks, green-eyed glares and all. It wasn't like he had to adopt her, too. "I'll give it a shot," he said, rising and heading for the door.

"Be nice," she said again. "That's all I ask."

Leanne and Sonya and Robb, leaning on the deck railing, watching the other four adults battling it out in a badminton game, turned curiously as he strode down the steps.

"Where're you going, Tyler?" Robb grinned knowingly. "Need a white flag?"

Tyler gave him a rude gesture.

"Be nice!" Leanne and Sonya called simultaneously.

They sure were enjoying the hell out of this he thought darkly. No loyalty whatsoever. Disgruntled, he decided to go the long way around, by the street, instead of taking the shortcut through the azaleas. That way Eleanor might see him coming and hopefully decide not to answer the door.

Chapter Seven

Eleanor peeked through her raised bedroom window toward Rosie's yard. Through the drooping branches of the oak tree she could see the back lawn was a beehive of activity. Someone had set up a net over which Nancy and Joel and another couple, who must be Allison and Dave, swatted birdies with badminton racquets. Eleanor smiled, unconsciously moving in front of the window for a better look. In the sunniest part of the yard, three of the smaller members of the clan motored around inside a plastic pool, while the other children, and Robb, too, she noticed with a smile, raced around, firing streams of water at one another from guns of all shapes and sizes. And on Rosie's deck, the barbecue grill again emitted the most wonderful smells. Eleanor inhaled deeply and her stomach growled, reminding her she hadn't eaten anything but a suspiciously tough bagel, all day long.

Rosie phoned that morning to remind her she was invited to join them. Eleanor was afraid her excuse sounded lame, but it was true nonetheless; she really had accidentally fallen asleep, fully clothed, somewhere around two a.m., and hadn't awaken until late morning, gritty and aching and irritable. She had missed her long-awaited first bath in the romantic old tub the night before, and that, more than anything, really ticked her off. In a convoluted way, she laid blame for her long night squarely at the feet of Tyler Hurst. After all, if she hadn't felt compelled to trumpet her unarguable possession of the house, she'd have had her bubble bath and gone to bed at a normal hour.

But she'd finally dragged herself out of bed, had a good soak in the tub, washed and dried her hair---no small task---and now she was piddling around, trying to stir up some much-needed motivation. She really ought to set up the computer and work on her résumé. Getting dressed might be a good idea, too.

Rosie's back door creaked open and slammed shut, and Eleanor recognized Tyler crossing the deck. Her heart skipped a beat. She frowned. Why did the wretched man have the ability, at this distance, to make her feel wobbly? He didn't like her, for heavens' sake, and she liked him even less.

After exchanging words with some of the children, he began walking down the driveway toward the street. Maybe he was leaving, she thought hopefully. She craned, trying to see, but the trees and shrubs blocked her view. If he left, she'd definitely join Rosie and the others.

Losing interest in her limited view, she went downstairs and started a fresh pot of coffee. She smiled at her lovely kitchen, with its glossy granite countertops and shiny new appliances. Perhaps she would browse online for simple recipes because cooking in here was much more appealing than it had been at her apartment. There were so many things to enjoy about her new home.

A sharp rap from her porch interrupted her thoughts and she padded barefoot to the front door. A large shadow was visible through the opaque stained glass and her spirit plummeted. She drew in a deep breath and opened the door an inch. "Yes?"

Tyler's eyes flicked derisively over her disarray. "Rosie wants you to come over."

"Good morning to you, too," she said, holding the door firmly. "You're trespassing," she added sweetly.

"Hardly," he said. "Your closing's not for three and a half more weeks. Technically I still own this house."

"Technically Rosie does. Anyway, did you notice all the boxes? I'm all unpacked. Completely settled in. Not going anywhere. Staying right here."

Silence. She edged the door open a bit more to see his face, glaring at her.

"It's mine," she added for good measure. She was pleased to note the narrowing of his eyes. "All mine."

"Are you going to come over or not?" he bit off. "Rosie wants to know."

Ah, such a gracious invitation. "What about you, Tyler? Do you want me to come over?" She batted her eyes at him.

He looked positively pained.

No, he didn't want her to come over. So why was he the one issuing the invitation? Eleanor surveyed him thoughtfully. "Did Rosie make you come over here?"

"Do you really think it was my idea?" he replied tightly.

She edged the door open a bit more so he could see her clasp a hand over her heart. "And here I thought you just couldn't wait to see me again."

Tyler gave her a brutal and unfriendly glare. "Let's get something straight right now." He pushed the door open easily and filled the doorway. "Let me tell you how it's going to be."

He didn't intimidate her anymore, well, not that much. Eleanor shoved her hands into the pockets of her robe and gazed up, unperturbed. "How what's going to be?"

"This," he said, gesturing from her house to Rosie's. "This whole neighbor thing."

"You can tell me how you think it's going to be and I'll let you know if I concur or not."

Closing his eyes, he pinched the bridge of his nose with his thumb and forefinger.

"Getting a headache?"

"Don't worry about my headache. Be quiet and listen. For some unexplainable reason Rosie has taken a liking to you and I have to live with that, but there are a few rules you'd better remember. First of all, I don't want you coming over to Rosie's house, uninvited, ever. She's eighty-six years old and she has a right to her privacy."

Why, the big ox! As if she ever would.

"And I don't want you asking her for anything. Or anybody else in my family for that matter. I mean, not even a cup of sugar."

Fuming, Eleanor crossed her arms. "Anything else?"

He nodded. "I don't want any loud stuff going on over here. I don't know what you're used to, but this is a quiet neighborhood, and that's how it's going to stay."

"Damn, there go my plans for a wild, drunken orgy," she drawled as best she could.

"And just so you know, I come over all the time and I plan to keep a close eye on you. You won't get away with anything, I can

promise you that. Now, get a move on, Rosie's waiting for you."
He turned on his heel and strode across the porch and down the
steps.

She stared after him, and then took a deep breath. "Just give
me five minutes," she called back sunnily. "Save me a seat right
next to you and my joy will be complete."

He slowed, shoulders stiffening, as if he were battling the urge
to turn around and respond, and then picked up his pace again.

* * *

"Here he comes, and he doesn't look happy," Leanne announced,
standing sentinel beside the large kitchen window. Allison and
Sonya, heads together over a wedding magazine, leaned across the
kitchen table to see.

"I'd say you're right," Ally agreed blithely. "That definitely is
not a happy face."

"Is Eleanor with him?" Rosie asked..

"No, it's just him and his temper." Leanne grinned and waved
Rosie over. "Come see what you think."

Rosie peered through the window. Leanne was right; Tyler
didn't look happy at all. His jaw tight, he stomped across the
driveway. Robb called out something; something irreverent, Rosie
was sure, and Tyler responded with an evil glare.

"He looks a little annoyed to me, too," she agreed mildly.

"Is he coming inside?"

Rosie glanced outside again. Tyler had moved off to the side,
out of sight of his brothers and brothers-in-law, glaring in the
direction of Eleanor's house. No doubt about it, he was clearly in a
first-class temper. "In a few minutes, I'm sure." Nothing if not

predictable, Tyler wouldn't set a foot inside until he was calm and composed. Rosie could count on one hand the times she'd seen him truly fly off the handle. When irritated, he always took a moment or two to think, to put things into perspective. Maintaining his composure was imperative to him and had become second nature.

But collecting himself seemed to be taking an extra bit of effort in this instance, she thought, biting back a smile. Apparently his second confrontation with Eleanor had gone the way of the first. What a showdown that had been! Tyler had been seething but Eleanor hadn't backed down an inch. Today's visit must have degenerated into a rematch, and judging by the stony look on Tyler's face, he hadn't come away with the upper hand.

Rosie felt inexplicably pleased. Her intuitive feeling about Eleanor had been dead on. Poor Tyler, he knew a lot about women in general, that was an undisputed fact, but apparently he didn't know enough to realize he may have finally met his match in her new next-door neighbor.

Just as she hoped.

"I don't get it," Sonya frowned, reaching across her stomach and the table to take a tortilla chip. "Tyler gets along with everybody. He goes out of his way to be polite and put people at ease."

"Especially women," Ally said, waggling her eyebrows, pushing the bowl nearer her sister-in-law.

Heads nodded in fond exasperation. Though he was discreet, a trait she appreciated, Rosie and the rest of the family knew a bit more about Tyler's off-the-field prowess than he realized.

"I don't think I've ever seen him behave rudely to a woman until yesterday." Leanne smoothed the tablecloth thoughtfully.

"Rosie has a theory," Ally remarked.

"What kind of theory?" Leanne and Sonya looked at Rosie expectantly.

"Uh, oh, here he comes." Rosie moved away from the window hastily.

The screened porch door opened and closed, and then the kitchen door opened. Tyler ducked inside, nodded silently, and headed for the refrigerator.

"Where's Eleanor?" Rosie asked innocently.

Tyler opened the refrigerator door and dug an IPA from the vegetable bin before answering. "Unpacking her broomstick and cauldron, I guess."

All four women frowned at him.

"Tyler!"

"For heavens sakes!"

"Why in the world would you say something like that?"

"Gotta call them like I see them." Tyler twisted the cap off. "She's not as nice as you all seem to think," he said balefully. "And I'm not going over there again." He downed a long swallow of beer and wiped his mouth with the back of his hand. His stance, legs planted apart and shoulders stiff, clearly dared Rosie to contradict him.

"All right," Rosie replied mildly. "I suppose it was unrealistic of me to hope you would be nice and make amends. I suppose I was asking too much."

"Oh, no," he said, shaking a finger at her. "Don't even try to put that spin on it. You weren't there. You don't know. I went over there just like you wanted, against my better judgment, I might add, but she didn't even give me a chance. She's got a tongue that could peel paint from a boiler."

Leanne, Ally and Sonya burst out laughing. Rosie turned away so Tyler couldn't see her fighting a smile, too.

"It's not funny." He glared at them indignantly. "She's got all of you fooled."

"Ty, she barely reaches your elbow and you're scared of her!" Ally whooped, elbowing Leanne.

"Scared of her?" Tyler banged his bottle on the counter top. "Scared of her? What kind of stupid remark is that?"

Rosie masked her bubbling laughter with a cough. She could almost see the steam rising from the top of Tyler's head and the tips of his ears were fire-engine red. If he were holding a can instead of a bottle she had no doubt it would be crushed flat.

"I think you're right," Leanne managed, rising. "Don't worry, Ty." She put an arm around his waist and waved her free arm in front of him as if fending off an attacker. "We'll protect you."

"Very funny," he said, shaking free. "Glad I could amuse you all." Grabbing his bottle, he stomped outside.

Rosie felt a little guilty about Tyler's hurt feelings, but mostly she was gleeful over his rare, obvious foul temper.

"About that theory of yours," Leanne said, returning to her chair. "I think we've figured it out for ourselves."

"Doesn't take a rocket scientist, does it, girls?" Rosie beamed.

* * *

Eleanor was a little more than five minutes behind Tyler, thanks to an unexpected call from her father. Talk about your emotional roller coaster, she thought wearily, setting her phone on the kitchen counter. One minute she was flying high, jazzed about her newfound ability to annoy Tyler Hurst as much as he annoyed her, then she was breathless with fury over his dictatorial rules, and now, five short minutes on the telephone with her father left her as flat as a pancake. At least she could be grateful he hadn't phoned before Tyler's visit, she thought wryly, slipping through the back door. At least she'd had some measure of fun before the predictable paternal rain fell on her parade.

She closed the door carefully, and trudged down the steps. When she'd phoned her father on Thursday to remind him she was moving on Saturday, and invited him to come by to see her new house, she'd thought he might actually show up. Lectures were so much more satisfying in person than over the telephone, after all. But he didn't call, and he hadn't come by, and Eleanor knew why. Until she capitulated to his demand that she get back on her career track at CBB, she would be persona non grata.

Today's brief, one-sided conversation had centered on the problems she had created for CBB when she so recklessly turned in her resignation. Philip Conrad wanted her back, her father stated, and was willing to let bygones be bygones if she returned Monday morning. No apologies necessary, her week off would be considered paid vacation, and he would even give her back control of the Wilford case. Though her father didn't admit it, it seemed Wayne was already stumbling over his wingtips, and Mr. Wilford was less than delighted with his new lead counsel.

It wasn't easy---it never was---but Eleanor held her tongue while her father completed his speech before driving another nail into their relationship. She wasn't going back to Conrad, Berkley and Burns, period, and she simply couldn't put it any plainer than that. The conversation ended abruptly, and she didn't think her father would be dropping by to see her new home any time soon.

Eleanor rounded the azalea hedge and started down Rosie's wide driveway. Tyler Hurst better not give her any more trouble today, she thought vengefully. She'd had enough of tyrannical men and he might just draw back a bloody nub.

"Eleanor! We've been waiting for you." Leanne hurried in her direction. "In fact, I was just about to come get you since our first messenger didn't seem to get the job done." She draped an arm around Eleanor and gave her a swift squeeze.

Oh, how nice it felt to be greeted with a smile and a friendly word. Eleanor, taking another dip on the roller coaster, felt moisture catch behind her eyes.

Nancy joined them and Eleanor was surprised with a second hug. "We were beginning to worry Tyler locked you in a closet."

Eleanor spied him, his back to her, standing on the deck beside Robb and Joel and a fourth man. No warm welcome there, but she didn't expect one. Robb and Joel waved, and she waved back. The fourth man curiously looked her way.

"Eleanor, David; David, Eleanor," Leanne called.

"Hi," Eleanor called. "Nice to meet you."

"Likewise," he called back. Tyler stubbornly kept his back to her. Irrationally, it lifted her spirits.

"David's Ally's husband," Leanne told Eleanor, leading her toward the deck. "Come meet Ally."

Robb jogged over to meet Eleanor by the door. "Hey, I've got another joke for you," he whispered. "What do you call a thousand lawyers at the bottom of the ocean?"

Eleanor bit back a smile. "I have no idea."

"A good start." He winked at her. "Present company excluded, of course."

Eleanor grinned in spite of herself. "Of course." She watched him saunter back toward the other men. Amazing that he and Tyler were brothers. Too bad somebody couldn't drop them in a bag and shake them up, dusting some of Robb's perpetual good humor onto his cranky brother.

"About time you got here, young lady." Rosie swung the kitchen door open and gave her a big hug. Eleanor, finally overwhelmed, had to swipe away a tear.

After a leisurely lunch, which concluded, thankfully, without any embarrassing accidents, Leanne, Allison, Nancy and Sonya steered Eleanor and Rosie toward the glider beneath the oak tree and playfully ordered them to stay put and entertain one another. They then disappeared indoors to clean Rosie's kitchen and to put the smaller children down for naps. As much as Eleanor already liked the younger women, she was delighted to spend a little time alone with Rosie.

"I'm enjoying myself so much," she confided, giving the ground a push to set the glider into gentle motion. "I can't remember ever having such a pleasant afternoon." Especially since Tyler was making himself scarce. She glanced toward the deck, which seemed to be the preferred gathering spot for the men, to make sure Tyler was still keeping his distance. As had happened several times during the afternoon, Tyler's gaze fell upon Eleanor at just the moment she looked his way. She couldn't help herself; she gave him a big smile and a cheery wave. Folding his arms across his chest, he scowled and turned around.

He was so easy to provoke. She liked that about him.

In a short while, Leanne, Sonya, Ally and Nancy rejoined Eleanor and Rosie beneath the oak tree and conversation turned to the upcoming wedding.

"This is a nice upsweep," Nancy pointed to a model's hairstyle in the bridal magazine on her lap. "Simple but pretty."

"Hope's still leaning toward some kind of French braid updo for everybody, I think." Leanne leaned over to flip the pages in the magazine, and pointed to a photograph. "Something like this."

Sonya and Ally rose to look over Nancy's shoulders. "My hair's not long enough for that," Ally remarked, perching on the arm of Nancy's chair.

Sonya studied Ally's shoulder length hair for a moment. "I think it is. We could try. Hey, April!" Sonya waved across the yard.

April, Leanne's fourteen year old daughter, sunning in a chaise, looked up, shading her eyes with her hand. "What?"

"Come show us how to do a French braid?"

April rose and crossed the yard. "Yeah, sure. Who's my victim?"

"Aunt Ally. She doesn't think her hair is long enough for this." Leanne showed April the photo. "What do you think?"

April flitted around the chairs to study Ally's hair. "It's probably long enough." She glanced around the group. "But if I have to show you, I'd rather use somebody with plenty of hair." She looked at Eleanor. "You."

Eleanor blinked. "Me?"

April nodded. "That way they can all see what I'm doing." She circled around and patted Eleanor's heavy knot of hair that was, as usual, trying to escape the hairpins holding it in place. "You've got plenty to work with."

Eleanor couldn't possibly refuse, though the idea of letting her hair down, literally, made her a little queasy. "Okay," she replied, summoning a smile. "I have to warn you, though; my hair's usually got its own ideas."

April dragged a chair to the center of the circle. "Sit here." She tugged Eleanor's hand, towing her up from the glider and pushing her toward the chair. Eleanor was barely seated before April began plucking the heavy pins from her hair, and in seconds the knot of hair tumbled down. The women gasped collectively. Eleanor felt oddly naked and fought the impulse to scoop the untidy mess back up again.

"Wow, Eleanor, your hair is amazing!" April's spontaneous remark broke the hushed pause and initiated a flurry of conversation. Her voice carried, and the men, standing on the deck, turned around.

Eleanor threw a fleeting glance over her shoulder to gauge Tyler's reaction to the embarrassing furor. He wasn't frowning, which was something. Standing stock-still on the deck, he stared across the distance with a peculiar look on his face. It sent a chill down Eleanor's spine and she caught her breath.

But before she could blink, his expression went sub-Arctic and he turned away dismissively.

Eleanor, feeling vulnerable and idiotic, eased her death grip on the metal armrests of her chair, and squeezed a breath of air into her lungs. The conversation, rolling around her, became distinct again. "I really ought to cut it," she murmured, pushing it away from her face. "I'm far too old for so much hair."

"No, indeed, it's beautiful!" Rosie protested emphatically. "It would be positively criminal to cut that hair."

"You should wear it down all the time," Sonya said. "If I had hair like yours, I'd wear it down every day."

"Is it naturally curly?" Allison gently tested a curl. "It is," she announced to the others. "I hate you, Eleanor." She tempered her remark with a wide grin.

"Okay, this is what you do," April began, positioning Eleanor in the chair. "Put your hands down, Eleanor, and sit straight."

Eleanor obeyed promptly, and smiled weakly when Rosie winked at her. April gently tugged Eleanor's hair this way and that, explaining as she went to her audience. "There," she concluded, capturing the end of the heavy braid with a red scrunchie. She draped the heavy braid over Eleanor's shoulder. "One French braid, as requested. One extremely long French braid."

Eleanor reached to feel the smooth plait beginning at the crown of her head. She tilted her head left, then right. It felt light and wonderful. She beamed at April. "I love it. Can you teach me how to do this?"

April grinned back. "Sure. It looks really good on you. Way better than that grandma-bun." The others agreed, a tad more tactfully, but no less enthusiastically.

Eleanor patted the braid again, and then examined the scrunchie on the end of her hair. Bye-bye hairpins, she thought with satisfaction. The revised, summertime-edition Eleanor was going to need lots of scrunchies, all colors.

Chapter Eight

Tyler cast a brief glance at the large, utilitarian clock on the mirrored wall and touched the control panel to begin decreasing the speed of the treadmill. An hour was enough; his knees wouldn't forgive him if he ran too long. He grabbed the towel draped over the panel and wiped his face, slowing to an easy stride. He felt good. He'd done his lifting this morning without too much interruption, and he still had enough time to soak in the whirlpool for a few minutes before changing to take Rosie to lunch. Hopefully he'd be able to avoid any conversation about Eleanor today. He and Rosie would just have to agree to disagree on the topic of her neighbor. The memory of Eleanor on Sunday morning, planted behind the front door of the house on which he'd spent so much time and energy, threatened to make his mood plummet. What a ridiculous woman, wearing that fuzzy robe with her mess of hair tumbling down her back, purposely egging him on with her crows of ownership.

"Excuse me, Mr. Hurst. Do you have a minute?"

Tyler lowered the towel and turned his head to find a pretty brunette standing in the narrow aisle between his treadmill and the wall. The girl, willowy and curvy in all the right places, smiled at him winningly, if a little cautiously. Tyler was usually safe from feminine intrusion in the heavy weights room, but here in the common area, he seemed to be fair game.

"Sure," he replied, automatically lifting his mouth into an answering smile. He jabbed the 'off' button and eased into the narrow space. "But let's get out of the way here." With a hand at her elbow, he turned her around and guided her a few steps away from the row of humming machines. "What can I do for you?"

She responded with a blush and a slightly breathless laugh. "My name's Holly, and my friends and I---they're over there---," she gestured toward a cluster of leggy young women by the drink bar. "We were wondering if we could get a selfie with you."

Tyler sighed internally but raised a hand to acknowledge the avid group of---what? ---nineteen and twenty year olds? They waved back, enthusiastically, all atwitter.

She blushed again. "And maybe you could have lunch with us or something, our treat."

Ah, it was the 'or something' that bothered him. There had been a time, not so long ago, when he would have hustled her straight out the door, or maybe the whole flock, but he liked to think he was a little kinder than he used to be. And she reminded him of Hope, which made him feel a little queasy.

But he didn't want to hurt her feelings, either. With a hand at her back, he began propelling her toward the drink bar. "I'd be honored to take a selfie, sweetheart, but I'm afraid it's a bad day for lunch. Maybe another time?"

After some sweet talking and a round of selfies with several phones, and in a better mood, he managed to extricate himself and headed toward the locker room. He loved southern girls; he really did, with their pretty faces and prettier manners. He looked forward to perhaps finding an older version of Holly sometime soon. As he strode to the back of the club, an unwelcome image popped into his mind, of Eleanor Haley in that silly robe, all green eyes and startling wild hair. God, no, not her, he scowled mentally. Never her.

* * *

An hour later, Tyler pulled into Rosie's driveway, climbed out of the Mustang and whistled his way up the steps and into the house. "Paging Rosie Hurst, paging Rosie Hurst." He ducked through the kitchen and glanced into the living room. She was usually dressed and ready to go for their Wednesday lunch outings.

"Back here, Ty."

"Hope you're as hungry as I am," he called, moving down the hallway. "I thought we'd drive down to New Orleans to---" He drew up short in the doorway of Ally and Leanne's old bedroom, now Rosie's sewing room.

Rosie, still in her robe and slippers, was seated in the rocking chair, scissors in hand and pink fabric in her lap, while Eleanor Haley sat cross-legged on the floor with more pink fabric. His mood sank.

"Oh, Tyler," Rosie said, frowning. "I'm sorry, I lost track of time."

"No problem," he said, eyeing Eleanor with irritation. No problem except she was here.

"We've been cutting out squares for the rosebuds."

He had no idea what she was talking about.

"You know, rosebuds for the birdseed."

He shook his head.

"The little satin rosebuds filled with birdseed. Remember? Like at Robb and Nancy's wedding?"

He was pretty sure he hadn't tossed bird seed or anything else at Robb and Nancy but that wasn't the point. "Isn't there a lot of time before the wedding?"

"Eleanor and I were having coffee and I mentioned it so here we are. Such a help." She cast a fond glance at Eleanor, which he noted, sourly, was returned in kind. Yeah, she probably jumped at the chance to wedge her way more tightly into Rosie's good graces.

"You go get changed, Rosie, and I'll finish up," Eleanor said.

Rosie rose and patted Eleanor's head. "Such a help."

After Rosie disappeared through the door, Eleanor glanced up at Tyler. "Why don't you go wait in the kitchen?"

Why didn't he – what? Did she just try to tell him what to do?

"I don't need you standing over me, glowering," she added. "I'll be done in just a few minutes and back on my side of the hedge before you know it. Unless," she added with a sly smile, "you wanted to invite me to lunch, too."

He raised his eyebrows at her silently.

She chuckled. "Or maybe you should wait here and make sure I don't try to steal something."

"Maybe I will," he replied, easing himself carefully into the rocking chair. He didn't know why; the kitchen was a better idea but he hated that she had suggested it. He watched her measure and cut little squares of the pink cloth and wished she'd look up and see his glare.

* * *

It was very quiet in the room and Eleanor decided to gamble. She shot a sideways glance at Tyler. "So, you played football."

He glared at her. "So?" he finally replied.

She nodded. "For what---fourteen years?"

Another long silence. "Yes."

"That's a long time," Eleanor said, trying to summon a tone of awe.

Nothing.

O-kay. Eleanor pressed her lips together. This was clearly the Titanic of all sinking conversations, but damn it, she wasn't going to go down without a fight. "I don't know much about football," she confessed. "What part did you play?"

"Part?" Sounding oddly choked, he dipped his head and rubbed his eyebrows with his knuckles. "I didn't play a part, honey. I played a position."

Honey, again. Eleanor grimaced. Now wasn't the time to pick a fight, not if she was trying to make some kind of peace with him, but oh, how she hated being called honey. "Okay," she said tightly. "What position did you play?"

"Defensive end. Now, what, if anything, does that mean to you?"

It didn't mean a damned thing to her but he didn't have to be so sarcastic. "I just thought you might warm up a little if I asked you about your job," she retorted.

"I'm as warm as I'm ever going to get, Thumbelina," he drawled.

Thumbelina! Eleanor inhaled with a hiss, her good intentions forgotten. "Well, excuse me, Hulk. I had no idea football players were incapable of carrying on simple conversations."

He didn't like being called Hulk any more than she liked being called Thumbelina. Eleanor made a mental note to use it again sometime.

"It would have to be simple if we discussed football, wouldn't it, honey, considering how little you know? Why don't you study up a little, check out a book from that library of yours, and get back with me?"

Eleanor blinked in angry confusion. What the devil he was talking about? What library?

"And, incidentally, I can carry on a simple conversation," he continued smoothly. "I can even carry on a complicated conversation. Believe it or not, I've assimilated quite nicely back into society."

"Evidence to the contrary," she muttered darkly. So much for making peace with Tyler Hurst.

* * *

Later that evening, Rosie called Eleanor to come over for dessert and Eleanor was unable to resist. They sat together under the oak tree, and after an indecent slice of coconut cake, Rosie snapped beans and Eleanor drew her legs up on the blue lawn chair and wrapped her arms around her knees. "Rosie, tell me why Tyler hates attorneys."

Rosie picked a green bean from the bowl on her lap, broke it and tossed it into a second bowl on the chair beside her. "It all started with Rodney Stineman," she began. "After my son, Bill, and his wife, Miriam, died, Rodney Stineman came to the funeral and introduced himself as a good friend of Bill's." She sighed. "I was naïve and I believed him, of course. What I mean when I say that, is, I was a very sheltered wife, and I knew less than nothing about the world beyond my house and this yard. When Robert died---my husband," she explained, "Bill took up right up where he left off, looking after me and my finances and such."

Eleanor nodded, trying to reconcile the lively woman beside her to the picture Rosie was painting of a timid younger self.

"So when Rodney Stineman offered to help us, I was very relieved. There was a lawsuit, and insurance claims, and, oh, more problems than I could really understand."

Eleanor knew, without a doubt, where this was headed, and it made her sick to her stomach. She hated sharing a profession with the kinds of attorneys who preyed on vulnerable people. "And Rodney Stineman seemed like a blessing to you at the time."

Sighing, Rosie continued snapping beans, and nodded. "Very much so. In retrospect I can barely believe how naive I was, but to make a long story short, instead of helping us, he helped himself, and when the dust finally settled, there was very little money left."

Very little money, and six young grandchildren, Eleanor mused. "What did you do?"

"There was nothing I could do about the money," Rosie replied. "It was gone, so we just did the best we could. Ty was almost eighteen by that time, and colleges were beating our door down, trying to sign him to play football." Holding the sides of the bowl in her lap, Rosie gazed across the yard. "That was the one time Ty and I ever argued. He wanted to go straight to work but I wouldn't hear of it. He was too talented, and too smart, to miss the opportunity to go to college on a scholarship, but he was one stubborn young man. In his mind, he was convinced he'd failed me and his sisters and brothers by not protecting us from Rodney Stineman, and leaving us, to go to college, was absolutely out of the question."

A seventeen year old boy didn't have a prayer against an unscrupulous attorney. Eleanor chewed on her fingernail. But she could understand how a seventeen year old boy would feel, too.

"It wasn't until the LSU football coach sat him down and explained that he could have a successful future in professional football, that he finally agreed to accept the scholarship."

"And so, becoming a professional football player became his goal."

Rosie nodded. "To the exclusion of almost everything else. College football wasn't a game to him; it was a job. He signed up for the draft his junior year and the Renegades picked him in the first round."

Eleanor didn't need to understand the language; it was enough to understand Tyler had succeeded. It didn't surprise her. "And that's why he hates attorneys? Because of Rodney Stineman?"

Rosie shook her head emphatically. "There's more. Then there was Louis Terrell."

Eleanor's heart flopped. "Let me guess; another attorney."

"And Tyler's first agent." Rosie set the bowl to the side, losing interest in the green beans. "When Tyler went to Denver, he was determined to carve a niche for himself on the team, and he didn't want to be distracted by anything else. He relied on the advice of other players, men he felt were knowledgeable and successful, and he hired Louis Terrell. You know, to advise him about investments, that kind of thing. That way, he felt he could concentrate on his performance, confident he was making and saving more than enough money to put the other children through school."

"He was how old?"

"Twenty-one."

They shared grim looks. Eleanor sighed. "How much money did he lose?"

"Quite a bit."

Eleanor didn't need or want to know any more than that. "That's awful."

Rosie patted Eleanor on the arm. "There's more."

Eleanor gaped in dismay. "You've got to be kidding me."

"I wish I were. It was about that time, when Tyler was feeling really low, that he met a woman and got married."

Eleanor lifted her eyebrows in surprise. "Tyler was married?"

Rosie snorted. "Briefly and disastrously."

Eleanor was stunned. The idea of Tyler being married was, well, it was horrible, but she didn't want to think about why it bothered her so much.

"She had an affair, and there was an ugly divorce."

Eleanor dropped her head into her hands. "She took him to the cleaners." She already knew the answer she would hear.

"You got it. And then she married her boyfriend."

Poor Tyler. Eleanor slumped against the back of the glider, the bowl in her lap forgotten.

"Who was also her divorce attorney."

Eleanor felt faint. There was going to be hell to pay when Tyler learned the truth. Rosie patted her hand. "Now you know."

She wished she didn't.

* * *

Eleanor was astonished at how quickly she fell into a blissful routine in her new home. She slept until the morning sunlight peeked into her bedroom and she lazily enjoyed coffee in the rocker on her front porch or at Rosie's house. She gave away her drab gray sofa and bought cheerful, overstuffed furniture that suited her gingerbread house, discovered she had a real interest in the flowering plants that the home's previous owner had nurtured, and she spent time with not just Rosie but with Leanne, Nancy, Sonya and Ally when their busy schedules permitted. She'd grown up so alone and marveled at how quickly they accepted her into their close knit circle. With their encouragement she'd bought enough bright summer clothing and hair ties to almost make up for the years of dark tailored suits and hairpins, she enjoyed manicures and pedicures, and she helped however she could with plans for Hope and Adam's wedding. She knew the summer wouldn't last forever and she was soon going to have to think about finding a job, but for now she was delighted to discover that there could be much more to her life than law and work. And best of all, Tyler Hurst had made himself scarce, not just for the closing on her house but from her life altogether.

One humid afternoon in late June, Eleanor again found herself enjoying her newfound freedom, traipsing along with Rosie and Leanne, visiting antique stores along the main avenue in Ponchatoula.

"Eleanor, come see this!"

Eleanor peered around the corner of a walnut vanity table. "Where are you, Rosie?"

"Over here."

Well, that helped a lot. Eleanor grinned and wriggled through a gap between the vanity and a massive armoire. They had been browsing all day, exclaiming over interesting finds and debating the pros and cons of pieces that might suit her house.

"In the back. Hurry up."

"I'm coming," Eleanor replied. Weaving her way through the crowded showroom, she spied Rosie's white head across a battered

CHRISTY ST. ROMAIN MARCHAND

chest of drawers. The problem with going antiquing with Rosie, she had learned, was that it was awfully easy to get separated, and when they did, they had a hard time locating one another over the tall pieces of furniture. That's where Leanne came in handy. They used her as a human lighthouse of sorts. "What did you---" She rounded the chest of drawers and sucked in her breath. "Oh."

Leanne performed a very credible game show hostess flourish. "Ta da."

Before Eleanor was the most beautiful fairytale bed she had ever seen, with an ornate headboard, carved posts and an arching canopy.

"It's rosewood." Rosie showed Eleanor the price tag. "And it's a steal. Can't you just see it in your bedroom?"

Vividly. "I want it," Eleanor said, adamantly. "I want this bed." Out with her plain headboard, in with the princess bed.

"Do you want this bed, Eleanor?" Leanne teased.

Eleanor grinned unabashedly. "I have to have this bed." She bit her lip. "How will I get it home? Will they deliver, do you think?"

"Why don't I call Robb," Rosie suggested, taking her phone from her purse.

Eleanor was pretty sure calling Robb for help would fall under Tyler's "don't ask for favors" rule. "Oh, no, Rosie. I'm sure they'll deliver."

Rosie turned to face Eleanor, her hands on her hips. "Eleanor Haley, I declare you are going to have to stop worrying all the time about whether you're being a bother or imposing or whatever else convoluted notion you get into your head. Okay?"

Eleanor closed her mouth and nodded.

"Go find someone to ring it up." Rosie checked the price tag again and then squeezed Eleanor in a hug. "This is perfect for your bedroom, honey, and it's such a bargain, too

Several minutes later, Eleanor returned, receipt in hand, and beamed at Rosie and Leanne. "It's mine." She could scarcely wait to get it home.

An overall-clad man joined them, tools in hand. "We'll break it down, ma'am, so it'll fit in your truck."

Rosie paused thoughtfully. "Could you wait until my grandson arrives? That way he can see how it fits together."

The man nodded, placing the tools on the floor. "Good idea. Sometimes these old beds are a little tricky."

"Ty can handle it," Rosie said confidently. "We're just going to walk across the street and have a cup of coffee while we wait for him."

What! Eleanor looked at Rosie in horror. "You called Tyler? Not Robb?" It was a mystery how her heart could sink and beat faster all at the same time. "What happened to Robb?"

"Ty happened to be at the nursery and he offered to come straightaway." Rosie patted her on the arm. "Don't worry. He's happy to help."

The only thing Tyler would willingly help Eleanor do would be to move out. She knew he had been avoiding her the same way she avoided him. "Did you tell him it's me he's helping?"

"Why, I don't remember." Rosie replied absent-mindedly. She spied an upholstered rocking chair tucked into a crowded corner of the shop. "Oh, look. What a nice rocking chair. Did Leanne see this? She'll love it." Rosie, oblivious to Eleanor's consternation, moved away to admire the rocking chair.

Eleanor followed her, feeling desperate. "Rosie, call him back. Tell him never mind."

Rosie continued on toward the rocker. "He's already on his way."

Eleanor worried the end of her braid. Rosie might think he would be happy to help but Eleanor knew better. "You know how he feels about me, Rosie," she began. "And he doesn't even know the truth yet, about my being an attorney."

Rosie gave Eleanor a gentle push into the rocking chair, and sat on a pine chest beside her. "And what do you think he's going to do when he finds out?"

Well, she didn't really know; she just knew she didn't want to be around him when it happened. "He's going to be really angry." Not merely annoyed or irritated, really God-awful angry. "At both of us. At all of us. Keeping it from him."

Rosie patted her arm. "And he'll get over it."

Maybe in a hundred years. Eleanor shook her head emphatically. "I really don't think so." She knew he'd find out eventually but she hoped she'd be back at work when he did, too busy to care. Not relaxing and enjoying these lovely, leisurely summer days spent mostly with his grandmother and sisters.

"Oh, he'll fuss and stomp a little, but he'll get over it. You just be yourself and it will all work out. You'll see."

Rosie was nothing if not blindly optimistic. Eleanor tried one more time. "You do know that we can barely be in the same room together, don't you? I'd like to blame him completely but the truth is, I've been pretty spiteful to him, too."

"Good for you," Rosie said cheerfully. "Don't let him get the upper hand. He'll do it in a New York second if he thinks he can get away with it. And quit worrying about the attorney thing. He thinks you're a librarian, and he will for the foreseeable future unless you tell him otherwise."

Eleanor did a double-take. "He thinks I'm a what?"

"He thinks you're a librarian. When he asked me what you did, I remembered you said you spent a lot of time in the law library, and so, I just rambled a little without actually fibbing, and now he thinks you're a librarian. Now come on, let's have some coffee." Rosie headed toward the front of the store.

Forty-five minutes later, Eleanor was sitting with Leanne and Rosie at a table near the window of the coffee shop, clutching her coffee cup anxiously.

"There he is." Leanne nodded toward the street. Eleanor turned and watched a giant glossy truck maneuver into the curbside parking space outside the shop.

Rosie put her coffee cup down and reached for her purse. "He got here fast." She noticed Eleanor's nearly full coffee mug. "You barely touched your coffee, Eleanor."

Because her stomach was still a little queasy from finding out she was a librarian.

"Oh, man," one of the two women behind the counter exclaimed, elbowing her co-worker. "Oh, man. Look at him, Sylvia."

No need to wonder who they were talking about. Eleanor recalled, only too well, the first time she'd laid eyes on Tyler. She glanced, sympathetically, to watch Sylvia, heavily made up and poured into a tight pair of jeans and tee shirt, lean over the counter for a better look.

Just pretty packaging, Eleanor wanted to tell her, lifting her cup for a final sip of coffee. She heard Sylvia wheeze, as though she'd had the wind knocked out of her lungs. What now? Eleanor looked back out the window.

Long, tanned, powerfully muscled legs swung out of the truck and hit the pavement. In deference to the climbing temperature, Tyler wore khaki shorts, an LSU tee shirt, and canvas deck shoes.

"Good God," Sylvia breathed, smoothing her hands over her hips.

Like Sylvia, all Eleanor saw were his legs. Coffee splashed from her mug onto her sundress. Setting her mug down with a disgruntled thump, she dabbed at her bodice and shot a nasty glance in his direction. So he had legs. Most people did.

Tyler tossed his sunglasses onto the seat, then closed the door and glanced around. Some of the other female customers spotted him, and the low murmur of conversation heightened several notches.

Rosie and Leanne exchanged amused glances. "Let's get out of here before there's trouble," Leanne suggested, rising.

The real trouble was going to start when Tyler discovered realized who it was he had come to help, Eleanor thought, rising and following Rosie and Leanne to the door.

Leanne pushed through the door and held it open for Rosie. Tyler turned and smiled. "There you are. What have you gone and bought---" He saw Eleanor, bringing up the rear, and his smile downshifted to a frown. "You."

"Me," she agreed, trying for a blithe tone and flipping her braid over her shoulder. She clamped her purse under her arm and straightened her back.

"Hi, honey." Rosie smiled up at Tyler and slipped her arm through his. "Come see what we found."

Pressing his lips together, he returned his attention to Rosie with some effort. "You said it was a bed over the telephone. I didn't know you were interested in buying a bed."

"I bought a rocking chair, too," Leanne told him. "Will you have enough room in your truck?"

"Yeah, sure. Why another bed, Rosie?"

"Oh, I didn't buy the bed. Eleanor did."

A few steps behind them, Eleanor braced herself. Here we go, she thought fatally, watching him snap to a stop, his back and shoulders stiffening. She idled over to the window of the shop, gazing at the display as though the grouping of furniture was the most fascinating thing she'd ever seen.

"Is that so? Well, well, well, what do you know about that."

She wasn't fooled at all by his seemingly affable response, and wondered how Rosie and Leanne didn't notice the biting tone.

"We asked the man to wait until you got here before taking it apart, since it has to be put back together again in her bedroom."

Eleanor slanted a careful glance in his direction. He gave her a brief, black look, the pulse at his jaw working. "Does it, now."

Oh dear. She hadn't thought about who would be putting the bed back together. In her bedroom.

She might as well have been invisible, so completely did he ignore her while he, and the two men who worked in the store, dismantled the bed and carried the pieces to his truck. She and Leanne stayed out of the way, sitting at one of the small tables on the sidewalk in front of the coffee shop, while Rosie went back and forth, instructing Tyler on the best way to arrange the pieces in the bed of the truck. One thing Eleanor did like about Tyler was his deference and devotion to Rosie. He clearly appreciated his special grandmother, and for that, she could forgive him a lot.

Leanne elbowed Eleanor in the ribs gently, and nodded to her left. Sylvia painstakingly polished the front window of the coffee shop, all the while glancing over her shoulder to see if Tyler noticed her.

"Happens all the time," Leanne whispered. "You wouldn't believe what women do to get his attention."

Eleanor lifted an eyebrow questioningly.

"Just wait."

The window-washing effort didn't even garner Sylvia a glance, so she stepped up her campaign and took a broom to the sidewalk. Amazing, Eleanor thought, impressed in spite of herself. A girl would have to be pretty coordinated to sweep, twitch and thrust all at the same time like that.

Tyler, effortlessly carrying one of the last pieces of the bed under his arm, had to step around her and her broom, to slide the piece into the back of the truck. "Excuse me," was all he said, his attention focused on his work. Sylvia bit her lip and went back inside the coffee shop.

"She's giving up," Eleanor whispered to Leanne.

"How much do you want to bet?" Leanne laid a dollar on the table. Eleanor dug in her purse and put another one beside it.

Out came Sylvia, moments later, a reckless glint in her eye and a folded piece of paper in her hand. She lodged the paper beneath his windshield wiper and then, haughtily ignoring Leanne and Eleanor, sat down at the table nearest his truck. Leanne picked up the money and dropped it into her purse with a "told you so" grin. Eleanor smiled back wryly. Tyler made his last trip out, carrying Leanne's rocking chair as easily as if it were a child's chair, with Rosie at his side. Leanne and Eleanor rose to meet them.

"You know, Ty," Rosie began innocently, "I think we could put the rocking chair in the back seat of Leanne's car instead of trying to fit it into the back of your truck or in the trunk. Of course, that means there's no room for Eleanor in the car. You don't mind riding home with Tyler, do you, Eleanor?"

She very much minded riding home with Tyler. Eleanor gaped at Rosie in dismay, scrambling mentally for an appropriate objection. It seemed, since her own tongue was frozen, that the object of her horror was her only hope. Surely Tyler would balk. She caught his gaze and tried to convey her mental message. Get us out of this. He gazed back imperturbably.

"Whatever you want, Rosie." Tyler's dry tone sent a ripple of uneasiness down Eleanor's spine. "Where are you parked, Leanne?"

"Just down the street, see? Bye, Eleanor. Don't forget, lunch Friday. Good luck with the bed." Leanne squeezed Eleanor and then started off down the sidewalk toward her car, jingling her keys in her hand.

She needed good luck, all right, just to make it home alive.

"I'll see you tonight, Eleanor. Call me when the bed is up so I can come see how nice it looks in your room." Rosie gave her a hug as well. "Smile, honey, everything's fine. I'll see you in a little while."

Tyler shifted the chair and gave her a hard look. "Wait here."

Well, duh. Where else did he think she would wait?

His eyes narrowed as though he could read her thoughts. "Don't get smart with me," he muttered. It didn't take him very long at all to load the rocking chair into the back of Leanne's car and return. Silently he unlocked the passenger door and opened it, then stepped aside and looked at her with something suspiciously akin to anticipation. Looking past him, Eleanor suddenly knew why. His monster truck was high off the ground and had no running boards. She was wearing a long sundress and there was no way she could climb into it, not without help, and they both knew it. She sent one last desperate glance down the street, but Leanne's car was already out of sight.

"Problem?"

Tyler's expression was bland, but Eleanor knew he was smirking beneath the surface. Suddenly she had a lightning bolt of inspiration. "No, no problem," she replied, glancing around over the hood of the truck. Sylvia was still poised for action in the small wrought iron chair. "Excuse me, Sylvia; can I borrow that step stool you were using a few minutes ago?"

Sylvia, startled to be called by name, quickly recognized the unexpected opportunity. "Oh, yes, I'll get it!" She was a flash of movement, darting into the coffee shop like quicksilver.

Eleanor crossed her arms and looked smugly at Tyler. "That's Sylvia," she said unnecessarily. "She works in the coffee shop. I think she likes you."

"You don't say." Dipping his head, Tyler rubbed his brow with his thumb.

"Probably because she doesn't know you."

He had no time to reply before Sylvia, step stool in hand, burst back through the coffee shop door and cornered the hood of the truck. "Here you are," she said, shoving it in Eleanor's general direction, her eyes fixed on Tyler.

"Why, thank you," Eleanor said wryly, catching the stool before it clattered to the ground. "Sylvia, meet Tyler Hurst." She snapped the stool open and scrambled up into the truck, tucking the long skirt of her dress in neatly.

"Nice to meet you, Sylvia." Tyler, to his credit, didn't let his eyes drift toward Sylvia's impressive chest.

"You, too," Sylvia arched and preened. "I left this on your window," she said, retrieving the note and putting it into his hand. "To ask if you'd like a cappuccino."

Tyler gave Sylvia a smile that would melt the polar ice cap. "Well, as a matter of fact, honey, I'd love a cappuccino. You must have read my mind." He shot a smug look at Eleanor.

Sylvia looked as though she would explode with joy.

Eleanor stared at him. He wouldn't. He wouldn't just walk off and leave her there to wait in the truck while he schmoozed with Sylvia. Would he?

Snapping the step stool closed, he picked it up and put his hand on Eleanor's door. "Wait here." He closed the door and turned away.

Eleanor watched, eyes narrowing, as Tyler put a hand at Sylvia's back and sauntered into the coffee shop with her. Wait here? Oh, the nerve. The unmitigated nerve. She hoped he'd spill his hot cappuccino down his khaki shorts.

Chapter Nine

Fifteen minutes later, Tyler emerged from the coffee shop, traveling cup in hand. He opened his door, slid into his seat, and closed the door. Humming, he put the cup into the drink holder on the console and started the engine. Eleanor stared out the side window, refusing to acknowledge his return. The longer she'd been forced to sit there, trapped in his big Tonka truck, the madder she got. For two cents she'd have climbed down and called an Uber, but that was her bed in the back of the truck, and she'd be damned if she'd leave it in his possession.

Stretching his arm along the back of the seat, Tyler looked over his shoulder and began edging the truck out of the parallel parking spot. His hand bumped her shoulder and she squeezed closer to the door. He put the truck in forward, eased into the street, and started whistling.

Eleanor closed her eyes. In less than an hour, she'd be home and Gerald Moses would be there waiting to unload and assemble her bed. Tyler could just back his truck up and go on over to

Rosie's to wait because he wasn't setting foot into her house. Not today, not ever.

Tyler swung his truck onto the interstate and headed back toward Baton Rouge, and after thirty long teeth-gritting minutes of his tuneless, pointless whistling, she'd had all she could take. "Stop it. You're giving me a headache."

He broke off abruptly and gave her an innocent look. "Aw, a headache, huh? There's Tylenol in the console. Want to wash them down with my cappuccino?" He picked up the cup and took a swallow. "Mmm."

She narrowed her eyes and folded her arms across her chest. "I hope you choke on it."

He slanted a satisfied glance her way. "In a temper, are we?"

"Don't you worry about my temper."

"I promise to only get ten hours sleep tonight worrying about your temper, honey."

She hated him, she really did. "Don't call me honey!"

His tone and the topic changed abruptly. "You know, I distinctly remember telling you that you're not supposed to leech onto my family. Have you forgotten?"

Eleanor remembered it with painstaking clarity. "You mean when you were delusional and thought you could tell me what to do?"

He scowled at her, his veneer of affability stripped away. "When it comes to my family, you'd better know I can tell you what to do. I want to know what you're up to."

She scowled back. "What do you mean, what I'm up to? Why are you so damned suspicious? I'm not up to anything."

"Don't give me that. Why are you latching onto Rosie? I know all about your coffees in the morning and your lunches with my sisters. What is it with you? Don't you have a life? Your own family, your own friends?"

His hard words cut right through Eleanor, snatching her breath away. Suddenly she didn't feel up to a battle. "Actually, no," she replied quietly. She turned her head away and stared unseeingly out the window.

"What do you mean, 'no'?" he snapped.

"No, I don't. I don't have a family." She twisted so he couldn't see her face. Wrapping her arms around her waist, she leaned her head against the leather seat. Why was he digging at her like this? What awful thing did he suspect she was plotting?

His scowl deepened. "Rosie said you have a father and a brother. What about them?"

She winced. "My father and I haven't got any kind of relationship, and I haven't seen my brother in years."

"Hard to believe."

His thick-headed skepticism was infuriating. Who would lie about a thing like that? "Believe it," she said abruptly, twisting back to face him. "Not everybody has the kind of family you have, Tyler. Not everybody's that lucky. My brother wouldn't know me if we bumped into one another on the street, and as far as friends go, until I moved next door to Rosie, I only had one real friend. You remember her, don't you? Her name's Gracie. She's the one you thought would make a suitable neighbor because she comes complete with husband and child."

Tyler tightened his hands on the steering wheel.

"But now, Tyler, I've got six friends. Gracie, Rosie, Leanne, Nancy, Sonya and Ally." Eleanor counted them off on her fingers. "Imagine that! Six friends! I'm sorry that you don't like it but I'm not giving them up. I feel like I've won the lottery." She laughed, but it rattled in her chest and sounded more like a gasp. "And I'll tell you something else, since you think you have some right to know what I'm up to. I've been reinventing myself. What do you think about that? It's not hard, either, because, as it turns out, I'm pretty much starting from scratch. You like that, don't you? That's funny, isn't it? A thirty year old woman with no interests, no hobbies, and no life to speak of, but the really hysterical part, Tyler, the part that'll just make your day, is, I didn't even know it! How funny is that?"

Tyler glanced at her, expressionlessly.

Eleanor tried to stop but found she couldn't. "So let me tell you something you won't like a bit. This all started with me finding my house---mine, all mine, Tyler, whether you like it or not, and now I'm taking the first vacation of my life, for the whole damned summer, and if your grandmother invites me over for coffee or your sisters invite me to lunch, buddy, you can bet the bank I'll be there in a heartbeat. Whether you like it or not, do you hear me? It has nothing to do with you, so you can just mind your own business and shut the hell up!"

He gave her another one of those curiously blank glances, as though he could see her lips moving but didn't hear a word she said. Then he turned his eyes back toward the road.

Eleanor inhaled a long, piercing breath and made herself speak calmly. "Rosie is the kindest person I've ever met in my entire life, and if you honestly think I'd harm her in any kind of way, you're wrong. Every kind of wrong." She ran out of steam and her voice broke. Don't cry, don't cry, don't cry, she prayed fiercely, not in front of him. A tear slipped down her cheek anyway.

Tyler swung an arm toward her, his movement startling, and she flinched.

"What do you think I'm going to do, hit you?" He sounded furious. Yanking the console open, he dug around and pulled out a wad of paper napkins. "I don't hit women. Here."

She turned her shoulder to him. She didn't want his stupid napkins. Oh, why had she let her mouth run away?

When she wouldn't accept the napkins, he flung them on the seat, then swore and veered the steering wheel. Eleanor swiped her face with her arm and looked up to find Tyler had taken the wrong exit off the interstate.

"Where are you going?" She sat up straight, looking out the window anxiously. "This isn't my exit. Get back on. Take me home."

"I need tools," he bit out. "For the bed."

She shook her head vehemently. "No. I don't need you. I made other arrangements."

He brought the truck to a screeching halt at a red traffic light and turned to look at her, incredulously. "What do you mean, 'made other arrangements'?"

"I called someone."

His eyes narrowed.

"I had plenty of time stuck in this stupid truck," she said tiredly, "so I called someone. He's meeting me at the house."

"Well, pardon me all to hell for telling you otherwise, Eleanor," he drawled, "but I told Rosie I'd do it, and I'm doing it. That's all there is to it. Call him back."

"I will not. Take me home."

"Call him back."

"Take me home."

"Do it!"

"Home," she insisted, clenching her hands so tightly her fingernails bit into her palms. The cab of the truck felt claustrophobic. She wanted to shrink against the passenger door but she lifted her chin and stared him down instead.

A horn sounded behind them and Tyler jumped. The light was green and they were holding up impatient traffic. He snarled an expletive and stomped the accelerator, making the truck jump forward with a burst. "I'm getting my way on this," he bit out. Eleanor had to grab the door handle as he swerved to an abrupt stop on the shoulder of the highway. He killed the engine. "Call him back, damn it."

Eleanor felt as if her head were going to explode. She pressed her hands to her temples. "Why won't you just do what I say?"

"That would mean you'd win, and you're not going to win, I promise you. That's all there is to it. Make the call."

"I hate you." This wasn't about winning, this was about keeping the tenuous grip she had on her own emotions. He was maddening. She couldn't breathe. "I don't want your help. Just take me home."

"Make the call."

With a muffled growl of fury and frustration, Eleanor dug her phone out of her purse and jabbed the numbers. He listened while she asked for Gerald and explained she wouldn't need him to come by her house after all. Finishing, she dropped the phone back into her purse.

"All right, then," Tyler said calmly.

Eleanor stared at him, her heart beating in frantic cadence, as he restarted the engine and pulled back onto the highway. He made no sense, no sense at all. While he couldn't have made it any plainer how divinely uninterested he was in her rabid, pathetic confessions, just let her try to release him from the misery of her company, and all holy hell broke loose. It became a competition he was going to win at any cost.

She lifted her chin. Or maybe not.

* * *

Tyler glanced at Eleanor, but she'd turned her back to him again, and all he could see was the curve of her cheek, faintly tracked by that one renegade tear.

He returned his attention to the highway and the busy afternoon traffic. Soon they'd reach his house, where they could both escape the confines of the truck, at least for a few minutes. He needed to get out, that was for sure. The atmosphere inside the cab was so charged he could feel Eleanor, across the seat, struggling to collect herself, or maybe girding herself up for their next battle.

Well, she could rest easy because there wasn't going to be another battle. Tyler didn't feel like it anymore.

Not that he hadn't wanted one earlier. Oh, man, he had. In a bad mood already, he couldn't believe his eyes when he spied her coming out of the coffee shop door behind Rosie and Leanne. Floating along in that dress, her braid over her bare shoulder. And when he learned he'd dropped everything and run to Ponchatoula to help her, not Rosie; well, he was primed and loaded. He didn't like it and she was going to hear about it. When Rosie suggested he drive her home, he was elated, especially when he caught Eleanor's look of horror.

Then came the priceless opportunity to put her in her place, to make her wait and stew in his truck, and he couldn't resist, even if it meant suffering through fifteen minutes of the waitress's suggestive conversation. Tyler had to admit he felt pretty smug about making her wait. It wasn't like she was locked inside or in any kind of danger, and he'd kept his eye on her the whole time. When they eventually got on their way, and she sat without saying a word, he figured they might actually make it back to Baton Rouge without incident.

But, no, of course he was wrong. She said something, he said something, she pushed, he pushed back, and there they went, trying to rip one another up again.

Tyler sighed again. If he'd had any clue she was going to turn into a freaking runaway train, emotional cargo bouncing all over the place, telling him all manners of things he really didn't want to know, he'd have stopped the truck, leapt out, and run for cover. He recalled her face, white as paper, and that laugh that wasn't a laugh at all, more like a painful kind of wheeze that made him flinch again just remembering it. And when he thought it couldn't possibly get any worse, she topped the show off with tears and that panicky jump when he went for the console. He'd known men who used their size and strength to abuse women and he despised them. It infuriated him that Eleanor so quickly placed him in that same category.

In a matter of minutes she had him so unsettled he could barely stay on the road.

Then her announcement that she didn't need his help. Tyler gritted his teeth. Who the hell was Gerald? And then, go figure. Instead of being thrilled she had some other sucker lined up to take orders, he had to dig in his heels and make a big stand.

Maybe because it was a lot easier to react to her stubbornness over the fool bed than it was to think about the other things she revealed. Stuff he definitely did not want to talk about. Stuff he was pretty sure she regretted telling him. And, unfortunately, stuff that made him wonder, guiltily, if he hadn't been a little too tough on her, after all. Tyler turned into the entrance to his neighborhood, nodded at the security officer at the gate, and eased down the main boulevard. He turned into the driveway and pulled the truck to a gentle stop into the garage between the Mustang and the Harley.

"Want to come in?"

She gave him a disbelieving look. Her color was better, he noticed with relief. Not all pasty anymore. "No."

He tugged the keys from the ignition and tossed them in his hand. "I might be a couple of minutes."

"Whatever."

Tyler seized on a promising thought. "I've got something inside you might be interested in."

"I doubt it."

"You said something about not having any hobbies earlier and—"

She looked at him, eyes narrowing, warning written all over her face.

He held up a conciliatory hand. "Well, you did, and you don't have to rehash anything---," and God, he hoped she wouldn't, "but I really think you might be interested in something I'm working on inside. It's for your house."

She didn't blink. "The only thing I'm interested in that has to do with my house and involves you is my bed in the back of your truck."

He inhaled a big breath and blew it out noisily. She was still fuming over being out-maneuvered and in all fairness; he'd feel the same way if he were in her shoes. She just didn't understand it was a matter of principle and responsibility. He'd told Rosie he'd take her home and set up the bed and that's what he was going to do. Eleanor really didn't have any say-so. "Okay, then, I'll be right back."

She jerked her head in a mute, impatient nod, and folded her arms across her chest. Tyler slid out of the truck, went into the storeroom attached to the garage and dug around until he found what he needed, then strode back to the truck. She was still sitting, staring straight ahead.

"All right," he said. "That didn't take too long, did it?"

No reply. Not even a flicker of acknowledgment.

Damn, she was difficult. Here he was, trying to smooth things over, trying to initiate a little bit of normal, easy conversation, but she would have none of it. He wasn't used to putting out a whole lot of effort to make a woman agreeable. In his experience, they were just naturally agreeable. Until this one.

On the silent ride to Magnolia Drive, Tyler did some thinking and admitted to himself he'd behaved pretty poorly outside the coffee shop. He didn't like people treating him differently because he was big but he hadn't thought twice about mocking Eleanor because she was so small. And while he still didn't much care for the way she'd gotten into Letty's house practically overnight, while he was out of town, and for a song, he believed Rosie when she told him it had been all her doing. It was just the kind of warm-hearted, hare-brained thing his grandmother was notorious for and it really wasn't fair to keep holding it against Eleanor. And maybe she wasn't what he thought of when he pictured a perfect next-door neighbor, but the fact was, she had jumped at the chance to help Rosie with Hope's silly whatchamacallits, and Rosie seemed to honestly enjoy her company. His sisters and brothers and in-laws all liked her and the kids, well, they were completely smitten. Plus, if there was a more sedate occupation in the world than librarian, he didn't know what it was. Finally, and quite frankly, the idea of not having to go up against her tongue anymore did his heart a world of good.

By the time they turned onto Magnolia, Tyler had reached his conclusions and felt pretty magnanimous. He had no doubt he could tweak up the charm a little and bring her around. It was just a matter of a little time and a little attention. Childs play, he thought smugly.

Eleanor gripped her purse, clearly ready to escape the truck the minute it rolled to a stop. Scooting to the edge of the seat, she peered ahead and smiled.

What was she smiling at? Tyler looked past Rosie's driveway and spied a van parked along the street in front of Eleanor's house. Two men were waiting, leaning against the side of the van. They glanced up as Tyler and Eleanor approached, straightening and jamming caps on their heads.

Tyler passed Eleanor's driveway in order to back up, and read the lettering on the side of the van. Gerald Moses Moving Company. Gerald? He swung a disbelieving look at Eleanor, who was busy unbuckling her seat belt. Wait a minute. He heard her make the call. Though, technically, he realized with a start, he'd only heard one side of the conversation. Jerking the truck into reverse, he wheeled it down the driveway and across the lawn, coming to an abrupt stop near her front steps.

There hadn't been anyone else on the call. She had tricked him.

Eleanor reached for the door handle but he caught her arm with one hand. He was suddenly so mad he couldn't think straight. "You only pretended to make the call."

She pried his fingers from her arm and then lifted her face to give him a slow, evil smile. "You're just so easy." She jumped down out of the truck.

Tyler watched her skip around the front of his truck, all sweetness and light in her flowery dress, to welcome the pair of men who were already busy pulling pieces of her bed from the back of the truck. She was the most infuriating, irritating, irksome, crafty piece of work he'd ever had the miserable misfortune to encounter and it would be a cold day in hell before he tried to make amends with her again.

* * *

Later that night, Eleanor sat cross legged in her beautiful new bed with her laptop, reading up on gardening, when she became aware of a low rumbling noise, getting nearer and growing louder. Her neighbors were all fast asleep, there was rarely any traffic on their quiet side street this late at night, and she certainly wasn't expecting any company.

Rising, she went to the side window in her room and watched as a motorcycle, not big and loud like Tyler's, but definitely a motorcycle, came into sight and turned into her driveway. The helmeted rider, indistinguishable despite the bright moonlight, brought the machine only a quarter of the way down the driveway before stopping. When he killed the engine and turned off the headlight, Eleanor's skin went clammy. She wondered if the rider could see her, peeking around the edge of her window, and then she wondered, in a panic, if she'd remembered to lock her front door. By the time she flew down the staircase and satisfied herself that the bolts were fastened, the motorcycle revved up again. She peered through the living room windows and watched it back up slowly and rumble out of sight.

Perhaps the rider thought the house was still for sale, or perhaps he was simply lost. It was easy to get turned around in winding avenues of the old neighborhood, she reminded herself. A chill skimmed her skin and she rubbed her arms. At any rate, he was gone now. There was nothing to worry about.

* * *

Tyler turned into Rosie's driveway and was surprised to see no sign of her car in the driveway or in the garage. He glanced at his watch. One o'clock, right on time for their lunch date. Something unexpected must have come up; something wedding-related, no doubt. He sighed. Thank God there were only a few more days before the big event. The level of activity among all the women in his family had whipped to a fever pitch and every day brought some new crisis. What could today's big dilemma be? They couldn't find the right little people for the top of the cake? He grinned to himself. In his opinion, they were all getting a little bit punchy. Even Hope, normally so sweet-tempered, had been alternately weepy and short-tempered ever since she and Adam blew back into town. Tyler didn't recall Leanne or Ally's weddings being so burdensome; but then, he had been up in Denver and had only come in for the main event. He smiled at the recollection. Fly in, walk 'em down the aisle, jump back on the plane. He had been on to something and hadn't even known it.

He parked the Mustang in the shade and wrested the keys from the ignition. Well, soon it would all be over and things would get back to normal. Whatever that was. Off-season 'normal' used to mean hanging out here at home for a couple of weeks, spending a couple or three weeks traveling to some little bump or dip on the globe with or without female company, and then heading back to Denver to get back to business. Now he had to keep reminding himself this wasn't just another off-season. It was just---off.

Tyler exhaled a long whoosh of air and climbed out of the Mustang. He guessed he'd go in and wait around for Rosie. After all, it wasn't like he had anything else to do, or anywhere else to go. After his workout--- which, this morning, suddenly struck him as pointless---he'd stopped by the nursery to see what was new. He could usually rely on Robb to at least pretend like he needed advice on something, but today they hadn't talked business at all. Not that that wasn't good, Tyler reminded himself quickly; of course it was good, but at the same time, the nurseries were one of Tyler's favorite ventures, and he missed being involved.

Instead, they lounged around in his office for a while, boots up on the desk, cracking jokes about all the wedding fuss. The process seemed simple enough to them; a bride, a groom, a minister, a ring, and that was that. Robb's assistant manager, a pretty redhead, overheard them and tried to explain. Weddings, to women, she said, were like the Super Bowl, to men. Then it was their turn to laugh, and to agree women certainly must be from Venus or Pluto or wherever, because that was the silliest comparison they'd ever heard. Then a vendor dropped in, and Robb had to get back to work, so Tyler just scuffed on out of there.

About then was when he realized it wasn't just Robb and the nursery. It was the same thing with Ally's boutique, the same thing with Joel's insurance company, and the same thing with Lee and Elliot's veterinary hospital. Everybody was up and running, doing a good job, taking care of business. Tyler was starting to get the feeling his own brothers and sisters didn't know quite what to do with him now that he was a permanent fixture. Hey, that was understandable, he didn't know what to do with himself, either.

Suddenly thoroughly disgruntled by his negative train of thoughts, Tyler ambled to the house and ducked inside. Voices carried from the living room. He shook his head in fond resignation. Rosie liked leaving the television on.

"Ooh, Anna's in big trouble now, isn't she?"

Tyler flinched at the familiar, lilting voice floating from the living room. Aw, man. Not her. Not now. He grimaced as he approached the arched opening to the living room. Eleanor wasn't supposed to be here now. She came over in the mornings, that much he did know, and that was why he stayed away until the afternoons when the coast was generally clear. He got a knee-jerk headache every time he thought about the way she only pretended to call Gerald Moses. She'd set him up like a first-prize idiot.

Don't think about that, he warned himself. It still made him mad. Think about what she's doing here, when Rosie isn't even here. She was making herself entirely too much at home, that's what she was doing.

"It's gonna be all right, Eleanor. Watch and see." Tyler recognized five-year-old Shelly's slightly lisping voice and had to smile. Shelly was some sweet piece of work. He leaned around the door to look into the room and saw the pair, curled together in the deep, comfortable chair closest to the television. Shelly lay across Eleanor's lap, patting her comfortingly with one hand, unconsciously toying with the end of Eleanor's long braid with the other. He watched Shelly tug the tie from the end of the braid and begin untwisting the heavy strands.

Funny how all the kids had a kind of fascination with Eleanor's long braid. Just last Sunday, he'd watched as Shelly and Austin, with Seth toddling behind, lay in wait and converged on her as she slipped through the gap in the hedge to join his family. Then they led her toward the swing set before she could even say hello to Rosie or see he still wasn't speaking to her. Tugging her down to the grass, the trio promptly pulled her braid apart, arranged her hair over her shoulders, and began tucking bits of clover and who-knew-what else into the curls. It was when Ally gently elbowed him in the ribs to ask, apparently for the second time, if it wasn't a cute sight, that he realized he had been standing and staring. Snapping out of it, he'd told Ally somebody ought to do Eleanor a favor and tell her to put that mess back in a ponytail or something. Ally frowned at him indignantly, and left him without another word. He didn't know why; all he did was state facts.

That was the same day Eleanor and Hope met one another for the first time, and, naturally, Hope fell in with the rest of his contrary family and liked her right away. It was a constant source of frustration to Tyler how Eleanor behaved so nicely around all of them. None of them had a clue what she was really like. The screened door squealed and banged, jerking Tyler out of his sour thoughts.

"Oh, Ty, have you been waiting long?" Rosie pushed through the kitchen door with Leanne on her heels. "We just ran over to meet Hope at the florist."

"Just got here," he replied, hoping Eleanor didn't figure out he'd been spying on them for a couple of minutes.

"Hey, Ty." A bag of groceries on her hip, Leanne gave him a squeeze and continued on toward the kitchen counter. "Shelly? Come on, sweetie, we've got to go get April."

Eleanor and Shelly joined them in the kitchen. Shelly lit up when she saw Tyler. "Uncle Ty!" she crowed, "pick me up!"

He complied obediently, lifting her high in his arms. She beamed at him, patting his cheeks, while Eleanor maneuvered around him as though he didn't exist. "Hi, Eleanor," he said pointedly, just to make her look his way. She tossed a careless wave over her shoulder as she moved through the dining area toward the kitchen.

Women fell all over themselves trying to catch his attention, he wanted to tell her. Women with a lot more going for them than a messy yank of hair and squinty green eyes.

"Thanks for keeping Shelly, Eleanor." Leanne pulled grocery items out of the bag, then stopped and turned around, her expression suddenly concerned. "Rosie told me about the motorcycle and the weird calls. It sounds creepy. Have you filed any kind of report with the police?"

Tyler frowned at his sister. "What are you talking about, Leanne?" Nobody had mentioned anything about a motorcycle or weird calls to him. He turned to Eleanor, eyebrows lifted in question. "What's she talking about?"

Eleanor shrugged. "Nothing."

"It is so something," Rosie insisted. She turned to Tyler, her brow furrowed. "Twice now Eleanor's noticed a motorcycle turning into her driveway late at night, and she's gotten several hang-up calls in the last week."

"Probably just spam or wrong numbers," Eleanor said with a dismissive shake of her head.

Tyler wasn't convinced. "Tell me about the motorcycle." He juggled Shelly in his arm, his attention focused on Eleanor.

She took a glass from the cabinet and filled it with water at the sink. "Nothing much to tell."

"Can't I be the judge of that?"

Eleanor lifted the glass to her lips and drank a long swallow, eyeing him over the rim.

Tyler gritted his teeth. She couldn't even answer a simple question without challenging him.

"He's shown up twice, around midnight," she began indifferently. "He rides a little way down the driveway, kills the engine, sits there for a minute, then starts it up again and rides away. That's it." She drank another swallow. "I told you there wasn't much to it." Turning her back to him, she slowly poured the remaining water down the sink and rinsed out the glass.

Tyler didn't like it.

"Don't you think a big dog is a good idea, Ty?" Leanne held her arms out to Shelly. "Come on, honey, we have to go."

Shelly hung back, clinging to Tyler. "Kiss, Uncle Ty."

He obeyed immediately, and then returned to the topic at hand. "An alarm system would be even better."

"I don't need a dog; I have Walter." Eleanor slanted a mischievous grin toward Leanne and Rosie, and they laughed.

Tyler didn't get it. "Who's Walter?"

Leanne put her hands on her hips in mock amazement. "You haven't met Walter?

He shook his head impatiently. If he'd met Walter, he wouldn't ask who Walter was.

Rosie shook her head. "Walter is loud, I'll grant you that, Eleanor, but he won't scare away a burglar."

"Oh, you're not giving Walter nearly enough credit." Eleanor passed in front of Tyler again, but hesitated, then stopped to tie

Shelly's shoe. Tyler was struck by how tiny Eleanor seemed, when she was near and not moving past at the speed of light. "I keep telling you it's nothing to worry about, anyway." Flipping her braid over her shoulder, she gave Shelly a little tickle, but never rested her green eyes on Tyler's face. "Bye, Shelly. Thanks for watching 'Frozen' with me."

Shelly nodded, and then turned Tyler's face toward her own with an insistent little hand. "Did you know Eleanor's never seen "Frozen" or "Moana" or *anything*?"

"No, that's not true, Shelly. Remember I told you I've seen 'The Little Mermaid'?" Eleanor lifted a hand to brush a curl from Shelly's face. "It was my most, most favorite, and we're going to watch it soon, me and you."

Tyler caught Eleanor by the arm. "Who's Walter?"

She looked long and hard at his hand on her arm, and then lifted her face to his, her eyes narrowed dangerously. Tyler dropped his hand quickly. "Come over some time and meet him," she said calmly. "You'll love him; he's a lot like you."

Rosie and Leanne burst out laughing again, and Tyler felt his skin heat. Whatever she meant; it wasn't a compliment. "Fine, don't tell me." He didn't give a damn who Walter was, anyway. She didn't need a dog or a security system for protection from any criminal element; her tongue was enough of a damned lethal weapon.

Chapter Ten

Eleanor studied her reflection in the bathroom mirror. The new coral silk dress Rosie insisted was exactly right for a July wedding felt, well, awfully skimpy. Eleanor smoothed her hands over her hips. Thanks to Rosie's regular invitations to meals, she'd gained a little weight in the last few weeks and this dress, well, it clung. She turned around and glanced over her shoulder. Yes, it definitely clung. She smiled at her new curves.

Scooping up her brand new, glittery little purse, she skipped down the staircase in her brand new frivolous shoes. She was brand new clear down to her undergarments, she thought with a giggle.

"Time to get up! Time to get up!" Walter flapped his wings energetically as she dropped her bag on the table by the door.

She detoured by his cage hopefully. "Say 'looking good, Eleanor!'" she coaxed him. "'Looking good, Eleanor!'

Walter, predictably, two-stepped sideways down his perch and looked the other way. Eleanor put her hands on her hips. "You know, Walter, one of these days you're going to have to acknowledge me. Don't forget I'm the one who's trying to reunite you with Mrs. Dunlap." Shaking her head in exasperated amusement, she picked up her purse and slipped out the front door to make her way over to Rosie's.

She had to stop on the porch and take a look around first, though. Hope couldn't have custom-ordered a more beautiful wedding day. It was going to be everything a July wedding should be; blue skies and puffy clouds, a beautiful bride and proud groom, happy family and good friends. And she was a good friend, too, which was the most amazing thing of all.

Eleanor carefully picked her way across the lawn and through the azaleas. She pushed the screen door open tentatively. "Rosie?"

"Oh, good, Eleanor, thank heavens you're here!" Rosie sat on the edge of the sofa in her robe and slippers, her glasses on her nose, digging industriously into her sewing box.

Something was wrong if Rosie wasn't dressed yet. "What's the matter?"

"Rosie," Hope's voice filtered down the hallway. "Better bring two!"

"Hope's slip keeps sliding down her waist. We have to safety-pin it to her underskirt somehow. And where in the world are Nancy and Robb? They're picking up the bouquet, and they're late." Rosie seized something from the depths of the box. "Oh, here's another big one."

"Here, give them to me," Eleanor said, happy to be needed. "I'll help Hope with her slip while you get dressed."

Rosie placed the pins in her palm. "That would be wonderful." She rose and tugged her glasses off to look at Eleanor. "Oh, look at you, honey. You look beautiful." She turned Eleanor around by her shoulders, beaming proudly. "Your dress is perfect. I told you it was made for you."

Eleanor curtseyed. "You were right. I love it."

The porch door squeaked open and Eleanor recognized Tyler's heavy footfall. She knew he wouldn't spare a glance in her direction, new dress or not. She smoothed the silky fabric again, annoyed with herself. He'd never look at her and see anything but a red haze of irritation. But today was important and that was why she had decided she was going to make every effort to be pleasant with him. Hopefully he would cooperate and be pleasant in return.

"Mornin'," he called as he made his way inside. "I need some help with this damned necktie, Rosie. Something's wrong with it."

Turning, Eleanor watched him stride in the room, his faded blue jeans a startling contrast to his untucked, halfway buttoned tuxedo shirt. The crisp whiteness of the shirt against his tanned skin, his necktie dangling from his fingers; he looked like a barely tamed barbarian. Her legs suddenly rubbery, Eleanor put a hand on the back of one of the easy chairs. He took her breath away. She hated that about him.

"Doesn't Eleanor look beautiful in her new dress, Ty?" Rosie gave him a wave, then stopped and stared. "Why aren't you dressed?"

He tossed an uninterested glance in Eleanor's general direction, one she pretended not to notice, and then he nodded and squeezed Rosie affectionately. "Because, unlike the women in my family, it doesn't take me hours to get pretty.

Laughing, Rosie took Eleanor's hand and traded Hope's safety pins for Tyler's necktie. "Here, Eleanor, you help Tyler and I'll pin Hope's slip." She shook a finger at Tyler. "You just make sure you have your pretty self planted at the beginning of the aisle at four o'clock."

"Rosie!" Hope, down the hallway, sounded panicky.

"Coming, honey." Rosie set off toward the back of the house.

Flustered, Eleanor examined the narrow strip in her hand. Tyler leaned down and snatched it back. "Never mind, I'll do it myself."

All her good intentions flew out of the window. "Well, pardon me all to hell," she drawled, slapping a hand on her hip. "But Rosie told me to do it, and I'm doing it, and that's all there is to it."

Tyler immediately recognized that she was mocking him and his expression darkened.

Eleanor sank into a chair and grinned up at him. "Did it sound as silly when I said it, as when you did?"

He crushed the tie in his hand. "Look, Eleanor, I don't want to have to put up with you today. Just stay away from me, all right?"

Rosie bustled back into the room just as Robb entered the kitchen from the porch with an oversized florist box in his arms. "Finally!" she exclaimed with relief, taking the box and placing it on the kitchen table. "Where in the world have you been? Where's Nancy?"

"She and Austin are in the car. We have a problem." Robb pushed an agitated hand through his hair. "She and Austin are going to have to miss the wedding."

"What?" Rosie and Tyler asked simultaneously.

"We just left the doctor's office. Austin has chicken pox, and even though he's past being contagious, the doctor advised us not to take him to the wedding. I'm going to bring them home and meet y'all back at the church."

"Oh, for goodness sakes. Poor Austin." Rosie twisted her hands in agitation, "But Nancy's a bridesmaid, Robb."

"I know, and she's upset, too, but Austin's cranky and we'd be crazy to try to bring him along. It's going to be a long evening and he's just not up to it."

Tyler looked thoughtful. "Isn't there anybody who can look after him? A sitter or a neighbor? One of your employees?"

Robb shook his head. "We've already called around to everyone we could think of."

Rosie threw a helpless glance in Tyler's direction. "What should we do?"

Tyler shrugged. "There's not much we can do."

Tyler couldn't do anything, but she could. Eleanor stepped forward. "Let me babysit Austin."

Three heads turned simultaneously.

"I can watch him right here where he'll be comfortable," she continued, ignoring Tyler's sudden stiffening. "Nancy can't miss the wedding." Tyler might not like it, but it wasn't up to him; it was up to Robb and Nancy. She could do this. She could take care of Austin. Eleanor ignored the selfish voice that reminded her she was as excited about attending the wedding as anyone else. She nodded decisively at Rosie. "Don't you agree, Rosie?"

Rosie wasn't happy with her proposal, either. "Oh, Eleanor, you've been looking forward to the wedding every bit as much as we have. There has to be another solution."

"I'm sure there is," Tyler agreed, frowning. "She---," he said, jerking his head in Eleanor's direction, "probably hasn't got any experience nursing a sick child. It's a terrible idea."

Eleanor resisted the urge to jab him in the foot with her high heel. "Then you come up with a better idea."

"Don't be silly," Rosie reproved him. "Chicken pox is hardly life threatening. Austin's not that sick."

"Nope, just itchy and cranky," Robb agreed. "I think it's a great idea, Eleanor. Nancy will be so relieved." He hugged her warmly. "You sure you don't mind missing the wedding?"

She absolutely hated to miss the wedding but being able to save the day was more than worth the disappointment. "I'm absolutely sure, Robb."

* * *

The reception, escalating gradually from decorous to raucous, wasn't even close to winding down, but Tyler was tired of all the commotion. Not only that, if he was cornered by one more complete stranger who wanted to impress him with their crack-brained analysis on why the Renegades failed to win the NFC championship last season, he'd likely blow a fuse. Pushing up his white cuff, he glanced at his Rolex and exhaled a relieved whoosh of air. His commitment to Rosie to stay until at least ten o'clock was fulfilled. Now he could escape to Baxter's and unwind with friends and a couple of beers.

After tracking Hope across the room for a hug and kiss, Tyler looked for Rosie and found her sitting, wilted but triumphant, with some of her blue-haired friends. "Look," he said, leaning down to be heard, "If I'm done here, I think I'll go."

Rosie peered up at him. "So soon?"

He tapped at the crystal of his watch. "Ten o'clock."

She shook her head wryly. "And you're going to turn into a pumpkin, I suppose." He grinned in reply. "Well, all right." With a nod to her friends, she rose. "Will you do something for me on your way home?"

"Sure thing."

She gave him an approving pat. "Good. Wait here while I get the food I packed for Eleanor."

Tyler frowned. "Wait a minute. I didn't say anything about doing anything for Eleanor."

Rosie stopped and fixed him with a chiding glare. "Ty, she saved the day for Robb and Nancy. The least we can do is make sure she has something to eat. I don't think it will kill you."

Tyler guessed it wouldn't. On the short ride to Rosie's, he comforted himself that all he had to do was push the containers at Eleanor, make sure Austin was still alive, and get the hell out of there. Five minutes at best, and then he could go home, lose the tuxedo and head to Baxter's just like he planned.

Rosie's house, upon his arrival, was dark and still. Balancing the containers in his hand, Tyler tried the knob and found it locked. Well, at least she had the sense to lock the door, he thought with some asperity. After unlocking the door and slipping inside, he found the kitchen dim and there was no sign of life in the living room, either. He frowned. Eleanor said she was going to keep Austin at Rosie's house, so where were they? He deposited the containers on the counter and began his search. Quietly he moved through the house, glancing into each room along the way. The clutter and debris left over from the morning's mad rush had been cleared, and he realized Eleanor was responsible. Thoughtful of her, he acknowledged grudgingly. He came to the partially closed door to Rosie's bedroom, and pushed it open. A mountain of pillows lined the nearest side of the antique tester bed. Tyler entered, stepping around foam puzzle pieces and toy characters strewn about the floor, to take a closer look.

In the hazy light from an animated movie still playing noiselessly on Rosie's television, he gazed down at the bed's sleeping occupants. An unwilling smile curved his lips. Eleanor lay on her side, one arm draped protectively over Austin, and the other, pillowing her head. He pointedly avoided glancing down the length of slim, shapely legs drawn up beneath her. Austin was sprawled comfortably inside the curve of her arm, one hand clutching a toy super hero and the other fisted around a handful of Eleanor's loose hair.

That hair. Tyler shook his head in wonder. If there was anything at all appealing about Eleanor, it had to be her hair. She usually kept it under Nazi-like control, and even though the braid she now favored was a helluva lot better than that old ladies' bun, it was just natural for a guy to wonder what it would look like if she just let it alone. The reality, spread on the bed in disarray, was startling. It practically crackled with energy. He extended a cautious hand to move a strand that threatened to tickle Austin's face.

Green eyes opened and stared at him just as he touched the strand. He jerked his hand away as if he had accidentally burnt it.

"Hey," Eleanor whispered. She didn't move, she just stared up at him with sleepy green eyes. Tyler felt an unwelcome curl in his groin. "How was the wedding?"

This was the wrong damned place to have a conversation. He didn't want to look at her, see her all drowsy and rumpled, with Austin cradled in her arms. "Fine," he replied shortly, jamming his hands into his pockets. "Rosie sent you some food."

Eleanor tried to move away from Austin without waking him, and grimaced when she felt his tight grip on her hair. "Owee," she said, trying unsuccessfully to pry his little hand away. Her positioning was awkward, and she froze when Austin sighed heavily and curled deeper into her arms.

Tyler watched, feeling more and more disgruntled. "Here," he said finally, leaning down to uncurl Austin's fingers. He lifted him slightly at the same time to free Eleanor. She slid off the side of the bed, her dress twisting around her thighs, and deftly lined some of the pillows in the space she'd vacated. Tyler hung back, waiting as she circled the bed and moved toward the door. She stopped when Austin mumbled, and cast a worried glance over her shoulder.

"He's fine," Tyler said in a low voice. "He'll settle back down."

She nodded and slipped through the door, barefoot, and Tyler followed her down the hallway. Her hair curled almost to her hips, and she was already busy trying to capture it, her arms lifted, her dress hiked. A brief detour by her purse garnered a hair tie and before he knew it, it was pulled back again. He ignored the twinge of disappointment. Why even have all that hair if she kept it tied up all the time, he thought crankily. Why not just lop it all off? That wild hair, always so tightly bound, was just another good example of her contradictory nature.

They reached the kitchen in silence, and he nodded toward the boxes of food.

Eleanor turned on the light over the sink, bathing the kitchen in a soft, golden light. "So, how did everything go?" She opened a cabinet and withdrew a plate.

Damn, it annoyed him, how at home she was at his grandmother's. "Okay." He wasn't there to give her a news report. If she wanted details, she'd have to wait for Rosie. "How was Austin?"

"Oh, just fine. We watched TV and played games." Unaware of his scowl, Eleanor pried the first box open and sighed with delight when she saw the contents. "Rosie's so thoughtful," she murmured.

He almost pointed out that he was the one who delivered them, but caught himself in time. He didn't want her thanks because then he'd have to say 'you're welcome' and he didn't feel like it. She wasn't welcome. Leaning against the wall, he watched silently as Eleanor arranged the hors d'oeuvres on the plate before returning to the table. She sat down and smiled up at him. "Come on, Tyler, help me eat this. Rosie sent so much."

There wasn't enough food in both boxes combined to vaguely capture his interest. Not only that, the idea of sharing leftover wedding food with a suspiciously agreeable Eleanor Haley made him jumpy. "No, thanks."

Shrugging, she sat down and tried again. "Did Rosie convince Shelly to scatter the rose petals?"

Tyler was unable to suppress a smile at the memory. His reply slipped out despite his intentions to avoid a conversation. "By the hardest. They made a deal; Shelly scattered half and kept half."

Eleanor's return smile was so warm he felt a little guilty for being selfish with the tiny bit of information. "That's fair," she said, picking up a dainty crab-filled pastry shell. She bit into it, and ran her tongue past the edges of her mouth. "Mmm," she said, closing her eyes with pleasure for a brief moment.

Tyler felt the unwelcome curl of awareness again. She acted like she'd never enjoyed food before in her life. Skinny as she was, maybe she hadn't. He unwillingly recalled the shells were a little on the dry side, and crossed the kitchen to pour her the glass of water she was going to need. He didn't want to have to perform any Heimlich maneuver if she choked, that was for sure.

Eleanor smiled her thanks. Again, it wasn't her typically superior smile, so Tyler didn't know quite how to respond. He settled for a noncommittal grunt, and resumed his position against the wall.

"Was Hope just beautiful?" Eleanor asked, her expression dreamy. "Her wedding gown was so lovely. What did Adam look like when he saw her coming down the aisle?"

"Hope looked fine and Adam looked nervous."

Eleanor frowned at him, and then at the stuffed mushrooms on her plate. "Never mind. I guess I'll just have to wait and hear everything from Rosie." She pushed unhappily at one of the mushrooms with her small pink-tipped finger. "What time do you think she'll be home?"

"I don't know. At least midnight, more than likely," he replied. "She'll be too tired to stay up and answer questions."

Her shoulders drooped slightly in response to his statement but she nodded in prompt agreement. "Of course. Well, I'll hear all about it tomorrow, then."

Tyler watched her spurn the mushroom before moving her half-hearted attention to a dainty chicken salad sandwich. Eleanor had really wanted to go to the wedding, he realized with a blink. When she volunteered so swiftly to stay behind and care for Austin, he just figured it didn't make much difference to her and he hadn't given it any further thought. He took a fresh look at her dress, wrinkled and sporting a suspicious stain on one shoulder and sleeve. Rosie had said something about it, what was it? It was new. Tyler knew women, and if a new dress wasn't proof of her enthusiasm for Hope's wedding, he didn't know what was. But she'd only got as far as Rosie's house, and nobody saw her in her new dress but Rosie and Robb's family, and him, and now it was spoiled. Without thinking, he abandoned his position against the wall to gesture at the spots. "What's this?" Possibly a stupid move, he realized belatedly. He knew how much women hated it when their clothes were spoiled, especially brand-new big-occasion dresses, and he didn't much feel like listening to Eleanor carry on.

Eleanor glanced down and brushed at one of the spots. "Oh, some of Austin's ointment, I guess," she replied serenely, returning her attention to her plate. "No big deal. I'll take it to the cleaners tomorrow."

"I'll pay for it," he said automatically.

"I don't think so," she retorted, glancing up at him with affronted green eyes.

Why was she always so difficult? "Well, Austin can't." Tyler took care to speak in a nice, even tone. "As his uncle, I'd like to take responsibility for it. What are we talking about here, anyway? Twenty bucks?"

"Oh, get over your responsibility fixation," Eleanor shot back, clearly unimpressed with his pleasant tone or logic. "How do you know I didn't smear it on myself, by accident? You know how clumsy I am." She stabbed at one of the Swedish meatballs; her brow furrowed, then laid her fork down and pushed the plate away.

Tyler winced. He should never have called her clumsy. It had been a cheap shot and she was never going to forget it.

"And you're not responsible, anyway," she continued, looking back up and pinning him with her gaze. "You go to great pains to make it clear I'm not welcome here, I'm not part of your family, and then you turn right around and try to boss me around as if I were. You can't have it both ways, you know."

Stung, he stared at her, struggling to decide which remark to take issue with first. What did she mean, responsibility fixation? And he certainly didn't try to boss her around. He'd like to see the poor fool who did. He didn't boss his family around, either. Or did he? Tyler felt a prickle of uneasiness, but shoved it aside. As far as how the stuff got smeared on her dress, well, how it got there was beside the point. The bottom line was, Austin's medicine was supposed to be on Austin, not her dress. If she'd gone to the wedding like she was supposed to, instead of giving up her afternoon to babysit someone else's fretful four-year-old, her brand new dress would still look brand new.

Tyler drew in a sudden, quiet breath. And here he was, topping her evening off by picking a fight over a couple of spots.

She glared at him, small chin lifted, gearing up for battle.

Well, why not? All they ever did was bicker back and forth. He debated mentally whether to conform to their established pattern or to take a careful little step in a new direction. Slant left, instead of right. Though it pained him to admit it, she'd been halfway pleasant since he'd arrived. He supposed he could be agreeable, too. It had been peaceful in the dim kitchen before and he wanted it to be peaceful again. She deserved that much, considering how her day turned out. Tyler pulled out a chair and sat down. She watched him warily.

"You're right," he said. "Pay for your own spots." There. He waited to see what she would make of his grand concession.

Her brow creased again, in surprise, then she looked so pleased with him that he felt pleased with himself, and he guessed he could take a couple of minutes to hit the high points of the wedding before he left. "Hope looked beautiful," he said casually, "and Adam got all choked up."

Eleanor leaned forward, immediately enthralled. "Tell me more."

So he told her everything he could remember. She sat on the edge of her seat, her chin propped on her hand, green eyes sparkling while he told her how the altar boys had problems lighting the highest candles on the candelabra, how Rosie cried unashamedly when Hope and Adam presented her with a bouquet of white roses, and how Shawn and Thomas pilfered a tray of tiny cakes and overate themselves green beneath one of the buffet tables.

Tyler's knee began to throb so he pulled out another chair and propped his legs up, and was taken aback when Eleanor wordlessly fetched the bottle of pain reliever and a glass of water for him. When it became obvious that the stuffed mushrooms were destined for the trash, he tugged the plate over and put them out of their misery, and earned another big smile. Then they shared the next plate, and she asked a million questions and he answered them. Finally the conversation slowed, and Eleanor yawned and rose. "I think I'll check on Austin. Make sure he hasn't rolled off the side of the bed." She flashed an easy smile at Tyler and disappeared around the doorway into the living room, completely unaware, as usual, that her hair was escaping the elastic band.

Tyler felt unaccountably complacent. Funny how much more entertaining the wedding was, in the retelling, than it had been during the actual event. He rose to throw away the empty containers and put the dishes in the dishwasher, and then looked around. The kitchen seemed oddly empty so he decided maybe he ought to go along and see about Austin, too. He ambled through the living room and down the hallway. When he reached Rosie's bedroom door, he hung back, not wanting to startle them.

She sat on the side of the bed in the dark room, her back to the doorway, smoothing Austin's hair and murmuring to him in a low voice. Tyler strained to hear what she was saying, to no avail. His tow-headed nephew gave a sleepy nod and held his arms up. Eleanor lifted him and rose, nestling him close against her chest. Tyler was arrested by the tender expression on her face, by Austin's serenity in her arms. His chest felt oddly constricted and he drew in a careful breath.

Her attention completely focused on Austin, Eleanor turned and walked straight into him, sandwiching Austin between them. "Oops," she said lightly.

"Sorry," Tyler murmured, not sorry at all, automatically steadying her with his hands on her shoulders. Man, she was little. Barely big enough to hold Austin without buckling from his weight. Tyler caught a trace of perfume, something soft and sweet, mixed with the familiar smell of a warm, sleepy child. Fierce feelings of raw protectiveness surged, mixed with something else, something alarming. Unconsciously, Tyler dipped his head for a second whiff. Eleanor looked up, wide-eyed, and his breath caught again. Her luminous green eyes, and lips, parted in surprise, were raised dangerously near. She stood perfectly still but he could swear she was trembling. His mind, reliably sharp even under the most carnal of conditions, went a little foggy. Eleanor ran the tip of her tongue around her lips, and her unconscious gesture hit him with the staggering force of a 300 pound linesman. But in a good way, he thought with ragged amusement.

"Tyler?" She whispered his name questioningly, breathlessly.

He didn't answer her. Instead, he leaned against the doorway, favoring his bad knee, and deliberately slid his hands around her shoulders to draw her, along with her drowsy passenger, into the curve of his arms. This was what he wanted, he realized in astonishment. This was what he had wanted for God only knew how long. He didn't want to waste time analyzing his discovery; he just wanted to hold her. Eleanor didn't protest or pull away, a promising sign, but he could feel her wariness by the way she clung to Austin in her own arms. Instead of feeling mismatched because of their size disparity, Tyler was knocked out by how neatly she and Austin fit against him. Her cheek was level with his heart, which seemed to be beating in odd fits and starts. He wondered if she could hear it. One arm held them securely against his chest, while the other traveled across the soft, smooth fabric of her dress, to bump into the elastic thing holding her hair back. He toyed with the idea of tugging it loose. It wouldn't take much effort. He wanted to. He would. Tyler pulled at the hair tie, intent on his mission.

"Bathroom, Uncle Ty," Austin mumbled. Twisting and squirming in Eleanor's arms, he reached toward Tyler and he automatically caught him, lifting him into his arms. The movement effectively separated him from Eleanor, and Tyler watched with dismay as she took the opportunity to slip past and disappear down the hallway without a backwards glance.

* * *

What was *that*? Dizzy, Eleanor nearly stumbled in her haste to escape. In the kitchen, she leaned on one arm and shakily poured herself a glass of water at the sink. She drank the water in one long, parched drink, and then poured herself another. Had that just happened? Had Tyler Hurst really held her close for what felt like a second and an eternity, all at the same time? His hands roaming around on her back, up to her hair, down to her hip? Yes, he had. She knew because the path his hands had taken still hummed. She drained the second glass and it slipped from her hand and bounced noisily in the sink.

Okay, gather yourself. Standing upright, Eleanor held her right hand in front of her face, palm down, examined it, and snorted in disgust. Shaking like a leaf. Do better than that. Inhaling deeply, she closed her eyes and concentrated on exhaling slowly, carefully. It always worked before, when she was preparing to face a disgruntled client, or a jury, or her father. Her hand still trembled. Try again.

The hair on the back of her neck prickled and she knew without looking that Tyler had entered the room.

"Austin's back in bed, and I think we've got company." Without a glance in her direction, he moved to the window and looked outside. "Yep. Rosie's home, with Robb and Nancy." He turned toward her and she felt dizzy all over again just from his nearness. Damn him for affecting her like this, she thought, gritting her teeth. Ever since she'd awakened earlier to find him beside the bed, his pleated shirt wrested open at the neck, his expression inscrutable, she'd felt a little addled. Ever since, she'd battled to obtain a sense of balance but it wasn't easy because he kept switching gears on her. His jump from barely concealed animosity to easy companionship over the kitchen table was welcome but confusing all the same; so how was she supposed to react after that brief embrace? Pretend as though it hadn't happened? Okay, she could do that, at least until she reached the safety of her own home. She needed to get home. How quickly could she leave? Would Rosie think it odd if she rushed out?

Tyler disappeared into the living room as Rosie and Robb and Nancy entered the kitchen, plainly tired but satisfied. "Oh, Eleanor," Rosie said, stepping out of her shoes with a heartfelt sigh before gathering her into a warm hug. "I couldn't stop thinking about you this evening, here with Austin, both of you missing all the fun."

Pulling herself together, Eleanor gently hugged Rosie in return. "We had fun here, too."

Tyler returned to the kitchen, holding Eleanor's shoes in one hand and her purse in the other. "Austin's asleep in Rosie's room, Robb. I'm going to see Eleanor home now."

Eleanor shot a startled look at him, then Rosie.

"Good idea, hon," Rosie said casually, as though nothing were at all odd about Tyler's remark.

"It's not necessary, Tyler," Eleanor said, her response more abrupt than she intended.

"Maybe not," he replied mildly. "But you'll humor me?" He bent to place her shoes on the floor, and then offered an arm. Eleanor gaped at him, and then cautiously put her hand on his forearm to step into her shoes.

Yawning, Rosie missed Tyler's gallant gesture. "We'll see you tomorrow afternoon, won't we, Eleanor?"

Tyler's arm, through the crisp white sleeve, felt warm and solid. Eleanor glanced up at his face and found him studying her, hazel eyes glittering. Quirking an eyebrow, he nodded toward Rosie. Eleanor belatedly realized Rosie had asked her a question and it took her just a moment to recall what it was. "Oh! Yes, tomorrow," she managed.

Robb and Nancy thanked Eleanor again, good nights were exchanged, and Tyler led Eleanor through the porch and onto the deck. "There's no need to walk me home," she shot off shakily, desperately resorting to her old antagonistic behavior in an attempt to achieve some kind of control. "I'm perfectly capable of getting there by myself, you know." Give me one of those arrogant glances so I can grab onto it and pitch a fit, she begged mentally. Let's get that jaw ticking.

Her hostile remark didn't seem to surprise him in the least, however. Tyler gazed at her imperturbably. "Of course you are," he agreed, but he put a light hand at the back of her right shoulder, almost curving around her, and nudged her down the steps and across the shadowy lawn anyway.

He wasn't taking the hint and Eleanor didn't know how to make her desire to escape any plainer. Wordlessly they passed through the gap in the azalea hedge. "Nice night," Tyler remarked, glancing upwards when they reached Eleanor's open lawn. "Lots of stars."

"What are you up to?" she blurted, stepping away from the light touch on her back.

He slanted a puzzled look in her direction. "What are you talking about?" Eleanor's heel sank in the soft grass and Tyler caught her elbow to steady her. "I'm not up to anything, Eleanor. I'm just seeing you home." He began to propel her onwards, but she jerked away, moving quickly up the steps to the safety of her front porch.

"I'm home," she announced, fumbling in her purse for the single key she'd taken off her key ring. "Go on now."

Tyler waited on the steps.

Where was the damned key? Eleanor felt panicky. She had to find it and get inside, get away. She felt the key, got her fingers on it, but when she pulled it out, it slipped through her fingers, falling onto the porch with a, bouncing clink. "Dammit!" She dropped to her knees, aware of how comical she must appear but too flustered to care.

"Get up from there, Eleanor. I'll find it."

Bossing her around again. She ignored him, furiously feeling around the floral doormat. Tyler bent on one knee and immediately picked the key up, which, inexplicably, was suddenly right there in plain sight. She reached for it but he closed his fingers around it and rose, offering a hand to tow her up.

She scrambled up by herself and thrust out her hand. "Give it to me, Tyler."

He regarded her with blatant amusement. "Easy, honey." Stepping closer, he slid the key into the lock and turned the knob.

"I hate being called honey," she snapped, trying to squeeze past him. "It's chauvinistic and condescending."

Blocking her easily, he turned her to face him. She stared mutinously at the buttons on his shirt. "Rosie calls you honey," he replied smoothly, lifting her chin with his finger. "You don't mind it when she says it."

Oh, he was tricky, and he was smooth. Now that he knew he had her all tied up in knots, he was purposely toying with her and enjoying every minute of it. Eleanor narrowed her eyes and pursed her lips. "That's different and you know it. Back off, Tyler. I don't know what kind of game you're playing, but I'm not playing it with you."

Dropping his hand, he stepped back marginally and looked hurt. "What makes you think I'm playing a game?"

"This isn't how you act with me," she retorted.

"I've turned over a new leaf," he promptly replied. "I'm behaving myself. Haven't we been getting along tonight?"

"I think you're trying to manipulate me by being nice."

"And I think you're trying to pick a fight with me because I'm making you nervous, but it's not going to work. I don't want to fight with you anymore." He gave her a slow smile that sent her pulses racing. She was sunk. This was no ordinary man; he was a professional in more ways than one. If she could only figure out what he hoped to gain from his about-face. Eleanor opened her mouth to reply, but a droning hum down the quiet street caught her attention and she tensed. Tyler immediately sensed her distraction, and frowned. "What is it?"

"It sounds like the motorcycle," she whispered, suddenly glad he was there.

Tyler tilted his head, listening, and his face tightened. "Go inside," he murmured, prodding the door open with his foot.

The noise drew nearer, and Eleanor's pulse quickened. "What are you going to do?" she asked anxiously, catching his sleeve. "Don't do anything stupid."

A grin flashed across his face, and he stunned her by leaning to drop a swift kiss on her mouth. "I'll try not to. Go on, go inside." He pushed her through the door and pulled it closed behind her.

On the other side of the door, Eleanor's purse fell from her hands and the motorcycle was temporarily forgotten while she touched her lips in numb bemusement. Tyler had kissed her. On the mouth. No question about it. Inhaling sharply, she slid toward the window and peeked out cautiously. Tyler was sprinting toward the azaleas along the driveway, where he disappeared into the shadows just as the ominously familiar motorcycle reverberated to its usual stop on the end of the driveway. Her heart pounding, Eleanor crumpled the silk of her skirt into her fists. Careful, careful, careful, she chanted mentally. She didn't want anything to happen to him before she had a chance to tell him never to kiss her like that again.

Chapter Eleven

The rider silenced the motorcycle and lifted his helmeted head, looking toward the house as he always did. Eleanor watched, her heart jolting to her throat, as Tyler leapt from the shadows and pounced. The hapless rider never even saw him coming. Tyler plucked him straight off the seat of the machine as though he were weightless and jerked him around, pinning his arms behind his back. Swallowing in relief, Eleanor scrambled back toward the door and yanked it open. The trespasser, slim in build, twisted ineffectively as he was hauled toward the house.

"Call the police," Tyler's voice cut through the quiet night. His prisoner, still helmeted, struggled with renewed enthusiasm. "Quit fighting or I'll break you in half." Tyler jerked him off his feet and knocked the helmet away, revealing a white, pinched face and eyes wide with fear.

He was just a boy, Eleanor realized with a start. He couldn't be older than eighteen or nineteen.

"Let me go! I can explain!"

"You can explain to the police," Tyler snapped, roughly propelling him up the steps to the porch.

"I haven't done anything wrong," the boy protested, insistently thrashing against Tyler's superior strength. "I can explain!"

"You can, huh?" Eleanor skittered out of the way as Tyler shoved the boy inside and thrust him toward the sofa where he landed unceremoniously. "Let's hear it, then." Hands propped aggressively on his hips, Tyler towered over the boy. "You tell me why you keep showing up here in the middle of the night."

Righting himself, the boy pushed an unruly lock of dark hair from his forehead and jerked his head toward Eleanor. "Her."

Eleanor swallowed and offered a silent prayer of thanks that Tyler had insisted on walking her home.

"What the hell do you mean, 'her'?" Tyler jerked his head toward Eleanor and she was shaken by the fury on his face. "Call the police, Eleanor," he ground out. "Call them now."

Nodding, Eleanor shakily dug into her bag for her phone.

"She's my sister," the boy mumbled. "I just wanted to see her."

Eleanor froze.

"She's your what?" Taken aback, Tyler swung his head between Eleanor and the boy. "What did you just say?"

His chin down, the boy lifted his shoulders in a curiously defeated shrug. "My sister. I just wanted to see you." He directed his last comment to Eleanor.

Tyler cast an incredulous look at Eleanor. Stricken with shock, Eleanor could only stare at the boy.

"You don't have to call the police," the boy said, his head still downcast. He twisted his hands uneasily. "I won't come around anymore, I swear."

"Is this your brother, Eleanor?" Tyler glanced at Eleanor and, apparently not liking what he saw, took quick steps in her direction. "Sit down, honey." His large hand at her back, his brow creased in concern, he led her to the far end of the sofa. "You're white as a ghost."

Eleanor slipped out of his grasp to sit nearer the boy. He glanced at her warily; his eyes a familiar green, and then back down at his hands. She inhaled a trembling breath. "I have a brother named Scott," she whispered. "I haven't seen him since he was four."

The boy nodded jerkily. "That's right. Thirteen years ago."

Eleanor's gaze traveled to his hands, clamped together, trembling. A tumult of emotion threatened to overwhelm her and she couldn't find her voice.

The boy sucked in a deep breath. "I'm sorry for scaring you. I didn't mean to. I kept thinking I'd get up the nerve to knock on the door, but---" He hesitated, and then shrugged. "It was harder than I thought."

"Why do you come skulking around late at night?" Tyler demanded. "Why not come around during the day?" Clearly he wasn't satisfied, or completely convinced.

"I don't get off work till ten," Scott replied, reluctantly meeting Tyler's eyes. "And it takes me a while to get here." He turned to Eleanor. "I live in Lafayette."

Eleanor gasped. So close! All this time, he'd been only an hour away. If only she had known. If only she had made it her business to find out, she berated herself, instead of simply assuming that he was out of reach.

Tyler folded his arms across his chest. "Have you been calling her and hanging up?"

Scott flushed and nodded. "I kept losing my nerve," he mumbled. "I didn't know what to say in a text, and you're not on Facebook or Twitter or anything."

"Let me see your driver's license," Tyler ordered, holding out his hand. Eleanor shot him an impatient look which he ignored. Rising, Scott dug into his jeans pocket and obediently handed over his thin wallet. Tyler flipped it open and examined the license. "Scott Michael Haley," he confirmed, glancing into the money compartment as well. "You haven't got much money here, have you? Thinking of asking your long-lost sister for a loan?"

The boy shot him a disgusted look. "Yeah, right, that's it. A couple of mil at least." Retrieving his wallet, he jammed it back into his pocket.

Eleanor squelched a tiny smile at the evidence of Scott's mettle. She patted the sofa beside her encouragingly and he sat back down. "I'm really happy to see you," she finally managed, reaching out to cover his hand. "You can't imagine how happy. How is Monica?"

"Dead." His low tone conveyed his grief.

Eleanor's heart sank. "Oh, Scott." Her stepmother had been a warm woman who, for a brief time, brought laughter and affection into Eleanor's somber childhood. "I'm so sorry." What a hopelessly inept thing to say. She squeezed his hand helplessly.

"I live with my uncle now," he said. "My uncle's the one who told me to come see my father."

Eleanor inhaled sharply. "Have you seen him?"

"I tried, but he was busy."

"Too busy to see you?" Eleanor sat up, astonished. "When was this?"

"About a month ago, before I came to your house the first time." Scott didn't seem eager to go into details.

"And he knew it was you?" Eleanor couldn't fathom that their father would refuse to see his own son.

He shrugged. "I told the secretary my name. She went into the back, then came back out a couple of minutes later and said he was busy. I figured I didn't want to see him anyway."

Eleanor cast a distressed look at Tyler. He stood a few discreet feet away, looking out the window, his arms folded like a sentinel, but she knew he heard every damning word. "I don't know what to tell you," she said slowly. "I don't pretend to understand him. We're not very close."

"I guess that's good news," Scott said with a crooked smile. "I used to hate you, you know," he added.

"Hate me?" She sensed, rather than saw, Tyler shift a little in her direction.

Shrugging, Scott raked a hand through his hair. "I was little. All I knew was, you got to stay and I had to go. We didn't have it too good, but maybe you had it worse."

"Well, if it's any consolation, I didn't want to stay," she confessed, relaxing again. "I wanted to go with you and Monica." Eleanor clearly recalled the dreary morning when Monica, drawn and damp with tears, hugged her close before disappearing with Scott. Eleanor's father wasn't home when they left, and when he returned that evening, he acted as though Monica and Scott had never existed. In a few short days, all traces of their six years in the house were wiped away, and Eleanor again became the unhappy focus of her father's attention. And when it hurt too much to think about Monica and Scott, she learned how to push them to the back of her mind, and threw all her energy into her studies.

"I remember you being a lot bigger," he said, smiling.

Eleanor settled back against the sofa cushion, happy to recall gentler memories. "To a four year old, sure. What else do you remember?"

He bit his lip and squinted thoughtfully. "I remember sitting beside you in a room with the ceiling painted like the sky while you read out loud."

Eleanor remembered helping Monica create a crop of unlikely, puffy clouds on the soft blue nursery ceiling, with kitchen sponges, of all things, before Scott was born. She remembered feeling amazed that something as ordinary as a kitchen sponge could create the fanciful clouds, and was convinced Monica was capable of anything. Of anything, maybe, but enduring her father's cold temperament. "You used to beg me to read to you," Eleanor replied, kicking her shoes off and tucking her feet beneath her on the sofa. She yielded to the temptation to smooth back a lock of Scott's dark hair, rebellious like her own. "You loved Curious George the best." They shared a smile of remembrance.

"Anyway," he continued, "Mom and I didn't have much but at least we had each other. You didn't have anybody."

Eleanor knew she ought to deny his sympathetic assumption, but, well, he already had a glancing understanding of their father, and how was she going to dispute the truth, anyway?

Tyler cleared his throat. "What are your plans?" he asked Scott abruptly.

"What do you mean?"

"Tonight. Are you planning to ride back to Lafayette?"

"Well, sure," Scott replied. "It's an easy ride."

"Because I'm sure Eleanor wants to catch up with you, but it's been a big day and it's getting late."

Irritated with his high-handedness, Eleanor frowned at him. "Mind your own business, Tyler."

"So you can bunk at my place tonight, if you want and come back over tomorrow," he finished.

Eleanor blinked in surprise. Scott eyed him warily. "Who are you, anyway?"

Tyler crossed the room, hand outstretched. "Tyler Hurst." Scott accepted his conciliatory gesture and they shook hands. Eleanor felt a wave of unexplainable emotion and had to look away for a moment.

"Sorry about earlier," Scott said, looking Tyler in the eye. "About causing trouble the way I did, scaring Eleanor." He grimaced apologetically at Eleanor and she smiled her forgiveness. "I'm glad you were looking after her." Suddenly his eyebrows shot up. "I know who you are! Defensive end, Denver Renegades."

Tyler nodded, and Eleanor struggled with a response to Scott's assumption that Tyler was looking after her. "His grandmother lives next door," she explained lamely before returning her attention to Tyler. "He can stay here, Tyler." Ignoring Tyler's answering frown, Eleanor caught Scott's hand. "You will, won't you? I mean, you just got here, and we have so much to catch up on."

"I don't want to be any trouble," he said, halfway rising. She tugged him back to the sofa.

"You'll be less trouble at my place," Tyler said, earning another glare from Eleanor. "I promise to have him back bright and early in the morning, Eleanor."

Shaking her head, Eleanor rose and walked to the front door. "You've been a great help, Tyler, but you've worn out your welcome." Opening the door, she waved him out. "My brother and I have a lot to catch up on, and we don't need an audience."

"Can I talk to you outside for a minute?"

She could see he wasn't going to go anyplace until he had his say-so. "I'll be right back," she told Scott. Resignedly, she slipped through the door to the porch where Tyler waited, his hands braced on his hips.

He didn't waste a second. "Okay, this is well and good and everything, and I'm happy you've been reunited, but you really don't know squat about him, Eleanor. Use your head. He can stay with me tonight, and I'll bring him back tomorrow morning."

Eleanor sighed. "He's my brother, Tyler."

"Whom you haven't seen in thirteen years." Tyler was fast becoming agitated with her stubbornness. "You're taking a risk."

"My brother," she repeated, "whom I've missed for thirteen years." She didn't want to fight with Tyler about it; her feelings were too raw, too jumbled, not only about Scott but about Tyler, too. But he wasn't going to tell her what to do. "You're not my keeper, you know."

He snorted. "For which I'm very grateful."

She put a hand on her hip. "Then what's the problem?"

He stared at her a long minute, then ran a frustrated hand through his short hair. "I'll be damned if I know. Do what you want. You will, anyway." He turned on his heel and stomped across the porch.

"Tyler." She needed to tell him---tell him---what?

He stopped and turned around on the bottom step. "What?"

Eleanor inhaled deeply, stepped across the porch, and leaned on the railing. "It's been some night, huh?"

He pressed his lips together, clearly disgruntled. "Yeah. Some night."

"You kissed me." It was a light, wondrous accusation.

"I don't recall that."

"You know you did."

"Then I have mush for brains," he retorted, but the corners of his mouth lifted slightly.

"No argument there," she replied smoothly.

"It didn't mean anything."

"Of course not."

"I've kissed a couple of women here and there."

"So I've heard."

"We haven't even made a deal about not fighting anymore," he pointed out.

"And there's no guarantee we will," Eleanor shot back mildly, comfortable in her familiar combative role. She smiled at him from her safe distance, then straightened and stretched a little. "Well, good night, then."

He hesitated, and Eleanor thought if anything in the world would make her think twice about returning inside to her brother, it would be the chance for another kiss from Tyler. But he just nodded, and she didn't know whether she was relieved or dismayed. "See you tomorrow," he said, setting off toward Rosie's.

Eleanor watched him stride away in the dark night, all long-legged masculine grace, until he was out of sight, before going back inside, where her brother---her brother!---waited for her.

* * *

Tyler headed toward Rosie's, agitated on a whole multitude of levels. He didn't want to feel concern about leaving Eleanor alone with Scott, he didn't want to dwell on what kind of miserable excuse for a father they shared, he didn't want to know the whole story about why they'd been separated for so long, but most of all, he didn't want to wonder what might have happened between him and Eleanor if Scott hadn't chosen to make a return visit tonight.

Crossing into Rosie's yard, he frowned when he saw Robb and Nancy's car still in the driveway. It was late and Rosie ought to be in bed. He thought about going inside to shoo them out, but then it occurred to him they might be lying in wait to ask what was up with him walking Eleanor home. No, thanks, he thought wryly. He could do without an inquisition. The smart thing to do was to go home, even though he knew he was only postponing the inevitable. He couldn't answer Rosie's questions until he answered a few of his own. Like, exactly how stupid was he? Or, what the hell had he been thinking, following up the brainless clinch in Rosie's bedroom doorway with that lame kiss on the porch?

He veered toward his Mustang, quietly opening the door and sliding inside. He could've sidestepped the first incident, but the kiss wasn't going to be so easy to dismiss. It was just that when Eleanor tugged on his arm and told him not to do anything stupid, it just tickled the hell out of him and he couldn't help himself. Tyler grinned in spite of himself, realized he was grinning, and frowned.

He sure hoped Eleanor knew what she was doing, inviting her brother to spend the night. Granted, the kid looked harmless enough, but happy reunion aside, it was entirely too trusting of Eleanor to invite him to spend the night. What did she really know about him, anyway? They both admitted it had been thirteen years since they'd seen one another, and a lot could happen from the time a kid was four till he made seventeen. She really should have listened to him.

But it really wasn't any of his business. He wasn't her keeper. And he was damned glad he wasn't.

* * *

Eleanor tiptoed quietly down the stairs, not wanting to wake Scott. It was late morning and sunlight rippled through the windows. It was a beautiful day, as pretty as the day before, as pretty as a day should be when a girl's family doubled overnight.

She and Scott had stayed up half the night, propped on the kitchen barstools where they tried to cram the past thirteen years into a few late night hours. Right now he was asleep, sprawled across her old bed in one of the spare bedrooms. Eleanor couldn't help peeking in on him, just to make sure she hadn't dreamed the whole unlikely evening. But there he was, clutching his pillow around his head just like she did. Was that sort of thing genetic?

She passed Walter's cage and thought about uncovering it, but only briefly. Walter seemed to have a knack for knowing when she wanted him to be quiet, and delighted in making raising a ruckus accordingly. Damned cantankerous bird. Eleanor shook her head and moved on toward the kitchen where she automatically put on a pot of coffee. The debris from their very late night pizza delivery still lay scattered across the island. She shook her head, smiling, and cleared it away. Scott had a serious appetite, and if she succeeded in convincing him to move to Baton Rouge, she was going to have to do some serious grocery shopping. When he confided his ambition to attend LSU in the fall, she immediately suggested he move in with her. It made perfect sense. She had plenty of room, the house was close to campus, he could save the cost of room and board, and even though last night was a good start, they still had lots to catch up on. Now that she had him back, she intended to make up for their years of separation.

Eleanor stood sentinel before the dripping coffee maker, mug in hand, thinking about how she could convince him to move. He admitted he felt in the way at his uncle's house, but he balked at her invitation. Eleanor suspected their father's rejection was a primary reason. She was still astonished by his reaction to Scott's reappearance in their lives. There had to be some explanation and she was going to find out what it was. It was one thing for him to stomp all over her feelings--- she was used to it---but he wasn't going to be so heartless where Scott was concerned. And regardless of her father's feelings on the matter, she was going to let him know, in no uncertain terms, that Scott was going to be a part of her life from now on.

Scott was also hesitant to move because he already had a job in Lafayette. Apparently there hadn't been much money left after Monica's hospital bills were paid, but he was adamant about supporting himself. No way was he going to mooch off his sister, he said, and that was that. Eleanor resolved to help him find a job, and she knew she'd have to think about getting back to work, too. It was one thing to have a lackadaisical attitude toward work when she had only herself to think of, but things had changed again. Now she had her brother's welfare to consider.

The coffee maker finally gave its telltale last hiccup and she poured a cup, deep in thought over the startling events stemming from last twenty-four hours. Scott wasn't the only big surprise; there was Tyler, too.

Tyler. Eleanor sighed. Wresting her chenille robe in her free hand, she sank into one of the cozy living room chairs and wrapped her hands around the warm mug. In broad daylight it was painfully easy to understand that their accidental bump in Rosie's doorway had been prolonged simply to avoid startling Austin, and that his swift kiss on the porch was just a clever diversionary tactic to keep her from panicking. Eleanor stirred her coffee slowly. While she'd love to tell herself that Tyler was falling under her captivating spell, the idea was so outlandish she had to giggle. Last time she checked, one ointment stained coral dress did not a femme fatale make. And, honestly, the idea of Tyler in pursuit was the tiniest bit frightening, anyway. Eleanor was nothing if not pragmatic. Two fumbling, short-lived relationships in college with boys as geeky as she was didn't exactly prepare a girl for someone like Tyler Hurst. On the Richter scale of sexual experience, she imagined he'd rocket off the chart, whereas she, well, unfortunately she'd flat line on zero.

But, looking at the bright side, the slight shift in his disposition might mean he didn't still suspect she wasn't entertaining some kind of criminal intent. It sure would be nice to visit Rosie without pretending she didn't notice his constant disapproval. She sipped her coffee, thinking about how best to handle him later in the day at Rosie's. Just steering clear of him was a good start, and if they had occasion to speak, well, she'd pretend like nothing untoward happened last night at all. No silent embrace, no little kiss. Nothing at all. That was her plan, and she imagined he'd jump at the chance to go along with it.

Eleanor heard a rapping on the front door. Rising, she glanced through the side window and saw April on the porch holding a covered plate. She swung the door open, smiling. "Morning, April."

April held the plate out. "Hi sleepyhead, Rosie made muffins."

Eleanor took the plate and sniffed appreciatively. "They smell delicious."

Before April could answer, Scott appeared in the kitchen doorway. Barefoot, rumpled jeans riding low on his hips, he pulled his tee shirt over his head and bare chest before crossing the room. "Mornin'. What time is it?"

When April spied Scott, her mouth dropped open and she looked back and forth between Eleanor and Scott. Eleanor leaned to the left to see the clock on the wall in the kitchen. "Almost eleven thirty," she replied. "How did you sleep?"

"Great." He started down the stairs, raking his hands through his hair, eyeing April with interest. Eleanor followed his gaze and was amused to discover April standing dumbstruck. "April, I'd like you to meet my brother, Scott."

"Your brother!" April closed her mouth. "I thought---I thought---" She blushed prettily. "I didn't know you had a brother," she finally managed.

Eleanor didn't want to know what April's fertile mind had been thinking. "April is Rosie's oldest grandchild," she explained to Scott. Scott already knew a lot about Rosie from their late night of conversation.

"Hi, nice to meet you," Scott said.

April nodded, temporarily at a loss for words.

Eleanor viewed her with some amusement. "Would you like to come in?" she prompted her.

April snapped back to attention. "Oh, no, not – no," she managed. "But Rosie said come over whenever you can. She's got lots to tell you." She looked from Eleanor to Scott. "I know she'll want you to come, too. Please come." With a bemused smile, she backed up and departed.

Scott moved to the window to watch April leave, and then turned, smiling sheepishly. "I know I said I had to leave early to be at work for four, but maybe I could hang around just a little longer."

* * *

Tyler, arriving late at Rosie's house on Sunday, turned his truck into the driveway and sat for a long moment, hands on the steering wheel, wipers still sweeping. Nobody was outside so he could leave before he was noticed and no one would be the wiser. Join his family or put the truck into reverse? After a boring morning spent bumping around alone inside his house, he wasn't that enthused about joining his family, either. This restlessness wasn't any fun at all.

But he did want to see Eleanor; the sooner, the better, and this is where he would find her. Tyler was convinced that as soon as he saw her again, he'd be able to put his concerns about last night's odd reaction to rest. He figured the unexpected attraction he'd felt for her had more to do with Hope's wedding and her kindness toward Austin than anything else. It was just a reflex kind of thing, that's all, aggravated by the fact he was being so careful about women since he'd been home. He had to get out more, that was all there was to it. Accept some of the invitations that came his way. He didn't know what he had been waiting for; he wasn't going to find the right woman if he didn't look for her.

The sleepless hours had been spent reminding himself of the kind of woman he wanted, and of the land mines he was clearly going to encounter if he didn't nip this shifting relationship with Eleanor right in the bud. She was a walking recipe for disaster, that's what she was, from her sharp tongue and meltdown emotions to the fact she lived under the watchful eye of his grandmother. Tyler shuddered. For fourteen years, with the exception of his disastrous marriage, he'd successfully kept his grandmother and his personal life in two separate worlds. That's how it had to be, until he was one hundred percent convinced he'd found the right woman.

No matter what he told himself, though, he still had been unable to shake the mental picture of Eleanor leaning against the porch rail, stretching like a little kitten, accusing him of kissing her and daring him to do it again, all at the same time. So contrary; so typically Eleanor. A dowdy little librarian with the uncanny ability to hit every one of his switches.

So, he didn't want to go to Rosie's but he didn't want to stay home. He wanted to see Eleanor and at the same time he was uneasy about how he'd feel when he did. Finally he decided, the hell with it all, he'd postpone the inevitable and go for a long ride on the Harley in some other direction. Any other direction. A long, peaceful ride; just him and the bike and the wind and the road. He wanted some peace.

Tyler glared ruefully at the sky. But, no, of course he wouldn't get what he wanted. Damned contrary Louisiana weather; it began to pour down as soon as he set off, even while the sun shone, so instead of peace, all he got was wet, and now here he was after all. He killed the engine abruptly, freezing the wipers on their track across the windshield.

April burst through the azaleas, her arms shielding her head from the rain. She skidded to a breathless stop beside him, her face bright with excitement, as he eased from the cab. "Hi, Uncle Ty! Eleanor has company. It's her brother. He's gorgeous!" She made her announcement with undisguised glee.

"Oh?" Tyler elected not to pop her bubble by mentioning he already knew about Scott.

April nodded energetically. "I didn't even know Eleanor had a brother! They're coming over in a few minutes." She sped toward the house to impart her news to the rest of the family.

Tyler jammed his keys in his jeans pocket and glanced toward Eleanor's house. Should he go over and warn her that April was about to incite a riot of curiosity? He stood, oblivious to the rain, thinking about it. No, there was no point initiating anything; he'd see her soon enough. A smart man would hang loose, off to the side someplace. Use his big family for cover while he got a better handle on this dilemma.

He headed toward the house, wincing when he pushed open the kitchen door. It was bedlam inside. The women clogged the kitchen and breakfast area, and past them, Tyler could see his brothers and brothers-in-law lounging in the living room, guffawing over something on television. Nobody at all was supervising the kids, who were yelling and running around and between and under, adding to the chaos.

Nope. No way. It was too much. He wasn't in the mood. With a little bit of luck, he could slip back outside and make an escape. Trying to shrink, he turned on his heel to flee.

"Tyler!" Though he couldn't see her, Rosie's voice rose above the din.

Sighing, he stopped and turned back around, wearily forcing an imitation of a smile on his face.

Wiping her hands on a dish towel, Rosie met him at the doorway and tugged him down for a kiss. "I was beginning to worry about you. I tried phoning you this morning but it went to voice mail." She squinted at him speculatively. "And last night you didn't come back inside to say goodnight after you walked Eleanor home."

"Sorry, Rosie," was all he said, offering no explanation, looking over her head toward the living room. That's where he needed to be, in there, with the guys, where nobody cared about his comings and goings or whether he answered his phone or not.

Rosie's brow creased and he could tell she was trying to analyze his mood. Good luck, he thought wryly. She gazed at him a moment, then nudged him back through the door and onto the porch. "Come on, Ty, let's sneak out of this madhouse for a minute."

Tyler allowed her to propel him onto the porch. Rosie closed the kitchen door carefully and turned around, sighing. "If I'd had any clue it was going to rain, I think I would have told everyone to stay home." She reached up to brush at the drops of water on his shoulders. "You're all wet, honey. Let me go get a towel."

The noise inside was audible on the porch. Tyler jerked his head toward the door. "Do you really want to go back in there?"

Rosie shook her head emphatically. "Not really."

"Then stay out here with me." Relaxing marginally, Tyler leaned against the wall. "I doubt the rain will last much longer."

Rosie pushed the screened door open a crack and looked up at the sky. "I hope you're right." She closed the door and turned back to him. "April just told us Eleanor has company. " She tugged the small wooden step stool he'd built in high school from beneath the potting table and perched on it, waiting for his response.

Instead of being annoyed that Eleanor was the first topic Rosie chose to bring up, Tyler was almost relieved. He felt a little guilty about not returning last night to fill her in about Eleanor's reunion with her brother. "Actually, yes. He showed up last night. He was the one on her mystery motorcycle."

"Well, what do you know about that? Tell me what happened."

Tyler told her the whole story; how Eleanor recognized the sound of the motorcycle from a distance, his part in grabbing Scott, Scott's astonishing announcement, and Eleanor's elation at being reunited with her little brother. He wasn't surprised to see Rosie dab at the corner of her eye with the hem of her red shirt when he described Eleanor's need to pat her brother, to make sure he was really sitting beside her. "What do you know about her father?" he asked her when his story was finished. The little bit he'd learned last night really bugged him.

"Almost nothing. Eleanor doesn't bring him up. I do know he hasn't been over to see her one single time since she moved into the house. He doesn't sound like much of a prize to me."

That was an understatement. Tyler moved away from the kitchen door and tugged a threadbare lawn chair from the gap between the potting table and the porch wall. It had seen better days, and he sat in it cautiously. "Well, she's got her brother now, I guess."

"I'm happy about that." Rosie surveyed him thoughtfully. "You know, Ty, I couldn't help noticing last night that you two seem to have made your peace with one another."

Careful here. Rosie was fishing. Tyler nodded. "I guess." Rosie didn't respond and he realized she was waiting for more information. "It was nice of her to stay behind to look after Austin when she wanted to go to the wedding," he added lamely.

"You know, I wouldn't be a bit surprised if the next wedding we go to is hers," Rosie mused. "I wouldn't be surprised if she and her husband have a child right away, either."

Tyler gaped at his grandmother. In one short breath she had Eleanor tidily married off and already changing diapers.

"It does my heart good whenever I see Eleanor with the children," Rosie said. "She has a natural way with them, have you noticed? They love to see her coming."

"It's her hair," he said without thinking, distracted by the mental picture Rosie had conjured of Eleanor in a wedding gown. Or with a child propped on her hip. A little daughter with thick curls like her mother.

Rosie squinted at him. "It's what?"

"Her hair," he mumbled, studying his hands. "They like her hair."

Rosie looked at him pityingly, as though he were slow-witted. "It's not how she looks, it's how she acts. She talks to them, she listens to them, she loves to get down on the ground and play with them. Haven't you noticed?"

Yes, he'd noticed. Tyler's frown deepened. "Rosie, aren't you getting carried away? Eleanor doesn't even date." Not that his sisters and sisters-in-law weren't chomping at the bit to address that very problem, he thought sourly. Yesterday at the wedding reception, he'd overheard them batting around names of possible matches for Eleanor, as though it was their responsibility to fix her up. It occurred to him, with a nasty jolt; now that Hope's wedding was old news, they'd probably make Eleanor's love life their new, collective project.

Rosie brightened. "Oh, give her a little time. Earlier in the week we stopped by the bank on our way home from Leanne's, and she ran into someone she knew. A good looking fellow. I think he asked her out."

Tyler received Rosie's news with a distinct pang. Now that Eleanor was loosening up and had an appealing moment every now and then, he guessed it was only natural for men to glance her way. So, not only would his sisters and sisters-in-law be lining them up for her, she'd attract them all on her own. Rosie was right. She could be married within a year, a mother within two or so, and

Rosie would have the package unit of neighbors he had originally wanted. He should be glad. Why wasn't he?

"I truly believe it's just a matter of time," Rosie said with a convincing air. "Look," she said, rising and pushing the screen door open slightly. "You were right. I think it's stopped raining. Thank heavens. Let's get everybody outside, onto the deck." She slipped back inside the kitchen.

Tyler exhaled the long breath he didn't realize he'd been holding, rose and pushed through the screened porch door to walk outside onto the deck.

And ran smack into Eleanor, almost mowing her down in the process. Automatically he caught her in his arms before she stumbled, pulling her forward with his hands on her shoulders. "Ow," she said, muffled, pressed to his chest.

Scott stood a step behind his sister, and Tyler nodded to him over Eleanor's head as he steadied her before letting go. He stepped back a fraction and lifted her face with two fingers beneath her chin. "You okay?"

She nodded soundlessly, her green eyes wide.

As if they had a mind of their own, his fingers slid around the smooth curve of her jaw. She stood frozen, and he realized what he was doing. Touching her, for no good reason. Dropping his hand abruptly, Tyler stepped back. "You really ought to watch where you're going," he said weakly.

Eleanor narrowed her eyes but before she could respond, his gaze traveled down the length of her body and he received an unwelcome jolt. "What the hell are you wearing?"

A flash of uncertainty crossed Eleanor's face, and then she, predictably, lifted her chin. "What do you mean? I'm wearing clothes, genius."

He stepped back to get a better look. She had stopped dressing like she was going to a funeral all the time, but the little cropped blue shirt that didn't even met the top of her white shorts showed off a lot more than he was comfortable with. Careful, careful, he thought. Anything he said could start a fight.

"You have something else to say?" Eleanor tapped a small feet impatiently and planted her hands on her hips.

"No," he managed.

"Then move so we can go inside. I want everybody to meet Scott." Her belligerent stance hiked the hem of her shirt another fraction. Expression tightening, Tyler intentionally blocked the doorway. She couldn't go inside looking like that. He couldn't look at her all afternoon, with her looking like that.

Scott put his hand on Eleanor's elbow in a protective manner and surveyed Tyler silently as if to warn him not to think of getting personal with his sister. Tyler sighed. It sure hadn't taken long for the two of them to bond. Two green-eyed Haleys glaring at him. Great, just great. "How's it going, Scott," he said, holding out his hand.

Scott shook his hand solemnly. "Okay," he replied. "I think Eleanor looks just fine," he added, the glint in his eyes daring Tyler to disagree.

Eleanor gave her brother a bright smile. It was the same pleased smile she'd deposited on Tyler a time or two the night before, and he felt a little put out because it was aimed at someone else.

"You know, I think I'll keep you," she quipped to Scott as she elbowed past Tyler none too gently to get to the door. She gave Tyler a glance that clearly suggested nobody would be interested in keeping him. "Come on; come meet everyone."

Wincing, Tyler let her flounce past. He had nearly convinced himself that when he saw her again, he wouldn't be affected one way or another, but somehow he didn't think the overpowering need to pick her up, carry her home, and cover her from chin to ankle was a good sign. At all.

Chapter Twelve

If she didn't count Tyler's rude welcome, Eleanor would have to say her Sunday was about as good as it could get. The summertime air felt clean and sweet after the brief cloudburst, and the sunlight glinted off the damp grass. It was a little too soggy beneath the oak tree, though, so she and the rest of Rosie's crowd lounged on the deck instead, nibbling on a vast spread of leftover reception food and watching the children shriek and skid on a long wet strip of yellow plastic set out in the yard. A Slip'n'Slide, Austin importantly informed Eleanor from his seemingly permanent position on her lap. She may have missed the wedding but she clearly had a little pal for life, and she was convinced that, in the grand scheme of things, she'd come out on top. What's more, Rosie and the others seemed intent on spoiling her today as recompense for yesterday's little sacrifice, as if simply being with them wasn't reward enough.

The only unsettling note was the fact that, instead of steering clear of her like she expected, Tyler was always nearby. Almost underfoot, really, and several times she'd caught him eyeing her with a speculative gaze that made her pulse skip a little.

The easy conversation revolved around Scott's homecoming and the events of Hope and Adam's wedding and reception. Eleanor was proud of Scott's relaxed demeanor and good manners when she introduced him to Rosie and the other adults. They accepted him immediately, without any long explanations on Eleanor's part, as though there was nothing at all unusual about his sudden appearance. Scott stayed by Eleanor's side for a little while, then wandered off, ostensibly to get a closer look at the Slip'n'Slide. Eleanor wasn't surprised when she saw April meander after him, and she shared a little smile with Rosie, who sat beside her.

"Smell that?" Rosie leaned back and inhaled deeply.

Eleanor sniffed obediently. "Smell what?"

"Romance. It's in the air." Rosie leaned back, looking very pleased with herself.

Leanne and Robb, pulling up chairs beside Rosie and Eleanor, shared wry smiles. "Scott's a very nice boy," Leanne said, and Robb concurred.

Eleanor smiled, delighted they agreed with her own evaluation. "I'm trying to convince him to move in with me," she confided.

"So what's preventing him?" Leanne asked.

"He thinks he'd be imposing even though I keep telling him nothing would make me happier. I have plenty of room. Plus he's worried about finding a job."

"A job, huh?" Robb chewed his lip thoughtfully. "Well, that's easy to fix." Rising, he winked at Eleanor, and then strode across the deck and down the steps toward the teenagers.

Eleanor lifted a puzzled brow. "What's he doing?"

"Stealing my thunder," Leanne said with a mock frown.

Eleanor didn't get it. "Excuse me?"

"Offering him a job," Leanne clarified. "Before I even had a chance."

Eleanor gaped at Leanne, then Rosie. "Just like that?"

Turning to watch Robb cross the lawn, Rosie squeezed Eleanor's hand. "Why not? That's what families are for. And if Scott doesn't want to work at one of the nurseries, there's always plenty of work at the animal hospital or Joel's office or Allie's boutique. A job is the least of Scott's worries, believe me."

Eleanor felt a lump form in her throat at Rosie's breezy inference that she and Scott were family. She turned to watch Robb cross the lawn and approach the teenagers. Tyler crossed the deck and drew to a halt at her side, but her attention was riveted on the scene playing out on the lawn. Straightening, Scott wiped his hands on his jeans and nodded at something Robb said. Eleanor couldn't see Robb's face or hear their conversation, but judging from the look of surprise on Scott's face, followed swiftly by an emphatic nod, a wide grin and a firm handshake, she figured the job offer had been extended and accepted, and she was that much closer to achieving her goal of permanently reinstating Scott into her life. She hugged her arms around her waist and said a silent prayer of thanks as Scott shook Robb's hand a second time, shared a smile with April, and began walking toward Eleanor. Behind him, Robb gave Eleanor and Rosie a thumbs-up. Eleanor beamed at him in return.

"Guess what?" Scott called. "Mr. Hurst just offered me a job at his nursery."

She twisted around on the bench, shifting Austin on her lap. "You don't say! When do you start?"

He shifted from one foot to the other. "Right away, if you're serious about me moving in with you."

"I'll tell you how serious I am," Eleanor replied, her smile erupting into a full-fledged grin. "Why don't you take my car and go get your stuff?"

Tyler laughed out loud, startling Eleanor. "Your car? That's a good one. He couldn't fit much into your little car."

Eleanor stiffened and turned to glare up at him. "He can fit a lot more in my car than he can onto his motorcycle."

"Well, I'm not denying that, honey---" He broke off, his eyes widening in playful horror at the accidental endearment. She ignored the thrill his deep drawl sent charging down her spine, and pressed her lips together. "Sorry about that." He winked at her, effectively erasing the probability of any true repentance on his part. "But wouldn't a truck be better?"

"Oh! Here's an idea." Rosie appeared at Eleanor's side. "Why not let Scott use your truck, Tyler? He could drive it back tonight, pack his things, and come back tomorrow." Rosie nodded in satisfaction as though the matter were settled.

Eleanor shook her head swiftly. "Thanks, Rosie, but it's out of the question---"

"Great idea, Rosie." Tyler interrupted her easily.

Eleanor looked at Tyler with astonishment. This was a severe infraction of his own rule regarding favors.

"What do you say, Scott?" Tyler lifted a questioning brow. "Sound like a plan to you?"

Scott glanced back and forth between Eleanor and Tyler, clearly hesitant to accept the offer until Eleanor gave him a sign of approval. "I don't know," he said cautiously. "What do you think, Eleanor?"

"She thinks it's a wonderful idea," Rosie interjected. "Don't you, honey?"

Eleanor studied Tyler for a long moment. He gazed back blandly. Nobody else seemed to realize the significance of his offer. Eleanor hadn't thought, earlier, that it would be possible to feel any happier, but now she knew she'd been wrong. "My car is small," she agreed.

Rosie nodded emphatically. "Much too small, honey."

"Practically useless," Tyler added mildly. "Might as well drive a bumper car."

"Enough, already," she said, her happiness leaking out in the form of a silly grin. "You've made your point."

* * *

In no time, Scott was preparing to leave. "Be careful," Eleanor told him for at least the third or fourth time as she reached up to give him one more hug.

"Don't worry, Eleanor, I will. I'll be back early tomorrow. Thanks again, Ty." Scott shook Tyler's hand for at least the third or fourth time before closing the door.

"You're welcome," Tyler replied easily.

Eleanor gave Scott a little wave as he slowly backed the truck down the driveway, then she and Tyler walked to the end of the driveway to watch him disappear down the street. Tyler stood behind her, so close that if she leaned back just a little bit, she could probably rest against his solidness. Suddenly feeling a little tired, a little anxious, a little emotional at watching her brother drive away---Eleanor wished she had the right to lean back and rest against him. She stepped away to remove the temptation and turned around to face him. "He'll be careful."

"I know," Tyler replied. "I wouldn't have offered the truck if I didn't think he was responsible."

"Last night you thought he was dangerous," she reminded him, wrapping her arms around her waist.

Tyler shrugged. "I still think inviting him to spend the night was a little rash but things turned out okay." He tossed his key ring, minus one key, from hand to hand. "I need a ride home."

His comment didn't register right away. Eleanor watched the truck turn at the corner and roll out of sight.

"I need a ride home," he repeated.

Eleanor shielded her eyes from the sun's glare to look up at his face. "You want me to take you home?"

"Seems fair," he replied mildly. "Rosie didn't think you'd mind, but if it's too much trouble---" He trailed off smoothly, one blond eyebrow arched questioningly.

Eleanor stepped back some more and studied him. It would be pretty ill-mannered of her to balk at taking him home, considering her brother just drove off in his vehicle. "No, it's not too much trouble," she replied slowly. "Do you want to go right this very minute?"

He nodded.

How odd. He was usually the last to leave. "Okay, then. Just let me go tell everyone bye."

"Tell you what, you go get your car and I'll say goodbye for both of us," he said, turning on his heel. "Don't be long."

Eleanor stared at his rapidly retreating back, torn between vexation at his high-handedness and a tiny swell of anticipation.

Pivoting on one foot, he turned and walked backwards. "Don't just stand there," he called. "Go on, get your bumper car."

Eleanor bit back a smile. Sheer minutes later, heart thumping from her haste to collect keys and purse and sunglasses---at least that's what she told herself---she backed her car down her driveway and rolled forward to Rosie's drive where Tyler waited, his eyes shielded by his sunglasses. He opened the small car door and peered inside. "This thing's even smaller than I thought. Let's take Rosie's car."

"Oh, no," she replied promptly. "Get in. I insist."

Tyler obeyed, gingerly folding his long legs beneath the dash. He squinted at her, the corners of his mouth tilting. "You're enjoying this, aren't you?"

She nodded merrily.

Fastening his seat belt, Tyler flashed a grin. "Top speed's what – forty?"

"Quit maligning my car," she said sternly. "It fits me just right. I drove a big old Volvo until I got tired of police officers pulling me over all the time to make sure I wasn't some twelve year old kid out joyriding."

He chuckled.

"I really do appreciate you lending Scott your truck, Tyler." She was still a bit astonished by his careless generosity. It was the kind of thing he did for his family all the time, but she never expected him to make such an offer to her brother.

"No big deal," he replied.

It was a big deal to her, but he didn't seem inclined toward a lot of conversation so Eleanor concentrated on her driving. At the first traffic light, a low slung sports car rolled to a stop beside them and Eleanor automatically glanced over. The driver, an attractive dark haired man, looked back with undisguised interest. He smiled at her, then blinked and abruptly returned his attention to the road. Puzzled, Eleanor glanced at Tyler. He had pulled off his sunglasses and was eyeing the other man, expression forbidding and eyes narrowed.

"Stop that," she hissed automatically.

"I'm not doing anything," he replied, sliding his glasses back on his nose, clearly satisfied. He pointed a lazy finger toward the traffic light. "Green means go."

"I know that," she retorted, jerking forward with a screech.

"You have anything going on this afternoon?" He asked the question carelessly, his attention seemingly focused on the rapidly passing scenery on the right.

She shot a sideways glance at him. Earlier she thought she'd march herself right on over to her father's house to demand some answers, but right now she was feeling a little too happy to think about him. "I don't know," she answered vaguely, zipping her car onto the interstate. "Why do you ask?"

"I'm hungry. Want to stop and get something to eat?"

"But there was a ton of food at Rosie's, Tyler."

He grimaced. "I don't want leftover wedding stuff. I want real food." He lifted his sunglasses with a finger and peered at her. "Ever had tamales from Lupitas?"

Last time she looked, tamales weren't exactly real food, either. "No, can't say as I have."

He dropped his sunglasses back down on his nose. "You're in for a real treat, then. How about we pick up a couple dozen?"

She slanted another look at him. "I got the impression you were in a real hurry to get home, like you had something planned."

"Eleanor, you know I love my family, but if I had to spend one more minute with them today, listening to a rehash of the wedding, I promise you I'd go stark raving mad and it wouldn't be a pretty sight. Take this exit," he directed her, pointing to the right. Eleanor veered off obediently, astonished by his heartfelt remark. "It's up a couple of blocks; see the sign?" She followed his directions, pulled into a graveled parking lot beside an unpretentious building, and watched silently as he struggled to unbuckle his seat belt and unfold himself from the car. "I'll be right back." He rounded the car on his way to the building.

"Tyler, wait." She simply couldn't help herself. She had to ask.

He drew to a halt beside her door, an eyebrow tilted in question.

"Do you mean to say you'd rather spend your afternoon with me than with your family?" As soon as the words slipped out, she wished she could yank them back. He was hungry, he was polite, and she was his ride home.

Tyler gazed at her inscrutably for a moment, then reached in and gave her braid, resting over her shoulder, a gentle, playful tug. "You got that right, honey."

Eleanor gripped the wheel so tightly her fingernails dug into her palms.

"Dammit, I'm still having trouble with that," he said with a wink. "Sorry." He turned and strolled toward the shabby restaurant.

"It's okay," she managed. She guessed he could call her honey, if he really wanted to. Since he was having so much trouble with it and all.

* * *

Eleanor followed his directions and drove her car down a long, curving driveway to an enormous stucco home with a slate roof. It was huge and modern and not a little impressive. Tyler led the way from the triple garage to a covered walkway and through a wrought iron gate. Eleanor marveled at the expanse of patio, a pool, and a ridiculously green lawn that bordered a golf course. Tyler handed her the thick brown paper bag he'd carried out of Lupitas and unlocked the glass back door. "Come on in."

Eleanor followed him through the doorway and into the kitchen. She set the paper bag on a wide marble topped island and looked around. Tyler's house could have been lifted straight from the pages of an architectural magazine. Massive honey-colored timbers stretched high across the lofty ceiling of the great room. Bright sunlight poured through two levels of wide windows and a whole series of French doors. Three huge clear stained glass panels, a simple but majestic design of mountains and water and sky, hung in the second level windows. Tyler's furniture was simple, but plainly first class, and oversized enough to suit him. She walked farther into the living area and craned her head upwards to admire the timber-railed loft.

All this space for one man. Rosie certainly hadn't exaggerated when she said Tyler had done well playing professional football. Eleanor felt extreme admiration for the young boy who had set a remarkable goal for himself and achieved it. Which made her realize; what she didn't see, anywhere, was anything remotely related to football. She wasn't really surprised because, while the others loved to expound on his achievements, Tyler didn't talk about his career.

"Something to drink? He peered into his refrigerator. "Beer? Wine?" She hesitated and he noticed. He withdrew two bottles and held them up. "Root beer?"

"Root beer, please." He walked to her, stride loose and confident, and handed her one of the bottles. He seemed so much more in his element here than he did in Rosie's compact home, she mused. Even bigger, too, she mused, tugging at the hem of her shorts uncomfortably.

"Want the grand tour?"

"Sure," she replied. "This is some place." And that was some understatement.

"Yeah, it's okay." Tyler drank half of his root beer in one long swallow.

Eleanor watched his tanned throat working and went a little wobbly. Get a grip, she admonished herself. Don't look at him. Look someplace else. She crossed the room hastily to investigate a telescope positioned beside one of the windows. "You don't sound very enthusiastic."

Tyler finished off the root beer, leaned to place the bottle on the coffee table, and shrugged. "I can't get used to it. I liked it at first because it reminded me of my old place but the view's all wrong." He ate up the space between them in three long strides. "It doesn't get much flatter than that, does it?" he asked wryly, nodding outside.

Eleanor couldn't hold back a smile at his plaintive tone. "A bit flatter than the Rockies. I can see why you might be having problems adjusting."

"That's not all," he said slowly, pushing his hands into his jeans pockets. "I'm here too much."

Eleanor detected a different note in his voice, and she turned to look at him. Squinting slightly, he seemed to be studying the view but she suspected his mind was somewhere miles away. "Here too much?" she asked, prompting him. "How can that be? You're at Rosie's too much."

Tyler grinned at her sassy remark. "Hey, remember last time you were here you wouldn't get out of the truck?"

"Oh, I remember," she retorted, trying to hide her smile as she pretended to examine the settings on the telescope. "I also remember why. Something to do with being trapped inside your truck." He didn't offer a quick reply so she looked up to gauge his reaction, and found him studying her, his hazel eyes almost golden in the bright, airy room. "What?" she asked abruptly, suddenly uncomfortable again. "I'm not mad about it anymore."

Tyler gazed at her a long, silent moment. "It occurs to me I've got some apologizing to do," he said simply. "I'm thinking about where I ought to begin, and I'm ashamed I've got so many choices."

"Is that so," she murmured, taken aback.

Tyler nodded. "If I started with today and worked backwards, I'd apologize for criticizing your clothes." He swept her up and down with an appreciative gaze. "You look great, by the way."

Eleanor stared up at him, speechless. An apology and a compliment.

He gave her a slow smile. "If I started at the beginning, I'd apologize for calling you clumsy."

"Twice," she managed; suddenly shy under his warm gaze.

His grin broadened. "Twice," he agreed. "And there's so much more, in the middle---," he broke off and sighed deeply with affected chagrin. "Can't I just issue a blanket apology for everything?"

"That would be letting you off really easy," she murmured, tilting the telescope and peering through the eyepiece. "I don't know."

"Wouldn't it be nice to start off fresh? Let bygones be bygones?" Edging a little closer, he lifted her long braid and toyed with the curling end.

"I just don't know," Eleanor repeated, torn between confused delight and sheer panic. "I can't see anything out of your telescope. Does this thing work?"

"You're trying to change the subject." He pushed the telescope away and lifted her chin with his hand. "How about it? Give a guy a break here."

A girl couldn't say no to those green-gold eyes. "Oh, all right," she said breathlessly, curling her hands into fists to keep from sliding them up the broad chest that was only an inch away. She had to remind herself, adamantly, that he was only trying to make amends, not inviting her to think of him as her own personal playground. "You're forgiven."

"Great!" Tyler immediately moved away, proving her own point. "Come on, let me show you around." He led the way toward a wide hallway off the living area. She followed obediently. "My office," he said, gesturing toward a room on the right. Eleanor took a quick peek. Ah, so this was where he kept his memorabilia. Behind a massive leather-topped partner's desk, a lighted glass case was filled to bursting with trophies and balls. Framed photographs and more mementos crowded the walls. Eleanor was surprised when Tyler continued down the hallway, apparently uninterested in showing off his prizes. She hung back in the doorway and he turned questioningly.

"Can't I look at your stuff?" She'd done a little homework since the day Tyler accurately accused her of knowing less than nothing about football. It hadn't taken much research at all to figure out that his fourteen year career was nothing to take lightly.

Tyler seemed taken aback. "Sure, if you want to." He returned, flipping the light switch. "I didn't think you'd be interested."

"Why not?" She smiled at him. "I know more than you think I know."

He angled a lean hip against his desk, his half-smile clearly conveying his amused skepticism. "Oh, really?"

"A defensive end is positioned on the farthest end of the defensive line, next to the tackles, hence the name," she recited, "and his job is to minimize the amount of time the quarterback has to find an open receiver." She gave him a smug look. "What do you think about that?"

He grinned. "I think somebody's been studying."

"Yes, I have," she admitted. "I found a very helpful book titled 'Football for Dummies.'"

"There's a book called 'Football for Dummies?'" Tyler laughed out loud, a wonderful sound that sent ripples of delight down Eleanor's spine.

"Yep. I can talk football with anybody now. Ask me about zone defense or encroachment. Special teams or penalties. Ask me anything." Eleanor leaned against the cabinet; her hands clasped behind her hips, and dared him with a smile.

Tyler's smile disappeared. He pushed away from the desk and took a purposeful step in her direction, then stopped abruptly. "Let's save this for some other time, okay? There's something else I want to show you." He turned on his heel and moved to the doorway, turning off the overhead light.

Perplexed by Tyler's lightening-swift mood change and curious start-and-stop trek across the room, Eleanor slowly followed him down the hallway. Well ahead of her, he pushed another door open and stood back to let her pass. She looked around with interest. It was a workroom of sorts, with more wall to wall windows overlooking the golf course, dominated by a large, plain worktable in the center of the room. A curious assortment of tools were scattered on the tabletop, and a frame on one end held pieces of glass fitted together like pieces of a jigsaw puzzle. Eleanor stepped up to the table curiously. The colors of the glass in the frame were very familiar, and the number '421' was worked into the design. Her house number. She turned and stared at Tyler in awe. "You made the window in my front door, didn't you?"

"Yep."

"And the one hanging in your living room."

"Yep."

"I had no idea," she murmured, standing on her toes and arching forward to get a better look. "You're very talented."

Tyler pulled the board closer to the edge of the table and angled it so she could see it fully. "This is designed to fit into the small window beside your front door."

He must have started it when he still thought Hope was moving in. "I see," she said softly. She would treasure her glass door panel more than ever, knowing Tyler had crafted it with his own hands. A football player and an artist. He had many more facets than she had given him credit for.

"Want me to finish it?" He presented the question casually, laying the board back down.

She beamed at him. "Oh, yes, Tyler, but only if it's not too much trouble." She stroked the glass. "I don't want to be too much trouble."

"You've been too much trouble since the day you fell into the bushes, Eleanor," he replied slowly.

Eleanor felt her pulse begin to speed up under his solemn scrutiny and disquieting remark. She drew in a shaky breath and looked away, at a loss for a response. "I never meant to be," she said quietly.

He said nothing. He just looked at her, his eyes oddly narrowed.

"What's this?" she asked hastily, pointing to a piece of equipment on the table in a vain attempt to fill the charged silence.

He glanced at the table. "That's a grinder."

"What does it do?"

"It grinds. We have a problem, Eleanor."

She looked up at him, wide-eyed and more confused by the moment. "We do? What is it?"

He studied her for another long minute and then exhaled a long breath she didn't even know he was holding. "The tamales are getting cold. Come on, let's go eat," he said, pointedly nodding toward the hallway.

She obediently led the way back down the hall and through the great room. "What's up there?" she asked, waving a hand toward the loft.

"Bedrooms," he replied tersely, passing her on his way back to the kitchen.

She guessed the tour was over, and wondered what she'd done to make his mood shift. She followed him into the kitchen area. Rounding the island, he tore open the bag and began unfolding the layers of heavy paper insulating the hot tamales. For a simple task it seemed to take all his attention. Maybe he was trying to think of a way to speed through the meal and get her out of there. She decided to make it easy on them both.

"You know, I think I'm going to pass, Tyler."

He looked up, his expression unreadable. "What do you mean? You said you didn't have anything to do this afternoon."

Eleanor shrugged. "I'm tired. You know, yesterday, last night, Scott, you, me, everything---," she rambled and trailed off quietly, cursing her runaway tongue. She could have gone all day and left out the 'you-me' reference. Maybe he wouldn't notice.

Abandoning his task, Tyler circled the island slowly and drew to a halt inches away. "'You-me'?" he asked guardedly.

She couldn't look at him. She looked down at her sandals instead.

"I thought things were okay between us."

"They are," she agreed quickly. "Absolutely okay."

Tyler hunkered down, balancing easily; his hands braced his thighs, and looked up at Eleanor, studying her downcast face for a long minute. "So what's the deal? What's going on inside that head of yours, Eleanor?"

She wasn't the one having mood swings. "Get up from there, silly," she said lightly, trying to back away. He was entirely too close and yet completely, painfully, out of her reach. She looked over her shoulder to judge the distance to the door.

And felt a large warm hand on the back of her leg, pulling her closer, between his knees, wrecking her plan to escape. She froze, her gaze still turned longingly toward the door. With one light finger, Tyler turned her face, forcing her to meet his gaze. "But I don't want you to go."

Eleanor stared at him.

"I got all those hot tamales."

She bit back a strangled laugh.

"Friends don't leave friends alone with three dozen hot tamales," he continued. "I'd be forced to eat them all. Do you want my heartburn on your conscience?"

"Oh, all right," she said, torn between laughter and frustration. "I'll stay a little while longer."

Chapter Thirteen

Close call. Tyler rounded the island, astonished by the wave of relief he felt at convincing Eleanor to stay. It was no surprise she tried to bolt, as odd as he was acting. He dumped the hot tamales onto a platter and stuffed the heavy paper into the trash. He hardly recognized himself, running at the mouth about hot tamales.

But the important thing was to keep her there, at least until he decided what he wanted to do with her. Tyler grimaced. Wrong mental picture. He knew exactly what he wanted to do with her, but this was Eleanor. Things weren't simple. He had to keep reminding himself he couldn't just take her upstairs and then send her on home like he might have in the past. He'd had a dangerously close call back in his office, though. When she told him she'd been studying football, it had been all he could do not throw his misgivings out the window, charge across the room and haul her upstairs where he had all manners of rewards in mind for her adorable effort. He'd actually taken steps in her direction before his brain prevailed. And then in his workshop, when she said he was talented in that low, husky voice, well, he wanted to show her just how talented he was in other areas. He'd actually started to say something then, but, thank God, reason kicked in.

He had to continuously remind himself he'd be crazy to start something with Eleanor.

"Can I help?"

Shaking his head, Tyler grabbed plates and set them on top of the island. "There's nothing to do. You sit right there." He pushed the platter of tamales toward her before withdrawing two more bottles of root beer from the refrigerator. Was that everything? He hesitated, a bottle of root beer in each hand, to survey the spread, and felt a sinking sensation in his stomach. This was the best he could do---a pile of greasy hot tamales? It was pathetic. He was pathetic. He should have taken her out to eat someplace nice like he originally planned when he maneuvered her into giving him a ride home. He would have, too, if it hadn't been for the ass at the traffic light who couldn't keep his eyes in their sockets. Tyler had realized, right then and there, he couldn't deal with other guys ogling Eleanor, in a restaurant or anyplace else, and he knew they would---she was such a sweet eyeful in her little shirt and shorts. At the time, inviting her into his house seemed like a good idea. Now it seemed like criminal stupidity.

"Napkins."

Eleanor's comment startled Tyler from his musings. "What's that?"

She was eyeing the mountain of tamales skeptically. "There's a good chance we'll need napkins."

Of course, napkins. Tyler opened the pantry and pulled out a new roll of paper towels, then joined her at the end of the island. "I don't have cloth napkins like Rosie," he said somewhat defensively.

Eleanor smiled at him. "Neither do I."

With that one little smile she managed to soothe his uneasiness. She was a good sport. He liked that about her. Some of the prima donnas he'd dated would have pitched a screaming fit at the very thought of eating greasy food off paper plates at a kitchen counter. They wanted to be seen at trendy restaurants or hot clubs, and if there was any part of his house they were interested in, it generally wasn't the kitchen. Not that he made a habit of bringing women to his house; his house was pretty much hands-off to anybody but his closest friends and family.

And now, Eleanor. Sliding onto the stool beside hers, he tugged the platter nearer, and deposited three tamales onto her plate. "So," he began, determined to regain some control---of the conversation, if nothing else. He went straight to the topic that had been bugging him since the night before. "What's the story on your father?"

Grimacing, Eleanor immediately pushed two of the three hot tamales back onto the platter. "Do we have to talk about him?"

Better that than a continuing dialogue on hot tamales. Tyler plowed on. "Oh, come on. You know all about my family." He twisted the cap off a bottle of root beer and passed it to her.

Eleanor made a face. "Your family's different. I already told you that."

"How so?"

"For one thing, you like one another."

Tyler stopped and looked at her closely. "Come on."

"I'm a big disappointment." she said mildly, her attention focused on the single hot tamale in the center of her plate. She picked up her fork and prodded it doubtfully.

Startled, Tyler lifted an eyebrow in question. "I'm sure you're not."

"It's true," she insisted. "My first mistake was being a girl. He wanted a son, so you can imagine his disappointment to be presented with a four pound daughter. And then to make matter worse, my mother never came home from the hospital. She died from complications and there he was, stuck with a sickly daughter. Not a happy camper."

Tyler frowned. He didn't know what he liked less; her words or the carefully nonchalant way she spoke them.

"That's why I'm so baffled about his response to Scott." Eleanor's brow creased. "I vividly recall how pleased he was when Scott was born. I never knew the story of what happened between him and Monica---my stepmother---," she clarified unnecessarily, "but I always assumed he looked after Scott at least financially, if nothing else. It's not like he couldn't afford to. I see now I should have asked more questions. I'm going to go see him." She laid her fork down and tapped the tamale experimentally with one pink-tipped finger. "I'm going to get some answers." She looked like she'd rather be beaten with a paddle than confront her father. Tyler felt a trickle of anger on her behalf.

She studied the hot tamale, poked it with her fork again, and then lifted amused green eyes. "I don't want to hurt your feelings, Tyler, but this thing doesn't look very good. It's greasy and the crust is too tough."

Tyler decided to go along with her obvious attempt to distract him. "It's wrapped in a corn husk, honey. Look." He deftly unwrapped it and speared part of the previously concealed tamale with his fork. "Come on, try it." He carried the fork to her mouth. "One bite. If you don't like it, we'll eat something else." He realized belatedly he'd called her honey again but she didn't seem to notice. It was a good thing, since the endearment seemed to be rolling off his tongue with increasing regularity.

"One bite," she agreed, her nose wrinkled as she cautiously accepted his offering. Tyler bit back a smile of amusement when her eyes lit up. "Well," she said approvingly, "it definitely tastes better than it looks."

Tyler speared another bite for her. He figured he could sit there and hand feed her little bites all day long if it made her happy.

Eleanor shook her head and held out her plate instead. "Pile 'em on," she said. "And now let's talk about you."

"What about me?" Tyler began working on the half dozen tamales on his own plate.

"Tell me about your life in Colorado."

Tyler flinched in spite of himself. Lately he'd been going to great pains to avoid thinking about his previous life, not that it did much good. "Very different from here," he finally replied.

"I imagine." She unwrapped a second tamale and examined the corn husk with interest. "I bet it was hard being so far away, especially at first. I bet you hated being away from your family. You were how old? Nineteen? Twenty?"

He blinked. The only other person who really knew how hard it had been to move away was Rosie. Other people, even his brothers and sisters, had been carried away by the dazzle of his future and figured he was as thrilled as they were. "You'd win those bets," he replied simply.

"Rosie said you were in school at LSU when you were---," she hesitated. "Nominated?"

Tyler grinned. "Drafted, honey. Drafted."

Eleanor waved her fork dismissively. "Drafted. So you didn't get your degree."

She sure didn't mind digging up bones. He still had regrets about dropping out of LSU. "It was the right decision."

She nodded thoughtfully. "What did you like most about playing?"

"I liked making a lot of money." Tyler expected Eleanor to frown at him for his blunt reply but she surprised him by nodding again.

"To take care of your family," she concluded for him. "But did you ever resent the situation you were in? That you had to move away?"

Tyler sighed. No such thing as a simple conversation with Eleanor. "I resented losing my parents and I resented some other things that happened along the way, but I never resented Rosie or my brothers and sisters, if that's what you mean." He hoped she didn't ask for clarification on 'other things.' He for damned sure didn't want to talk about his experiences with thieving attorneys or his disastrous marriage.

"You gave up a lot to take care of them." She studied him admiringly.

Tyler shook his head dismissively. "Come on, let's face it, there are a lot worse ways to earn a living than by playing a game."

"A game," she repeated thoughtfully. "Did you think of it as just a game? It seems like pretty serious stuff to me. I read somewhere that a man who plays just one professional football game will never be physically fit again."

Tyler was taken aback. "Did you read that in your dummy book?"

Eleanor completely missed his reproving tone. "If not there, someplace else," she replied carelessly. "I told you I've been doing a lot of reading on the subject." She began cutting her third tamale into perfectly uniform pieces. "I imagine the more games you play, the more damage is done. Rosie says you hardly ever missed a game."

He blinked at her cleverly camouflaged insult. "Is that so?" He leaned forward and stilled her hand as it aimed for the tamale. "Do I look physically unfit to you, Eleanor?"

"Rosie says your knees hurt all the time, and I've noticed how often you rub your neck and shoulder. She says you should own stock in Icy Hot."

"Oh, really."

"Rosie also says you've dislocated your shoulders more times than she can remember. By the way, what's the difference between a dislocated shoulder and a separated shoulder? She says you've done that, too."

Rosie talked too damned much. Tyler leaned forward, still holding her hand captive. "Eleanor, do I look physically unfit to you?"

Unhearing, she pursed her lips together thoughtfully. "And I've seen, for myself, how slowly you get up sometimes. Just like an old man."

He narrowed his eyes. An old man? He'd like to see an old man who could bench press three hundred and ten pounds.

"Then there are your headaches. Have you ever had a concussion?" Eleanor looked worried at the possibility. "I've read about quarterbacks who can't remember their names for days after being hit."

Just who in the hell did she think was hitting the quarterbacks? "Eleanor," he began mildly. "I asked you a---"

"Because that would explain your headaches."

"Eleanor, did your books tell you what this means?" He jabbed his right hand fingers into the palm of his left hand.

"It means 'time out!" She looked positively joyous at the opportunity to expound on her newfound knowledge. "Each team is allotted three time outs per half and they're used for regrouping and planning strategy."

"Exactly right, honey," he said, amused and irritated all at once. "I'm calling one right now. Be quiet for a minute. I asked you a question."

"I heard it," she retorted, pulling her hand away. "I just didn't want to hurt your feelings by answering it, that's all."

He lifted his eyebrows in surprise. "What the hell is that supposed to mean?"

Eleanor shook her head sorrowfully. "I'm the very first to admit you've held up well externally, Tyler, but let's face it. Basically you're a human car wreck. Rosie says you've got more pins in your joints than a pincushion." She raised one of her perfectly proportioned bites of tamale to her mouth.

Held up well externally? A human car wreck? Tyler's mouth fell open, and that was when he spied the smile playing around the corners of Eleanor's mouth. She had been playing him. He bit back a smile of his own. "You're messing with me," he said accusingly.

"Who me?" Eleanor gave him a close-to-perfect innocent, perplexed look, then grinned and gave herself away.

Tyler tried hard to look disgruntled. "Better be careful. You might start something you can't finish."

"Yeah, yeah, right. Had you going, though, didn't I?" Clearly pleased with herself, she carried another bite to her mouth. "You should've seen the look on your face."

It was her face he was interested in; her dainty heart-shaped face, her green eyes sparkling with mischief. Her tempting little mouth. A warning bell went off in his head, bellowing he was about to mess up. Tyler ignored it. "Come here," he said soberly, catching her hand.

Her smile stilled. "What?"

"Come here," he repeated, tugging her hand gently. "Closer."

Eleanor obediently, albeit hesitantly, leaned toward him.

"Got a little bit of something here," he lied, stroking the corner of her soft mouth with the pad of his thumb. Her skin was soft as silk. "There, all gone."

"Thank you," she whispered, running her tongue over the spot he'd touched.

Her innocent gesture sent a bolt of desire coursing through him. He wasn't hungry anymore, not for food. He wanted Eleanor. He might as well admit it. He might as well deal with it. "You remember talking about the two of us getting off to a fresh start?"

She nodded as she reached for fourth tamale; apparently uncaring that he still had possession of her hand. "Of course."

Tyler balked. Once he set off down this path, there would be no turning back. Did he really want to do this? There would be nothing casual about a relationship with Eleanor. He reminded himself of all the problems that would fall in his lap if he insisted on pursuing this course of action; if he insisted on pursuing her. He clamped his mouth shut.

"And now you've changed your mind?" She slanted a teasing smile in his direction.

Things were happening too fast, and nothing was going according to plan. Instead of the nice, easygoing girl he figured he'd eventually find, here he was, twisting in the wind over his grandmother's pet project. He didn't know what scared him more; the fact that Eleanor and Rosie seemed to keep no secrets from one another, or the prospect of trying to sneak in and out of Eleanor's house. He didn't want to have to explain himself to Rosie, and he didn't want Rosie to get any ideas. She didn't understand casual relationships and he wasn't ready for anything more. Was he willing to give up the little bit of privacy he'd managed to retain since moving back home?

Eleanor's expression tensed. "Tyler?"

Tyler shuddered. No, he wasn't. He had enough problems right now just trying to figure out what he was going to do with the rest of his life without complicating things further.

"Tyler."

That's what Eleanor was, a complication he couldn't afford.

But maybe there was a way around it. Maybe he could explain to Eleanor how it would be in both their best interests to keep their private business---private. It could work. He felt suddenly optimistic. Sure, it could work. She probably didn't want his family in the middle of her personal business, either.

Eleanor laid her fork down and began to pry at the fingers clamped around her hand. "Tyler, you're hurting me."

Her words cut through his fog of panicky rumination like a stiletto. Tyler cursed and jerked his hand away, horrified.

"I won't kid you anymore about being weak or unfit, I promise," she managed to joke as she gingerly waggled her fingers.

Damn it. He could easily have broken every bone in her hand. He rose abruptly, his bar stool screeching in protest as he kicked it away. Eleanor gave a little gasp when he hooked the leg of her stool with a booted foot and pulled it away from the island, then went still with surprise as he effortlessly scooped her up and carried her, cradled against his chest, across the expanse of floor toward a deep leather sofa.

"What are you doing?" she squeaked, clutching at his tee shirt.

Making a big mistake but what the hell. Tyler sank onto the sofa with every intention of shifting Eleanor to his side, but somehow or another she ended up in his lap, her back resting against his chest. He expected her to simultaneously slap him and leap away, but after a long, frozen moment, she surprised him by drawing up her slim, bare legs and, if anything, nestling closer into the curve of his arm. Well, okay. Tyler exhaled carefully. No big deal. They could probably sit this way for a second. Just a second, though. Just long enough for him to reassure himself he hadn't hurt her. "Let me take a look at your hand, honey."

She lifted the offended item to his nose for his inspection. "It's okay," she said in a comforting tone. "See?"

Tyler slipped an arm around her waist just to give her a little support. He liked how she felt, light as a feather yet warm and snug against him, the tiny wisps of hair that had escaped her braid, tickling his jaw. "Are you sure?" He caught her hand, gently massaging her delicate little fingers. His mouth was inches away from her ear so he spoke in a low tone. A dainty little ear, perfectly shaped. "I could have really hurt you."

Eleanor silently flattened her hand against his, palm to palm. The tips of her fingers barely reached his knuckle joints. The unlikely juxtaposition of her flawless, pale little hand against his ruthlessly abused and scarred counterpart blew him away. Eleanor seemed similarly mesmerized.

Enough was enough. "We have a problem," Tyler said hopelessly.

"Not tamales again, please," she breathed, softly tracing the deep creases in his palm with her index finger.

Tyler choked back a startled laugh. "Forget the tamales," he managed. "We have a much bigger problem." Eleanor let go of his hand and twisted in his lap to study his face. Tyler inhaled sharply at the effect of her movement. Make that two bigger problems.

"Tyler, I have a question. Can I go first?"

"Sure," he managed. As long as she stopped wriggling.

"We've covered a lot of ground in the last twenty four hours or so, wouldn't you say?"

He'd like to cover more. "No doubt. That's what I'm---"

She cut him off by pressing a finger against his mouth. "That's not my question. I have to clarify a thing or two before I get to the main question, okay?"

Whatever she wanted, as long as she sped things up a little.

"Do you consider us friends now?" She chewed on her lip, and then continued before he could respond. "That wouldn't be an excessive exaggeration, would it?"

Shaking his head, he wished he could adjust his ever-tightening jeans somehow.

"And you would agree that there are lots of different kinds of friends ---casual friends, childhood friends, co-worker friends, family friends---"

Tyler waved a restless hand to hurry her up. She clearly had no idea what she was doing to him, wriggling around on his lap. "Sure."

"So my question is simple. What kind are we? What exactly is your position on our friendship?"

Eleanor sat on his lap, wrapped in his arms, and she could ask him a question like that? Tyler felt a rush of tenderness combined with amusement. "You're sitting on my lap," he couldn't help pointing out. "What does that tell you?"

Eleanor flushed. "To be perfectly honest, Tyler, I'm not sure what to make of it," she confessed. "I'm a little surprised to be here."

The feeling of tenderness came back and threatened to swamp him. She felt so good in his arms. Tyler slid his hand along the curve of her flushed cheek and around the nape of her neck. He could feel her pulse racing beneath his fingertips as he gently worked to free the fat braid sandwiched between them. "It's like this, Eleanor," he began, nonchalantly slipping the fabric band from the end. "I seem to be cruising right on past feeling friendly to---well, feeling really friendly." His eyebrows lifted meaningfully. "And I hope I'm not the only one here who feels this way." He began sifting her braid loose and her heavy, wavy hair felt just as silky as he'd imagined.

Eleanor bit her lip, her brow furrowed. "Define 'really friendly,' Tyler."

He had a much better idea. "I'm an action kind of guy, honey. How about I show you?"

He was about to kiss her. She forgot all about her confusion as he purposefully dipped his head. She closed her eyes in painful, breathless anticipation. And---

Nothing.

O-kay. He wasn't going to kiss her. She had read him wrong. Eleanor trembled, her discomfiture threatening to swallow her whole. She felt tears well up in her closed eyes.

"Look at me, Eleanor." Tyler's voice was a low rumble.

She couldn't look at him.

"I want to see your eyes, honey," he coaxed, his breath mingling with hers. The touch of his mouth on hers, gentle as a whisper, sent a jolt through her body from head to toe. "Please?" He kissed her again, lightly but for a moment longer. Helplessly she obeyed, faint with both panic and longing. Tyler gazed down at her, a smile playing around the corners of his mouth. "That's better. This is what I'm talking about. Really friendly."

A tiny tear trickled out of the corner of her eye, and Tyler's half-smile turned into a frown. He drew away slightly to take a careful look. "What's the matter?"

Eleanor shook her head and dashed the telltale tear away.

He tilted his head, his expression bewildered.

"I'm sorry. I'm so embarrassed. I'm no good at this," she confessed miserably. Too bad there was no dummy guide for romance.

She needed to hear it straight out. He could do that. Tyler lifted her chin with his finger, his green and gold gaze sincere. "Oh, honey, listen to me. I'm seriously attracted to you. I guess I have been for a while. How do you feel about me?"

Eleanor didn't know whether to feel grateful for his candor or ashamed she had to be led through the process like a kindergartner. "The same way," she managed.

He looked relieved, which struck Eleanor as nothing less than astonishing. "Good. Then this is what I think. I think we ought to spend some time getting to know one another. Just the two of us. Nobody else. No Rosie, no sisters, no brothers, no nieces, no nephews, nothing. Starting right now. What do you say?"

Eleanor's eyes widened. Time alone with Tyler? "Yes."

He nodded firmly, clearly satisfied. "All right, then." He cast an almost predatory nod toward her partially loosened hair. "I've got to tell you, Eleanor, I've got a real thing for your hair." She thrilled to his unexpected confession. He made short work of the rest of the braid, and then slowly, deliberately slid both of his hands through the heavy mass to hold her head gently captive between his warm hands. "Yeah," he said in a low, rumbly tone. "I like this." Eleanor went weak at his touch and at his narrowed, glittering gaze. "Ready or not," he murmured, bending his head to hers again.

His kiss began like the first two; light and experimental, but when she slid trembling, tentative hands up his hard chest, over his broad shoulders and twined her arms around his neck, she was rewarded with a husky groan that curled her toes, and Tyler's kiss instantly took on a whole new tone. He slanted his lips on hers and launched a full-scale attack; his mouth and tongue alternately demanding and coaxing, teasing and thrusting. His skill terrified her even as she shivered with desire. She didn't want to think about how much practice he'd had at this kind of thing, or about how badly she wanted to please him, and she especially didn't want to think about how completely clueless she was about pleasing any man, much less a man like Tyler---but then he nudged her chin upwards and slid the tip of his tongue down her throat, then back up the curve of her neck to her ear, and when he slowly, deliberately licked the hollow of her ear, the last functioning corner of her mind melted into a hot pool of desire, which was a huge relief because she didn't want to think about anything, she just wanted to feel, and he was making her feel plenty.

Still holding her head captive, still paying delicious, wicked attention to her ear, he pulled one hand away from her hair to begin a torturous exploration of her body. He skimmed over the curve of her hip and tickled the skin just beneath the hem of her shorts, making her breathe faster, and then slid his hand beneath the hem of her shirt. Eleanor caught her breath as he unfastened her bra with an experienced flick and pushed it away to give himself room to caress the curve of her breasts. When he teased one curiously aching nipple, then the other, she wanted to weep. She'd never felt anything like it before in her life, and she cursed herself for being so backwards, then she gave thanks that it was Tyler who was inciting her body to riot level, and then she wondered if what he was doing to her would feel good to him, too.

Suddenly bold, Eleanor tugged at his shirt and slid a hand beneath the thin cotton to touch the muscles of his stomach and chest. Her bravery earned her another groan and he abandoned her ear to return to her mouth even more possessively than before. She pulled frantically on his shirt, wanting more of his warm flesh, wanting the shirt gone, wanting more of everything she knew Tyler could give her, and suddenly Tyler lifted her again, and she found herself straddling his lap, clamped against his chest, his arms wrapped around her like steel bands. She could feel his heart pounding as madly as her own, and that wasn't all she could feel. The almost frightening bulge beneath the fly of his jeans sent shivers down her spine because she knew she did that, she caused that bulge, and Eleanor felt dizzy and triumphant and terrified all at once.

"Don't move," he murmured, nibbling along her neck.

Was he crazy? He was the one who put her in this unladylike position. It wasn't her fault she had to move, that she had to wiggle against him just a little---

"Stop," he half-groaned, half-laughed, grabbing and stilling her hips with his hands. "For God's sake, Eleanor, stop."

"I don't want to." But she obeyed because he knew much more about what they were doing and why they ought to stop or go. As long as they didn't stop for long.

"We're going too fast," he explained, sliding his hands beneath her shirt and refastening her bra without even looking.

She hated how experienced he was, and glared at him.

He smoothed some of her wild hair away from her face. "We have to slow down."

She sighed with disappointment. "Why do you get to make that decision unilaterally? Shouldn't it be a joint decision? Isn't it negotiable?

He did laugh then, and leaned his forehead against hers. "Sometimes you scare me, you know that?"

"Oh, sure," she said, frustrated and suddenly very cranky. "I'm a hundred pounds of pure terror."

"You are. Sometimes you sound just like a damned attorney, with all your negotiating and clarifying and arguing." Tyler shook his head in mock-horror.

Cold dread snaked down Eleanor's spine. The secret of her profession had weighed heavily on her in the past; now it threatened to overwhelm her. She had to tell him the truth. Just maybe not this minute. She changed the subject. "Tell me why we have to slow down," she ordered, draping her arms around his neck.

"I have some concerns. I just think it's smart to reach a mutual understanding before we go---too far."

He sounded awfully business-like all of a sudden. "What's your concern?"

"You live next door to my grandmother, Eleanor."

"Yes?"

"Bottom line is, I've always made it a point to keep my private life---private, and I'd like to keep it that way. Your living right next door to Rosie is a problem."

Puzzled, she sat up and studied him. "What do you mean?"

He looked as though he were choosing his words with extreme care. "I'd rather Rosie and the others not know about us. Our feelings, our --activities."

Eleanor gazed at him, his words echoing back at her. She frowned. Don't jump to conclusions, she admonished herself. Hear him out.

"Think about it," Tyler said quickly. "You know how they all love to talk everything to death."

"Because they care about one another," she reminded him quietly. They cared about her, too, amazingly enough, and she treasured that gift. Did he want to keep his feelings for her, whatever they were, whatever they became, secret from his family? Did he expect her do the same?

Tyler sighed. "But we won't have a minute's peace, and I don't want them to get any kind of ideas---" He broke off uncomfortably

"What kind of ideas are you afraid they might get, Tyler?" Suddenly Eleanor felt obscene, straddling his lap, and she scrambled off awkwardly, evading the hands that tried to stop her. Her legs felt a little noodly beneath her as she backed away from the sofa, and her hair stuck to her suddenly clammy skin.

Tyler sat forward on the sofa, his hands clasped between his knees. "I'm just saying we should have some time to ourselves before we go public."

Go public. He made them sound like stocks and bonds. "You mean, keep our relationship a secret from your family." Please tell me I misunderstand, Eleanor begged him mentally. Please think more of me than this.

He looked pained. "I mean we should just low-key it, that's all."

"Exactly how would we do that? I don't understand the mechanics. Am I supposed to stay away when you're there?"

"No, of course not."

"Then what? Act like we're still fighting?"

Tyler sucked in a breath. "No, just---I don't know---act like regular friends."

Eleanor looked at him for a long moment, thinking hard about whether she was willing to accept his stipulation. In Tyler's own way, he was just as controlling as her father, and caving in to his wishes today would set a terrible precedent. "Here's the thing," she said finally, "I've hidden my feelings for years. I'm not doing that anymore."

Tyler sucked in a deep breath. "Not even for a little while?"

"Define 'a little while.'"

He was beginning to look slightly annoyed. Women probably didn't often quibble with him over the details of their affairs, Eleanor thought disjointedly. "I don't know exactly," he said. "Just a little while."

Until he decided differently. Eleanor started to feel annoyed, herself. "Let me ask you something, Tyler. Do you think it's reasonable and fair to ask me to engage in an emotional and physical relationship with you while simultaneously hiding that relationship from your family, who are my friends, for an unspecified length of time, while you try to resolve vague, nameless issues that you can't even *explain* to me?"

Tyler gaped at her.

Well, she didn't think it was reasonable. Not today, not tomorrow and not in a million years. It would be a betrayal; not only of Rosie, but of herself as well. Eleanor believed, with her stunted but still incurably romantic heart, that when she fell in love, she'd have the inherent right to shout it from the roof tops. Not that she was in love with Tyler; of course. She was just in lust with him, like every other woman who met him. She'd get over it. "I guess I really should thank you for putting on the brakes, then," she said shakily, "because I'm not going to be your embarrassing little secret."

Tyler leaned forward, his mouth dropping open in objection.

Eleanor batted at her hair and looked around for her hair tie. Don't cry, don't cry, don't cry, she ordered herself. "Where's my scrunchie?" she asked, trying to sound calm and collected. "Are you sitting on it?"

"Embarrassing little secret? No, honey, you're taking this all wrong."

"And don't call me honey," she said.

He pushed his hand through his hair. "We're back to that?"

"I am not your honey in private and your---your---pal around your family." Eleanor moved to the side of the sofa, spied her hair tie and snatched it up. "I'm not embarrassed to tell Rosie how I feel about you, Tyler." Her implication that he was, was clear, and she could tell it hit home because the tips of his ears went red. Eleanor turned her back on him and started toward the kitchen in search of her purse and keys.

He leapt up from the sofa and dogged her steps. "I never said anything like that. I'm just suggesting we give it some time, that's all. I mean, for God's sakes, Eleanor, yesterday at this time we didn't even like one another."

Eleanor spun on her heel, her mind clicking reliably again. "That's where you're wrong. Deep down I always did like you, even when you were awful to me, because I could see how much you love your family, and I love them, too. That was always your one saving grace, Tyler, but now you say you have no problem lying to Rosie and you want me to lie to her, too. Well, I'm not going to do it. I'll choose the truth and my own self-respect over your kisses and secrets any time." She managed to bind her hair in a ponytail, then picked up her purse and keys and headed for the door. "See you around."

Tyler beat her to the door, flattening his hand at the top to prevent her from opening it. The muscle in his clenched jaw throbbed. "You're overreacting," he ground out. "I guess I

CHRISTY ST. ROMAIN MARCHAND

should've taken you upstairs after all. Maybe you'd be more reasonable if we'd finished what we started."

In a perverse way Eleanor almost wished he had, too, before he'd opened his big, stupid mouth, so she'd have at least one golden memory to hold on to in her old age, but she'd die before she'd admit it. "You overestimate yourself," she shot at him. "It would take a lot more than anything you have to offer to make me lie to Rosie." She tugged on the doorknob. "Move out of my way."

He stood back. "Fine, then."

Eleanor slipped through the door and made a run for her car.

Chapter Fourteen

"So, let me see if I've got it straight. You missed the big wedding, gained a brother-slash-roommate, stopped fighting with Tyler, fell in love with Tyler, and then completely and irrevocably lost your ever loving mind and told him no when he made a major pass at you?" Gracie sat back in her chair on the sunny patio of Madre Tierra with a look of disbelief.

Eleanor squashed a wedge of lemon into her glass of iced tea and stirred vehemently. "I never said one thing about falling in love with Tyler, Gracie, and you're missing the whole point. He wanted me to lie to Rosie. I won't do that."

"Maybe you didn't give him enough of a chance to explain."

Eleanor sighed and sipped her tea. Maybe it hadn't been such a great idea to keep her lunch date with Gracie. She didn't want to think about Tyler, much less talk about him, but Gracie was determined to ferret out every last detail. "He said he didn't want his family to get any ideas. What does that say to you? It tells me he wants to make a brief little affair as convenient for himself as possible, that's all, and I really didn't see what he could add that would have changed anything. It's common knowledge he goes through women like Kleenex. Do I look like Kleenex?"

Gracie shook her head in confusion. "What?"

"I'm not affair material," Eleanor clarified.

"I still say you left too soon. Maybe he just wasn't good at explaining himself."

Eleanor shook her head. "He was crystal clear, Gracie." She frowned at the beverage. It was tasteless compared to Rosie's iced tea. She flagged their waitress down. "I think I'll have a margarita, please."

"Large or small?"

"Large," Eleanor replied. "Definitely a---"

"Small," Gracie broke in. "She'll definitely have a small. What are you doing this afternoon? Not driving around, I hope."

"I don't know. I can't go home." Eleanor pushed her place setting away and dropped her forehead on the table with a gentle thud. "Not until I figure out what I'm going to tell Rosie."

"Why do you have to tell her anything?"

"Because the first thing she's going to ask me is what we did when we left her house Sunday. I've managed to avoid her so far, what with helping Scott get settled, but I can't keep it up. I don't want to, anyway. I miss her. I hate Tyler for this whole mess," Eleanor lamented, her voice muffled against the tablecloth.

Gracie patted her on the head. "Then why can't you just tell her what happened? Tyler's a big boy and it's all his doing so he ought to be able to handle the backlash."

"Because I care about Rosie and I don't want her to know what a louse her precious grandson is. It'll hurt her feelings to find out he didn't want her to know anything about us." Us? she thought miserably. There is no us. There can never be an us. And though Eleanor knew she was throwing away the most exciting offer of her life, she had to say no. She had to keep reminding herself that Tyler's stipulations were unacceptable. She'd been alone too long, damn it, to agree to a relationship where she'd still be alone. She would hold out for the special man who cared enough to---how had Tyler put it? ---go public with his feelings.

And Tyler wasn't that man.

"Excuse me, is she all right?"

Eleanor lifted her head from the tabletop to find their waitress regarding her anxiously. She held a goblet the size of a fishbowl along with a platter piled with nachos.

Gracie waved a careless hand. "She's just having a dramatic moment."

A dramatic moment? Eleanor glared at Gracie. Some sympathy and understanding right about now would be nice.

"Okay, well, here's something to think about," Gracie said, unfazed. "What was your worst problem, say, two months ago?"

Eleanor frowned, thinking back. Nothing came to mind. How odd. How could she not remember? She stirred the margarita with its tiny striped straw. "Trying to get the deposition from Alcord Chemical?" She bent her head to try to get some margarita through the little straw but it was impossible.

Gracie nodded. "Whatever. What's your worst problem now?"

So many choices. "My father, my lack of a job, Scott's tuition--"

Gracie smacked Eleanor on the hand with her fork. "Your worst problem."

"Tyler."

Gracie grinned at her triumphantly. "Exactly!"

"I don't understand what you're getting at, Gracie." Eleanor gave up on the straw and lifted the glass to her lips and gasped when the margarita heaved forward and went up her nose. Good God, she was so unsophisticated, she couldn't even manage a frozen drink. Eleanor sighed and slumped in her chair.

Gracie was kind enough not to laugh. "Okay, I'll make it simple." She held out her right hand, palm side up. "Here we have a deposition. A dry, boring piece of paper. I'll even throw in Phillip Conrad and Wayne Patterson." She held out her left hand. "Now over here we have a gorgeous six and a half foot tall football player who ought to come with a warning label, who told you, to your face, he wants you." Gracie raised and lowered her empty hands as if she were weighing the make-believe contents. "Oh, gee, which problem would I rather have?" she asked in an exaggerated tone. "Oh, my, I don't know, that's a tough one."

Eleanor made a face and swatted Gracie's hands. "I'm just a temporary distraction. I don't mean anything to him. Why else would I have to be a secret?"

Gracie shook her head vehemently. "Then why you? Why not any one of the many, many women who would be more than happy to be his secret distraction?"

Eleanor's antennae went up. Gracie sounded like she knew something specific. "What many, many women?" she asked casually.

"Ben sees him at the health club and says he has to swat women away like flies."

Eleanor ignored the frisson of jealousy curling its way down her spine. She didn't want to think about Tyler roaming around a health club. She wondered if he wore shorts there. He probably did. Swarms of nubile young women, with touchy-feely hands and chiseled bodies of their own probably ogled him in his shorts every day. Eleanor gritted her teeth. "He's a competitor, he likes to win, and I'm this week's challenge. That's all there is to it."

Gracie shook her head vehemently. "I think you're wrong. You've been hitting sparks off one another since the day you met."

"No, I'm telling you, it's true. He's bored. And did you know he still thinks I'm a librarian? Wait until he finds out I'm an attorney, and it won't be long now, that is, if I ever manage to find another job. I've made some calls and I'm not getting anywhere." Eleanor stabbed her fork into a nacho and dropped it onto her plate.

"What about Sternberg and Associates?"

"I called Maury Sternberg the same afternoon you told me they were looking, but Maury said they'd already hired someone."

Gracie looked perplexed. "That doesn't make sense. I heard Wayne saying something just this morning about the problem Sternberg is having finding someone with the right background." She leaned forward, her brow creased. "Do you think Phillip has something to do with this?"

Eleanor sat back, her expression grim. "He might. He's still trying to convince me to come back to CBB before Wayne makes a complete hash of things, and his tone's been getting pretty nasty. I guess blacklisting me so I can't get a job anyplace else would fall within his bag of tricks."

"What are you going to do about it?"

Unhearing, Eleanor continued. "If we're right, I bet my father's involved with it, too. He's single-minded about me becoming a senior partner at CBB."

"Even if you don't want to work there."

Eleanor laughed a painful laugh. "Even if."

* * *

Enough was enough, Rosie thought unapologetically, rapping on Eleanor's front door. Three whole days had passed since Tyler and Eleanor left her house together, and she'd seen neither hide nor hair of either, since. Most unusual, since Eleanor drifted over almost every morning and Tyler showed up almost every afternoon. Also, the telephone conversations she'd been forced to initiate with each of them had been supremely unsatisfying, to say the least. Something had happened between them, neither one was talking, and Rosie's curiosity was about to eat her alive.

Eleanor swung the door open, a welcoming if somewhat wary smile on her face. "Morning, Rosie."

"Morning, honey. Hungry? I baked cinnamon rolls." Rosie didn't wait for a return greeting or an invitation; she simply pushed the tray into Eleanor's arms. "They're straight out of the oven. Got any coffee?"

Eleanor propped the tray on her slim hip and closed the door. "Just made a fresh pot."

Walter sidestepped down his perch and stretched his neck flirtatiously. "Hallo, good looking," he crooned in his falsetto.

"Hello, Walter," Rosie replied, giving Eleanor a speedy squeeze before marching toward the kitchen. "Any signs of the retirement home relenting on their pet policy?"

Eleanor followed her. "As a matter of fact, yes. They finally admitted that the policy is silent on the inclusion of birds as pets so they've agreed to let Walter stay with Mrs. Dunlap on a trial basis. She's so happy about it. I'm taking him over there tomorrow. Of course," she smiled ruefully, placing the tray on the island, "they may change their minds again when they realize how loud he is."

She crossed the kitchen to pour Rosie a cup of coffee. "Aren't you supposed to be at art class this morning?"

Rosie nodded. "Yes, but I'm tired of painting fruit. I want to paint something interesting and I told the instructor to call me when they're done with fruit." She eyed Eleanor as she climbed onto a stool at the island. She looked pale to Rosie; pale and tired, and she was still wearing her pajamas and robe even though it was almost ten o'clock. "Robb called last night and said he can already tell Scott's a hard worker."

Eleanor smiled, this one sincere. "Scott was chomping at the bit yesterday morning, and he came home raving about his day. I'm so grateful to Robb for offering him the job."

"No more grateful than Robb and Nancy when you saved the day for them last Saturday."

"Oh, that was nothing," Eleanor said, uncurling the ring of her roll. "Austin and I had a good time together."

Enough small talk. Rosie was much more interested in the time Eleanor spent alone with Tyler Saturday evening. Her vague but hopeful plan to somehow push the two of them together at the reception had come to nothing when Eleanor stayed behind with Austin, but when Tyler paid absolutely no heed to any of the pretty women clamoring for his attention, and then agreed, albeit grudgingly, to detour back by Rosie's to bring Eleanor some supper, she'd said a tiny little prayer that somehow the two of them would finally stop sniping at one another. She could see how perfect they were for one another; why couldn't they? So when she got home and found Tyler so curiously amiable and Eleanor clearly flustered, well, it seemed her prayers had been answered. And then on Sunday; Tyler's peculiar mood and the way they disappeared together---well, it was very encouraging.

And then, nothing. Just baffling silence.

Rosie sighed. She'd just have to carefully work her way to the topic she was most interested in, then. "So Monday you helped Scott settle in, and Tuesday---," she prompted.

"Tuesday we went to LSU to see what we need to do to get him enrolled for the fall semester." Eleanor frowned slightly. "I had no idea how high tuition is now. And yesterday, after lunch with Gracie, I went by my father's office, and then started working on my résumé'."

"How was your visit with your father?"

Eleanor meticulously unwound the ring of her spiraled roll. "Typical. I don't know much more than I did before about why he refuses to see Scott. He assumed I was there to tell him I'd changed my mind about going back to Conrad, Berkley and Burns, so we got off to a bad start right away when I told him otherwise. When I finally had an opportunity to ask him why he didn't tell me anything about Scott, he told me it wasn't my concern." She shook her head, her brow furrowed. "Can you believe that? It went from bad to worse when I told him Scott has moved in with me."

"How so?"

"He started lecturing me about minding my own business and getting my priorities back in order." Eleanor propped her chin on her hand and sighed. "That's when I had to get up and leave. My priorities are in order, with Scott at the top of the list. I don't mind going back to work," Eleanor continued, "but my motivation has changed. I don't care about making senior partner in some stuffy old firm anymore. I just want to make enough money to get along and to help Scott with college."

Rosie studied Eleanor thoughtfully. "Let's say money wasn't an issue. What kind of practice would you choose?"

Eleanor didn't hesitate. "That's easy. I'd work for people who need help but don't know where to turn and can't afford it, anyway. Elderly people, for example."

"Like your friend, Mrs. Dunlap."

"Exactly!" Eleanor sat upright, cinnamon roll forgotten. "Every time I visit her, she introduces me to more of her friends and it seems like the majority of them don't really have anybody to look after them. They ask me to look at paperwork that they can't read anymore, or ask my advice on problems with insurance or trust accounts."

Rosie knew about Eleanor's weekly sojourn to the Willow Lake Retirement Home, with Walter's travel cage in tow, and wasn't a bit surprised by her reply. Eleanor would make a wonderful advocate for the elderly. There had to be a way to make it happen.

"I tried to squeeze as much pro bono work as I could in at CBB, but the senior partners didn't have much social conscience. Everything there boiled down to prestige and billable---"

"Answer the door, Hazel! Answer the door, Hazel!"

Eleanor shook her head in mock vexation at Walter's raucous interruption. "Be quiet, Walter!" she called, and then turned back to Rosie with a rueful smile. "He's got a new trick. He pretends like somebody's at the door just to make me get up and look, and then he smirks."

Rosie smiled back. "I didn't know birds could smirk."

"Walter smirks."

"Eleanor?" A deep voice carried from the living room. "Can I come in?"

Walter wasn't playing tricks after all. Eleanor's skin went cold, then hot, and her mug of coffee, mercifully empty, slipped from her fingers and clattered onto the granite island top. She'd worked very hard at avoiding Tyler since Sunday, and she certainly wasn't ready to face him right now, especially not in her pjs and robe. Why on earth was he here?

He was in search of Rosie, of course. Eleanor glanced at Rosie and smiled, or at least tried to. "Tyler," she said unnecessarily. "Looking for you, I'm sure."

Rosie shook her head. "I doubt it."

Well, she hoped he hadn't come over to see her. What could he possibly think he had to say that she was even remotely interested in hearing, anyway? He'd said more than enough at his house on Sunday.

"Eleanor?"

"In here," Eleanor called in a slightly strangled voice. She tried again. "In the kitchen." She tried to hold onto her anger and not pay any attention to the thrill his rumbly voice generated.

Tyler stepped through the wide doorway from the living room, filling it up. His tentative smile turned to open-mouthed surprise when he spied his grandmother on Eleanor's right. "Rosie," he managed, drawing to an abrupt stop.

"Ty," Rosie replied with a wave. "Fancy seeing you here. Have a cinnamon roll."

Tyler glanced back and forth at Eleanor and Rosie, obviously unsettled. "No, thanks," he finally replied, stepping into the kitchen. "I thought you had art class this morning."

"She's boycotting," Eleanor reported, trying to look relaxed, making a big production out of uncurling a second cinnamon roll.

"Too much fruit," Rosie added.

"Ah." Tyler acted as though Rosie's explanation made perfect sense. "Funny you didn't mention that when we talked yesterday," he added belatedly, slightly accusingly.

Rosie shrugged carelessly. "It was how I felt this morning. What about you? Did you come straight from the gym?"

Tyler glanced down at his damp tee shirt and sweat pants, and then shot a pained glance at Eleanor that seemed to smack of an apology and a cry for help all at once.

Eleanor gazed at him, suddenly calm. Poor Tyler, he was clearly in a quandary. Whatever his reason for coming over, unannounced and uninvited, he was either going to have to come clean with it in front of his grandmother, or think fast and make something up.

"Well?" Rosie asked. "What are you up to today?"

Tyler shrugged. "It was just an idea, but---," he paused.

"But what?" Eleanor prodded.

"I thought I'd see if you maybe wanted some help with---" Tyler hesitated again, his expression becoming grim.

He was racking his brains to think of a plausible lie to tell his grandmother. Enough of this. Eleanor gripped her coffee cup tightly. "With what?" she challenged him impatiently. He wasn't going to play games with her, not in her own house, not in front of Rosie. "Help me with exactly what, Tyler?"

Tyler glanced at Rosie and back at Eleanor, and his gaze rolled over her like a steamroller, from the bare toes peeping from beneath her shaggy chenille robe to her shiny face and messy ponytail. Eleanor swallowed and stiffened under his intense scrutiny. She knew she wasn't a beauty like the women he didn't mind being seen with, but who asked him to come over, anyway?

Then Tyler's expression softened visibly. He stepped over to tuck a strand of hair behind her ear. "Help you explain, honey." He tore off a piece of her cinnamon roll and popped it into his mouth.

Eleanor stared at him as he chewed. Explain? What was she supposed to explain?

"Explain what?" Rosie surveyed them eagerly. "What in the world are you talking about?"

Tyler pried Eleanor's empty coffee mug from her hand. "Go on, tell her." He looked around for the coffee pot and, spying it, crossed the kitchen to refill Eleanor's mug.

"Tell me what?"

Eleanor shrugged helplessly at Rosie's question. "I don't know what he's talking about."

Leaning against the counter, Tyler shook his head in mock dismay. "Sure you do, honey." He took a sip of coffee from her cup.

Rosie spun on her stool and fixed Eleanor with her bright blue gaze. "For heaven's sake, Eleanor, what on earth is he rambling on about?"

Eleanor found her voice. "Tyler's playing games."

He managed to look offended. "No, I'm not."

Eleanor hugged her arms around her waist. "Please stop, Tyler," she said softly, dropping her gaze.

Tyler's smile vanished. "Okay, then, I'll tell her. The truth is, Rosie, Eleanor and I decided we didn't want to fight anymore."

Eleanor's head snapped up at his abruptly serious tone.

"Oh?" Rosie leaned forward on her barstool. "I'm glad to hear that."

Tyler nodded. "We also decided we wanted to spend time together. Alone," he added deliberately.

Eleanor began to tremble.

"But then I hurt Eleanor's feelings by suggesting we keep our relationship to ourselves. I think she got the idea I was embarrassed to let you and the others know I feel about her, but that wasn't it. I've been thinking about it, a lot, and I realize it was more of a control thing." He spoke to Rosie, but his gaze was trained on Eleanor. "I guess I've picked up some bad habits living by myself for so long, like expecting the people I care about to let me meddle in their business but forgetting it gives them the right to meddle in mine."

Eleanor stared back at Tyler, her heart thumping painfully as she comprehended his remarks.

"I guess a better way to say it is I've figured out it's okay to trust the people who care about me. Hopefully Eleanor still fits in that category." Crossing the few feet between them, Tyler lifted Eleanor's cold hands from her lap. "I'm here to tell you I'm sorry." He chafed her hands gently. "I didn't expect to say all this in front of Rosie, but it's just as well, don't you think? Now there aren't any secrets."

Eleanor nodded, her eyes welling with tears.

"Time for me to go," Rosie said, slipping off the bar stool.

Eleanor snapped her attention to Rosie. "You don't have to," she objected weakly.

"Yes, she does," Tyler said with an unapologetic wink at his grandmother.

"Yes, I do," Rosie echoed, her blue eyes twinkling in return. "My mission this morning was to find out why you were both acting so strangely and now I know." Rosie patted Tyler's cheek. "You've made an old woman happy, honey, but it certainly took you long enough."

"Been matchmaking all along, huh? I should have known." Tyler said, releasing Eleanor's hands to give Rosie a gentle nudge toward the living room. "We'll see you later on." He disappeared around the doorway, his hand on Rosie's elbow.

Slipping off her bar stool, Eleanor followed them into the living room and found Tyler closing and locking the front door. He turned, gave her a slow smile and held out his arms.

Eleanor flew across the floor toward him. Tyler bent to catch her, folded his arms around her, and lifted her to put her at face level. "All better now?"

Eleanor nodded, not trusting her voice. She twined her arms around his neck, loving his strength, loving the gleam in his hazel eyes, loving---

Him.

Eleanor's heart did cartwheels. Gracie had been right all along. She loved this great big handsome, bossy, wonderful man. She buried her face against Tyler's warm shoulder, afraid to look at him. Her feelings, staggering and raw, had to be written all over her face.

"Spend the day with me?"

She nodded again.

"Good." Tyler held her tightly for a long moment, and then placed her back on the floor. Bending over, he pulled the lapels of her robe together and secured her belt. "I want to go about this the right way, Eleanor," he said. "Wine you, dine you, all that stuff. I think it's important to take the time for that kind of thing in a real relationship."

A real relationship. Eleanor's heart sang with delight.

"Because that's what I see happening here with you and me."

Lightheaded, Eleanor caught his hand and tugged him up and toward the sofa. "I have to sit down," she breathed. "Just for a minute."

Grinning, he sat down and promptly pulled her into his lap. "I have all these good intentions to behave myself," he complained, "yet here I am on a sofa with you again."

"We're not misbehaving," she argued mildly. "We're just talking. You were saying something about what you see happening with us."

"Right. Well, see, it's like this. I think the way you start out sets the whole tone for a relationship. Don't you?"

Eleanor wouldn't know; she'd never had a relationship. Tyler, on the other hand, had had plenty of relationships so she guessed, on this issue; she'd have to defer to his knowledge and experience. And if he was right, well, she wanted to start out being honest. "To be perfectly frank, Tyler, I'm in uncharted territory here."

"Me, too."

"Oh, come on," she said, disbelieving. "You've had lots of relationships."

"Not that many," he objected. "And not the kind where we spent a lot of time talking."

Eleanor didn't know whether to feel jealous of or sorry for the women with whom he hadn't spent a lot of time talking. They all looked pretty happy in the photographs she'd seen online so she figured they didn't mind the not-talking part all that much. There was one particular relationship she was curious about, though. "Rosie said you were married once."

He expelled a disgruntled breath. "A long, long time ago." She looked at him expectantly. "You really want to hear about that right now? It's not a pretty story, honey."

Eleanor didn't want to make him drag up unhappy memories. "You don't have to tell me about it if you don't want to.

"What the hell," he said, slipping a hand behind her head to tug the hair tie from her hair. "It'll take all of two minutes. Her name was Elizabeth and I met her at a place in Denver where a lot of the guys used to hang out. I didn't know it at the time, but she was quite a regular there." He twined a curling lock of hair around and around his finger.

"A football groupie." Eleanor had learned more than she anticipated in her football books.

"That's right, and some of the other guys tried to warn me but I was too stupid to listen."

"You were young, away from home for the first time, and lonely."

"And really stupid," he repeated wryly. "Anyway, we went out for a while and when she told me she was pregnant, I did the good southern boy thing and married her." Tyler collected a bigger handful of Eleanor's hair and slowly sifted it through his fingers. "And then I found out she wasn't really pregnant. She'd made it all up. The sad fact is that I was more relieved than anything. Elizabeth was definitely not mother material."

Eleanor wondered if Tyler thought she was mother material. There was no question in her mind that he was father material; the way he doted on his nieces and nephews never failed to make her biological clock go one on one with her heart. "What happened then?"

"I told her I wanted a divorce." Tyler was silent for a long moment. "She had a great fondness for my paycheck, though, so she fought the divorce for a long time."

"How long were you married?"

"Just under three years."

Eleanor mulled over his story. Trapped in an unhappy marriage for three years with a woman he didn't love and couldn't trust; it was no wonder Tyler had avoided serious relationships ever since. "What ever happened to her?"

"She married her divorce lawyer." He looked disgusted.

Eleanor's blood congealed. Oh, God. She had to tell him about being an attorney. She couldn't put it off any longer. "Tyler, I have something to tell you," she started off haltingly. "Something important."

Shifting away from her, Tyler put a finger over her mouth. "I can't sit here like this any longer, honey, not with you like that and your bed right upstairs. All my talk about going slow will go up in smoke."

"It'll just take a minute," she said desperately. If she didn't tell him now, she'd lose her nerve.

Tyler shook his head. "I'll be able to listen a lot better after you're dressed." He rose, tugged her from her seat and nudged her toward the staircase. "Go on, honey, get dressed so we can get out of here."

Maybe she wasn't supposed to tell him right this minute. Maybe a better opportunity would come up later in the day. They'd be spending the whole day together, after all. Eleanor started up the stairs.

"Wait a second."

She turned around, her hand on the rail, and watched Tyler spring up the steps after her. "Here," he said, pressing the hair band into her hand. "Wear your hair up so I can take it down again later." He pulled her close for a bone melting kiss.

"I can do that," she replied breathlessly.

Brief minutes later, Eleanor hurried back down the steps and glanced around. There was no sign of Tyler in the living room. "I'm ready," she called, bubbling with anticipation. She'd tugged on jeans and a tee shirt appliqued with smiling hearts. The silly shirt just exactly fit her mood. "I just need to lock the back door." As she reached the bottom of the stairs, she caught a glimpse of

Tyler in the dining room where she'd left her laptop. He stood beside the table, turned away from her. His back was rigid, his shoulders tense, and he held papers in his hand.

Her résumé'. Horror drained the blood from Eleanor's face.

Tyler turned slowly, his eyes narrowed, expression stony. He held the papers out and deliberately let them fall, fluttering to the floor. "You're an attorney." He spat the word as though it tasted vile.

Eleanor reached a hand toward the door casing for support and nodded. Her heart shuddered almost to a standstill. "That's what I wanted to tell you," she managed in a whisper.

He stared at her, the pulse at his jaw throbbing. "Does Rosie know?" The question barely made it through clenched teeth.

Eleanor nodded again and watched as he absorbed the knowledge that his grandmother also had conspired to keep him in the dark. "I wanted to tell you, Tyler," she said, knotting and unknotting her fingers. "I didn't like keeping it from you. Everybody said---" She dropped off when his expression grew blacker.

"Everybody?" he bit out. She couldn't even nod. She didn't have to. "Everybody," he repeated carefully. "Well, what do you know about that. Aren't you all clever?"

Eleanor didn't feel clever, she felt panicked and paralyzed. She tried to think of the right words. "Tyler, you have every right to be angry---"

"No shit." He turned his back to her and looked out the window. "I guess you feel really smart, getting me worked up enough to spout off all that crap in front of Rosie." He drew in a deep breath. "You think you've got me backed into a corner, don't you?"

"I don't think that." Eleanor stepped forward and tentatively touched his arm. "Tyler, please let me explain."

He jerked away from her. "You know, you really had me going, Eleanor," he said in a dangerous yet conversational tone. "All your righteous indignation, that great speech about how you couldn't lower yourself to keep secrets, while, all along, you were keeping a whopper of a secret, yourself, weren't you? You and my entire family. Whose idea was it to tell me you were a damned librarian?"

Eleanor's stomach pitched. She couldn't let him blame Rosie. It was obvious he would never forgive her, but she had to at least try to make things right for his family. She couldn't live with herself if she spoiled his relationship with Rosie.

"You didn't let me finish," she said, drawing herself up tightly. "Everybody said I ought to tell you," she lied, "but I decided to wait. It wasn't any of your business, what I do for a living, and there was no love lost between us, anyway. And I still don't think I have to apologize for my work. Why should I? I don't go around stealing children's inheritances or bilking my clients out of money or sleeping with their spouses."

Tyler's gaze narrowed again, to the merest of slits, at her direct references to his personal experiences, and Eleanor felt a wave of nausea, but once started, she couldn't seem to stop. She had nothing, personally, to lose anymore. "Maybe I don't think much of football players," she said, drumming up a note of derision. "What do you think about that? Maybe I think it's stupid, even criminal, for a big dumb jock to earn so much money just for playing a game. But you know what? I'm not so narrow-minded that I can't respect you for doing it well. I can give you that. But you can't do the same for me, can you? I'm the same person I was before I went upstairs." Eleanor tried to squelch the pleading tone in her voice. "I'm the same person I was before you knew my great, horrible secret, but it doesn't matter to you, does it? You're too comfortable in your ridiculous prejudice." She ran out of breath and drew to a ragged halt.

Tyler stared at her coldly for an endless moment. "You can't live here. You need to get out of this house."

So that was that. Eleanor lifted her chin another fraction and sighed dramatically. "The more things change, the more they stay the same," she said with mock-weariness, then turned to yank open her front door. "It's my house. You get out."

Chapter Fifteen

"Earth to Eleanor." Leanne waved a hand in front of Eleanor's face. "Hello, anybody home?"

Eleanor broke out of her listless reverie to catch Leanne and Rosie exchanging worried frowns. "Sorry," she said, offering an apologetic smile. "What did you say?"

Leaning over to pat Eleanor's hand, Rosie nodded toward the raised stage and runway. "It's about to be Tyler's turn, honey." The lights in the elegantly decorated room dimmed as she spoke.

Eleanor drew in a ragged breath. She didn't want to be here. She had told Rosie and the others repeatedly that she didn't want to come to the charity bachelor auction but her protests fell on deaf ears. The others didn't know what had transpired between Eleanor and Tyler; they thought she was down in the dumps because she was having problems finding a new job, and they were convinced that the charity dinner and auction would cheer her up. Only Rosie knew the real reason for Eleanor's dejection, because Tyler had lit into Rosie, too, before disappearing for the past week and a half. In fact, Rosie had been worried that Tyler wouldn't return in time to participate in the auction, but Eleanor knew he would. He had made the commitment to Leanne's pet charity and nothing would prevent Tyler Hurst from fulfilling a commitment.

"Okay, ladies, it's the moment you've all been waiting for." The emcee's announcement was met with a roar of female cheering and she was forced to wait a moment for the noise to subside. "Yes, indeed, our final bachelor of the evening is about to make his stroll down the runway. This thirty-five-year-old star athlete says he plans to take the woman who wins his company on a very special evening for two down in romantic New Orleans."

More whoops of delight interrupted the emcee's introductory speech. "Picture yourself at world-renowned Brennan's for a candlelight dinner, followed by a romantic carriage ride for two through the French Quarter. Then, if you're not too tired, you'll share cafe au'lait and conversation at Antoine's, and finally, if you're a really lucky lady, maybe he'll show you some of the moves that made him so successful for fourteen years in the National Football League. It could give new meaning to the terms tackle and sack." The emcee's final quip sent another wave of wine-generated hysteria through the room.

The orchestra played a drum roll and the spotlight careened crazily around the room. Even though she knew firsthand how Tyler affected women, Eleanor was still astonished by the shrieking but otherwise elegant women who were practically spinning in their seats to get an unobstructed view of the stage and runway. She propped her chin on her hands, thinking of the million other places she'd rather be than in this room right now. She eyed the exit longingly.

"Can you believe how women behave at these things?" Nancy planted her elbows on the white linen tablecloth and grinned at Eleanor. "Isn't it fun?"

Not trusting herself to speak, Eleanor bared her teeth in what she hoped resembled an answering grin.

The emcee broke off in laughter at the increasing noise level and waved a graceful arm in the direction of the parting curtains at center stage. Eleanor's breath snagged painfully when Tyler stepped out and the roaming spotlight zoomed in on him. The furor of voices died to a breathless hush and all eager, feminine eyes trained on him as he sauntered down the center of the runway in a finely-cut suit, clearly as comfortable ambling down the runway, the object of unadulterated feminine awe, as if he were strolling down the rows of Rosie's vegetable garden. His severe hair style was razor sharp, his greenish blue gaze clearly amused at the ruckus his participation was generating.

Reaching the end of the lighted runway, he drew to a halt and the noise level in the room lifted again. He scanned the room, searching until he found his sisters and Rosie. Eleanor, on Rosie's left, shrank away. Tyler winked at Rosie and the clamor peaked. Rosie was forgiven, Eleanor realized with relief. Then Tyler spied Eleanor and his expression visibly tightened. He stared at her coldly and Eleanor gazed back, determined not to show any emotion, for what felt like an eternity.

"All right, ladies, let the bidding begin. Who will start the bidding off?"

Tyler glanced away, clearly unaffected by their combative staring match, while Eleanor sagged in her seat.

"Five hundred!" An excited voice at the rear of the room sang out.

The emcee clucked admonishingly. "Five hundred? My heavens, ladies, look at the man."

The ladies were looking, all right, thought Eleanor. Given half a chance they'd be scrambling onto the runway to touch, too.

"Do I hear a thousand?"

Eleanor heard a thousand, then two thousand, then three, and soon it was clear Tyler would easily surpass the highest bid of the evening; the five thousand dollars that had been bid for the good looking television anchor. In fact, he'd probably break the record and then some, which was wonderful for Leanne's charity. Just wonderful. And soon it would be over, and she could go home.

After a few wild moments of bidding and counter bidding, it became apparent that the war for Tyler was being fought between a pretty redhead in a shimmering white tube of a dress and a second woman just beyond Eleanor's line of vision, sitting behind a fluted column. Eleanor watched Tyler as the bidding escalated. He stood motionless; the only hint of his interest in the battle an occasional glance of curiosity at the two determined bidders.

"I have eight thousand five hundred dollars going once," sang the emcee after a few wild minutes of bidding. "I have eight thousand five hundred dollars going twice, I have eight thousand five hundred dollars going three times and--- Mr. Hurst is sold!" She referred to the list on the podium which matched bidder placard numbers to names. "Congratulations to Miss Eleanor Haley!" The audience broke into applause.

Eleanor's heart stopped beating. She cast a frantic look at Rosie. "Eight thousand---I didn't---you didn't---oh, God---oh, no---" The room went hazy and she clutched the table edge. "Oh, no, Rosie, you didn't."

Rosie nodded, a mixture of concern and determination on her face. "I did," she confessed in a whisper. "You can be mad at me later, but first you have to go up there and get Tyler."

"Eleanor!" Rosie's granddaughters laughed, unaware of Eleanor's horror.

"You sly thing!"

"How did you manage that?"

Rosie pried Eleanor's fingers from the tablecloth. "Go on, honey, everybody's waiting."

"Congratulations, Miss Haley!"

* * *

Un-effing-believable. Tyler unconsciously clenched his fists in response to the emcee's exclamation and watched as Eleanor cast a frantic look at Rosie. Tyler avoided Rosie's hopeful smile when Eleanor finally rose and began making her way toward the stage. He had figured out something was going on, something he wasn't going to like, when he recognized one of Rosie's elderly friends repeatedly flashing her bidder card aloft, but he couldn't believe Rosie would go so far as to kiss more than eight thousand dollars goodbye to throw him and Eleanor together again when she knew all he wanted was to stay as far away from Eleanor Haley, Esquire, as possible.

Eleanor slowly wound her way through the tables and carefully climbed the steps to the stage. Tyler watched her approach. He forced himself to relax, clasping his hands behind his back.

He guessed he shouldn't be surprised by anything Rosie did because she firmly believed Eleanor was the wronged party in this whole stinking mess. When he confronted Rosie after discovering the truth, his grandmother actually had the audacity to suggest he was overreacting. Overreacting! When Rosie knew, better than anybody, how he felt about attorneys and why. He had lived his entire life trying to compensate for wrongs committed by attorneys, not just against him but against Rosie and his sisters and brothers as well.

And the secrecy. Rosie knew all along that Eleanor was no damned librarian and had kept it from him. Her disloyalty had been a hard pill to swallow, but what really made the whole mess so damned unbearable was the fact that if he had only obeyed his original instincts and controlled himself, he'd never have gone over to Eleanor's like some lovesick moron and admitted, for the record, in front of God and Eleanor *and* Rosie, that they were headed into a real relationship. Rosie was on a mission now, even though it was a fool's mission, to try to put them back together.

The emcee took Eleanor's hand and led her toward Tyler, placing her hand on Tyler's arm, initiating another wave of applause before turning to the crowd. "Thank you so much, everyone, for your participation and generosity tonight!"

Tyler felt Eleanor flinch when cameras flashed. Against his will, he dropped his gaze to her face, and was, for an instant, unsettled by her pallor. Then he steeled himself by recalling how she'd so effectively manipulated him. She was a true credit to her profession.

As soon as he could, Tyler led Eleanor off stage; his smile plastered in place, and kept walking until they reached a relatively quiet corner of the busy backstage area. "Rosie should have saved her money, honey," he said in a low, cold tone, dropping her arm as though she had the plague. He wrestled his tie from his neck and stuffed it into his pocket. "She just made a bad buy."

"I don't know why she did it," Eleanor said, stepping away from him, unconsciously rubbing her arm where he'd held it. "It's a big mistake."

"You got that right," he said, before walking away. If Rosie wanted him to treat Eleanor to an eight-thousand-three-hundred dollar night to remember, well, hell, he guessed he'd just have to oblige.

But it would be on his terms.

* * *

"Your father can see you now," his secretary told Eleanor with a kind smile.

Eleanor managed a smile in return and rose from the deeply tufted leather chair in the waiting area. "Thanks," she replied, straightening her shoulders. One issue at a time, she reminded herself. First ask him about the suspicious reluctance of any law firm to accept her résumé, much less schedule an interview, and then talk with him about Scott. One issue at a time.

She lifted her chin and entered her father's sedate office. He sat behind his massive desk, ramrod straight, his attention focused on the legal brief laid neatly before him. Eleanor eased across the room and sat quietly until he lifted his silver head, his sharp green gaze slicing through her self-confidence before she uttered the first word.

"Eleanor," he said.

No 'good morning,' no 'nice to see you.' Nothing new. "Thanks for taking the time to see me."

"I'm sure it's important, for you to rouse yourself out of your very busy schedule."

Eleanor inhaled carefully. He wasn't wasting any time, so she wouldn't, either. "Yes, it is. I'm wondering if you can shed any light on the fact that neither Maury Sternberg nor Jack Caillier will return my telephone calls about positions available at their firms."

Judge Haley leaned forward, steepling his hands together. "Am I to assume that you're thinking of returning to your career?"

"You know I am if I've called Mr. Sternberg and Mr. Caillier. Have you had conversations with them lately; conversations where I was a topic?"

Her father lifted an eyebrow at her combative tone. "Are you suggesting I have something to do with your inability to secure a position?"

Here goes nothing. "Yes, I am." Eleanor met his affronted gaze squarely. "I think you've warned other firms away from me in an attempt to force me back to CBB."

Judge Haley looked away first, picking up his Mont Blanc pen and rolling it between his fingers. Eleanor knew a diversionary tactic when she saw one. "But, frankly, I have trouble understanding why you would go to such lengths. Why is it so important to you that I go back to CBB?"

Judge Haley set the pen down carefully. "Very simple. You belong at Conrad, Berkley and Burns. Until your recent---," he shook his head in disgust, "---inglorious lapse, you were on the verge of becoming the first female senior partner in what I consider to be Baton Rouge's finest firm. Your name would be on the letterhead, Eleanor, and you would have the respect and admiration of every other attorney not only in Baton Rouge, but throughout Louisiana and beyond. That's what I want for you."

No, not her, Eleanor realized abruptly. It wasn't about her at all. Her father was the one who wanted to bask in the glory he described. He had never been proud of the slight, shy daughter who had entertained childish ambitions of teaching or nursing, but he could be proud of a daughter who had risen above the confining, masculine walls of Conrad, Berkley and Burns to become the first female senior partner. He simply didn't want to wait while she began all over again at another firm. Clearly he had selected CBB, years back, and there could be no deviation from the master plan. But when she became senior partner, then what? Now she was sure there must be more. What was next on his agenda? "Then what? After I become senior partner as you've planned---a certain number of years, a number you've predetermined, and then what?" Eleanor sat forward on the edge of her seat. "Can't I have a copy of this blueprint you've designed?"

Her father pressed his lips together. "I won't tolerate that tone, Eleanor."

"I'm thirty years old and you're scolding me on my tone instead of listening to what I'm saying. I'm not going back to Conrad, Berkley and Burns. I've told you a dozen times and it's still true. Eight miserable, stifling years was enough, thank you. Now I want to help people, people with problems, not faceless corporations."

Judge Haley leaned back in his chair. "That's all very noble, Eleanor, but it won't get you very far. You're a single woman and you have to think of your future."

"I hope to heaven there's more in my future than just work, father."

He snorted. "Oh, that's right. You have a boyfriend now. You bought him, I understand?"

Eleanor blinked in dismay.

"Did you think I wouldn't hear about it? I've received more than one telephone call about your behavior last weekend. What did he cost you---over eight thousand dollars, I believe? A football player," he scoffed coldly. "Simply outstanding."

Eleanor struggled to gather her wits for a response. "It wasn't as it appeared," she managed. How stupid she had been to not realize her father would have heard about the auction.

"It is the height of ill-taste and will have repercussions you haven't begun to imagine," her father shot back. "I want you to come to your senses and start concentrating on your career again instead of adolescent romances. Frankly, I don't think you're quite mature enough for a relationship, Eleanor."

Eleanor gaped at him, at a loss for words. It was hard to fathom that a man who purportedly cared for her could say such hurtful things. If she wasn't woman enough for a relationship with a man, it was because she'd been tucked away on a shelf her entire life. Didn't he understand she didn't want to wither away in a law library or courtroom, to going home to an empty house every night with nothing but a briefcase for company?

'That's why it's better that you concentrate on your career," he said.

One issue at a time, she reminded herself, and she hadn't come here to discuss her own personal problems. Eleanor found her voice. "I promise you there is nothing at all between Tyler Hurst and myself, and I won't discuss it with you any further," she said as firmly as she could manage. "I do, however, want to talk with you about Scott."

Her father's eyebrows lifted derisively. "I've already made my feelings on that issue perfectly clear."

"Clear as mud," Eleanor replied wearily, resigned to a contentious outcome. "For heaven's sake, why won't you acknowledge your own son?"

"Eleanor, I'm telling you to leave this matter alone."

"And I'm telling you I want to know why." Eleanor trembled with both determination and anxiety. She'd never pushed her father before.

He leaned forward, his face mottled with anger. "All right, then. I'll tell you why, since you're so eager to know. He's not my son. He's not your brother. His mother had an affair while we were married, and the boy you're convinced is your brother, the boy you've invited into your home, is the result of that affair."

Eleanor jumped up from her chair. "I don't believe that for a minute!"

"Control yourself, Eleanor. You wanted to know and now you do."

Eleanor didn't know how he came to his conclusions, and she didn't care. The important thing was Scott. "Father, all you have to do is look at him and you'll see you're wrong. For heaven's sake, he's your image! But you refused to see him so you wouldn't know that, would you?" Eleanor felt as tired as if she'd just run a mile uphill, and she knew that simply telling him would never convince him. "Scott works at Southern Heritage Nursery on Government. Go there and see for yourself. Do blood tests if you still aren't convinced, but you will be. He's your son, and you'll know it the moment you lay eyes on him."

* * *

Despite every attempt Eleanor made to get out of the scheduled evening with Tyler; from trying to reimburse Rosie for the fortune she had donated to the charity, to countless unreturned telephone calls to Tyler, the evening arrived and she had no choice but to prepare for a night of – she didn't know what to prepare for, really. Rosie had repeatedly insisted Tyler would be over his initial distress---she actually used the word 'distress' as though they both didn't know Tyler was seething with fury---by Saturday night. Eleanor knew better than to believe her.

All she knew was, thanks to one very terse voice mail, he would be picking her up at seven o'clock. And it was seven o'clock now.

From her upstairs bedroom she heard a knock on the front door, and then Scott called from downstairs. "Eleanor! Tyler's here."

Drawing in a deep breath, she took her time walking down the stairway to the front door. She opened her front door and blinked. Instead of a coat and tie, Tyler wore an aged leather jacket over a beer advertisement tee shirt, a geriatric pair of jeans, scuffed cowboy boots and an insolent expression. He gave her dress a disparaging once-over. "If I've been tricked into taking you out, we'll go where I want to go, not to some over-hyped, waste-of-time exercise in embarrassment," he drawled.

Eleanor felt the stirring of a healthy dose of irritation. He was the one insisting on this debacle. She tossed her purse on the table beside the front door with a disgusted thump. "Why are you even here? You know it wasn't my idea. Can't we just forget the whole thing?" She wished she had the gumption to slam the door in his stony face but in deference to her stained glass panel, she resisted the temptation and closed it gently.

Or tried to. Tyler wedged a boot in the door, pushed it back open and pressed his way inside. "No way." He folded his arms across his chest. "You're not going to get out of this that easily. Rosie threw away over eight thousand dollars and I'm going to make sure you get your money's worth."

"What's wrong with you?" Eleanor pushed ineffectually against the door but might as well have been pushing against a brick wall. "It's not that complicated. I'm sure even you can understand. You don't want to go and I don't want to go. You're off the hook."

He looked her over insolently. "You have five minutes to change or you go as you are."

Eleanor gaped at him, astonished at his arrogant attitude. "You can't make me." The words popped out of her mouth before she could think twice. Mistake, she thought. It was like flapping a red flag at a frothing Texas longhorn.

"Sure I can, but you won't like it. If I were you, I'd go change and I'd be quick about it. Otherwise you'll look a mite silly on the bike."

The what? Eleanor's eyes opened wide. Oh, no, he couldn't mean the motorcycle. No way was she straddling that noisy monstrosity. Eleanor felt renewed determination to end the farce. "You have got to be kidding."

He quirked one eyebrow and glanced pointedly at his wristwatch. "Four minutes."

He meant it. Eleanor stared at him; her irritation bubbling into fury, then gave a little shriek of frustration and pounded up the stairs.

"What's going on, Eleanor?" Scott called.

"I'm changing my clothes," she called back, unwilling to drag him into her problems.

"Hey, Scott," she heard Tyler say. "Tell your sister she's down to three and a half."

"Hey, Eleanor, Tyler says you're down to three and a half," Scott called upstairs obediently.

Biting back an epithet, Eleanor stripped off her dress and struggled into her blue jeans. They were tighter than she remembered, probably thanks to Rosie's baking prowess. She yanked a blouse off its hanger and wrenched her arms through the sleeves, buttoned as fast as she could, then dropped to her hands and knees to rummage desperately for a pair of shoes. I'm doing this for Rosie, she reminded herself. I'm doing this for Rosie.

But the truth was, she was doing it for herself. Tyler might despise her, but she was still infatuated with him. How pathetic was that? Eleanor stilled, reflecting on her own idiocy.

"Time's up."

She gave a muffled shriek and rocked back on her heels, out of the closet. Instead of clomping up the stairs, Tyler had sneaked up as quietly as a mouse. She glared at him as he leaned against the jamb of the door, his face remote and forbidding. "I need shoes, you big oaf."

Stepping over her, he leaned down and picked her pink athletic shoes. "Here," he said, pushing them at her. " "I'm tired of waiting." He turned on his heel and disappeared through the door.

"Y'all have fun," Scott called, oblivious to the situation.

Yeah, right. Fun. "I won't be late," Eleanor called back. She tugged on one shoe at the top of the stairs, rushed down the steps, and tugged on the second shoe. By the time she got them tied and hurried down the porch steps, Tyler was already outside on the driveway, climbing on the bike. "Get on," he said peremptorily, handing her a helmet.

Exactly how? She propped the helmet on her hip and eyed the machine doubtfully.

He exhaled impatiently. "The helmet goes on your head.

Hurry up."

"I know that," she shot back. She jammed the ungainly black helmet over her head, consigning both Tyler and her neat French twist to hell. It felt like she was wearing a bowling ball. She struggled with the chin strap and then almost pitched over sideways because it was so damned heavy. Tyler didn't offer help, but then again, she didn't expect any.

"Now, put your right foot on the foot peg and throw your left leg over the seat," he said slowly, as if she were slow-witted. "It's not that complicated. I'm sure even you can figure it out."

Glaring at him, Eleanor followed his instructions, and found herself astride the motorcycle, plastered against his back. She wasn't going to cling to him, no matter what. She tried to inch backwards but the sloping seat wouldn't allow it. The machine roared to life and she gave a little shriek, clamping her arms around Tyler's waist. He steered it onto the street and then took off. "Not so fast!" she shouted, clinging to his leather jacket in spite of herself. Naturally Tyler ignored her. When he veered around a corner, Eleanor was sure she was going to fly right off the motorcycle in the opposite direction.

Okay, be rational, she told herself. Rosie wouldn't let Tyler ride her great-grandchildren around and around the block if he didn't know what he was doing, and even if he did hate her guts, he wouldn't let any harm come to her because then he'd have to explain her death to Rosie. Eleanor began to relax slightly once they turned onto the main thoroughfare, and after a couple of blocks, she decided that riding Tyler's motorcycle was kind of fun.

A few blocks more and she decided it was downright exhilarating; whooshing past cars with a roar, the raw power of the Harley between her legs. It was a sultry, sticky summer night and the wind felt wonderful. Eleanor felt reckless and wild. She wanted to go faster. She wanted a leather jacket of her own with the Harley eagle on the back. She wanted somebody she knew from her old life to see her, because, for once in her life, she was part of something big and erotic and exciting, and she wished the ride could go on forever. Tyler might think he was punishing her traveling on the motorcycle, and he might think she was at his mercy for however long their mystery trip took, but in fact the exact opposite was true. He was in for a big surprise. Eleanor stopped trying to preserve any modicum of distance between them on the narrow black seat. Instead she slid forward and boldly squeezed her thighs around Tyler's hips. When she could tell, by the tensing of his shoulders, that he'd noticed, she bit back a smile and slipped her hands from his waist around to his chest. He reacted with a slight shudder and she felt an intoxicating ripple of power. There would be hell to pay later on, she was sure, but for the duration of their ride, there was nothing Tyler could do to stop her from copping a nice feel. Eleanor laughed, uncaring if he heard, and caressed the flat, tense muscles of his abdomen and chest through his silly Voodoo Ranger tee shirt. She considered toying with his belt but changed her mind and deliberately scraped his nipple with her fingernail instead. She heard Tyler bark something, but couldn't make it out. Oh, what the heck, she thought gaily, and dropped her other hand below his belt buckle.

Tyler turned sharply off the road into a grocery store parking lot, making her abandon her mischief and hang on for dear life. He jerked the motorcycle to a stop, kicked the kickstand down and practically leapt off the machine. Eleanor, a smile still twitching around her lips, casually propped her feet on the foot pegs and watched Tyler struggle to unfasten and yank away his helmet. His eyes blazed with fury. Eleanor didn't give him a chance to speak. "This is fun, Tyler! What a good idea!"

He stepped forward, that wonderful, reliable pulse at his temple pounding. "Keep your hands off me, Eleanor," he said through gritted teeth.

She laughed at him. "I have to hold on to something!"

He glared at her for a long minute and she could see him struggling to contain his temper. "Just keep them where they belong," he bit out. "Quit all that funny business."

She held her hands up innocently. "Where do they belong? Maybe you should be more specific."

"I'll be specific," he said, leaning down in what Eleanor figured was supposed to be an intimidating stance. He took her hands, planted them on the chrome grips beside the seat, and then jerked away from her. "Here, not squirreling around on my chest."

She curled one hand around the grip, arched her back, and patted the seat in front of her. "Oh, all right. Come on, then, Easy Rider. Quit wasting my time and Rosie's money."

He opened his mouth, clamped it closed, jammed the helmet on his head and threw his leg back over the seat.

Eleanor laughed out loud. He was just so easy to provoke. She loved that about him.

Chapter Sixteen

Tyler turned his head to see what his table mates were grinning at, afraid he already knew.

Yep. He rubbed his brow forcefully, willing his headache to go away. On the front row of the rowdy crowd, both arms locked up with brawny, fuzz-faced wanna-be cowboys, Eleanor kicked and scooted like she had the sense God gave a cricket. Her fancy twisted hairdo was unwinding down her back, a few long, wavy strands falling into her face as she whipped her head back and forth, laughing with her dance partners.

Laughing and having a good time.

More than a little disgruntled, Tyler leaned his chair back on two legs and watched. She acted like she didn't know or care she was the worst dancer on the floor. When she stumbled, instead of being embarrassed, she threw bright grins at her besotted pair of partners, who were more than happy to hold her up. In fact, they had their hands all over her, holding her up, and she didn't even notice. Tyler picked up an empty beer can and crushed it.

She had no shame at all, the lying, conniving---attorney.

Well, what did he care? He was just doing what had to be done; getting this farce of a date over with. Blame it on his responsibility fixation, he thought irritably.

"And remember what happened next? Ol' Martin picked up the football and kicked it up into the stands!"

Tyler glanced around the table at some of his oldest friends, men he'd played high school and college ball with, as they laughed uproariously at a story they'd all heard a thousand times before. Some things never changed, and that's what he liked about Baxter's. He could always count on good country music, cold beer, and endless football stories around the big table beside the dance floor rail. It was one of his favorite places.

Until tonight. Eleanor was actually ruining Baxter's.

Russell Rivera slapped Tyler on the back. "What's wrong with you, Ty? You're sitting there like a lump on a log! What're you doing, sitting here, anyway, while your date's out there on the dance floor?"

"She's not my date," Tyler said, signaling the waitress. "Bring us another round," he called over the din. She gave him a thumbs-up.

"You came in with her, didn't you? I saw you come in with her."

"Yeah," Tyler replied grudgingly, kicking his chair back from the table so he could stretch out his legs. "I came in with her."

Russell eyed Eleanor, flushed and laughing, approvingly. "Cute little thing. Great ass." He whistled appreciatively. "Don't you think so, Gus?"

Tyler contemplated breaking Russell's front teeth.

Gus Baxter, Tyler's retired, grizzled high school football coach and his managing partner in the bar, leaned across the table. "Whaddja say, Rusty?"

Russell jerked his head toward the dance floor. "Ty's date. Did you meet her? I noticed he didn't bring her over to introduce her to any of us. Hurts my damn feelings."

Gus nodded. "I met her at the door. She's a nice little girl." He squinted at the dance floor. "But what's she doing out there dancing with them other fellers, Ty?"

Tyler grunted in reply.

"I think she's shopping around for a better time," Russell joked. "Ty sure ain't much of a damn date. Whatcha think, Gus? She going to leave with Ty? Russell kicked his chair back beside Tyler's, and folded his arms across his broad chest to watch Eleanor. "Or is she going to leave with one of her dancing boys?"

The electric slide ended and a slow ballad began. Muscles tightening, Tyler watched as Eleanor thanked the bozo on her left before waltzing away with her clearly delighted right hand man.

No. Tyler rose, his chair crashing to the floor. Eleanor wasn't going to slide all over Bozo Number Two on the dance floor, not in his bar, in front of his friends, not tonight, not ever. She was leaving all right; this minute, with him. Tyler heard Russell hooting with laughter as he strode away and it galled him further.

A couple of women tried to catch his attention as he circled the railing separating the dance floor from the tables but he barely noticed. It took him a couple of minutes to shoulder his way through to the middle of the dance floor where she was busy leaning and dipping with Bozo Number Two. Bozo's hands were gripping her hips like they were community property. Tyler felt a blinding rush of rage, and he didn't know if it was aimed at

Eleanor, the bozo, or himself. He grabbed Eleanor's arm and spun her in his direction. "You're making a spectacle of yourself," he growled in her ear. Bozo looked suddenly uncomfortable, as though he were trying to decide whether he should reclaim his dance partner or beat a hasty retreat. He even went so far as to square his shoulders and step forward, his jaw thrust out. Tyler straightened and glowered down at him. "Don't even think about it," he hissed.

Bozo blinked, nodded and hurried away.

Tyler returned his attention to Eleanor, ready to chew her out, but she was busy watching her dance partner disappear into the crowd with a disappointed expression on her face. Glaring at her was ineffectual as hell if she wasn't looking at him so he put a hand under her chin and tilted her head up. "A freaking spectacle," he repeated grimly, "and your hair's a mess. Why don't you cut off that tangled mop?"

To his satisfaction, Eleanor's smile faltered for the briefest instance. He began to tow her toward the exit, anxious to escape the crowded room and, ultimately, Eleanor's exasperating company. By God, she made him mad. Frothing, spitting mad. Every time he thought he had the upper hand, she faked him out. Instead of pitching a fit about him dragging her to a bar instead of the promised fancy night in New Orleans, she bounced right back with some neat little tricks of her own. Like the ride over to Baxter's. The motorcycle ride from hell. Her little traveling hands had him so damned aroused he thought he would explode. And then she sat there, perched on his motorcycle in the Winn Dixie parking lot, laughing at him. It made him livid, and the madder he got, the more she laughed.

And now that they were here, at his place, with his friends all around, she couldn't just sit still at his table and be unhappy like he wanted her to be, like she deserved to be. Oh, no, not Eleanor. She was the freaking belle of the ball. In the club crowded with long, tall, cowboy-booted women, Eleanor was tiny and curvy and having way too much fun letting her hair down, figuratively and literally, with guys years too young for her and years too innocent to realize there was a cold, calculating attorney hiding inside that innocent Tinkerbell exterior. He would be doing everybody a huge favor by getting her out of there. Himself, most of all.

Eleanor allowed herself to be towed along in the wake created by Tyler's charge to the door for, at most, three steps before Tyler felt her put on the brakes and attempt to retrieve ownership of her arm. He sensed more than saw the interested eyes turning in their direction when Eleanor balked. Gritting his teeth, he tightened his already firm grip on her slender arm and cast a warning look over his shoulder.

Eleanor threw her shoulders back as best she could with her right arm still captive and, eyes narrowed, looked pointedly at the big hand encircling her arm. Tyler felt a swift, annoying stab of conscience for manhandling her and loosened his grip slightly.

She immediately yanked her arm free and lifted her chin defiantly, rubbing her arm as if to wipe away the feel of his touch, then stepped forward, almost onto his toes, and jabbed him in the chest. "All right, Tyler, let me tell you a thing or two. You know good and well you brought me here to try to teach me some kind of stupid lesson. What did you think, I'd tag after you and sit at your elbow like a trained monkey all night? You abandoned me as soon as we hit the door, and now it's ticking you off that I'm having fun in spite of your petty little plan." Her raised voice carried over the music and more heads swung in their direction. Yanking the few remaining, valiant pins from her previously upswept hair, she waved them under his nose for a moment before purposefully flinging them to the floor. "And my hair's none of your damned business!" She shook her head ferociously and her hair tumbled around her shoulders and down her back.

Tyler gaped at it, horrified. She couldn't leave it like that. She had to put it back up. He felt a little desperate.

"Go ahead, abandon me," she railed. "I'm not complaining. Far from it! Go on back to your table full of jocks. Talk football all night long and keep reminding yourself and everybody else how great you used to be." Eleanor emphasized the 'used to be' and Tyler; paying attention again, felt his blood rise. "Just because I came with you doesn't mean I have to leave with you. I'll find my own way home, you big, big---" She pushed him in the chest with both little hands. "Gorilla!" Spinning on her heel, she stomped back toward the dance floor, hips twitching and hair rippling.

Gorilla? Tyler gaped at her swiftly departing form and clenched his fists in impotent, inexplicable rage. And what did she mean; she didn't have to leave with him? What did she think, he would just sit back down and watch while she sidled up against every panting, two-stepping loser on the dance floor, and then wave goodbye when she swayed out the door with somebody else? No, by God, she came with him and she left with him.

Eleanor threw a last defiant glare at Tyler before disappearing back into the crush of people on the dance floor. Taking a deep breath, Tyler reached down and snatched three or four hairpins from the floor, jammed them into his front pocket, and started after her. Her hair was going back up and those tight jeans, well; they'd never see the light of day again. That's all there was to it. Tyler elbowed his way through the crowd on the dance floor in baleful pursuit.

Eleanor found her dance partner---Bill? Phil? --- On the opposite side of the room, leaning against the bar looking slightly disconcerted. Waving, she began to make her way toward the empty bar stool at his side, a bright, empty smile pasted across her face, her heart thumping ninety to nothing against her ribs. Bill/Phil brightened for a moment, and then looked past her, his face falling again. Eleanor knew, with frustrated certainty, the cause of his mood swing. She looked over her shoulder and sighed. Yes, here he came. Tyler was bearing down, eyebrows drawn together in a menacing line, fists clenched.

"That's it," he said when he reached her. "I've had enough. Don't give me any trouble or I'll throw you over my shoulder. And don't drag anybody else into this because I'm telling you right now there's not a man in here that can stop me." He caught her arm again and started shouldering his way around the parameter of the room toward the exit. "You're going home."

Eleanor shivered with rage. "When I get home I'll just get in my car and come back."

"After I take you home I don't give a damn what you do." He towed her out the door, ignoring the hoots of laughter and risqué bits of advice that followed them, along the parking lot toward his motorcycle, parked beneath a bright light.

"I hate you," she said fiercely, trying to wrench her arm free. "I hate your guts. You're nothing but a bully, Tyler Hurst. I'm going to tell Rosie everything you've done tonight. She's going to be so ashamed of you." Tyler stopped abruptly and Eleanor felt a wave of relief. "Every last thing," she emphasized for extra measure.

"Is that so," he hissed, hauling Eleanor up against his side with one arm, turning on his heel and stomping toward the narrow alley running between the side of the bar and the neighboring building.

"Where are we going?" Eleanor pried at his arm and kicked futilely as he strode down the dim alley. Maybe bringing Rosie up had been a mistake.

Ignoring her, Tyler turned the corner at the end of the alley and set her on her feet. He stepped forward, crowding her, forcing her to take a step backwards. Eleanor's shoulders bumped the brick of the back wall of the building and her eyes widened when she realized she was trapped. Tyler felt violent and, contrarily, aroused; two emotions he had never simultaneously felt before. Not before Eleanor, anyway. He scowled, loathing the way she made him feel.

But only the narrowest of margins separated them and if he didn't feel the weight of that wild hair in his restless hands, or the taste of her perpetually pursed lips on his mouth just once more, he was going to go up in smoke. Tyler ignored the instincts that screamed at him to stop and think about what he was doing.

"Okay, this is it, Tyler. I am going to tell Rosie. I mean it, Tyler. Rosie's going to---"

"Shut up, Eleanor." He was tired of stopping and thinking. Where had it gotten him?

Eleanor looked around, swiftly weighing her options. On her left was battered pickup truck, on her right was a storage building, and a security fence with strands of barbed wire running along the top circled it all. Her back was against the brick wall of the club, a neon beer light blinking cheerfully in a window above her head and the raucous music from the dance floor was loud enough to drown out any calls for help she might make. She had nowhere to go. She would have to talk her way out of this, and quickly. Eleanor drew in a preparatory breath before raising her eyes and opening her mouth to speak.

Tyler took another step and, towering above her, flattened her against the wall. The lucid argument she intended to launch began and ended with a tiny squeak when without any warning, Tyler slid one powerful arm around the small of her back and drew her up, again lifting her feet from the ground. Before she could react, he clamped her effortlessly against his chest. Voice stolen, she felt like a rag doll, obediently limp with surprise as he tangled the fingers of his free hand into the hair at the nape of her neck. She watched his rigid face, his tight, frowning mouth, as he clenched a fistful of hair and pinned her with his accusatory gaze. He was so angry with her. He was never going to stop being angry with her. Eleanor shuddered. He could break her in half with little or no effort at all. He could crush her against the wall.

"What do you think you're doing," she managed in a tiny, breathless voice.

"Shut up," he repeated, his voice low and dangerous. Eleanor felt another thrill, not of alarm, but of sudden awareness. Tyler seemed to be losing a battle between his celebrated control and a reckless desire and she realized she could continue to fight him or she could go under with him. She seized the fabric of his shirt that strained across his broad shoulders, raking his skin beneath, and pulled him closer .

Tyler pulled her head back with a none-too-gentle tug on the handful of hair. Held motionless, Eleanor watched, helplessly mesmerized as he lowered his face toward her own. She could see, in his half lidded eyes, the battle he was fighting with himself. He hovered for a moment, wavering, then with an unmistakable hiss of resentment, dropped his head lower. There was nothing wavering or halfway about his kiss; she was overwhelmed by the combination of his crushing mouth, the hand holding her head just where he wanted it, and the arm that held her so close, so easily, against his powerful frame.

He shifted and deepened the punishing kiss and Eleanor made a tentative foray with her own tongue. He froze for an instant, and Eleanor's fists uncurled from his shirt and began traveling over the breadth of his shoulders, around the back of his tensely muscled neck. She could feel the pulse at his jaw, echoing the pounding of her heart. The kiss was hot and crushing, and she loved it, she reveled in it, she wanted more. She pressed her hands flat against his temples, holding his face prisoner, as though she, and not Tyler, were the one in control. As if she were captivating him, inciting his body to heights of awareness with savage kisses instead of the other way around. As if it mattered.

Tyler gave a groan and lifted his head, eyes glittering, to glance about. With one swift movement, he tightened his grip and shifted again; raising one booted foot to the low bumper of the truck on Eleanor's left and she found herself straddling his powerful leg. Before she had time to gasp at the intimate positioning or clutch at him to keep from toppling sideways, he dropped his mouth to hers again. The arm clamped around her back drifted lower, curving around her hips to grind her closer, while the other tugged her silk shirt out of the waistband of her jeans. Ignoring her half-hearted moan, he slid his big hand under the cool silk and launched an assault on the fastening of her lacy bra. It was stubborn and he lifted his mouth from hers for the briefest of moments, swearing in a muffled tone as he attempted to concentrate on the tricky fastening. Not like last time, Eleanor thought disjointedly. Last time he'd had no problem; this time he was struggling just like she was. Eleanor gasped when he conquered the hook and cupped a freed, aching breast with his warm hand. He gave a grunt of satisfaction and began to tease the peak of her breast just as he was teasing her mouth with his tongue.

The music and voices from the noisy club fell away and Eleanor lost all desire for anything but more of Tyler's relentless mouth and forceful caress. One hand gripped the neckband of his damp shirt as if she might slip if she didn't hold on; though she knew on some foggy level she wouldn't be returned to the ground until he was good and ready, while the other hand crept boldly to tug at his shirt. His jacket was in her way and she pushed at it, and he swiftly shrugged it off, uncaring when it slid to the gravel. He felt as hot as a raging furnace and she wanted---no, needed---to feel his body heat with her own hands, his bare skin beneath her touch. The thin barrier of cotton was more than she could tolerate. She yanked at the hem up and slid both hands beneath to the fabric to feel the taut, rippling muscles of his back as he curved closer and ground her on his rock-hard thigh.

Tucked against his chest and inside his arms, she was pressed as tightly to him as she could be without being inside his clothing, and when he began rocking his leg, rhythmically and suggestively, in time with the thrusts and dips of his tongue, Eleanor moaned and clamped her legs around his hips, her nails raking down his back. Hazily she wondered if it was possible to faint dead away from excitement. Nothing in her life had prepared her for the waves of need Tyler whipped within her. She began imitating the parrying and thrusting of his tongue and felt triumphant when he shuddered and groaned in response.

Suddenly abandoning her mouth, Tyler encircled her waist easily with his hands and pushed her away slightly, his leg still rocking. Mourning the loss of contact with the warm skin, mindlessly clutching the fabric of his shirt, Eleanor instinctively arched her back and wriggled on his leg, her head lolling sideways. Tyler supported her back with one hand tangled in her long hair while his other hand stumbled over the small buttons of her blouse. When he succeeded in unfastening her blouse, he swept it open.

The cool night air on her skin startled Eleanor and she drew in her breath with a gasp. Tyler hesitated, then abruptly put her on her feet, took her arm and tugged her along as he crossed the few feet to the storage building. Eleanor clutched the front of her shirt closed as she was swept along. When he twisted the door knob and found it locked, he cursed, knocked it open with one ferocious kick and pushed her inside. Before he yanked the battered door closed behind them, Eleanor was dimly aware of freezers and cases of beer and alcohol stacked around the walls. When the door closed, the room went pitch black, and Eleanor reached out for him. Filling up the inky emptiness, he lifted her onto a chest freezer and moved between her legs, slipping an arm around her hips to pull her to the edge. Eleanor wound her legs around his waist and, with hungry hands, pulled him closer still. He pushed her arms away to tug her shirt and bra off her shoulders. Her vague thought to try to tug his shirt off as well flew out of her head when he cupped a breast in his hand, his head dipping, his mouth zeroing in on her aching nipple. Eleanor inhaled long, ragged breaths, fierce flames of need curling and climbing, as he licked and sucked first one aching peak, and then the other. Robbed of her sense of sight, unwilling to break the spell of silence, Eleanor gave herself up to the tumultuous sensations only to find she wasn't satisfied; she wanted more. When Tyler straightened, cupping her breasts in his hands and crushing his plundering mouth to hers again, that was better, but she craved more still. He had taken her too far to turn back, he had created a monster, and she yanked at his belt, struggling with the buckle.

Tyler froze, and Eleanor froze in response, paralyzed with fear that she'd triggered his comprehension. She didn't want him to think, she wanted him mindless and explosive with passion, she wanted him to do something about the molten lava spinning through her veins and pooling between her legs in her deepest feminine part. He had started this and by God, he had to finish it. Eleanor caught his face between her hands and kissed him desperately, trying to pull him back under, and when he groaned, a deep, visceral groan, and dropped his hands to the zipper of her jeans, she went weak with relief. She wriggled farther back on the freezer while Tyler wrenched at the stubborn zipper. She braced herself with her arms and lifted her hips to help him as he tugged the tight jeans from her legs. Her shoes hit the store room floor, and her jeans and panties followed. Naked, uncaring, she leaned forward to help him, to hurry him up, but he pushed her hands away. She heard his own ragged breathing and a terse epithet, the sound of his jeans zipper, and then he moved back between her legs and tugged her forward. Eleanor gripped his shoulders as he guided his swollen flesh to her opening.

No. She felt an overwhelming tide of panic. He was too big, she was too small, and though she was wet and aching, it couldn't be physically possible, so she bucked and pushed at his shoulders to escape. Tyler gave her no mercy. He caught her easily, pulled her back, and gripping her hips, lifted her so she had no choice but to cling to him, and began prodding insistently, pushing his way into her inch by throbbing inch. Eleanor moaned with both fear and need, and he stilled, turning her head to lick the rim of her ear, his hot breath on the sensitive flesh distracting her for a tiny moment, then took advantage of her distraction by thrusting farther, and she gasped. He stopped again, giving her time to adjust, laving her ear and the pulse point behind her jaw, then thrust again, and Eleanor knew the measure of his control by the timbre of his rumbling groan. She felt herself stretching to accommodate him, and, delirious with relief that perhaps it was possible after all, she rewarded him for his effort by gritting her teeth and clamping her legs around his hips, and he understood, and gave a last, emphatic thrust that she felt all the way to her womb.

They remained carefully still for a long moment. Tyler withdrew slightly, and then returned, and Eleanor clung to him, astonished by her body's rippling reaction to his minimal movement. Inhaling sharply in the silence, he moved again, carefully, and Eleanor's head lolled backwards in answer. She wanted to tell him to hurry, to do it, to take her over the crest, but she didn't want to break the bond of silence that had enabled them to start their journey so she showed him instead by sliding her hands down to his lean hips to push him away, then pull him back fiercely. It was all the encouragement he needed to begin driving into her, warily at first, then with increasing, reckless intensity until Eleanor's breath came in short, shallow pants and she knew she was on the edge of something fierce and wonderful. It was all she could do not to cry out as the teasing pressure deep inside her womb coiled until she was sure she wouldn't survive the wild ordeal, and then a tiny quiver of something startling began rippling and then flowing, and finally pounding through her veins, and she had to bite her hand to keep from screaming. Tyler pushed her hand away to cover her mouth with his with another savage kiss and then she felt his shoulders tense, his whole body go rigid beneath her stroking hands when he found his own deliverance, and she clung to him while he braced himself over her, shuddering in the aftermath as their joint spasms subsided.

Exhausted but exultant, Eleanor swept a gentle hand back and forth over Tyler's shoulder. It was the most astonishing, satisfying thing that had ever happened to her. He was magnificent. She loved him so much. He had to know it; he had to care in return. Things were going to be okay. Things would be wonderful. She was startled out of her reverie when the door to the store room creaked, a sliver of light widening as it opened. Tyler jerked away, yanking up his jeans, to slam it closed again.

"What the heck? Who's in there?"

"It's me, Gus," Tyler replied, his voice guttural, his shoulder against the door.

"That you, Ty? I found your jacket. What're you doing in there? Did you break the door?"

Tyler ignored his friend's questions. "I need a minute," he called through the door. "Just leave the jacket and go on."

"Is everything okay? I can't believe you broke the door," Gus complained on the other side.

"Everything's fine, Gus. I'll fix the door. Go on."

Chilled without Tyler's heat, and suddenly horribly aware of her nakedness while Tyler was only slightly disheveled, Eleanor carefully moved off the freezer to try to locate her scattered garments, her legs weak. Incapable of speech, she was surprised by Tyler's steady voice. She found her jeans and shoes, but no panties, and as she untangled the inside-out legs, it dawned on her she seemed to be much more affected by their experience than he was.

"You got that little lady in there with you, son?"

Tyler cursed under his breath. "Yeah, Gus, she's here."

Suddenly uncaring about her lost panties, she pulled her jeans on, wincing at the harsh denim against her tender flesh, and jammed her feet into her shoes.

"She want to be in there?"

"What do you think? Now mind your own business, you nosy old bastard, and go away."

"Not until she tells me something, Tyler Hurst, because the last thing I saw was you yanking her out the door and she didn't look none too happy about it. It ain't like you to throw your weight around, sonny, and you just remember you ain't so big I can't still knock you down a peg or two."

"Say something or he'll never leave." Tyler's tone was abrupt and passionless.

Eleanor put a hand to her throat, swallowed past her sudden nausea, and complied. "Everything's fine, Gus." Her voice sounded unnatural; high pitched and quivery. She desperately groped around for her shirt and bra.

"Oh, that'll convince him," Tyler muttered darkly.

Those weren't the words of a man who was as affected by what just happened as she was. That wasn't the tone of a man who cared for her. Perhaps it had been his plan all along to seduce her and then walk away. He'd said he was going to give her her money's worth. An icy shiver swept Eleanor from head to toe.

She swallowed and tried again. "I've taught him who's the boss," she called, forcing a light note to her shaky voice. "We won't have any more trouble with him tonight."

Gus guffawed. "That's the way, little lady. Sugar catches more flies than vinegar, I allus says, but there's better places for canoodling than a dirty old storeroom. Y'all go on home now, you hear?"

Tyler hit a light switch on the wall and the store room was bathed in a harsh yellow light. Wincing, Eleanor automatically turned her back to Tyler, crossing her arms in front of her breasts, and looked around desperately for her lost garments. When she found her bra and shirt, jammed between the freezer and a stack of cases of beer, she worked with stiff fingers to put them back on.

Tyler was silent as she struggled, and when she finally turned, his expression was impossible to read. "Let's go," he said, opening the door and bending to scoop his jacket from the ground. He started off down the alley, sparing no glance to see if she followed. Eleanor stared after him dumbly. He stopped and turned around, his eyes icy. "I said, let's go."

Eleanor couldn't walk if she were under threat of death; in fact, it was all she could do to simply stand upright. It had just been payback for him. It hadn't meant a thing. She was the stupidest woman on the face of the earth. She wrapped her arms around her waist, trembling. "Go ahead. I'll be there in a minute," she said in a frozen little voice. She could see Tyler's jaw working. "Can I just have a minute? Please?" He started back toward her, cursing under his breath. Eleanor wrapped her arms tighter around her waist and tried to shrink against the door. Her teeth started to chatter and she clamped her jaw as tightly closed as she could. He peeled her away from the door and pushed the jacket over her shoulders. The heavy jacket hung, comically, to her knees. Eleanor felt a hysterical giggle bubble up in her throat.

"I'm not waiting around for you," he said, putting a hand at her back and propelling her down the alley toward the parking lot. Instead of going to his motorcycle, he opened the passenger door of an old pick-up truck. "Get in."

Eleanor clumsily obeyed without a word, and watched, her teeth still chattering, as Tyler strode toward the club's front door, had a brief conversation with Gus, and returned with Gus' keys in his hand. He opened the driver door and climbed in without as much as a glance in her direction. Eleanor hugged the door, her tumbled hair hiding her face, her gaze locked outside the window while a million fragmented thoughts floated around in her mind.

The ride back to her house was thick with silence until they rolled into her driveway. Eleanor pulled Tyler's jacket off with numb fingers and then wrestled with the stiff door handle. It was stubborn, it wouldn't work. Tyler gave a snort of impatience and reached across to yank it open for her, then caught her arm before she could slide out of the cab.

"Nothing has changed," he said, his eyes even colder than his tone. "Nothing."

Everything had changed, but Eleanor nodded anyway. She slid out of the cab and ran for her house and didn't look back.

Chapter Seventeen

Sunk low in his Adirondack chair, hands clasped behind his head, Tyler squinted at the horizon and wondered how long it would be before the sun rose over the golf course, lighting the view he hated. He glanced at his Rolex. Ten minutes past four. It would be a while yet.

He sat up and rubbed his aching neck. All night in a wooden chair hadn't done anything for his body or his disposition, but what difference did it make where he spent his night? He couldn't have bought sleep for a million dollars and this chair was as good as anyplace else for sitting and trying to figure out how the hell he could have made such a mess of things.

And every time he closed his eyes, all he saw was Eleanor, anyway. Flushed and laughing in Baxter's, vivid with fury when he dragged her out of there, stark white and shaking after---

After he completely and totally lost every vestige of self-control he ever thought he possessed, with a woman he despised, on top of a freezer in a filthy store room.

Oh, man. Tyler leaned forward and held his head in his hands. At some point, early on, in the alley, he was pretty sure Eleanor started to believe he was having some kind of change of heart---it was the only way he could explain her own startling about-face--- but she was wrong. He hadn't given half a damn what she thought or wanted or didn't want; he was out of control the minute she walked away from him on the dance floor.

Only he hadn't meant for things to go so far. The pitch black darkness and the profound silence between them made it easy for him to do what he liked with her without thinking; only feeling, but he hadn't meant to use her so fiercely. All night he'd been trying to convince himself he would have stopped if she had told him to, but the fact was, he wasn't so sure. That moment when she realized his size, when she panicked, he may have hesitated but he really didn't know if he would have stopped. Nothing cerebral about it; just simple reaction to weeks without sex and all the pent up irritation he'd been stoking against Eleanor for days. Anger and lust and a skewed desire for revenge, all mixed and all boiling, all callously taken out on a woman he outweighed by well over a hundred pounds.

Nauseated, Tyler cursed proficiently. Yes sir, he had a lot to be proud of. No matter what she was, how she'd fooled him, Eleanor didn't deserve what he'd done. He tried to piece together some of his anger but now all he felt was shame, sharp as knives and bone-deep.

Bottom line, it was done, he couldn't undo it, and the way he saw it, he now had three new problems. The first and most alarming problem had to do with the fact he hadn't used any protection and he'd bet his bank account she wasn't using anything, either. Experienced, Eleanor wasn't.

But, damn it all, experienced or not, honest to God, Tyler couldn't recall better sex in his life. She had been on fire for him, scorching him, taking all he had to give, and when the magnitude of his madness was beginning to sink in, then she had to go and start with those feather light strokes and kisses, like it had all been her choice and her pleasure. Against his better judgment, Tyler dug his hand into his pocket and pulled out the panties she'd so enthusiastically abandoned. Even now, as ashamed as he felt, all he had to do was think her slim legs wrapped around his hips, her mane of hair, her fluttering hands, her sighs, and he got hard all over again.

Studying the tiny bit of pink silk dangling from one finger, Tyler dragged in a deep breath, and then stuffed them back into his pocket. Move on, he told himself.

Problem number one; no protection, so there was a chance she could be pregnant. Slim, maybe, but a chance nonetheless. And if she was, what then? What was he going to do, marry her? That would be great, just great. Thirty-five years old and still making the same mistakes.

On the other hand, what if she was pregnant but didn't want the baby? His baby. Tyler felt a ripple of panic. Things might be different for other people these days and he might be old fashioned but he hoped to hell she wouldn't want to get rid of it. It would be a cold day in hell before he'd let her get rid of it.

Okay, get a grip, he coached himself. Cross that bridge when you get to it

He'd just have to go talk to her and find out how long before she knew one way or the other.

His second problem was Rosie. She was going to ask about their evening and what was he going to say? Tyler couldn't quite envision telling his grandmother how he'd dragged her beloved little neighbor into a dirty storeroom, ripped her clothes off and banged her on top of a freezer. How did he maneuver around that happy little truth? And it wasn't just Rosie, either. The rest of his family would be gathering later in the day, avid for details about their night out. Smiling, winking, expecting to hear a charming story.

Tyler dropped his head back into his hands. He should have just suffered through the scheduled evening in New Orleans instead of trying to outsmart Eleanor, to put her in her place. Experience should have taught him that plans to best Eleanor always backfired, only this time the ramifications were merciless. He'd completely lost control, behaved like an animal, gone too far. Even if Eleanor wanted revenge, even though she deserved revenge, he hoped his family would never know how cruelly he had behaved. But if they did, he'd own up to it.

But he had to know her intentions. Which meant, again, he had to talk to her.

And finally, he had to get her out of that house. Whatever it took, whatever it cost, he had to get Eleanor out of that house because there was no way he could ever look at her again without remembering last night, remembering how angry he'd been, how badly he'd wanted her, how good it had been. He didn't want to be reminded of it. So she had to go. He'd make it worth her while; he'd make her an offer she couldn't refuse. She could still be friends with Rosie; she just couldn't live next door.

And to make any offers, he'd have to talk to her.

Tyler glanced at his Rolex again. Four-thirty. Still too early. He wanted to get it over with as soon as possible and then he was going to get out of town for a few days. He'd had about all he could stand of being home these days.

* * *

"You sure you're okay, Eleanor?" Scott patted Eleanor on the shoulder awkwardly before jamming his Southern Heritage Nursery baseball cap on his head. "You want me to get you anything before I go?"

Eleanor reached up to squeeze his hand. "I'm just tired. You go on to work." Sleep had been impossible, and she had finally given up sometime in the middle of the night, climbing out of bed and trudging downstairs to huddle inside one of Rosie's gifts, a pastel patchwork afghan that smelled of baby powder and sunshine.

He looked at her doubtfully. "I know I told Robb I'd meet him at six but I can call him if you want me to stick around a while. You've been sitting there for hours. I'm worried about you."

Eleanor wanted to reassure him she was fine but she wasn't so sure. "Don't be. You know what? When I get up, I'm going to plant those petunias," she said, changing the subject. "They're going to be pretty by the front steps."

Scott, bless his heart, was easily distracted. "That's what I thought. Robb always tells customers to put bright colors by their front door."

"Well, he should know what he's talking about," she said, working up the energy to smile. Scott quoted Robb right and left and was beginning to talk enthusiastically about studying for a degree in horticulture. Eleanor didn't care what he studied as long as it was something that made him happy.

"Well, I'll be going, then. Call me if you need anything." With one last pat, he disappeared through the front door.

When the door closed, Eleanor pillowed her head on her arm, closed her eyes, and willed herself to fall asleep, but it was no good.

She could sit here all day but she wouldn't be able to turn off the maelstrom of thoughts spinning in her head. It was time to recognize some hard truths and there were plenty of them just waiting to smack her in the face. Things like how she needed a job to keep the house and to help Scott with tuition. How the only firm who would have anything to do with her was the one where she didn't want to work.

But all of that paled beside the worst cold, hard truth of them all; that she was stupid, stupid, stupid. She'd made up a fairytale in her mind that all the anger and betrayal Tyler felt would just dissipate after their tumultuous lovemaking. It wasn't lovemaking to him, it was nothing to him. She was the idiot who thought it meant more, who had urged him on.

Well, she'd gotten what she wanted. The bruises on her hips and the soreness between her legs were proof of that. Even if she managed to convince herself that for a sweet, short while last night, she'd believed his anger had burned itself out, that he'd forgiven her, in the cold light of morning she couldn't pretend there was any justification for that hopefulness. For Tyler there had been no gentle emotion, no tenderness behind what happened in that dark store room; only spiraling anger and lust, and she had brought it all on herself by recklessly goading him all evening long. She had stupidly assumed she could hold her own with him.

Now he had a whole new reason to despise her but he couldn't hate her any more than she hated herself. Eleanor huddled deeper into her corner of the sofa and sobbed.

* * *

Tyler turned his truck into Eleanor's driveway and was taken aback to discover her sitting at the foot of the steps to her porch, an untouched flat of flowers at her side.

Her eyes grew huge when she saw him. Tensing, Tyler drove to the very end, out of sight if Rosie happened to glance out of her windows, and saw with some relief Scott's motorcycle was nowhere in sight. Climbing out of his truck, he closed the door carefully and walked around to the front of her house.

Well, she hadn't run inside and locked the door, but then, that wasn't Eleanor's style. She still sat on the step, swathed in her fluffy pink robe, gripping a trowel with both hands as he strode forward.

Tyler nodded, his throat oddly tight. "We need to talk."

She didn't acknowledge his words; she just looked at him through shuttered green eyes.

Tyler raised a hand to rub his throat. "Do you want to go inside?" He didn't relish the idea of having this conversation out on her front steps.

She shook her head.

Well, okay. Tyler hunkered down and mindlessly touched one of the flowers before speaking again. "Things got out of hand last night." He glanced at her to gauge her response to his ridiculously obvious remark. She just continued to look at him unblinkingly. Tyler felt a ripple of unease. He didn't know this Eleanor; so subdued and quiet. He'd much rather her rage at him. "I didn't plan for things to go so far." He watched her swallow, her skin so pale it was almost translucent in the bright morning light. "I didn't use anything."

Her expression didn't change, and he wondered if, in her innocence, she didn't immediately understand his point. "For protection," he clarified. "I'm clean, but if it'll make you feel better,

I don't mind testing again to prove it." He regretted his choice of words; probably nothing was going to make Eleanor feel better.

She shook her head. "Do I need to prove anything to you?" she asked in a hollow voice.

Tyler inhaled and looked away. "No. The other thing is---," he trailed off and gazed across the lawn. "I guess you realize there's a chance you could wind up pregnant."

"I'll know in a week or so," she said quietly, tugging one of the flowers from the tray.

So apparently the possibility had occurred to her, too. Maybe it accounted for her very un-Eleanor-like behavior. "I'm going out of town for a few days," he said. "Would you-"

She interrupted. "I'll let you know."

"If it turns out that you are---"

"I'll cross that bridge when I get to it."

She was excluding him from the equation. If anybody knew how seriously he took his responsibilities, it was Eleanor, but there was no point in arguing about it now. "Okay," he said reluctantly. "I also want to talk about---"

"Rosie," she said before he could finish. "I don't want to upset her any more than you do."

He was startled by her paralleling train of thought.

"Just tell me what you want me to tell her." Stabbing the shovel into the soft dirt, Eleanor accidentally chopped the plant in half and stared at it with horror. She carefully picked it up to look at the damage and Tyler heard her draw in a deep, rattling breath. It twisted something in his chest and he moved closer to take the damaged plant from her hand. She snatched it back and clutched it protectively. "Just tell me what you want me to tell her," she repeated.

She was letting him off way too easy. Tyler's guilt churned. "That it was — that we had an okay time?" Repelled by his gross misstatement, he grimaced. "Without encouraging her to think---"

"That we've made amends?" Her face averted, she carefully chiseled some earth from the flowerbed. "Okay. Did we go to Brennan's or Baxter's?"

Tyler was confounded by Eleanor's willingness to concoct a story to spare Rosie. His level of shame spiked higher. "Baxter's. Let's keep it as close to the truth as possible."

Eleanor gave him an incredulous glance, a spark of her usual feisty self glinting for a brief instant. "Absolutely, knowing how important the truth is to you."

He took that one on the chin, and unable to meet her gaze, had to look away.

"Anything else?" She carefully tucked the injured plant into the ground, patting the dirt around it gently.

"I want to buy you out of this house."

She glanced up sharply. "What?"

"I'll make it worth your while. I'll give you enough to buy a nice house someplace else."

Eleanor rose awkwardly, dusting her hands on her robe. "I don't want another house."

"Well, you can't stay here," he said. "I'm not asking you to stop seeing Rosie. I just think it's best if you find someplace else to live."

"Best for whom?" she asked, two spots of color vivid on her pale face. "Best for me or you?"

"Both of us." Pulling his wallet from his back pocket, Tyler withdrew the check he'd written earlier and held it out to her. "Hold on to this and just think about it." Eleanor made no move to take it so he picked up her hand and pressed the check into her palm. "Just think about it," he said again. "And lastly---"

She looked at him.

"I'm sorry," he said clumsily. "Sorry about all of it."

She stared at the folded check in her hand. "Okay, well, I'm busy, Tyler, so if you don't mind, you can just go away now." Her words came out in a strained whisper. "Please just go away."

Tyler saw a tear glisten on her cheek before she could twist to turn her back to him. He missed his scrappy Eleanor, the one who would tear the check up into a thousand tiny pieces and fling them into his face. He frowned and reached a hand out to turn her back around, thinking crazy thoughts about snatching the check back, gathering her up to kiss away her tears. But before he could even begin to assimilate his shifting mood, he was distracted by a shiny black Lexus turning into her driveway. Glancing down, he saw she was trying hard to maintain her composure and wasn't yet aware she had another visitor.

"You have company," he said.

Eleanor turned her head to see, and he heard her inhale quickly, saw her shoulders sag. "Well, there you go," she said, her voice low. "Just when you think things can't get any---," she broke off and swallowed.

Tyler knew she didn't intend him to hear her words, and he didn't need to hear the rest of the remark to appreciate she was about to receive an unwelcome visitor. Another unwelcome visitor, he reminded himself, and he'd done a fine job priming her for it. By the anxious way she tugged her robe tighter and smoothed her already vanquished hair, her attention focused on the car gliding to a stop, Tyler realized he was already all but forgotten. He watched the sedan to see who Eleanor was girding herself to face.

315

The driver door opened and an older man of average height and slim build stepped from the car, dressed in an impeccably tailored suit. He closed the door, eyeing Tyler and Eleanor across the distance. Tyler, struck by his resemblance to Scott, knew he was Eleanor's father.

"You need to go," Eleanor whispered, pushing the check into her robe pocket.

"I can't," he replied promptly. "He's got me blocked in."

"Go around him. Or go over to Rosie's."

"In a minute," he said, despite her pleading tone.

Eleanor's father rounded the hood of his car and started down the walkway toward them, his stride clipped, his bearing stiff. He drew to a halt and addressed Eleanor, ignoring Tyler. "I see you got your money's worth."

What did he mean; money's worth? Frowning, Tyler glanced at Eleanor. She swayed slightly as though she'd been struck. "It's not what it looks like. He didn't spend the night."

Ignoring the voice reminding Tyler his actual behavior had been infinitely worse than what Eleanor's father suspected, he took a step toward the older man. "What the hell kind of remark is that?"

Judge Haley studied him with a frosty green gaze, and then turned back to Eleanor. "You look unkempt. Go inside and get dressed while I have a private word with Mr. Hurst."

Unkempt? Tyler clenched his fists and willed Eleanor to go inside. He had some words of his own for her pathetic excuse for a father and he'd just as soon she not hear them. Then he faltered; he wasn't Eleanor's champion and what went on between them was none of his business. He didn't want it to be any of his business, either. He'd done what he came to do and now he could leave.

Eleanor's response echoed Tyler's thoughts. "No, I don't think so," she said quietly. "There's nothing to say to Tyler. He's leaving now anyway."

Tyler just thought Eleanor looked pale earlier; now she was colorless, and he wavered again. He wouldn't pretend to be any great prize but he was still the only line of defense she had at the moment. He couldn't just walk away. "I think I'll stick around a minute after all, honey, and see what your old dad here has to say," he drawled. "Why don't you just go on inside."

"I am not going inside," she repeated with just a glimmer of her usual spirit.

Judge Haley pressed his lips together disapprovingly before turning to Tyler with a challenging glare. "I don't want you interfering with my daughter. I want you to stay away from her. You are completely inappropriate for one another."

Eleanor laughed, a choking sort of laugh, and Tyler instinctively moved closer to her, between her and her father. "You'll be relieved to know we feel the same way," she said, edging away from him, standing alone. "Right, Tyler?"

Tyler narrowed his eyes. How he felt, one way or the other, wasn't any of her father's damned business.

"Tell him, Tyler."

Tyler didn't want to tell him anything but to go to hell, but a swift glance at Eleanor told him she was barely hanging on. "Yeah," he said grudgingly. "That's right."

"Very good," Judge Haley said coolly, moving past him toward the steps. "Then our conversation is concluded." Effectively dismissing Tyler, he took Eleanor by her arm. "Come inside, Eleanor. I have another matter to discuss with you."

Eleanor didn't spare another glance for Tyler. She climbed the steps impassively, opened the front door, and followed him inside, then gently the door behind her without meeting Tyler's frowning gaze. She turned around to face her father. "Would you like a cup of coffee?" she asked numbly, politely.

"No," Judge Haley replied, glancing about her living room critically. "I think you should know I've decided to acknowledge Scott."

Startled, Eleanor sat down. "You have?"

Judge Haley nodded tersely. "I went by the nursery and saw him but I didn't speak to him."

"He looks just like you, doesn't he?" Eleanor couldn't help it; she wanted to hear him admit he had been wrong.

Her father chose not to respond. "Before I speak to him or make any kind of provision for him whatsoever, you and I have to come to an agreement."

Eleanor smoothed her robe over her lap. It was nothing less than she expected. There was always some kind of stipulation where her father was concerned. She braced herself. "What kind of agreement?"

Her father lifted a vase from the mantle and examined it. "I will fully fund his postsecondary and graduate education and I will set up a substantial trust fund in his name if---," he set the vase down and pinned Eleanor with his chilly gaze.

"If?" she repeated questioningly.

"If you sell this ridiculous house and return to work immediately. Another condition was to have been your disassociation with Tyler Hurst," he added nonchalantly, "but I believe that's already been covered. Well? Is your brother's education and financial well-being enough of an incentive to return to your career?"

"You know it is," she said, utterly defeated. She could fight Tyler or her father individually but she no longer had the energy required to fight them both. And she had Scott to think of. Her father had trumped her soundly. "Of course you know it is."

"Very good," he said, almost cheerfully. "There are one or two smaller issues but we can discuss those later. I'll have Jean notify Phillip today that you'll be back at work tomorrow."

"Fine," she said listlessly. Tomorrow was as good as any other day. No point in avoiding the inevitable any longer.

"And I'll begin drawing up the papers for Scott's trust fund myself. Perhaps we three can have dinner one night later in the week. I assume you can be trusted to set the wheels in motion on finding another place to live?

"Sure. Any suggestions?" She offered her question with a twinge of wryness.

"As a matter of fact, yes. There are some new apartments going up only a few blocks away from CBB. Shall I have Jean call and inquire?"

"Why not," she said, rising and moving toward the door. "Is that everything?"

Her father followed her to the door. "This is for the best, Eleanor. You'll come to realize that, I'm sure."

"If you say so," Eleanor said. She opened the door and stepped aside to let him pass, then closed it behind him. Leaning against the frame, she closed her eyes and drew in a long, rattling breath. She wouldn't think of this as a surrender; she would view it as a choice for Scott.

And she simply wouldn't think about Tyler at all.

* * *

"Eleanor, you simply cannot allow your father to manipulate you this way." Rosie was distraught. Her Sunday morning had been filled with unpleasant surprises, one right after the other. Returning home from church, she barely had time to put her purse down before the telephone began ringing. First it was Ty, calling to say he was catching a flight to Phoenix, no time to come by, he'd see her in a few days. And scant moments later, Eleanor phoned to say she had things to do and would have to take a rain check on the afternoon get-together.

The two calls, alarming in their similarity, prompted Rosie to march across the lawn to find out what happened the night before, during the evening she had forced upon Eleanor and Tyler. She had knocked, and waited. And waited. And waited. When Eleanor finally came to the door, tear stains evident on her face, Rosie knew something terrible had happened. No amount of coaxing could get Eleanor to explain, and before Rosie could even ask about the evening in New Orleans, Eleanor had informed her she was putting the house up for sale and going back to work at Conrad, Berkley and Burns. Rosie knew how to count, and in this case, she suspected one plus one equaled Eleanor's controlling father, and her own domineering grandson.

Eleanor, still pale, stirred her coffee listlessly. "It's really for the best, Rosie."

"For whose best?" Rosie demanded gently.

Eleanor hesitated, and then replied. "Scott."

"What has Scott got to do with this?"

Eleanor sighed. "All right, Rosie, I'll tell you what you want to know, but it's in the strictest of confidences."

Rosie nodded. "I understand."

Eleanor gazed across the room. "It's simple. Father will acknowledge Scott and provide for him financially if I move and go back to work."

"Why, that's criminal," Rosie sputtered. "It's practically blackmail!" What a horrible, horrible man. Eleanor simply couldn't cave in to him this way. "And otherwise, he wouldn't?"

Eleanor shrugged. "I don't know, he might, but I've decided not to risk it. It's very important to him that I go back to CBB, and it's very important to me that Scott be acknowledged."

"But what about the house? Why do you have to give up your house?"

Eleanor turned the spoon over and over in her hand. "I guess he sees it as a distraction."

Rosie suddenly wondered what else Eleanor's father saw as a distraction. "Was Ty also part of your his conditions?"

Eleanor hesitated just long enough to answer Rosie's question, and she knew it. She reached out and covered Rosie's hand. "Rosie, it didn't matter. Last night we got along fine but there won't be any romantic reconciliation. We're too different. We want different things. We both agreed."

Horse feathers, but Rosie decided she wouldn't challenge Eleanor's well-rehearsed spiel right now. She'd just pray that Tyler would come home quickly, before this mess spun out of control. She wasn't giving up on them yet.

* * *

Damn, it was hot. The minute Tyler stepped out of the climate controlled Baton Rouge airport, the humidity hit him like a fist. Reaching his truck, he threw his bag inside and dug his phone out of his pocket to check it again. No message. She'd said she'd call; so why hadn't she? The waiting and wondering was driving him crazy. Sighing, he started the engine, hit max on the air conditioning control and sped out of the parking lot.

Now, did he go home, or straight to Rosie's where chances were good he'd bump into Eleanor and maybe find out what he wanted to know? It wasn't exactly something he could come right out and ask her in front of his grandmother. Might as well go home first, cool off and gather his thoughts.

He guessed he shouldn't have stretched his five day trip into ten, but it wasn't like he'd stayed away on purpose or anything. Hank and Warren were in the mood for some golf and when they suggested flying down to Naples, it wasn't like anybody was waiting for him at home so he figured, what the hell. Naples was nice. Golf was good. Then Hank and Warren decided, at the last minute, to pack up the wives and kids, too. Which was, again, okay, because Tyler liked Lynda and Connie and all their kids, but it had only taken a couple of days of playing crappy golf, being elbowed in the ribs constantly because he wasn't paying attention, and feeling like the odd man at dinner every night, to decide he'd had enough fun. So then he flew up to Denver to run around with Garrett for a while but that was no good either because Garrett had a new lady and she had an unending supply of girlfriends who kept showing up, and while the idea of going out every night seemed like fun in theory, in practice it stank.

Tyler drove into his driveway and stopped to collect his mail before letting himself in to his silent, empty house. He tossed his bags onto the sofa and checked his phone again. Nope, nothing.

Frustrated, he returned to the kitchen where he opened a bottle of beer, propped a hip on a barstool at the island and began to sift through his mail. He paused when he came to an envelope with no return address, his name and address written in small, neat script. Tyler studied it for a moment before ripping it open. A shower of minuscule pieces of paper drifted onto the counter, the tiny scraps a familiar blue, the blue of his checks. Frowning, Tyler pulled a plain white piece of paper from the envelope and unfolded it.

The succinct message, "Breathe easy," was written in the middle of the paper in the same small script, and it was signed with an "E."

Tyler stared at the message.

Breathe easy? Breathe easy? Was this some kind of joke? Was this Eleanor's unique way to give him the news he'd been losing sleep over for almost two weeks? Instead of calling him like she said she would, she decided to trust the U.S. Postal Service with something as important as whether or not they were going to be parents?

And the best message she could come up with was 'breathe easy'?

Tyler read the note again, and his outrage fizzled. She wasn't pregnant. It was great news. He should be relieved. Elated, even. He traced the "E' with his finger. It was the best possible news.

He absently scooped up a few of the blue scraps. Yessiree, she'd torn up his check. He guessed it meant she wasn't going to give up her house. Tyler tried to stir up some anger over her defiance but he couldn't. What the hell, let her keep the damned house. What did he care. Tyler slowly swept the tiny pieces back into the envelope, then refolded Eleanor's note and shoved it into his pocket.

So that was that. No baby. Huge relief.

He guessed he'd go on over to Rosie's for a while. Nothing else to do. Maybe he'd see Eleanor while he was there and tell her she could keep the house.

Tyler pulled the note out of his pocket, unfolded it, and read it one more time. Breathe easy. Was that what Eleanor was doing now, breathing easy? Because it was the damndest thing; he should be, too, but his chest felt just as tight as it did before.

In record time Tyler pulled into Rosie's driveway, frowning when he saw her empty garage. What day was this? Thursday. What did Rosie do on Thursdays? He couldn't recall, and he wished for once he had a grandmother who stayed home occasionally. He edged the truck a little farther to get a clearer view at Eleanor's house. Scott's motorcycle was pulled off to the side but there was no little gray Prius in the driveway. Tyler saw something, though, that made him bring the truck to a jerking stop; boxes, lots of them, lined up neatly on Eleanor's front porch.

Moving boxes.

Frowning, Tyler killed the engine, slid out of the truck and automatically started toward her house for a closer look. This didn't make sense. He tried to push away the sinking feeling those boxes gave him. If she had decided to move, then why tear up his check? In his experience, attorneys were more than willing to take money, big sums of money, deserved or not, without a backwards glance. He climbed the steps to the porch, studied the row of boxes and then looked into the window. No sign of life, just more boxes. Tyler felt a stab of worry, and an unreasonable anxiousness to find Eleanor right away, to tell her she could stay, and while he was at it, maybe try to make amends for everything bad that had gone down between them. It had been impossible to forget how defeated she looked when he last saw her, walking inside her house with her father, closing the door between them. It was impossible for him to forget what a bastard he had been.

Tyler heard the back door open and close, and hurried around the house where he met Scott, heading for his motorcycle. "Hey, Scott, how're you doing?" he asked casually.

Stopping a few feet away, Scott gave Tyler a narrow look. "Eleanor's not here, Mr. Hurst."

So he was 'Mr. Hurst' again. "Yeah, I see that," he replied slowly. "I need to talk to her. You know when she'll be back? Or if she's with Rosie?"

"She's not with Rosie and she won't be home until later." Scott turned his back on Tyler and began walking toward his motorcycle.

Tyler walked along with him. "Where can I find her?"

Scott bit his lip, clearly debating whether to provide the information. "I don't think she wants to see you."

Tyler still had to see her. He tried for a reasonable, even tone. "I appreciate the fact you're looking out for her, but the fact is I have to talk with her and you can either tell me where to find her or I'll just plant myself here and wait until she comes home. It's up to you."

Scott stared back at him for a long moment. "She's at work," he said finally, grudgingly.

Work? Tyler blinked in surprise. "Since when?"

"Since last week."

"Where?"

Scott picked his helmet up from the motorcycle seat. "You shouldn't bother her at work, especially if she doesn't want to see you."

What Scott didn't understand was Tyler wasn't going to let him go anywhere until he found out what he wanted to know. "Come on, Scott, tell me where she's working."

Buckling his helmet beneath his chin, Scott glared at Tyler. "Where she used to work. Conrad, Berkley and Burns."

Tyler frowned. Wasn't that where Rosie said Eleanor worked before? The place she hated? He tried to recall the conversation he had with Rosie the day he found out Eleanor was an attorney, but he'd been so ticked he hadn't really listened to anything Rosie tried to tell him. Now he wished he had.

"I guess you're going to go right on over there and make her even more upset, huh?"

"No," Tyler said quietly. "That's not what I have planned at all."

Scott took his helmet back off. "She's been different ever since that night you picked her up on the Harley. Did you know that? You want to tell me why?"

Tyler met Scott's accusatory gaze levelly. "It's got nothing to do with you."

"The hell it doesn't! She's my sister. Anything that makes her unhappy is my business."

Tyler felt perversely proud of Scott's belligerence on Eleanor's behalf. "I already told you I'm not planning on doing anything to upset her," he said calmly. "I guess you'll have to trust me on that."

"Yeah, well, you'd better not," Scott said, jamming his helmet on his head. "You'd just better not."

Tyler stepped aside to give Scott room to maneuver his motorcycle around on the end of the driveway, and then started back to his truck. He looked up the address and made the short drive downtown. As he parked along Third Street, Tyler tried not to dwell on the fact he was actually, of his own volition, paying a visit to a law firm. He always made his lawyers come to him and they were always happy to do so. He tried to work up some hostility toward attorneys in general, usually an effortless exercise, but today it hardly seemed worth the effort. Rosie had tried to tell him he was making a big mistake by lumping Eleanor into the same category with Mattingly and Terrell and Stineman, but years of fury ran deep, the shock of discovery was great, and he had been incapable of listening. Now Tyler wished he'd paid better attention to Rosie's fervent defense instead of ranting like a wounded bear. Bits and pieces came back to him; how Eleanor's father pushed her into law, how unhappy she had been, how she wanted to help people who couldn't afford help.

In retrospect it all rang true. Maybe it was time to put his demons to rest.

Once the receptionist realized he didn't intend to waste time chatting, Tyler caught the elevator and set out to find Eleanor on the tenth floor. Ignoring curious glances and a couple of half-hearted attempts to stop him, he strode down the sumptuous corridor until he recognized Eleanor's blonde friend ---Stacy? ---Tracy?--sitting at a desk outside a glass-walled office. He veered in her direction. She looked away from her computer monitor, her automatically friendly smile vanishing abruptly when she recognized him. Tyler glanced at her desk plate. Gracie. Gracie looked about as happy to see him as Scott had been.

"Hi," she said warily, closing a file folder.

"How're you doing, Gracie?" He came to a stop at the edge of her desk, glancing nonchalantly into the office over her shoulder.

"Fine, thanks." She didn't waste any time. "Eleanor's not here."

"She coming back anytime soon?"

"Maybe."

"Mind if I wait?"

Gracie studied him thoughtfully, and then seemed to come to a conclusion. "No, I don't mind. You can wait in her office." She rose and waved him past her desk, through the open door and into a somber office. Tyler ambled in and looked around. He had a really hard time picturing Eleanor in here, sitting in the tufted leather chair behind the mahogany desk piled high with stacks of papers and files. He glanced up and noticed two female clerks sitting at their workstations, staring at him through the glass wall. Sighing, he turned away.

"I'm a little worried about her."

With a start, Tyler realized Gracie was still hovering in the doorway.

"Actually, a lot worried," she clarified, twirling a blonde curl around her finger.

Tyler leaned against Eleanor's desk and gave Gracie his full attention. "I'm listening."

She chewed her lip for a moment before slipping all the way into the room and closing the door. "She said she'd never come back to CBB in a million years and she meant it, so what is she doing back here, and what on earth is *wrong* with her?"

Tyler felt a rush of acute apprehension. "Could you be a little more specific?"

Gracie noticed the women, still gaping, and efficiently closed the blinds before sinking into a chair. "Okay, specifics. She despises Philip Conrad but she's back here working for him. She adores her house but she's moving out. She's had dinner with her father twice in the last week." Gracie began counting the items on her fingers.

"She never laughs; she hardly talks; she cut her hair; she actually went out with Mal---"

Tyler jerked away from the desk. "She cut her hair?"

Gracie nodded mournfully. "And she went out to dinner with Wayne Patterson. She hates Wayne Patterson."

Forcing himself to focus on one of the more important issues, Tyler folded his arms across his chest and tried to maintain an even tone. "Who's Wayne Patterson?"

"Philip's nephew and a major loser. They've been trying to set them up forever." Gracie gave Tyler a speculative look. "And if I even mention your name she shuts down completely."

Tyler tried to interrupt but Gracie shook her head and continued. "I know you've got something to do with it, so if you're here to try to fix whatever it is you've screwed up, then I'm on your side; otherwise, you'd better go right now. Think about it."

Tyler watched Gracie rise and walk out the door.

Gracie ducked her head back inside the door. "And you'd better think fast, because she's coming down the hall right now and you're a little too big to hide."

Ignoring the way his heart seemed to beat a little harder, Tyler moved to the corner of the office and cautiously pushed one of the blinds aside a fraction.

A woman came into view at the end of the corridor but it wasn't Eleanor. Tyler squinted and leaned forward for a better look.

Aw, man, it was Eleanor. Unnerved, he put a hand to the wall for support. Eleanor, minus about four pounds of hair. She wasn't exactly bald, not quite, but all that was left were short, wispy little curls, feathering around her jaw. She was wearing one of those ugly dark suits again, but now it fit her snugly, showing off the curves she'd acquired over the summer.

Without warning, Tyler felt like he'd been clipped by a locomotive. Walking toward him, he realized with blinding clarity, was the reason he felt out of place everywhere he went. Disconnected with his friends, uncomfortable in his own skin, restless, irritable, and frustrated beyond bearing. It was all because of Eleanor. Tyler sucked in a long, deep breath and struggled to get a grip.

Looking neither right nor left, she moved smoothly down the corridor, flanked by two suited men who laughed and conversed with one another over her head. They said something to her; she stopped and responded solemnly, and they gave her a little salute before veering away toward offices on the left of the corridor. Another man appeared at her elbow, and Eleanor glanced at him, a frown marring her brow. When the man slipped a casual arm around her shoulder, Tyler tensed instinctively. Eleanor plucked his arm away, said something that made the man's face fall, and promptly turned her back on him. She continued without a backward glance.

When she stopped to speak with Gracie, Tyler moved away from the window and sagged against the wall, head tipped back and eyes closed. In the space of a ragged heartbeat everything had changed and now he had to think fast. Eleanor was about to walk through the door and he suddenly had no clue what he was going to say. All he knew was, he never should have stayed away so long, dodging his feelings and pretending he didn't care about her.

The door opened. Tyler straightened, his heart slamming against his ribs just the way it used to when he was in his stance, waiting for the snap.

Chapter Eighteen

"The files you wanted are on your desk," Gracie told Eleanor. "And here are your messages."

Thanks," Eleanor said, remembering to smile. Eleanor knew Gracie was worried about her, just like Scott and Rosie, and it was important they understood she was perfectly fine. Things were progressing smoothly; not just her readjustment to work but the preparation for the move, too. The trick was just concentrating on one thing at a time.

Gracie gave her a curiously weak smile in return. Picking up her briefcase, Eleanor entered her office and quietly closed the door, her attention fixed on the first message in her hand. Her father wanted her to call him. Eleanor pressed her lips together. He was becoming downright chatty lately, so pleased with himself, with her return to docile-daughter status, and most of all, with Scott. True to his word, he was taking quite an interest in Scott. Scott wasn't altogether pleased by the attention, though. In fact, he was highly suspicious. Eleanor pushed away the prickle of anxiety she felt whenever she thought about the bargain she and her father had struck. She didn't want Scott to find out about it.

And who closed the blinds? she wondered distractedly. She liked them open; that way she felt less confined. She stepped toward the corner of the office to pull the blinds open, and her heart vaulted into her throat.

Tyler. Unexpected, uninvited, and unsmiling, leaning against the wall and sucking all the oxygen out of her office.

"Tyler," she said simply, drawing to an abrupt halt. What in the world was he doing here, deep in the land of the enemy, surrounded by a host of lawyers and all their trappings? Why hadn't Gracie warned her?

"Eleanor," he said in return.

Maybe she'd leave the blinds drawn after all. Circling her desk, Eleanor lifted a trembling hand to smooth her hair, then winced and straightened her collar instead. She laid her briefcase on top of her desk, sat down and allowed herself the joy of looking at him for one brief moment. He looked tired and unkempt. "What are you doing here?" She studied one of her messages intently but Gracie's rolling handwriting was more of a blur than usual.

"I wanted to talk to you."

And just like that he assumed she wanted to talk with him in return. How typically Tyler. Well, she didn't. "This isn't a very good time. I'm due in court in less than an hour." She rolled her chair forward, grateful for the bulk of the desk between them. "Who told you where to find me?" she asked, resuming her review of the sheaf of messages.

"Scott. I saw him at your house. He was a little reluctant to tell me where you were." Tyler clasped his hands behind his back and leaned forward to study one of her framed diplomas.

Like Scott didn't have enough to deal with, Eleanor thought with dismay, without Tyler getting in his face, demanding information.

"So, how're you doing?" he asked casually.

Astonished by Tyler's offhand question, by his mild manner and his very appearance in her office, Eleanor grappled mentally. His question wasn't difficult, but she had trouble with it just the same. "I'm very busy," she finally managed. "What do you want?"

"A few things. This, for example." Turning toward her, Tyler withdrew a folded piece of paper from his pocket and held it up. Eleanor recognized it immediately. "Before I left you told me you'd call when you found out whether you were pregnant or not. It wasn't until I got home this morning and went through the mail that I found this." Tyler unfolded it and read it aloud. "Breathe easy." He lifted his gaze to hers over the piece of paper. "Kind of cryptic."

So that was what this was about. She assumed he'd be delighted to get the news in any form. "I thought it was pretty plain, but okay. I'm not pregnant."

He stepped sideways to look at the next diploma and lifted a hand to straighten it slightly. "How come you didn't call like you said you would?"

"I didn't want to talk with you," she replied calmly. He glanced at her, frowning, and then glanced away again quickly, as though he couldn't stand looking at her. Well, it was hard for her to look at him, too, especially here at CBB where neither one of them could pretend she was anything but the enemy.

"And it wasn't that important."

That made him turn and stare, and she saw he wasn't as unaffected as he pretended. "Wasn't that important? Are you kidding? It was important to me. I wanted to know as soon as you knew." He stuffed the paper back into his pocket. "You weren't the only person involved, you know."

What did he mean, it was important to him? Eleanor was startled to realize she was beginning to feel a little bit angry. "Maybe I didn't care if you had to wait a day or two to find out," she added flatly, pushing the anger away. "Seems to me you've got very little to complain about, Tyler. Seems to me you ought to be dancing for joy. I know I have been."

Lie, lie, big fat lie. For almost a week she'd thought of little else but the fact she might be carrying Tyler's baby, vacillating between deep dread and boundless hope. There had been no dancing when she found out she wasn't; just another flood of unreasonable tears for what would never be.

Tyler stared at her for a long, long moment. Eleanor could see the pulse throbbing at his jaw but it gave her no joy. He nodded abruptly. "Okay, then tell me about this." He dug an envelope from his other pocket and upended its contents onto her desk.

Oh, the check. His conscience money. Eleanor lifted a shoulder dismissively. "I don't want your money." She blew the pieces off her desk, onto the floor, reminded herself to apologize to the cleaning crew, and opened a file folder lying on top of her desk. "Is that all?"

"Nope. Mind if I sit down?" Without waiting for her approval, Tyler sat down in one of the chairs opposite her desk. "I want to talk to you about the house."

She didn't want him getting comfortable in her office. She wanted him to leave. "We'll be moved out by the end of next week."

"Well, you see, that's just it. You don't have to move."

Taken aback, Eleanor glanced up. "Excuse me?"

He leaned forward, his hands clasped together. "You don't have to move. I changed my mind. Keep the house."

"No, thanks."

He frowned. "What do you mean, 'no, thanks'?" I'm telling you it's okay for you to stay."

"That's very kind of you," she said calmly, leaning back in her chair and examining a polished fingernail, "but unnecessary."

He looked more and more disconcerted. "But you love the house."

As if she needed him to remind her. Eleanor began to feel zips of irritation. She tried to quell them.

He frowned. "And Rosie; what about her?"

The irritation escalated to boiling anger in less than a heartbeat. "Don't be asinine. I care very much for Rosie but I don't have to live next door to see her." Eleanor leaned forward. "What's the problem, Tyler? You're getting exactly what you've wanted all along."

"Well, it's not what I want anymore."

She drew in a breath, composing herself again. "I can't help that."

He looked more worried than irritated. "Eleanor, stop it."

"Stop what?"

"Acting like this. Acting like the house doesn't matter to you. You don't want to move out."

How dare he come into her office and tell her what she did and didn't want to do? Eleanor gripped the armrests of her chair but managed to speak evenly. "Shall I tell you what I don't want? I don't want to see you anymore, Tyler, anywhere or under any circumstances." She didn't want his puzzled concern any more than she had wanted his cold fury.

CHRISTY ST. ROMAIN MARCHAND

Tyler flinched openly but Eleanor didn't allow herself to dwell on it. "I understand," he said in a low voice. "But Rosie needs a good friend like you next door."

Unfair. Completely unfair. He couldn't just springboard back and forth like this, and it didn't matter anyway. It was out of her hands now. She had Scott to think about.

"This conversation is over." She had to get away from him, and if he wouldn't go, well, then she would. She stuffed the messages and papers on top of her desk into her briefcase, clamped it closed, and rose.

Tyler stood up, his expression intense. "Eleanor, wait a minute. I have something else to say---"

"Not interested," she interrupted, swinging the briefcase from the top of her desk. The fragile grip she held on her composure was rapidly slipping away.

"Listen to me, Eleanor. I want to make things right."

She shook her head, trying not to listen. "Impossible."

He moved swiftly and blocked the door. "Don't say that. I want to make things up to you. You still care for me, I know you do, you have to."

She couldn't take this. "Why is that?" she hissed, reaching for the knob, trying to shoulder him out of her way. "Because I'm a glutton for punishment and you think there might be one tiny corner of my heart left to destroy? Well, forget it. I'm an attorney, remember? Attorneys don't have hearts. That's what you believe."

"Because I love you."

Eleanor felt the air in her lungs evaporate. She struggled to breathe. They were the words she had dreamed of, but they were too late. She'd made her choice. Scott's future was at stake.

"I do," he said insistently, putting his hands on her shoulders, trying to pull her close. "I do love you, and if you'll just trust me, I'll prove it to you. Give me a chance---"

Eleanor couldn't listen. "No. Stop saying that. It doesn't matter."

"Look at me and tell me it doesn't matter." Tyler forced her to look up at him and she was shocked by the intensity of his expression. "You can't, can you? You do care about me. I know you do."

"There is no future for us," she said finally, avoiding his question, wrenching away from him. "That's what you have to understand. That's all there is to understand." Desperate to escape, she managed to slip past and flee.

* * *

Rosie turned into her driveway and saw Tyler's truck parked beneath the shade of the oak tree. Thank heavens he had finally come home. Pulling her car into the garage, she blinked with surprise when she spied him, lying motionless in the hammock in the far corner of the yard. Getting out of her car quietly, Rosie slipped her purse strap over her arm and tiptoed across the grass.

Completely still, an arm flung across his face, he seemed to be fast asleep. Rosie studied him for a moment, torn between relief that he was home safe and sound, and irritation that he'd been gone so long. He was a little old for running away from home and she had a lot to say to him on the subject. But he must be bone weary to be dozing in this stifling heat, so Rosie decided to let him have his nap. She turned around to go inside the house.

"Rosie, I'm in trouble."

Startled, she froze, and then turned. Tyler's arm still shielded his face. "You mean, with somebody besides me?"

He lifted his arm slightly to look at her. "I'm in trouble with you?"

"Big trouble," she confirmed, somewhat taken aback by his haggard appearance. "You've been gone far too long, and you didn't answer my calls or call me back."

"I'm sorry." He dropped his arm back down. "I've been pretty stupid lately."

"Well, 'stupid' is rather harsh, honey."

He shook his head. "Stupid's an understatement. You don't know."

"What don't I know?" Despite her increasing concern, Rosie was careful to keep her tone light. She wondered if she was finally going to get some answers to the questions Eleanor so carefully deflected, on the rare occasions when Rosie even saw her lately.

"How stupid I've been." Tyler sat up carefully, swinging his legs out of the hammock. "I've made a pretty good mess of things with Eleanor, Rosie, and I don't think I can fix it."

Rosie stared at him, astonished. Tyler never, ever doubted his ability to solve any problem that came his way, or the way of anyone else he cared about.

Tyler dropped his head in his hands. "I love her, Rosie." He sounded pained and determined all at once.

So he'd finally figured it out. Rosie swept a loving hand against his lean cheek. "I know you do, honey."

"I tried to talk to her today but she doesn't want anything to do with me."

Rosie pressed her lips together. When Eleanor confided in her about Judge Haley's machinations, Rosie agreed not to tell Scott, but she never promised not to tell Tyler. Just in case Tyler needed a little extra motivation. "There are some things you don't know, honey."

"There are some things you don't know, either," he said quietly.

"Involving her father," Rosie added. Tyler's head jerked up and she knew she had his complete attention. She held out her hand. "Well, come on, let's go inside and talk. Two heads are always better than one, you know that. And I don't recall there ever being anything that you and I couldn't overcome, do you?" Abandoning her own plan to chastise him since he was doing such a good job of punishing himself, Rosie led the way to the house.

* * *

Finally home after her hellish day, Eleanor tried not to notice Tyler's truck parked in Rosie's driveway as she pulled into her own. It had taken all her effort to compose herself after his unexpected visit this afternoon and the last thing she wanted to think about right now was the look on his face when she fled her office. Even if she were crazy enough to believe what he said, the staggering things he said, she couldn't afford to have anything more to do with him. Some things just weren't meant to be. Sighing, she climbed out of her car, wrestled her briefcase from the passenger seat, and trudged up the walkway. A glance at the garage told her Scott was home. That, at least, was something to be happy about.

Eleanor opened the front door and blinked in surprise. Scott sat on the bottom step of the staircase, his hands knotted together, clearly waiting for her. His face was pale. "I talked to the judge today," he blurted. "He came by the nursery to give me a check for fall tuition."

She leaned to place her heavy briefcase on the floor. "I told you he was serious about helping you with school."

"He doesn't just want to help. He wants me to tell me what to do. He wants me to study law."

Eleanor stared at him. "Law? You told him you were thinking of horticulture, didn't you?"

Scott nodded. "But he says you and he had plans for me all along to study law."

"That's not true," she said, startled. "You can study anything you want."

"He said you and he made some kind of deal. What deal, Eleanor? What was he talking about? When I asked him, he clammed up. "

"But he never said---" Eleanor murmured, aghast, and then caught herself before saying too much. Turning, she started toward the kitchen, her mind racing in an effort to come up with a plausible explanation.

"What deal, Eleanor?"

"It's nothing for you to worry about." Her father never said anything to her about pushing Scott into law, but she should have seen this coming. She should have realized he would have his own ambitions for Scott, just like he did for her. And now Scott suspected there had been more to his sudden interest in him than long overdue fatherly concern. That was the last thing she wanted.

Scott followed her doggedly. "I've been worried for days already, Eleanor, wondering what's going on with you. I thought it had to do with Tyler but now I think it has something to do with me and the judge, and I want to know what it is."

Eleanor winced. She didn't want Scott to feel responsible for any of the changes they were going through. She had explained she meant to go back to CBB all along, and that they'd be just as comfortable in the new apartment as they were in the house. All fabrication, of course, but it was so important that Scott believe their father had simply seen the error of his ways. Now she realized she had only been playing with dynamite. Putting her purse on the island, she turned around to face him. "Believe me, Scott, I don't have any desire to see you study law."

"I don't know what to believe," Scott said, pushing a hand through his hair in agitation. "I believed you before, when you said I could live here with you and how you weren't ever going back to work at that firm. Now you're working all the time and he said it would be better if I lived with him."

Scott, going to live with their father? Eleanor felt gripping fear. He'd stifle the spirit out of Scott, too. No, no, she couldn't let that happen. "I'll talk to him," she said forcefully.

Scott grimaced. "I don't want you to talk to him. I don't want anything more to do with him. I never did, except it seemed important to you. I don't need him or his money."

What Scott didn't understand was that their father's financial support would make all the difference to his future. Eleanor tried to pull herself together and present a convincing front. "I'm sure we can straighten this out. Let me take care of it." She didn't know how, but somehow she would convince her father to let Scott make his own choices.

Scott shook his head vehemently. "Eleanor, you've got to be honest with me. I want to know what he was talking about."

"No. It's between me and him."

Scott glared at her. "No, it's between me and you. I've already told him to go to hell. Now I want to know about this deal, and I want the truth."

Or he'd tell her the same thing? Eleanor sank into a chair at the kitchen table. There didn't seem to be any other choice. She propped her elbows on the table and dropped her face into her hands. "He promised to pay for your education and put money in your name---," she stopped, unable to continue. If she told Scott the truth, any chance for him to have a good relationship with their father would be completely destroyed.

"If---?"

Suddenly unbearably weary, she laid her head down on her folded arms. "If we moved out of this house, I went back to work at CBB and I stopped seeing Tyler." But that wasn't enough, she thought disjointedly. Now her father had to go and start trying to run Scott's life, too, which was completely unacceptable.

"But, Eleanor, why'd you do that? That's crazy! You don't make deals like that!"

"I wanted to make things easier for you," she said quietly, straightening and meeting Scott's angry eyes. "If I didn't agree, he wouldn't have acknowledged you."

"Who cares?" Scott burst out. "Not me! I didn't want anything to do with him, anyway. I knew that after the very first time I went to see him." He pushed a hand through his hair in agitation. "You should have told me, Eleanor. Making deals like that without telling me anything was wrong."

Eleanor swallowed. "You're right. I'm sorry, Scott. I just wanted what was best for you." Suddenly her words echoed in her ear, and she realized that, in assuming she knew what was best for Scott, she was as culpable as their father. Eleanor felt nauseous.

"Well, you were wrong," Scott said flatly. "I'm going out."

Eleanor watched silently as he turned and disappeared through the doorway to the living room, and then listened as the front door opened and closed. Numb with self-loathing, she pushed away from the table and walked through the living room and up the stairs with the vague intention to change her clothes and continue her packing. When she entered the haven of her bedroom, though, she kicked off her shoes and climbed onto the bed instead. Drawing her knees up, she curled into a ball and closed her eyes.

Things had gone from terrible to unbearable, and she had nobody to blame but herself. Scott was right; it should have been his choice whether he wanted any relationship with their father. By going behind his back, no matter how noble her intentions, she betrayed his trust in her. He didn't want anything more to do with their father, which meant her capitulations had been in vain, and Scott might decide he didn't want anything more to do with her, either.

A knock downstairs on the front door interrupted her bleak thoughts. Not Scott, she thought, after a short-lived burst of hope. He wouldn't knock. Perhaps Rosie. Dragging herself back off the bed, she made her way downstairs and opened the door to discover her father waiting impatiently.

"I want to talk to you," he said abruptly. "I had a very disconcerting conversation with Scott today."

"I already know about it," she said tiredly, moving aside to let him enter and leading the way to the kitchen. "He said you told him he was expected to study law."

"Of course he is. That goes without saying."

"He wants to study horticulture. Didn't he make his feelings clear to you today?"

"Horticulture! I want you to talk sense into him, Eleanor."

Eleanor leaned against the kitchen counter, wrapped her arms around her waist, and studied her father. He was a handsome man for his age, with his silvery gray hair and proud bearing, but there was no kindness in him, no warmth or affection. It was time she stopped looking for those things. "Scott's got more sense at seventeen than I do at thirty," she said. "You made a big mistake trying to ram your goals down his throat."

"If I am funding his education, then I will have a voice in his future."

"You've ignored him for thirteen years. That kind of thing doesn't just wash away with a flood of money. And now that he knows about your plot, I don't think you're going to have to worry about what kind of voice you have in his future. He's not going to let you dictate the rest of his life." Eleanor shook her head. "And, starting now, neither am I."

Her father seemed untroubled by Eleanor's statement. "Are you quite sure you know what you're saying?"

Eleanor nodded. "I was willing to sacrifice my own dreams if it meant helping Scott achieve his, but you've overplayed your hand."

He clasped his hands casually and nodded. Eleanor wasn't fooled by his change in demeanor. She'd seen him go for the kill in just such a relaxed manner countless times before. "Your own dreams," he repeated mockingly. "I suppose these dreams include that football player."

Eleanor flinched in spite of herself, and her father nodded again, thoughtfully. "Marriage and children and this humble little cottage?"

"My dreams are my own business," she said coldly. "We're talking about Scott."

He lifted a dismissive shoulder. "Indeed. So Scott will work his way through college."

"People do it all the time."

"With no help from you."

"Of course I'm going to help him."

Her father drew to a halt and lifted a narrow eyebrow. "That will be difficult if you are unemployed."

What was he talking about? She was back, firmly ensconced at CBB, just like he wanted. "I'm hardly unemployed."

"I'm sure Philip will be most annoyed by your departure," he continued calmly.

Eleanor felt more confused than concerned. "I don't understand."

"And I doubt very seriously that any firm, anywhere, will want anything to do with you after they are made aware of your on-again, off-again interest in employment." Her father resumed his casual pacing. "You are already aware of how quickly rumors of that nature fly. And then what will you do? How will you help your brother?"

"You're threatening to have me fired from a job I hate?" Eleanor laughed in spite of herself. "Sorry, but you've pulled your last string. We'll manage one way or another. I don't care about winning your approval through some stellar legal career. The only things I care about are making amends to Scott for my meddling, unpacking these boxes, and---," she hesitated, and then drew in a deep breath. "And Tyler Hurst."

Judge Haley's face tightened.

She nodded emphatically, suddenly light-hearted, feeling awake and alert for the first time in days. "That's right, my football player. Today he told me he loves me, and you know what? I love him, too."

"Well, that's the best news this football player's heard all day."

Eleanor gasped at the familiar, rumbling drawl and spun around. Tyler, his gaze soft, the corners of his mouth tilted slightly, filled the doorway, with Scott at his elbow. "Tyler," she breathed, grasping the back of the kitchen chair with both hands. A swift glance at Scott, grinning broadly, giving her the thumbs-up, added to her giddiness.

Tyler ambled across the kitchen and curved his arm around Eleanor. She leaned into him, overwhelmed by a rush of emotions. "Don't go giving up on your career so soon, honey."

Her career? But Tyler hated her career. Didn't he?

"The Hurst Foundation needs you," he continued, lifting her chin and smiling into her eyes.

"What kind of nonsense is this?" Judge Haley snapped. "What are you talking about? I've never heard of any such foundation."

"Probably not," Tyler replied smoothly, returning his attention to her father. "It's brand new."

Her father looked grim. "It's some kind of gimmick, Eleanor."

"No gimmick. The Hurst Foundation is a non-profit organization that provides legal assistance to elderly people who can't afford it on their own. Eleanor's going to be the chairman. Chair-woman," he corrected himself.

Eleanor gaped at Tyler. He held her securely, as though he knew his arms were the only thing between her and a prone position on the floor.

"Why, that's ludicrous," her father sputtered. "Eleanor is a senior partner at CBB. She's not going anywhere."

Eleanor turned to gape . He never sputtered, never. Maybe she could get him to do it again. "You just said I was going to lose my job," she reminded him. "That I'm as good as unemployed."

"Yep, she's the head honcho, all right," Tyler continued affably. "She'll have a big budget, nice offices, a whole team of assistants if that's what she wants. And she's got the CEO right where she wants him."

"And that, of course, would be you," Judge Haley said caustically.

"Right again," Tyler replied, dipping his head back down to Eleanor. "You want to do anything for abused children while we're at it?" he asked, an eyebrow tilted engagingly.

As long as the earth was spinning off its axis, why not? Eleanor nodded.

"Battered wives?"

A smile breaking loose all over her face, she nodded again.

He grinned. "Emotionally challenged ex-football players?"

Eleanor laughed out loud. "My new specialty," she managed, lifting a hand to stroke his jaw, oblivious to her father's outrage.

Tyler pressed a swift kiss on her mouth. "Glad to hear it."

"This is the most preposterous thing I ever heard." Judge Haley was red in the face.

Ignoring him, Tyler snapped his fingers. "Oh, one more thing. Since you're representing me now, honey---you will represent me, won't you?---do you suppose you could get with LSU to find out what it takes to set up some kind of horticulture scholarship program?"

"I can do that," she replied promptly, winding her arms around his waist, laying her cheek against his chest.

He smoothed gentle hands up and down her back. "Knew I could count on you. I was thinking maybe we could name it after Rosie, and, hey, why don't we let Scott, here, be our first recipient?"

Eleanor stole a glimpse at Scott, who suddenly looked as dumbstruck as she felt. "I think it's a wonderful idea."

"I've heard all I want to hear." Eleanor's father spun on his heel and stomped toward the living room. Eleanor, Tyler and Scott listened as the front door opened and closed with a bang.

"Yes!" Scott whooped and pumped his arm in the air.

Tyler used his free hand to dig his keys out of his pocket, and tossed them to Scott. "Tell your sister good night, Scott, and beat it."

Catching the keys, Scott grinned at Eleanor. "I've got Tyler's place tonight, Jacuzzi and all. See you tomorrow!" He disappeared through the doorway.

"Late tomorrow," Tyler called after him. "And call first."

"Gotcha," Scott called.

With a second closing of the front door, they were alone. Not wasting a second, Tyler lifted her and placed her on the kitchen counter. Eleanor tugged him close, looping her arms around his neck. He smiled at her, hazel eyes warm. "You scared me half to death today," he said, smoothing one of her short curls behind her ear. "When you said there was no future for us, I thought I'd lost you for good, but then Rosie told me about your deal with your father, and I realized you never said you didn't care about me."

"It was a stupid deal to make with him," she said, tracing his brow with a finger. "I almost lost everything."

Tyler shook his head. "You aren't giving me enough credit, honey. I may be a slow starter but eventually I recognize a good thing when I see it." Leaning back slightly, he surveyed her cropped head and gave a mock sigh. "Even when it's almost bald."

* * *

in place along the altar; and Austin and Shelly had effectively charmed all guests and participants in their roles as ring-bearer and flower girl. The gentle music came to a halt and the organist launched into the Wedding March.

Still no sign of Eleanor. Tyler leaned forward a little farther, and then smiled when he caught a glimpse of her at the end of the long aisle. Despite her worry, her ivory gown still fit her sleek little body perfectly, and nobody except Tyler and an ecstatic Rosie knew there was any reason for it to be a little snug around the middle. Tyler realized he was grinning like a fool.

And then he frowned. Eleanor, taking her first smooth steps down the aisle, was flanked on both her right and left; Scott on her left, and---Tyler's muscles tightened fractionally---her father on her right. What the hell was he doing here? Tyler knew Eleanor had sent him an invitation, but despite her quiet hopefulness, there had been no response, and he had reminded her that the next move was up to her father. Apparently Judge Haley had figured that out for himself, and since right now, heading towards him with a radiant smile on her face, Eleanor looked about as happy as he'd ever seen her, Tyler guessed he could be generous, too.

He stepped away from the altar to collect his bride, nodding at Scott, sharing a long, level look with her father. Eleanor put her hand on his arm and looked up, her eyes brilliant with unshed tears. Tyler felt his throat tighten. Surrounded by family, creating their own.

Tyler Hurst was happy to be home.

Acknowledgements

Thank you so much for reading my book! I'm an independent author so every single time a reader downloads my book, I do a happy dance.

Self-publishing has been quite an adventure, and I couldn't have done it without a lot of help. Huge thanks to my friends and family who took the time to read my scribbles and give me feedback. This includes Amanda, Kado, Debra, Alicia, Joanne, Eve, Lenora and Alexandrea. Love you guys.

Special thanks to Shin Hyun Jeong of South Korea for the beautiful watercolor painting of my imaginary 621 Magnolia Drive, to Kimolisa Mings of Antigua for so adeptly formatting my manuscript into the correct form for several platforms, and Zainab Amin of Pakistan for understanding my idea and designing my pretty book cover. Thanks also to the members of the self-publishing groups on both Facebook and Reddit for great information and advice.

I've worked hard to eliminate any typos and errors, but if you spot any, please let me know: CMarchandauthor@mail.com

If you have enjoyed this book, please leave a review on Amazon and/or Goodreads, and if you think your friends would enjoy reading it, please share it with them.

Many thanks,

Christy Marchand

Email: CMarchandauthor@mail.com

Made in the USA
Coppell, TX
06 April 2020